"Urban fantasy at its best, combining spectacular magic and deeply explored character."

—*Publishers Weekly* (starred review)

"The arc begun in *Peace Talks* comes to a deadly, destructive finish in the seventeenth Dresden Files book—and nothing will be the same again."

—*Library Journal* (starred review)

"*Battle Ground* is an urban fantasy done at its best. Indeed it is the bar [to] which other authors should strive."

Grimdark Magazine

"One of my favorite urban fantasy series."   —Fresh Fiction

Additional praise for Jim Butcher and the #1 *New York Times* bestselling Dresden Files

"I've been waiting years for *Peace Talks*. This wasn't the book I was hoping for. It's better."

—#1 *New York Times* bestselling author Patrick Rothfuss

"Buckle up. It's going to be one, hard, ride. Jim Butcher has long proven he can juggle multiple threads of political intrigue, personal drama, and threat with a masterful use of action and tension."

—#1 *New York Times* bestselling author Kim Harrison

"Harry Dresden is a wholly original character in a wholly original world. Every book in the series is a great adventure."

—#1 *New York Times* bestselling author Charlaine Harris

JIM BUTCHER

BATTLE GROUND

A NOVEL OF THE DRESDEN FILES

ACE
New York

ACE

Published by Berkley

An imprint of Penguin Random House LLC

penguinrandomhouse.com

ACE is a registered trademark and the A colophon is a trademark of
Penguin Random House LLC.

ISBN: 9780593199312

Ace hardcover edition / September 2020
Ace mass-market edition / October 2021

Printed in the United States of America
5   7   9   10   8   6

CONTENTS

Chapter
One

Apocalypses always kick off at the witching hour.

That's something you know now.

It makes sense, if you think about it. An apocalypse, by its nature, is kind of doomy and gloomy. The best time for gathering energy for that kind of working is when you're in the deepest, darkest, coldest part of the night. That time of stillness between, oh, two in the morning and dawn. There're a lot of names for that time of night. The witching hour. The hour of the wolf. The dead of night. I could go on and on, because we all have names for it.

But they're all talking about the same time. The hour when you sit up in bed, sweating from nightmares. The hour when you awaken for no reason but to fear the future. The hour when you stare at the clock, willing yourself to sleep, knowing it isn't going to happen, and weariness and despair beat upon the doors to the vaults of your mind with leaden clubs.

That's when an apocalypse begins: the witching hour.

And I was charging straight into one as fast as I could.

My brother's old boat, the *Water Beetle*, a seedy,

beat-up twin to the *Orca* in *Jaws*, was too dumpy to skip over the waves of Lake Michigan as we headed for the blacked-out city of Chicago, but it bulldogged its way through them nonetheless.

An Enemy, capital E, was coming for my city, and the small portion of forces that the Accorded nations could gather in time was all that stood between the unknown power of the Fomor nation, led by a mad goddess bearing a supernatural superweapon, and about eight million powerless people with very little means of defending themselves.

I tried to give the boat's old engine a little more gas, and it started making a weird moaning noise. I gritted my teeth and eased off. I wouldn't protect anybody if the engine blew up on me and left us bobbing in the lake like a Styrofoam cup.

Murphy came limping up the stairway from belowdecks and eased into the wheelhouse with me. I was about six eight or six nine, depending on my shoes, and Murph had to wear thick socks to break five feet even, so I took up a little more space than she did.

But even so, she slipped up next to me and pressed herself against my side.

I put my arm around her and closed my eyes for a second and focused on nothing but the feel of her against me. Granted, the battle harness and the P90 she carried (illegally, if that mattered at this point) made her a little lumpier and pointier than the dictates of romance typically mandated for a love interest, but all things considered, I didn't mind. She was also warm and soft and tense and alert beside me.

I trusted her. Whatever was coming, she'd have my back, and she was tough and smart.

(*And wounded,* whispered some doubting part of me. *And vulnerable.*)

Shut up, me.

"How much longer?" Murphy asked.

"If any of the lights were on, we'd be able to see the skyline by now," I said. "How are our guests?"

"Worried," she said.

"Good. They should be." I looked down at her and said, "If anything happens, it will be near shore. Makes the most sense for the enemy to post their people or whatever there. Better tell everyone to be ready."

Murphy frowned at me and nodded. "You expecting trouble? I thought this Titan lady—"

"Ethniu," I supplied.

"Ethniu," she continued, without perturbation, "said she wasn't showing up until the witching hour. But it's midnight."

"For practitioners, the witching hour is between two and three in the morning. And besides. I think a revenge-obsessed goddess might not make the most reliable newspaper or clock," I said. "I think the Fomor are an aquatic nation. I think if she's really bringing an army in, she'll have scouts and troublemakers already in position. And I think that even taken off their guard, without their armies, there are beings in this town that only a fool would fight fair against."

"I guess there's no honor among demigods," she quipped.

I didn't say anything.

That got her attention. I saw her study my face and then ask, "How bad does it have to be for you not to be making jokes?"

I shook my head. "It's not just what's happening tonight. It's what it means. A supernatural legion is coming to murder everyone in the city. Whether Chicago stands or falls, it doesn't stay the same. It can't. This is going to be too big, too violent. The mortal world isn't going to be able to ignore it this time. No matter what happens tonight, the *world. Changes*. Period."

She considered that seriously for a moment. Then she said, "The world's always changing, Harry. The only question is how."

"Maybe," I said. "But I can't see how this one is going to be for the better. Mortals versus the supernatural world gets bad, Murph. Ugly. For all of us." I shook my head. "And that's going to happen now. I don't know when. But no matter what happens, it's coming. Now it's coming."

She leaned against me silently and said, "What do we do?"

"Hell if I know. The best we can."

She nodded. Then she looked at me and said, seriously, "Then get your head right. Leave that war for tomorrow. We've got plenty on our plate tonight."

I took a deep breath, closed my eyes, exhaled, and walled away a small ocean of fear that had begun roiling in my mind. By my own words, that worry was coming, no matter what I did. And I would face it when it arrived. Compartmentalize and conquer.

Because for tonight, there was only one thing that needed to be on anyone's mind.

"Defend Chicago," I growled.

"Damned right," Murphy said. "So how do we do that?"

I shook my head. "Way I figure it, Ethniu is our main worry."

"Why?" Murphy asked openly. "She's a big gun, but she's still just one person. She can only be in one place at a time."

"Because she's got the Eye of Balor," I said.

"Of who?"

"King of the original Fomorians," I said. "Archnemesis of the Tuatha, who I gather were some kind of proto-Sidhe. Ruled Ireland in prehistory. There was a prophecy that he would be killed by his grandson, so he locked his only child up in a tower for a few thousand years."

"Ethniu," Murphy guessed.

"Got it in one."

"Thousands of years as a prisoner. She's probably stable and well-adjusted," Murphy said. "So did he loan her the Eye or what?"

"Kind of. He died hideously, after some good-looking Tuatha snuck in and knocked Ethniu up. The child born of it eventually killed Balor. Maybe the kid gave the Eye to his mom as a Christmas present. I don't know."

She eyed me. "What do you know about it?"

I shook my head. "Mostly mortal folklore, which is sort of like trying to understand history through a game of telephone. But the Eye . . . it's a weapon that is beyond what the world has seen in millennia. Anyplace we gather to fight the Fomor's troops, we're just bunching ourselves up for the Eye to wipe us out by the boatload. And from what I heard, we've got very few ways to actually hurt Ethniu. But if we stand by and do nothing, she'll literally level the city with the damned thing."

"So how do we win?" Murphy said.

"Hell if I know," I said. "The Senior Council will have been gathering information this whole time. It's possible they'll have come up with options."

"That's why you went out to the island," Murphy said. "You think you can lock her up out there."

"I think if I tried to walk up and bind her, she'd rip my brain apart from the inside out," I said. I had to force myself not to rest my hand on the knife I was now wearing at my hip. In fact, it would be best if I didn't think about it at all. Too many things in this world are way too good at catching glimpses of your thoughts. "Maybe she can be worn down. I might have a chance then."

"Maybe," Murphy noted. "Might. I'm hearing a lot of waffle words."

"Yeah, that's because I'm speaking optimistically," I said, glowering.

"Let's call that one Plan B, then."

"Plan Z," I said. "This isn't like our usual mess. I'm still a heavy hitter in those. In the league these people are operating in, I'm a middleweight at best. I . . ." I shook my head. "I'm hoping someone has a better idea of what to do than me." I felt myself growing instinctively tenser and cut the throttle by half. "Okay. I think we're getting close. If there's going to be trouble, it will be between us and shore. Better let them know."

She bumped her head against my arm, leaned for a moment, and then pushed away. "I'll tell them."

She limped out carefully to go belowdecks again, and I began to cut the throttle a bit more, peering out into the night. There wasn't much to see. There was some city light against the belly of the cloud cover, south from way down past Aurora, and from the far side of the lake, but Chicagoland was wrapped in utter blackness.

Except . . . it wasn't.

I just hadn't been able to see the firelight from quite so far away.

The tall, dark, silent cliffs of the city's skyline appeared against the not-quite-black overcast. There were candles in windows, hundreds of them in sight, but they were lonely little points of light in all that darkness. Fires had to have been burning on the streets, because they cast ruddy cones of light dimly over the lower levels of some of the buildings.

I cut the throttle even more. I had a pretty good idea of where I was on the lake, thanks to my mental connection to the island behind us, but I was only sure of my position to within maybe a hundred yards, and the dark made things tricky. I didn't want to miss the channel into the harbor and gut the boat on the rocks.

The electric bow lights I would normally have used to help pilot my way in had been blown out when the Last Titan had unleashed the Eye of Balor on the roof of the nigh-indestructible castle of the Brighter Future Society. The Eye had blown a hole clean through it and simultaneously sent out a pulse of magical energy that had blown out the city's grid completely, including the electronics on cars and airplanes and the electrical systems on the boat. The old diesel engine was still chugging away, but that was about the only thing on the boat that had survived the super-hex the Eye had thrown out. Chemical lights hung at the bow and stern, but that was just to keep someone else from running into us, as if anyone else was out on Lake Michigan that night.

I peered through the dirty glass of the wheelhouse, searching for the white painted markers of the channel, which should have been all but glowing in the gloom. The harbor's lights were out, of course, and eighteenth-century lighting was not highly conducive to proper boat-handling safety.

Abruptly there was a crunching sound, squeals of protest from the *Water Beetle*'s hull and superstructure, and the boat went from moving slowly to not moving at all in the space of several seconds. I staggered and had to grab at the ship's console to keep my balance, and the wheel spun suddenly in my hands, the grips smacking my fingers hard enough to leave bruises before I could whip them away.

I lurched out of the wheelhouse as the boat began to pitch sharply to the left and front, timbers groaning.

Murphy appeared from belowdecks, a chemical light hanging from her harness, her little rifle at her shoulder. She staggered into the bulkhead with her bad shoulder and hissed in discomfort, then made it out onto the deck and braced her feet, holding on to the rail with one hand. "Harry?" she called.

"I don't know!" I called back. I reached into my shirt and pulled out my mother's old silver pentacle necklace with the red stone in the center of the five-pointed star. I held it up, murmured a word, and let out a whisper of will, and the silver of the amulet and the chain began to glow with soft blue wizard light. I made my way quickly forward as the ship rocked back the other way, groaning and squealing, holding up the light so that I could see a little ahead of me. "We must have run aground!"

But when I stepped over a thick clump of lines and got to the ship's bow, I could see only dark water in front of me. In fact, the light from my amulet picked out strips of reflective tape and plastic reflectors on the docks, ahead of me and slightly to the left. Which was to port, on a ship, I think.

We were still in deep, clear water.

What the hell?

The ship moaned and rocked the other way, and that was when the smell hit me.

It was an overwhelming odor of dead fish.

Oh crap.

I turned and held my amulet out over the clump of "lines" I had stepped over.

It was a thick, rubbery, pulsing, *living* limb, a tentacle, deep red-purple in color, covered in leathery, wart shaped nodules and lined with toothed suckers—and it was maybe half again as thick as a telephone pole.

I wasn't telling my body to move in nightmare slow motion, but it felt like that was happening anyway, as I followed the tentacle to the side of the ship, where it had slithered up the hull and seized the superstructure, attaching itself to it with dozens and dozens of limpet suckers—and went down to a vast, bulky *shape* in the water, something almost as massive as the boat itself.

That tentacle *flexed*, distorting in shape, and the ship screamed again, rocking the other way.

And a great, faintly luminous eye glimmered up at me through the waters of Lake Michigan.

A colossal squid. A kraken.

The Fomor had released the freaking kraken.

"Stars and sto—" I began to swear.

And then the waters of the lake exploded upward as what seemed like a couple of *dozen* tentacles like the first burst from the depths and straight at my freaking face.

Chapter

Two

Tentacles. That's what I remember of the next several seconds.

Mostly tentacles.

Something hit me in the face and chest and it felt like getting slugged with a waterbed's mattress. I was knocked sprawling back from the rail, and even as I went down, something began crushing my ankles together. I looked down to see a couple of winding tentacles holding my legs together, toothed suckers seeking purchase, fruitlessly for the moment—Molly's spell-armored spider-silk suit still had enough juice in it to hold them off, and the gripping teeth couldn't get through the fabric.

Then a third tentacle, this one much slenderer, whipped around my forehead, and I could *feel* the crackling sound as dozens of tiny teeth crunched through my skin and found purchase in the bone of my skull.

That's the kind of noise that will make you panic right quick.

My head slammed against something and there were a

lot of lights, and then my head and my feet suddenly got pulled in opposite directions.

I seized the tentacle that had me by the head and pulled hard enough to get enough counterpressure to keep it from snapping my neck—and it left me suspended uncomfortably, stretched out between the overwhelming opposing forces, just trying to hang on.

Story of my freaking life.

Harry Dresden, professional wizard. I'm a little busy or I'd shake hands.

I pulled hard with my entire upper body, and the tentacle, though incredibly powerful, stretched like a rubber band and loosened slightly, enough to let me gasp out a quick incantation: *"Infusiarus!"*

A sphere of green-gold fire, bright as a tiny sun, kindled to life in the cup of my right hand—which happened to be grasping a freaking tentacle of a kraken.

The creature itself apparently couldn't make sounds—but it shuddered in pain, twisting and jerking away from the sudden fire, and the *Water Beetle* screamed in agony as the beast thrashed.

I shrieked as my head was encircled by a band of fire from the tentacles biting in—only to vanish into the weird cold-static sensation that the Winter mantle had used to replace most sensations of pain. The noise of it was incredibly loud, at least to me, as the scraping against my skull conducted the sound directly into my ear bones. Hot blood began to trickle down my face and ears and the back of my neck—scalp wounds bleed like you wouldn't believe, and I'd just gotten dozens of them.

I cried out and forced more energy into the spell in my

hands, and my little ball of sunshine blazed like an acetylene torch. There was the sharp scent of scorched meat, and the tentacle suddenly snapped, burning through, and I came down on the deck hard, forearms slamming against the boards.

An instant later, the tentacles that were wrapped around my ankles whipped me into the air and slammed me into the bitterly cold waters of Lake Michigan.

The impact with the surface of the water felt like hitting a slab of brittle concrete. I managed to curl defensively, spread the impact out a little, but it wasn't enough to keep from having the wind blown out of my lungs just as I was plunged into frozen blackness.

There's no cold like the cold of dark water. It's . . . almost a predator, a living thing, and you can feel it ripping the heat out of you the instant you're immersed in it. Go down past the first couple of feet, even in summer, and that water gets seriously chilly, fast. Get dragged to the bottom, with the sudden pressure on your ears, the shock of the cold on your body, and it would be real easy to panic and drown, regardless of what the damned kraken had planned.

I frantically searched for options. Water and magic mostly don't mix. Water is considered, in many ways, the ultimate expression of the natural world. Water restores balance—and if there's one thing wizards ain't, it's balanced. We disrupt the world around us with our very thoughts and emotions, violate the normal laws of reality at a whim. But there's a reason dunking was used by the Inquisition and others, back in the day—surround a wizard with water, and he'd be lucky to be able to create the simplest little wizard light, or a spark of static electricity.

Which . . . left me with very limited options for dealing with a goddamned giant squid.

On the other tentacle, if there's one place you don't want to fight the Winter Knight, it's in the dark and the cold.

I could *see* the thing down here in the black, my eyes picking up on subtle purple and blue hues of bioluminescence, too dim to be easily noticed in any setting less umbral, and I was uncomfortably reminded of what it was like to use standard antiglamour unguents to see through illusion, only backwards. Maybe the kraken wasn't actually emitting light—maybe the faesight was simply illustrating it as something familiar for my human brain. But I could see it, plain as day, even down here in the frozen dark. Or maybe especially down here in the frozen dark.

The tentacles wrenched me this way and that, and I felt more of the things attaching themselves, some to my back, one across the backs of my thighs, one around my left arm—and I felt it when they started drawing me closer.

I got to see one great glassy eye the size of a hubcap, and then against the illuminated flesh of the kraken, I saw the black outline of its beak, an obsidian mass of hard, slicing armor that could snip me in half as easily as a gardener's shears take a blossom.

Then there was a dim, burbling sound of impact, and a second later someone came slicing through the water, swimming with an inhuman speed and grace, moving more like a seal than a human being.

She was wearing nothing more than black athletic underwear, inhumanly pale skin all but glowing in my faesight. Her silver eyes threw back the limited light like a cat's, and she bore one of my brother's backup kukris in her hand, doubtless taken from the arms locker below-decks. She darted through the water, seized me by the front of my coat, and then twisted one cold hand into my freaking belt and braced a foot against my hip, to give her a point of stability as she swung the knife with inhuman strength and speed against the resistance of the water.

The blade sliced into the warty skin of the kraken, unleashing a gouty cloud of purple blood. The creature twitched and writhed, and the hull of the *Water Beetle* screamed in the water as she hacked down at my feet like a frenzied axe murderer while somehow never striking my flesh.

A second later, the pressure on my ankles loosened, and then the thing ripped its tentacles away from me, taking half a dozen small bites of flesh out of my ankles and calves as it went.

Lara Raith, the queen in all but name of the White Court of vampires, watched the thing retreat for a second, knife gripped in her hand. Then she shifted her grip from my belt to under one arm, kicked off the bottom, and started dragging me up to the surface.

We broke into air and I wheezed as much of the precious stuff as I could into my lungs. Lara's hand was like a slender iron bar under my arm, firmly holding my head up out of the water. "Wizard, get back to the boat," she snapped. The water had pressed her coal black hair to her head. It made her ears stand out noticeably and somehow made her look a decade younger. Her eyes were bright with anger. "I will not have my brother trapped out on that island because you are too stupid to avoid swimming with a kraken."

"How is this my fault!?" I glugged, spitting out water.

There was a sudden cough and a hissing sound, and brilliant light flooded the surface of the water. Murphy had popped a flare on the bow of the *Water Beetle*, maybe twenty yards off, and stood holding it aloft in her hand, peering out at the water.

"Ms. Murphy!" Lara called sharply, and Murph swiveled to peer out toward us. The flare had blinded her to anything beyond the immediate reach of its light, but she'd ignited it to show us where to find the boat once she'd realized I'd gone into the drink.

The water suddenly thrashed with nearby motion.

"Go!" Lara called, and upended into the water as smoothly as an otter, vanishing with a kick of legs that were way too distracting, even in this mess. I spun in the water and started thrashing toward the boat. I was in good shape, but swimming was not my thing. I churned at the water and slowly drew closer to the ship's side. Murphy hustled over with the flare and said, "Over here!"

A lean, dangerous-looking Valkyrie came vaulting over the locker at the back of the main deck, where we stored the ship's lines, a coiled rope gripped in one hand. Freydis had short red hair, bright green eyes, freckles, and a boxer's scars and was dressed in black tactical gear. Her hands blurred as she unknotted the line and flung it out toward me.

The coil hit the water a foot from my head, and I seized it. Freydis started hauling me in, hard enough that the counterpressure from the water made it difficult to hang on to the rope.

"Harry!" Murphy screamed, pointing behind me.

I whipped my head around in time to see a bow wave

rushing toward me as something massive gathered speed in the water.

I started hauling myself up the rope, but the harder we pulled me, the harder the water pushed back.

"Harry!" Murphy shouted again—and flung the marine flare at me.

It tumbled through the air, dizzying in its brightness. At my size, I'm not an acrobat or anything, but my hand-eye coordination isn't too shabby. I reached out, batted it into the air instead of catching it, then with a last desperate clutch managed to grab onto it—just as the tentacles chewed into me again and dragged me under, the magnesium flare blazing even brighter as it hit the water with me.

Magnesium flares burn at about twenty-nine *hundred* degrees Fahrenheit. So when I shoved it against the tentacle around my waist, it peeled away as swiftly as a snapping rubber band—and the spider-silk suit reached the limits of its endurance, tearing off me like tissue paper, leaving pinched bruises all over my torso in its wake.

I looked down through the dark water and saw the kraken spreading out beneath me. It was . . . vast, its eyes gleaming with feral awareness, throwing back the light of the flare like eerie mirrors. For a second, I hovered there, meeting that gaze . . .

. . . feeling a dark, horrible awareness suddenly swelling unbearably inside my head.

What happened next would haunt me a while. The eyes are the windows to the soul. And wizards, if they meet your gaze for a moment, can sometimes get a peek in there. In the frozen dark of Lake Michigan, in the blazing, limited light of the flare, I soulgazed a kraken.

Soulgazes are serious business, because whatever you see there gets burned in. It never fades, never diminishes in horror or awe. If you see something bad enough, such as the n—

—something bad enough, it could do horrible things to your head.

I don't even know what I saw that night. A blur of images, alien and strange and somehow nauseating. I felt my limbs, spread out and floating in the water. I sensed other creatures like me, writhing in obscene embraces on the floor of the ocean, amid broken columns and ancient statues of things that somehow seemed to bend themselves into more than three dimensions. Sensation flared through my thoughts, so absolutely alien to anything in the human experience that it might as well have been pure agony.

I heard myself screaming, felt the bubbles pouring up over my face.

But here's the thing.

When a wizard looks into your soul, you look *back* into his. You see him the same way he sees you, clearly, a gaze that pierces veils and deceptions to see the world for what it truly is. The kraken stared back at me, and its warty hide began to ripple through fluttering bands of color, the skin distorting, becoming spiky, its tentacles coiling and curling in upon themselves.

I ripped my gaze away from the thing, my brain screaming in protest, but somewhere deep down, the instinctive part of me that almost enjoyed the benefits of the Winter mantle recognized something crucial.

Whatever it had seen when it looked back inside me

had, for that moment, terrified it utterly. And something abruptly changed inside me, like a switch had been flipped.

The not-squid, the kraken, was afraid.

I was still stunned by the soulgaze, and so was the squid.

It never saw Lara coming.

She hit it from behind and beneath, knifing through the water as if she'd been wearing a jet pack. She slammed the point of my brother's kukri into the warty flesh of its head, then used the viciously sharp blade on its curving inner edge to begin opening up the creature's flesh.

Hell's bells. She meant to cut out its brain.

The kraken abruptly thrashed and twisted, its skin rippling with colors and textures as it turned on her, tentacles questing. It seized her around the hips and whiplashed her back and forth in the water, ripping her hands free of the knife and aiming to break her neck with the force of it.

The knife was still sticking out of the back side of its head. Or body. I'm not sure which it was—the whole thing was just warts and tentacles and that vicious biting beak. So I began kicking down, ignoring the burning in my lungs. Lara hadn't gotten to cut very far before the thing had seized her, maybe twelve or fifteen inches.

But that was an opening more than big enough for the magnesium flare.

I shoved it into the kraken's flabby skull, all the way to my elbow.

It went mad.

I was battered by something, shoved back three or four feet, and if I'd had any breath left it would have been knocked out of me. I dimly saw Lara struggling, enwrapped in tentacles, until with her skin glowing like marble she seized one of the tentacles in both hands and simply tore it in half.

Fluid stained the water in a cloud the size of a swimming pool.

And through that cloud suddenly appeared lean, sinuous shapes, striking fear into the base of my brain that no amount of being a grown-up would ever entirely erase.

Sharks.

Bull sharks, blunt-nosed and with that glassy, quietly desperate stare. Maybe a dozen of them emerged from the murk, the smallest one at least twelve feet long.

Oh come on. This isn't even fair.

Someone, I reminded myself, *and I'm not sure who, just got done telling Murphy that when Ethniu's forces came, they would have no intention of fighting fair.*

The kraken thrashed in agony in the water.

And the sharks rushed the monster.

And, man, did *that* get messy fast. Tails threshing. Teeth flashing. Eyes rolling back white. Earth's oldest superpredators went up against a monster out of a madman's nightmares, and the result looked deadly and savage and beautiful.

Lara's eyes widened as two more sharks, fifteen-footers, came gliding out of the darkness straight toward her—and between them, gripping a pectoral fin of each, came the Winter Lady, the deputy to the Queen of Air and Darkness—my friend, Molly Carpenter. Molly had been tending to her duties as the Winter Lady all evening, but she'd still found time to provide me with sneaky backup magic in the true tradition of the Fae. She must have had the Little Folk keeping a watch along the shoreline for my return from the island.

Molly wore one of those surfer's wet suits, with patterns of deep purple and pale green on it in the streaks and rings of a highly venomous sea snake, her mouth stretched into a madwoman's grin. Her hair, luminous silver in the weird light, spread out around her head in an otherworldly aura.

She and the sharks went at the kraken. She bore a knife in her hand and immediately went to Lara's aid. The kraken wasn't done, though. Its jaws gaped and the beak came down on one of the smaller sharks like a pair of enormous scissors. One bite and snip, and it had cut the thing neatly in half.

There was a splash from above, and then Freydis arrived, the lean woman cutting through the water with nearly as much grace as Lara. She swooped down, kicking smoothly, headed for the knife at the back of the thing's head. Tentacles threatened her, but the Winter Lady flicked her wrist and half a dozen bull sharks rushed in, jaws ripping and tearing.

Freydis reached the knife, seized it in one hand, ripped the pin out of a freaking grenade that she'd been holding, and shoved it in the same hole where I had put the flare. I could see the outline of her fingers and hand through the creature's flesh in the illumination of the still-burning magnesium.

I started kicking for the surface as fast as I could. I wasn't worried about shrapnel from the grenade, but water is a noncompressible liquid. The blast would carry through it excellently, causing far more damage than the same explosion in open air. If anyone was too close to it, they'd get their lungs pancaked, and I had no way of knowing exactly how far the force of it would carry.

Freydis pushed off the thing contemptuously with her legs and had caught me in an embarrassingly short amount of time. I looked back to see Molly gripping the dorsal fin of the largest bull shark, rushing away from the wounded monster. Lara held on to Molly's ankles, dressed in the shreds of her underwear now, her pale skin covered in cuts and circular sucker marks, oozing slightly-too-pale blood in little streamers, and we all ran like the last fighters at the end of *Star Wars*.

The grenade went off behind us, wrapped in the flesh of the kraken, and maybe a quarter of the thing's head just turned into a cloud of chum. Its skin suddenly flushed pale, and the tentacles stopped thrashing so much as just spasming wildly. Leaving a cloud of blood and meat behind it, the thing started sinking toward the frigid bottom of the lake.

I broke the surface, gasping in a lungful of air, and started coughing. My head felt decidedly odd after that soulgaze, drunken in the worst kind of way. But, God, the air felt good. It felt so good I just sucked it in for a while, and only dimly realized, a moment later, that Molly and her big shark were just sitting there in the water next to me.

"I swear," she said. "I look the other way for like five minutes, and already you're in trouble."

"Bite me, Padawan," I muttered.

The smile she gave me grew extra sharp.

"Sharks, seriously?" I asked.

"They've been finding decades' worth of bull-shark baby teeth in the Great Lakes for years now," she replied.

She ran a hand fondly over the beast's back. "Plenty of these bad boys around."

"Lara?" I called.

"Here," said a voice behind me.

I looked over my shoulder. Lara looked like hell. She'd had no protection at all against the toothed suckers on the tentacles, and it showed. Her pale eyes were steady, though, glistening like the edge of a sword, as Freydis trod water beside her, helping her keep her head above the drink.

I kicked at the water a few times and said, "Uh. How do we get back up to the boat?"

In answer, a line fell over the side again, splashing into the water near me. Murphy appeared in the glow of chemical lights and said in a hushed, angry tone, "Jesus Christ, people, keep your voices down. If someone onshore has a night scope and hears you, they'll pick you off like cans on a fence." She looked down at me, and some kind of strain eased out of her face. She made a snorting sound. "Well? It's not like *I'm* going to pull you all out."

Wearily, I started lugging myself toward the boat through the water and made sure the others were coming after me. It took a hell of a lot of effort, but I hauled my bloodied ass to the boat, braced my foot on the hull, and climbed up it like the old Adam West version of Batman, only clumsier and a lot more bedraggled.

I made it to the deck, flopped over the railing, and just lay there for a minute, weary.

"You all right?" Murphy asked quietly, as the others began to climb out the same way.

"Gotta tell you, Murph," I sighed back. "I got a bad feeling about this."

"Speak for yourself," Murphy said. "I just gave my last grenade to a Valkyrie and ordered her to blow up a kraken. I'm having a ball."

Well.

Wasn't much I could say to that, all things considered.

Murphy and Molly between them had just saved our collective bacon.

I closed my eyes for a second.

I hadn't even seen what was coming for Chicago, and I was already bloodied and exhausted.

This was going to be a long night.

Chapter

Three

I piloted the *Water Beetle* back into dock, while Molly and her squadron of sharks escorted us the rest of the way in. I secured the ship, and by the time I'd gotten the last line tied off, there was a crackling sound, and the end of the dock was suddenly coated in ice. Molly stepped up out of the lake on the icy stairs she'd created, patterns of frost forming in her wet hair. She studied the city as she came, her eyes distant.

I lowered the boarding plank and shambled down to join her on the dock. "What do you see?" I asked quietly.

"Spirits," she said. "Messengers, I think. Hundreds of them."

"Martha Liberty," I said. "She's in tight with the loa. She'll have them watching for the Fomor."

"More than that," she murmured. "Angels of death . . ." Molly stared sightlessly toward the city for a long moment in cat-eyed silence. Then she shivered.

"What is it?" I asked.

"We should get moving," she said. "We need to get back to the castle."

I eyed her. Her face was blank, distant.

Lara Raith strode out onto the deck of the *Water Beetle*. The battle had done for her change of clothing. She'd had to make do with some of Thomas's stuff, stored in the ship's cabin—leather-look tights and a big white Byronic poet's shirt. My brother was not above embracing the classic stereotypes. The pale skin of her arms, where I could see it, was covered with dark, vicious bruises and round, mostly closed wounds, courtesy of the kraken.

Lara noticed me looking. "Not one quip about hentai, Dresden." She glanced at Molly and nodded. "Thank you for the assistance."

"It is no more than is due you under the mutual defense stipulations of the Accords," Molly replied in a rather frosty tone.

Lara stared at Molly carefully for a moment before inclining her head. "Ah. Of course."

Something like real anger flickered over Molly's face for a second and then was gone.

I glanced back and forth between them.

I hate it when I miss things.

"We need to coordinate with the rest of the Accorded nations immediately," Lara said to Molly.

"I concur."

"Yeah," I said. "You guys do that. There's something I have to do first."

Lara blinked. "As I understand it, Dresden, you may have a role to play tonight. And you have seen to it that I have an additional vested interest that you survive to do so. That being the case, I will not countenance you traipsing around the city alone."

This could get complicated. Lara had already used two of the favors owed her by the Winter Court, but apparently she had one remaining on credit with Mab. If she cashed it in, I wasn't sure I would be able to stop myself from cooperating.

I liked it way better when I could just be openly defiant, rather than being forced to resort to reason.

"Hey," I said, "do you hear that?"

Lara cocked her head. "Hear what?"

"Exactly," I said. "It's quiet. Barely after midnight. There's time."

"Time for what?" she demanded.

"To warn them," I said. "The community in Chicago. Someone has to let them know what's going on. Take me half an hour. Don't bother arguing."

Lara's expression flickered with exasperation and her jawline twitched. "Empty night, Dresden. Why must you make everything more complicated?"

"It's kind of my best feature," I said.

"It should be done," Molly observed, her tone remote. "If you will excuse me, there is something that requires my immediate attention."

She took a step forward and vanished into a curtain of cold wind and mist that whipped about her and then dispersed, leaving only empty dock in its wake. I blinked and tried to look as if that was something I had been expecting to happen for at least ten minutes.

Lara shook her head. "I won't try to stop you from fulfilling an obligation of Winter, if that's what this is," she said.

Ah. On her way out, Molly had set up cover for me. "That's as easy a way to explain it as any," I said.

"I need you alive if I'm to save my brother. I would feel better if you weren't going alone."

There were footsteps on the gangplank and Murphy said, "He isn't."

I looked up to see Murph in her tactical gear. If you didn't know what to look for, you almost couldn't tell she'd been crippled, when she was standing still like that.

"I don't doubt your loyalty to him, Ms. Murphy," Lara said. "Only your current limits. Time is critical. He needs to move."

"She's not going to slow me down," I said. "You and Freydis should hit the castle. Riley was assembling your people when we left. They'll need you."

"Very well," she said. "But don't waste time. The Fomor could appear at any moment."

"Aw," I said, "you're worried about me."

Her smile had a little poison in it. "Yes. Which we will discuss, when time serves." She raised her voice and called, "Freydis."

The Valkyrie came up the stairs from the cabin and vaulted lightly to the dock. Lara nodded, murmured, "Good luck," and then the two of them darted off toward the city, Lara in the lead, running in almost complete silence. They were out of sight in seconds.

Murphy exhaled slowly. "Hey, Harry?"

"Yeah?"

"My everything is broken," she said frankly. "How the hell am I going to keep up with you?"

"Yeah," I said. "Um. Work with me, here."

She arched an eyebrow at me.

*   *   *

Murphy gripped the edges of the shopping cart with both hands as I ran, pushing it down the middle of the street. "If you tell anyone about this, Dresden," she said, "I will murder you slowly. With dental implements."

I leaned down and kissed her hair. "Now, now. If you're good, we can get you a piece of candy at checkout."

"Goddammit, Dresden."

I grinned, and then the wheels of the shopping cart hit a crack in the road and Murphy hissed in pain. I tried not to flinch in sympathy and to pilot around the rougher bits that I could see.

Murphy could limp along, but there was no way she could have moved through the city quickly enough to keep up. I could have carried her, but it would have bounced her around even worse than the shopping cart. So we just had to make do.

It wasn't hard to move, really. The cars that had died on the streets blocked them to vehicular traffic, but there was plenty of room to maneuver around them for pedestrians, bicycles, and lanky wizards pushing shopping carts.

CPD had come out in force, armed and armored to the teeth. There were at least four officers posted at every major intersection, where they had lit the streets with road flares and trash-can fires. It didn't make the streets less dark or threatening, really, but it did the most important thing it could have done—it threw a spotlight on the police officers themselves. If you were looking around outside that night, practically the only thing you *could* see reliably was the police in their uniforms and badges, standing their posts at each intersection. They were showing the flag for civilization and law, reassuring people that there were still boundaries that would be defended.

But the looting had started, here and there. I saw several window fronts that had been broken out, though not as many as it could have been. Officers were advising people to get home and get off the streets, and we got the fisheye from more than a few uniformed guys as we went by. Murphy made me stop to talk to a couple of the uniforms she knew, and she passed on warnings for the people in law enforcement whom she still had contact with—that this was a Special Investigations problem, and that this was a time for all hands on deck, fully armed tactical teams on standby, right the hell now, and why are you still standing here?

Things hadn't gotten bad, at least not yet. But there was something in the air that hadn't been there before— the psychic stench of a widespread terror that was slowly gathering momentum.

The city's residents had begun to realize that something was very, very wrong.

The firelight, almost alien to mortal cities for a century or more, cast high, deep shadows that made buildings loom threateningly in the night and turned alleyways into pits of blackness. The presence of the police had to be reassuring—but it was also a warning, that things were bad, and that city hall was worried. The people who were walking on the street did so briskly, in tense silence, and tended to move in groups of three or four. I saw very few women out in the open.

I felt myself getting more tense. You couldn't have fear

spreading like this without building up considerable psychological pressure. Sooner or later, that pressure was going to cause something to burst.

They say civilization is a thin veneer over barbarism.

Chicago stood waiting for the first tearing sound.

We arrived at McAnally's Pub to find it . . . well, like always, only a lot more crowded.

Mac's place was a basement pub underneath an office building. You had to descend concrete stairs from the street to get in, and it featured a constantly irritating combination of a fairly low ceiling and ceiling fans. The entire place was done in old, stained wood, with thirteen stools at the crooked bar, thirteen tables for customers, and thirteen carved wooden columns featuring images mainly inspired by Grimms' fairy tales.

The usual candles and lanterns burned, lighting the place. Mac's charcoal grill was alight and covered in the various foods he offered to his customers, and the ale flowed freely.

When we came in the door, nothing happened for a second, and then a cloud of silence began to spread out from my feet until it had engulfed the room. All eyes were on me. These were people who knew who I was.

I could hear whispers. *Harry Dresden. Wizard.*

I adjusted the strap on the nylon backpack I had taken from the *Water Beetle*. "Mac," I said clearly. "Storage room. We need to talk."

Mac was a lean man around six feet tall with broad-knuckled hands and a shining bald pate, dressed in his usual black slacks, button-down shirt, and spotless white apron. He'd been a friend for a long time. He looked at me and then nodded toward his pantry and office.

Karrin and I walked over and went in. Without a word, I opened up the backpack, took out the little wooden sign, and put it down carefully on his desk.

Mac saw the sign and his eyes widened. He looked at me, his face written heavily with consternation.

"You know what it is," I said.

Mac rocked back half a pace. He looked from the sign to me. He didn't quite lick his lips in nervous guilt, but it was pretty clear that he didn't like that I'd realized what he knew.

"A lot of the Paranetters are here tonight," I said, "because we put out an alert yesterday and this is one of the designated shelters."

Mac nodded firmly.

I met his eyes for as long as I dared and said, "What's coming could kill every one of them. So I need your help."

Mac looked from me to the sign and back, grimacing.

"Mac," I said quietly. "Not just anyone would recognize that sign. I mean, it's just an old piece of wooden board, right?"

His expression became pained and he held up his hands.

"There's a Titan coming to Chicago," I said, "with an army, courtesy of the Fomor, to burn the place to the ground. They'll be here in maybe an hour. There's no time to get cute. Are you willing?"

He frowned. He stared at the sign for a second and then away.

"Mac," I said, "there's no time for this." I bowed my

head, rested the fingertips of one hand against my temples, and began to call up my Sight.

A wizard's Sight is a powerful tool for perceiving the energies of the universe. It gets called a lot of things, from dream sight to the third eye, but it amounts to the same thing—adjusting your thoughts to be able to perceive magical energies as they move around and through the natural world. The Sight shows you things in their purest nature, reveals fundamental truths about people, creatures, and things that you look at.

A while ago, some of the Outsiders had come looking for trouble at Mac's.

They'd recognized him.

I didn't know what Mac was, but it seemed clear that he wasn't just your average bartender. I figured it was about time we got to know each other a little better.

But before I could look up, Mac pressed my hand gently against my face, making it impossible to open my eyes.

"Don't," the mostly mute man said gently. "Hurt yourself."

He didn't let me move my hand until I'd released my Sight—and there was no way he should have been able to know that. But he did anyway. Which put him in a relatively small pool of beings—those with a connection to divine knowledge, to *intellectus*, and given what the Outsiders had called him, I was pretty sure I knew what Mac was now. Or at least what he had once been.

He lowered his hand slowly, his expression resolved. Then he took a step back, pursed his lips, looked at me, and shook his head. After that, he moved briskly, opening a storage cabinet and taking out a small, efficient toolbox.

A moment of effort and he'd put a couple of screws in the back of the sign, connected by a strand of wire.

"What is it?" Murphy asked as he worked.

"The placard from the Cross," I said. "The one that said, 'Here is the King of the Jews.'"

Her golden eyebrows went up. "From the vault?"

"Yeah," I said.

"What does it do?"

"It's embodied intercession. . . . It focuses energy on an individual," I said. "Something about pouring out the accumulated sins of humanity onto Christ, maybe. Hang it up and it puts up a kind of threshold that will hold off just about anything supernatural, as long as the property's rightful owner is alive."

Mac took a small folding knife out of his pocket, opened it, and pricked his thumb. A drop of blood welled.

"So everyone here will be safe," Karrin said.

Mac hesitated for only an instant. Then he took a deep breath and pressed his thumb against the back of the placard, smearing his blood there.

"Anything that wants to get to them will have to go through Mac first," I clarified quietly.

Mac took out a nail and a hammer; then he tucked the placard under one arm and walked out with them. A moment later, we could hear him using the hammer as he hung up the sign.

I turned to Murphy and said, "Here's where we part trails."

Her eyes flashed. "Harry," she said warningly.

I spoke in a flat, harsh voice. "You're slowing me down."

Karrin's eyes blazed. And then they shone and over-flowed.

"Goddammit," she said, looking away.

I could have hit her, hard, and hurt her a lot less.

I sighed and put a hand on her shoulder. "I saw Will and the Alphas out there," I said quietly. "Look. I have to go work with the Council. But the Accorded nations don't really care about regular people so much. Someone has to look out for them. I want to put you in charge of the Alphas and the Paranetters defending one another and anyone around here who needs help."

"You want me to be safe," she said harshly.

"If I wanted that, you'd be on the island," I said. "You're hurt. And you're a goddamned adult, Karrin. This is a war. I want you where you will do the most good."

"And where I won't distract you," she said.

I sighed and mopped a hand over my face. "If I could fix your injuries, I would. But the fact is that you can't keep up right now. It's just that simple."

"Fuck you," she said, her voice raw, and turned away. Then a moment later, and very wearily, she murmured, "Goddammit."

I put a hand on her shoulder. "Take care of our people. You're one of the few I'd trust to do it anyway."

Without turning, she gave a single severe nod.

Then she whirled, seized my coat, and dragged me down to her for a kiss. It was sharp, sweet, fiercely and desperately hot.

When she let me go, it took me a second to open my eyes and straighten up again.

"Harry . . ." she said.

"Be careful of the big bad Titan?" I said.

Her eyes wrinkled at the corners. "You're not going to do that," she said. She put her hand on my arm and squeezed, her eyes intent and ferocious. "Kick. Her. Ass."

Chapter

Four

We left Mac's office to find the common room silent. Everyone was staring at us. I'm used to the people in Mac's place sneaking covert glances at me, but it was rarely this crowded there, and the effect was disconcerting.

We stood there for a moment before Murphy nudged me and murmured, "Say something."

"What?" I asked.

"They're scared," Murph said quietly. "They know you have power. They want to hear from you."

I scanned the room of anxious faces.

Will and Georgia Borden were there, along with Andi and Marci, Chicago's very own vigilante werewolves. Will and Georgia made an odd couple. Will was about five and a half feet tall and must have weighed two hundred pounds, all of it muscle. Georgia was nearer six feet and looked like she ran a marathon a week. Both of them, as well as Marci and Andi, were dressed in loose, easily removed clothing.

But among those present, they were the only ones

with anything like a chance on the streets given what was coming.

The Ordo Lebes was there, kitchen witches with too little power to be considered for bodies like the Council but who had already fought its battle by providing safe houses around the city, warded very nearly as well as a wizard's premises. Think of it as the magical equivalent of a barn raising—dozens of minor talents working in unison to accomplish much more than they could have alone.

Everyone else was just folks, people with enough talent or the right circumstances to be connected to the supernatural community but who didn't have much in the way of power. Hell, even Artemis Bock was there, though he kept his head down and didn't look at me, since he'd kicked me out of his store for good several years ago.

God, that seemed so petty and unimportant now.

I walked by him to get to the center of the room and put a hand on his shoulder encouragingly on the way by.

"Hello, everyone," I said. "I guess you know me. But if you don't, I'm Harry Dresden, wizard of the White Council."

For the moment, anyway.

I took a deep breath. "There's not a lot of time here. So I'm going to give it to you straight. We're looking at an apocalypse."

That got me dead silence and stares. Murphy elbowed me in the ribs.

"Little A," I said in protest, then clarified. "The Fomor, those kidnapping bastards, are coming with an army. And they mean to kill everyone in the city."

That got me more dead silence. You could have heard half of a pin drop.

"What do we do?" Georgia asked into that void. "What *can* we do?"

Nervous whispers began to spread.

"You're not alone," I said instantly. "There's considerable power getting ready to argue with them about it. Names out of storybooks are getting ready to fight the Fomor. But that means it's going to be big-league bad out there," I said. I blew out a breath and pushed my fingers back through my hair. "Here's how it is, people. The wolf is at the door. So if you've been meaning to take a martial arts class, or you thought maybe you should learn to shoot a gun, it's too late. You've only got three choices now."

I held up a finger. "You can run, and they'll chase you." I held up another. "You can hide, and they'll hunt you." I clenched my hand into a fist. "Or you can fight. Because they *are* coming to kill you."

I pointed at Will and the Alphas. "These guys have made themselves ready and can maybe survive. But we don't need theoretical warriors out there. If you don't think you could win a scrap with Will and his people, the only business you have out there tonight is dying. The safe houses, like this place, will probably be the last to fall. But if the enemy takes the city, they *will* fall.

"So make your choice. Run. Hide. Or fight. Any of them could get you killed."

"Jesus," someone whispered.

Someone's baby made a fussing noise and was shushed.

"What about the army?" Bock asked quietly.

I shook my head. "They'll be all over the place. In the

morning. The leading elements of the enemy's forces are already here."

That went over with a round of whispers.

"I'm sorry, guys," I said into the sotto voce aura of fear. "But that's how it is. Choose now and stick with it. The more you dither, the more dangerous changing your mind gets." I gestured toward Murph. "You all know who Karrin Murphy is," I said. "She's going to be coordinating defense here. Will, that all right with you and your people?"

Will didn't need to check in with the Alphas. He simply nodded and said, "It is."

"Thank you," I told him, and meant it.

Georgia was studying Murphy's expression intently, and the two of them traded a look I couldn't read. "Of course, Harry. Whatever we can do to help."

"Mac, that all right with you?"

Mac didn't look up from the mug he was polishing with a spotless white cloth. He let his silence be taken as assent.

"Right," I said. "Gotta move. Saw a bike chained up outside. Whose is it?"

There was a profound silence in the room.

"Oh, come on, guys," I said plaintively. "It's not a violation of the Laws of Magic. I just really need wheels to go save the city and whatnot."

In the back corner of the room, a hand went up, and a skinny kid in sunglasses and a raised, tied hoodie spoke in some kind of Eastern European accent. "It is my bike."

I squinted at him and said, "Gary?"

Crazy-but-Not-Wrong Gary, the Paranet guy, hunched

down so hard that he looked like a cartoon buzzard, and his narrow shoulders nearly knocked off his own sunglasses. "Christ, Dresden," he said, in a plain midwestern accent, "just out me to everyone."

I eyed him for a second.

Then I said, "Guys, who knew this was Gary?"

Approximately eighty percent of the people in the room put up a hand, Murphy's and Mac's among them.

Gary looked sullen.

"You're among friends, man," I said. "Of course they know who you are."

Gary eyed me suspiciously over the rims of the sunglasses.

"Gary," I asked, "can I borrow your bike?"

He shrugged. "Sure."

He threw me a key. I caught it without dropping it, which made me feel cool. Then I said, to the room, "Things are going to be bad tonight, kids. I'm not your father, but if you're staying here and you want to live to see sunrise, I'd do whatever Ms. Murphy asks you to do."

"First thing we're going to need is a triage area," Murphy said to Will. "One way or another, people are going to get hurt."

"Georgia, get started on that," Will said. "Marci, Andi, with me. We'll go round up some more supplies from the drugstore."

The Alphas got to work with an immediate will, hehheh. They were good people.

I wondered how many of them would still be alive in the morning.

Will and Georgia had a kid.

I shook myself. I was terrified for them, for the people who were my friends—but if I stood there feeling terrified and sick and worried and helpless to protect them, I wasn't going to do them any good.

From where I stood, their best bet was for me to coordinate with the rest of the Accorded powers to hit the incoming enemy with as much muscle as could be mustered. The White Council could hit harder than just about anybody else on the planet. I'd personally seen members of the Senior Council tangle with small armies, wrestle with shapeshifting arch demons, and pull satellites down from the sky onto their enemies' heads, wiping them out by the hundreds.

And, Hell's bells, my place was among them.

I might be the dumb kid with the sledgehammer from his father's toolshed, compared to the sword-saint samurai who were the Senior Council—but I had discovered, in my time, that no matter how skilled and elegant a foe might be, a sledgehammer to the skull is a sledgehammer to the skull.

I bounced the binding crystal from the island in my hand and slid it into what was left of my suit coat's pocket.

I'd find something useful to do.

But I couldn't do it here. I couldn't watch over my friends. I couldn't be the one to protect them. I had to trust that what they'd learned from me, and from the community I'd helped to build, would see them through.

Well. That and an artifact that had been literally stored on the same shelf as the goddamned Holy Grail, and what was left of an ex-angel.

Along with the knife now resting on my left hip and humming with quiet power.

Stop thinking *about that, Dresden.*

I traded a last look with Karrin. Then I took the key, went out and unlocked Gary's red twelve-speed, put it in twelfth gear, and pedaled furiously into the night.

I mean, yeah.

I could have run, but come on.

There's no one human who likes that much cardio.

I had gone only a couple of blocks on the bike when I heard someone say, "There he is."

Another voice shouted, "Dresden! Stop! CPD!"

I thought about not doing it for a second—but assuming the bad guys got stopped tonight, the city would still be here tomorrow, and that would mean dealing with the law. Hell, I was trying to get Maggie into a good school. She'd never get admitted if her dad was, for example, on trial.

So I hit the brakes and let the bike skid to a stop in the darkness between a couple of guard posts. I waited there impatiently as two sets of footsteps came up, one tall and built light and one short and built heavy-duty. The taller, thinner shadow was breathing harder than the massive shorter one.

"Detective Rudolph," I said. "Detective Bradley. Out for a run?"

"You can fu . . ." Rudolph began, gasping.

Bradley elbowed him in the ribs and said, "Get your breath, sir."

"Bradley," Rudolph gasped, barely able to breathe, "goddammit."

Detective Bradley turned on Rudolph and pointed a finger. Just that. He said nothing and did not move. Bradley was built like an armored vehicle and had hands like a gorilla.

Rudolph, handsome as ever, even with his porn 'stache, wilted.

Bradley held his finger pointed a moment more, nodded, and then turned to me. "Excuse me, Mister Dresden. Lieutenant Stallings has asked you to come in on a consult."

"No can do," I said. "You need to seek cover in strong positions. Didn't you guys get Murphy's warning?"

"We got it," Bradley said. "But she ain't exactly in good odor right now, you know?"

"Because of you twits," I snarled, about ninety-nine percent of it at Rudolph. "Well, tell Stallings my official consulting advice is that he'd goddamned well better listen to every word she said."

"I knew it," Rudolph said to Bradley. "It's some kind of terrorist attack and he's in on it."

I stared at him, in my smudged, soaked, slashed suit that still smelled like dead fish and lake water, on my kind-of-stolen twelve-speed, and said, "Yeah, I'm Osama bin Laden over here. Hell's bells, I don't have time for this."

"You should come with us, sir," Bradley said.

The timbre of his voice had changed. He meant business. He hadn't changed his stance yet, but he was the kind of guy who would let you know his intentions—and I was still standing there astride a bicycle.

"Bradley," I said, "I know you're doing your job right

now. But you don't know how much you could be screwing things up for, um, everyone. Just everyone."

"Mister Dresden," Bradley said, "you've done some good for us before. You know this drill by now. Just come in. You'll be done in a couple of hours."

"We don't have a couple of hours," I said. And because I can let people know my intentions, too, I met Bradley's gaze and said, "Any of us."

When I give people that look, they look away.

Bradley didn't.

The eyes, they say, are the windows to the soul. They're right. How long it takes to trigger the soulgaze varies, but it seems to work faster for people in heightened states of emotion—and we were standing in the middle of *millions* of people in heightened states of emotion. It was fertile ground for such a connection.

So I got to See Bradley, and where he stood was not only a man in a modest custom suit, but also the spreading trunk of some oak tree so enormous as to look squat, rising to branches that cast far more shade than its source occupied.

It didn't take a genius to realize that I was looking at the man's character—that he bore the burden of his duty with stolid responsibility. It didn't mean that he was impervious to corruption or anything—but, like that solid tree, barring some injury or illness of character, it would hold up under the strain for a good long while. The image hit me with the same kind of impact you might experience in the ocean, as a wave lifts you off your feet. I had to take a stagger step to keep my balance, fighting to break the connection.

I don't know what I look like in a soulgaze. The only mirrors for the human soul are the people around us. All the people who had been my mirrors hadn't generally reacted with great positivity to what they'd seen.

Bradley let out a sharp, huffing cry and took a staggering step back. He stumbled and went down, catching himself awkwardly on his elbows and wrenching his neck. He lay there for a second, gasping.

"The fuck!" Rudolph screamed. He'd cleared his jacket from his gun and had his hand on the grip. "The fuck! The fuck did you do to him, Dresden!?"

I shook out my shield bracelet, just in case, and said, "Nothing! Just give him a minute!"

Rudolph drew the gun and aimed it at me, his voice panicked. "Goddammit, what did you do?!"

His finger was on the trigger.

Rudolph was one of those blessed idiots who thought that the world was a rational place. Though he'd been repeatedly exposed to the real score with the supernatural when he had worked at Special Investigations, he'd somehow remained impervious to reality, or at least gave every outward appearance of doing so. I guess it had made him really good at writing the reports Special Investigations had to turn in, where they reduced the paranormal into lowest common denominators until everything fit neatly inside all the categories.

Rudolph wasn't stupid. You can't be entirely dim and manage as a police detective and smarmy politico. His denial was less a function of intelligence than a complete lack of the moral courage necessary—a paralyzing inability to face truths that he found personally terrifying.

Rudolph was a coward.

"Trigger discipline, Detective," I said in a quiet voice, not moving. "I'm not close enough to get to you, and I've got this damned bike between my legs. There's no need to have your finger on the trigger yet."

"Shut the fuck up," he snarled, making a little gesture with his shoulders on the expletive. "Put your hands up! Slow!"

The Winter mantle didn't appreciate the aggression in his voice—or maybe it appreciated it way too much. My first blind instinct was to lunge at the screaming twit, take my chances, and break his scrawny neck. But that would have been impolite.

I did what he said, slowly, seething with rising impatience and anger the entire time. Hell's bells, of all the times to have to tangle with the normie bureaucracy, this was not it.

Unless . . . Maybe that wasn't what was happening here.

Rudolph had been on someone's payroll for a while, we'd been pretty sure. Suppose he'd been given orders to stop me and take me out of the picture for the evening?

Or for keeps.

And that accidental soulgaze with Bradley had just given him an excuse.

Rudolph might have been someone's creep, but a creep he remained, and he was scared. If I brought up a shield or tried any of my usual tricks, he'd pull the trigger before he even thought about it, and he was too close to miss. My suit would probably stop the rounds when whole—fae tailors seemed to regard bulletproofing as a standard feature—but the kraken had slashed sections of it to ribbons, and there was always the chance he'd aim for the head or neck, or that the shot would go up the sleeve or something. He could get off three or four shots while I was calling up my shield.

I might chance that. But it wasn't really Rudolph that was the problem.

The problem was what happened after I openly resisted a duly enabled officer of the Chicago Police Department. Once he started shooting at me, I'd have to disarm him at the least, and after that it might get really complicated, really fast. I preferred to be something other than a wanted fugitive.

Unless I just killed them both.

It was dark. There weren't any street cameras, any instant backup. We were playing by old-school rules, the Winter mantle suggested. Rudolph had crossed a line. It would be too bad about Bradley, who seemed a decent sort, but there were about eight million reasons around me why the logic came down on the side of eliminating both of them and proceeding to the defense of the city. For all I knew, Rudolph was a Fomor agent trying to take out one of Chicago's heavyweights. Well. Middleweights.

And it wasn't as if the two of them could stop me, unless Rudolph got lucky with the first shot, and that happens a lot less in real gunfights than you'd think.

Kill them, said a quiet, hard voice inside me.

I closed my eyes for a second. Maybe I should have run instead of taking the bike. The Winter mantle was apparently reacting to the fear in the air, and it sensed a city full of cowering prey to be enjoyed. It paced the length of the cage I'd built for it in my head like a hungry, restless animal.

No, I said back to the voice in my thoughts. *Killing*

your way to answers is never as simple as it seems. The best way to survive is to keep it simple.

I didn't bother trying to argue about right and wrong. Those are concepts beyond the scope of that kind of magical construct.

Assuming that's who I was talking to, instead of, you know. Myself. Gulp.

I opened my eyes and kept my hands up. "Rudolph, man, this is so not the time."

"Shut up!" he shouted. "If your teeth come apart again, I'll shoot."

I gritted my teeth and prepared my shield. Crap. If the idiot started shooting, I'd have to take my chances, raise the shield, and run away. There was no way these two could keep pace with me for long. Dammit, I just needed a second or so to get the shield up. I decided to lunge away from Rudolph, over the far side of the bike. In the dark, it might take him a second or two to find me and realign the weapon. I might have time to pull up a shield before he could even start shooting.

I heard the faintest scrape of movement in the shadows.

I looked beyond Rudolph, across the street, and saw the gleam of eyeshine in the darkness. One, two, three, four sets of eyes approached through the night, gleaming, low to the ground, vanishing into the particularly dark patches.

There was a sudden chorus of bubbling, throaty canine growls that came from the night on every side.

Rudolph's eyes went very, very wide. He took a panicked little step to one side, flicking his eyes left and right. "What was that?"

I made mumbling sounds without opening my mouth or moving my jaw, wobbling my hands a little without lowering them. "Oilcan," I said. "Oilcan!"

"Goddammit, Dresden!" Rudolph screamed. "Answer me!"

"They're wolves, Rudy," I said. "Timber wolves. They were in the neighborhood and they're friends of mine."

The growls grew louder. Will and the Alphas had been on the streets a long time. They knew how to survive there, how to fight, how to win, and how to be scary when they needed to be.

Ever heard a pack of wolves growling in anger? It's less than restful.

"Ever seen what a wolf's jaws can do to a buffalo bone?" I asked. "It's impressive. Next to that, human bones are like corn nuts."

Rudolph was well armored against reality. "There are no wolves in downtown Chicago!" he shrieked. "This is a trick!"

"Technically, you're right," I said. "They're were-wolves. But it's no trick."

Rudolph made a high-pitched sound, like a door opening on a frozen hinge.

On the ground, Bradley groaned and said, "Jesus, Mary, and Joseph. What the hell are you doing, Rudolph, you idiot?"

Rudolph's eyes snapped down to Bradley.

That was the opening I needed. I unleashed my will into the shield bracelet on my left wrist, raising it as I murmured, *"Defendarius."*

By the time Rudolph's eyes had come back to me, a

glowing quarter dome of translucent force had glittered into existence between us. The distortion of the shield made him a little wider and squatter. The gun in his hand shook. It was a miracle it didn't go off.

"Goddammit, what is happening!?" Rudolph demanded.

Bradley came to his feet, looking disoriented and annoyed. The first thing he did was stare, agog, at the glowing light of my shield. He shook his head a little. Then he went to Rudolph and, carefully, put his hand on the other man's forearm and pushed down.

Rudolph tried to shrug him off. "The fuck are you doing?"

"Saving your stupid career," Bradley said. He kept pushing. The cubic man was stronger than half a dozen Rudolphs. After a brief second of resistance, Rudolph relented and lowered the weapon.

He looked up at me and then out at the dark, where the growls had not stopped bubbling out of the night. "Dresden. Call them off."

I looked at Bradley and then called, into the dark, "Okay, guys, thanks. I think we've got things cleared up."

The growls vanished. There was no sound, but I was pretty sure the Alphas had cleared out. The only reason I'd seen them coming in the first place was because they'd shown themselves to me intentionally.

Like I said. Good people. But even better wolves.

"Put the piece up," Bradley said. "Now."

Rudolph glared at him, but he did it. I lowered my left arm and relaxed, letting the shield wink out. It left us in gloom that made us all into dark outlines while our eyes struggled to adjust.

"I'm writing this up, Bradley," Rudolph said.

"Go ahead," Bradley replied, his tone bored. I couldn't see much of him in the dark yet, but I could feel that he was focused on me. "I got a pen, too. You just drew on a civilian with no cause."

"Whose side are you on?" Rudolph hissed.

"Dresden has places to be," Bradley said.

"What?" Rudolph demanded.

Bradley's voice went flat. "Don't be stupid. He could have gone through us if he wanted to. You're lucky you're still alive. And your trigger discipline sucks."

Rudolph spat an oath and stalked away.

I watched the good-looking man leave and then turned to Bradley. I offered him my hand. "Thanks. And I'm sorry about that."

Bradley shuddered and took half a step back from me, turning his head away. "Don't come anywhere near me," he said. He jerked his jaw at my bike. "Now go do what you have to do. And stay away from me."

Like I said. The only mirrors we have are other people.

I didn't stare at Bradley's shadowed form in pain for very long. The witching hour was near.

The Titan was near.

I got on the bike and started pedaling.

Chapter
Five

I rolled up to Castle Marcone at half past midnight. It was an enormous, blocky house of stone with a raised tower at each corner. Honest-to-God torches burned in ancient sconces on the battlements. Guards in a mix of modern and classical armor manned the walls. Out front of the building, the useless autos had been rolled onto their sides and rearranged into a couple of concentric barriers in front of the entrance to the castle. You had to start at one end of the first barrier, then walk all the way to the other end in an S-line style to get into the castle—all of it under the gaze of the armed Einherjaren on the walls.

Messengers were coming and going on the ground, all of them on bicycles, moving by the dozens. Flickers of magical energy were pulsing through the air all around me as well—spells and wards that were being brought to life, major-league stuff that took a good long while to spin up. Meanwhile, in the air above the castle, darting winged forms swarmed *everywhere*.

It didn't look intimidating or anything.

Standing on either side of the doors to the castle was a

tall woman in black leathers and mail. Their hair was buzzed short on the sides and much longer on top. Neither woman was visibly armed, except for particularly hard-looking black fingernails, and their eyes were black all the way through the sclera, gleaming with a sinister intelligence.

I slowed down as I approached the doors, and the attention of two sets of all-black eyes settled on me like the barrels of guns.

"Look who it is," I said. "H and M. How's tricks, kids?"

"The *seidrmadr*," said the one on the left. I'll call her H, because honestly I couldn't tell them apart.

"The starborn," murmured M. "I still think we should shred him."

"It is the most logical course of action," H agreed.

Four hands tipped with very nasty-looking talons flexed.

These two were Vadderung's personal bodyguards, and they scared me. Anything that could be violent enough to be the last line of defense for freaking One-Eye was nothing I wanted to tangle with for fun.

Of course . . . I don't react well to bullies.

"Easy there, ladies," I said. "Or we'll find out how well you operate at absolute zero."

Two heads tilted sharply.

"The Winter Knight," M said.

"At the weakest portion of the seasonal cycle," H noted.

"Fifty percent chance he neutralizes one of us before termination."

"Conflict with the *seidrmadr* results in approximately a twenty-five percent reduction in the principal's personal defenses."

"Unacceptable," said M.

"Unacceptable," agreed H.

The pair returned to parade rest, hands and talons behind their backs. Their eyes returned to scanning the surrounding night, ignoring me.

"Well. It was nice to see you again, too," I said. "Do you guys like those little seed bells or would you prefer live mice in your Christmas basket?"

That earned me their attention again, and another head tilt.

"Levity," said H.

"Madness," said M.

And then they both blurred toward me.

It's hard to explain how fast the movement was. I threw up my hands. I'd gotten them almost to the level of my waist when something hit me and drove me flat to the concrete. There was a high-pitched, cawing shriek, louder than an air horn at close range, and then tearing sounds, snarls, and . . . splatters.

I lay there stunned for a second, the wind knocked out of me, unable to get a steady breath in. H, maybe, was crouched over me, her feet on either side of my ribs, the heels of her hands on my sternum. She wasn't looking at me. I followed the direction of her gaze.

M was crouched in exactly the same pose as H, only she was hovering over a mess. Her arms were soaked black to the elbow, as was a circle of sidewalk five feet across. What was left at the center of the circle was little more than maybe fifty pounds of tissue and bone. There were some scales involved there, and some limbs with too many joints, but I had no idea what kind of creature had been there a moment before.

I looked down at my own body. There was a distinct lack of gore. I finally got a breath. Whatever that creature had been, it had gotten to within ten feet of my back before H and M had dealt with it.

"The hell was that?" I asked.

"A scout and assassin," H said.

"Swift," said M. "Difficult to see."

H nodded and rose away from me. "The enemy prepares."

M rose and offered me a hand up. Her hands dripped with black gore.

"Levity, huh?" I said to her.

One corner of her mouth quivered.

No matter how severe Vadderung's people might be, they're always cheered by the chance to give you a hard time.

"Harry," Ramirez said as I got to the bottom of the stairs that led up onto the roof of the castle. "*Dios*, where have you been?" He paused and said, "What the hell did you get on your hand?"

I sighed. "You got some kind of scraper?"

He came down the stairway to me on his cane, looked at the knife on my belt, then up at me, and lifted an eyebrow.

"Ritually purified," I said. "Don't want to use it until it's time."

Ramirez eyed me for a moment before he grunted and produced a gravity knife from his pocket and flicked it open. He was a good-looking man, dark of complexion and eye, a Spaniard by way of California. He flipped the knife, caught it by the blade, and offered me the handle. "You hear what happened?"

"Yeah," I said, and took the knife. "Had to go grab some tools." I started trying to scrape the black gunk off my hand. I'm pretty sure it wasn't actually burning, and that was just my imagination, but as it had cooled it had taken on the consistency and adhesive properties of honey and smelled like offal. My progress was dubious.

"Just keep the knife," Ramirez said, his expression faintly nauseated.

"Thanks," I said, and forced myself to keep my tone calm and natural. "Where's the old man?"

"Roof, with everyone else," he said. "Everyone's rushing to bring in all the help we can. Don't really have many skills in that area. I feel like a fifth wheel."

"Yeah, well. We'll get our chance once the fighting starts."

Ramirez grimaced down at his cane. "True."

"Hey, at least you aren't in a wheelchair."

"True," he said, more brightly. His expression then sobered. "Harry, I need to talk to you about something."

"Always the very best way to set up a conversation for success," I noted drily. I tried to pay no attention to the way my stomach jumped.

"Yeah, well," he said. He pulled up on the stair above me, so that he could look me more or less in the face, if not in the eye. He regarded me for a moment before he said, "Where did you go tonight?"

My belly tightened even more. I felt everything shutting down, my expression locking into my best poker face.

Regret passed over Carlos's face. "You can talk to me."

"What?"

"Harry," he said slowly, "you and I are friends, right?"

"We've heard the chimes at midnight more than a few times," I said.

He nodded. "And seen a few bad places."

"We have."

"Well. Maybe you should . . . at some point . . . consider treating me like a friend."

I held myself perfectly still. "What?"

Carlos lowered his voice, but it remained intense nonetheless. "I don't mind that you think of me as the little brother, Dresden, but don't think I'm a goddamned idiot. Don't think I can't see what's happening."

I stared through him and said nothing.

"If you're in trouble," he said, "if you need help, you can talk to me, man. You *should* talk to me."

"Why is that?" I said.

"Because big and goddamned scary things are happening," Carlos said, his voice hard. "The knives are coming out, and it's my job to keep them from going into the White Council's back. Because you are in close alliances with scary creatures who are doing scary things to you, and you barely seem to acknowledge it. And because you've got access to way too much power, and you could do way too much damage, man. I know you, Dresden. I love you. But too much is at stake right now to let things slide."

"Is that a threat?" I asked him. It came out a lot more gently than it could have.

"If I can see it," he said, "others can, too. Talk to me. Let me help you, Harry."

I stopped for a second and thought about it.

Ramirez was a formidable ally. And, good God, it would be nice to have a skilled wizard in my corner. Ramirez was popular among the younger members of the Wardens. If I had his help, I'd have their help as well.

But Ramirez was also popular among the establishment. Granted, I wasn't entirely bereft of allies there, but increasingly as time had gone on, Carlos had come to represent a new ideal for the new generation of Wardens—more compassionate than those who had come before, quicker to investigate and slower to conclude, but every bit as dedicated to the Laws of Magic and the security of the White Council of Wizardry.

My friend Carlos would be an enormous amount of help—but Warden Ramirez would be honor bound to inform the Senior Council about my relationship to Thomas, if I told him the truth. I wasn't even sure that he would be unwise to do so, all things considered. But if that happened, I might as well leave my brother in the fridge—the White Council would never, ever leave my relationship to Thomas as a potential handle to be used against them. They would either reverse that pressure preemptively or else . . . remove the handle.

The White Council had never been a source of anything but grief to me.

Carlos Ramirez was my friend.

But Thomas was my brother.

"I don't know what to tell you, 'Los," I lied. "I was doing liaison stuff for Mab."

"Liaison stuff," Carlos said. "Rumor calls it something else."

Hell's bells, Freydis and her stupid illusion. "Stars and stones, it's like a British sex comedy around here," I said. "Look, there are shenanigans happening between Mab and Lara. I'm . . . moderating things."

He gave me an uncertain look.

"I'd tell you more if I could," I said. "But this is internal Winter stuff. And, honestly, man, we don't have time for this."

Ramirez looked away from me and sighed. "Dammit, Harry."

"Hey, I don't like it any more than you do," I said. "But I need to talk to the old man. We have work to do."

"Yeah," he said. He took a slow breath and then nodded once, decisively. "Yeah, we do. Come on up."

We went up the stairs together. Ramirez had a bruise forming on one cheek. There were ligature marks, sharp bruises, forming on his neck where his cloak had hauled him around.

Injuries I'd decided he needed to have.

Right before I'd lied to him.

Dammit.

I felt awful.

Chapter

Six

You look a little green, Hoss," Ebenezar said.

The old man was holding down one corner of the castle's roof, along with Martha Liberty and Listens-to-Wind. Martha Liberty was seated in a chalk circle, speaking to about half a dozen poppets—dolls, forms that spirits could animate to communicate with the mortal world—and then reporting in crisp, terse sentences to Warden Yoshimo, who lurked outside the circle with a notepad and pen.

Listens-to-Wind sat on the corner battlement of the castle, his legs hanging over the edge. He'd taken his sandals off and his feet were swinging idly. Every few moments, some kind of animal would come fluttering or sprinting up to him, mostly small birds and squirrels. They would chitter or tweet and the old shaman would tilt his head and listen gravely before nodding and speaking in quiet replies and sending the animal messengers off again. Wild Bill lurked at his shoulder, leaning in and tilting his head with a scowl, as if trying to pick up a new language and having only moderate luck. He also wrote down messages.

Both Wardens would tear off notes and pass them back to Senior Councilman Cristos, who was moving back and forth between them and Childs and Riley, each of whom was operating a ham radio.

"Ran my boat as hard as I could for a couple of hours," I replied. "My stomach didn't care for it."

The old man lowered his voice. "Don't expect me to feel sorry for you, boy. You're a goddamned fool."

Ebenezar didn't much care for the White Court of vampires. My grandfather had objected to my "helping" my brother. When I'd told him that he had another grandson, he had objected to that, too. He'd objected loudly enough to sink several boats in the harbor, and the only reason one of them hadn't been the *Water Beetle* was that I had stopped him, and gotten away with it.

The anger around him was still a crackling cloud of unreleased lightning.

But the old man was no fool. And he'd taught me how to reason when it came to supernatural conflict. He knew the direction of my thoughts, and what priorities would help us survive the night. "How far can you snare her from, do you think?" he asked me.

I made an effort not to put my hand on the knife at my side. "The lakeshore. If we get her there, she'll be in range."

Ebenezar grimaced. "And that's just close enough for you to make the attempt?"

I nodded. "From what the island says, it's a standard binding."

"Whoof," Ebenezar said, breathing out. "That changes things."

"Why?"

"Ethniu is a *Titan*, boy," he said. "Can you imagine trying to bind *Mab*?"

I shuddered.

"Well, she's an order of magnitude beyond that in power and will," Ebenezar said. "You can't just go straight up against a mind like that. Not when she's wearing Titanic bronze."

"Why not?"

"The stuff . . . it affects Creation on a fundamental level," he said. "As long as it has enough will behind it, the physical world is going to have a very limited effect on her."

I squinted at the old man. "So as long as she thinks she's invincible, she is?"

The old man lifted his eyebrows. "Haven't ever heard it summed up that way before. But, yes, that's accurate enough for our purposes."

"Denial armor," I muttered. "Hell's bells. So how do we get through it?"

"We'll have to soften her up first."

"How?"

"Whole lot of fighting, I reckon," the old man said. "Wear her will down." He sucked in a breath through his teeth. "Think of it like a bunch of farmers fighting an armored knight," he said. "The knight can take plenty of hits from us, but she'll hit just as hard or harder, and none of us can take a hit back."

"So we have to get her where we can come at her from multiple sides," I said. "Pack tactics. One attracts her attention and another hits her when she isn't looking."

"And enough hits will wear her down," Ebenezar replied. "Of course, the armored knight knows this. She'll play to avoid it if she can, but she has an objective to complete, so she can't afford to stay where it's safe. But if too many of us gather in one place, we'll be juicy targets for the Eye."

"So this is as much a deception as anything else," I said. "We've got to get her to commit somewhere hard enough that we can pound her enough to wear down her will. But she'll be expecting that—so it has to be a juicy enough target that she can't resist exposing herself." I shook my head. "That's not a good situation for us. We're depending on her to make a mistake."

Mab was suddenly there, in her battle gown, a sheath of mail beneath a cloak of flawless white and silver. Her hair spilled down around it like white clouds and silk.

"I assume, my Knight," she said, "that you consulted with your island?"

I produced the binding crystal from my pocket and showed her.

"Excellent," she said. "I do not believe Ethniu is aware of the danger the island could pose to her. She has no concept of professionalism. We can expect more mistakes from her."

"Why do you say that?" I asked.

"She is *here*," Mab said. "She could have chosen any city and accomplished her greater goal. But instead she is here."

I tilted my head and frowned before I understood. "Because you're here," I said. "It's personal."

Mab's mouth ticked up at one corner. "It is an old

score, between her people and the Sidhe. An old hatred. The hardest kind to resist."

I glanced aside at my grandfather. The old man didn't react.

"She must cast down what I have wrought," Mab said. "And she seeks to drive away my peers and allies by demonstrating my weakness—now, on the shortest night of the year, when my power is at its nadir."

I looked over at the other side of the roof, where the Summer and Winter Ladies both stood in the center of a swarm of glowing, winged Little Folk that came streaking in and away in blurs of colored light. Both Molly and Sarissa had their eyes closed, and their lips were murmuring.

"Given the power of her will," I said, "I'm not so sure the island is that big a threat. It's still got to be me who shoves her in the bottle."

Mab gave me a look that reminded me of why she was the Queen of Air and Darkness, and her eyes were as cold and grey as chains. "Any will can be broken."

I shuddered a little. On the inside. Because I really didn't want Mab to see it.

"A lot is going to rest on his shoulders," Ebenezar said gruffly. "So it'll be critical to keep him out of the fighting until it's time."

Mab gave Ebenezar a glance and what could only be in the most technical sense considered a tiny snort. "If you wished an instrument of careful precision and restraint," she said, "you chose the wrong champion, Blackstaff."

The old man glowered at the Queen of Air and Darkness and said, "Nonetheless."

"When horrors begin to tear apart the people of this

city," Mab said calmly, "when its women and children cry out for help, I should find amusement in seeing you at tempt to restrain him."

I lifted a hand and said to Mab, respectfully, "He's right. If I'm the play, then I've got to be ready when it's time."

Mab gave me a look with something in it that was almost like pity. Or possibly contempt. "As if you could restrain yourself any more ably than he could." She shook her head. "Be comforted, my Knight: I chose you for times precisely such as these, when an elemental of destruction is what is most needed."

"What?" I said.

Mab did something more frightening than most monsters *could*.

She smiled.

It was genuine.

"Harry," she said, her voice almost warm. "From the first time I laid eyes upon you, I saw a being who had the potential for true greatness." She laid a slim, cool hand on my forearm, and pride joined the smile already on her face. "It is almost time for you to begin to understand it yourself. And once you do, once you understand, we will do great things together."

The old man stepped between us, between the Queen of Air and Darkness and me. And he said, in a voice like granite, "He is not your weapon, Mab."

Mab's smile gained a hungry, wolfish edge. "He is *exactly* my weapon," she hissed. "By his own choice. Which is more than *your* people ever gave him. And they call the Sidhe wicked and deceitful."

I blinked and shot a glance at Ebenezar.

The old man wouldn't meet my eyes.

Mab laughed, low and amused. She stepped around Ebenezar, running a hand along my shoulder as one might the fender of a car one was particularly proud to possess. "Do what you can to stay within sight during the battle, my Knight. And be what you are. Ethniu will be what she is. She has no other alternative." She nodded to Ebenezar and said, "Br—"

There was a harsh buzzing sound that started faintly and grew louder in a rush. I moved without thinking. I swept my right arm out and shoved Mab behind me as my left came up, my will coalescing into a shield aimed primarily at the sky. I barely got the shield together in time for something behind a veil, diving at approximately peregrine falcon speeds, to splatter itself across a good three-foot-radius area of invisible force.

Even as I watched, maybe six or seven pounds of . . . meat, mostly, kind of appeared from behind a shattered veil and slid slowly down the sphere-shaped plane of my shield. It landed on the ground with a wet, slapping sound. I stared down at the remnants of the thing. It looked like some kind of mix of a bat, a lizard, and a squid, all rubbery and leathery and grey and pink, like ground beef left out too long. It smelled absolutely foul, as if some kind of venom bladder had been ruptured. Parts of some yellowish mucus were actively dissolving the flesh of the creature as it died, and its tentacles were thrashing, sliming more of the stuff onto the castle's roof, where it sparked and sputtered against the warded stone.

I lowered the shield warily and rose from my crouch. "What the hell was that?"

Suddenly I became acutely aware that the Queen of Air and Darkness was pressed against my back, and I was holding her there with one arm in a fashion that could accurately be described as undignified. I moved my hand hurriedly and glanced back at the monarch of the Sidhe. "Are you all right?"

Mab met my gaze, her eyes all but glowing. I looked away quickly. Her eyes shifted to Ebenezar, something triumphant in them, and she murmured, "Yes. Well done, my Knight."

"I mean, you're immortal, right?" I said. "Why would you need a bodyguard anyway?"

She nodded toward the yellowish mucus sputtering on the stones. "Something meant to weaken or incapacitate me for the coming battle, doubtless," she said. "Immortality offers a significant advantage, but it is no substitute for intelligence. Remember that, young wizard."

Ebenezar scowled and opened his mouth.

"Should it for some bizarre reason ever be necessary," Mab said smoothly, before he could speak.

I stared back and forth between the pair of them for a second.

Yeah. Time for things to change. Just as soon as we dealt with Ethniu and the Fomor.

"I find Corb's assassins wearying," Mab said calmly. She narrowed her eyes in thought for a few seconds before nodding firmly. "Very well, fishman. Have it your way." She snapped her fingers, and over by Molly, the Redcap whipped his head around as if Mab had called his name. The Sidhe warrior, tall and lean and good-looking in that wickedly youthful, long-haired way, the jerk, approached immediately and bowed, sweeping off his Washington Nationals baseball cap.

"Loose the malks," Mab said.

Holy crap.

Malks were . . . not so much cats as nightmares that happened to be shaped like cats. Imagine a lynx, only a little taller and thicker, weighing in at about fifty pounds, with human intelligence and a serial killer's bloodlust. Whatever you're imagining, unless you've been up to some damned peculiar things, the real deal is worse. Malks had claws that could shred through stone and some metals, were supernaturally stealthy and approximately as strong as a chimpanzee, and they resented taking orders, even from the Queen of Air and Darkness herself.

They might get the job done. But they'd hurt a lot of other people on the way, just for kicks. It was in their nature. If Mab turned a pack of those little psychos loose on Chicago, it would be a bloodbath, and they wouldn't care who got slashed to ribbons.

"Wait!" I said.

Mab's eyes turned to me like gun turrets.

The Redcap stared at me with wide eyes and shifted his weight slightly away from me, as if he was getting ready to dive for cover.

Even Ebenezar gave me a look that doubted my mental capacity.

"Uh, please," I added hurriedly. "There's a better way."

Mab's eyes narrowed. "Explain."

"You're irritated with Corb, and that might have had an effect on your judgment," I said.

The air grew several degrees colder in the immediate area. Mab didn't move.

"Save the malks for something more important," I said. "You want these . . . squidwards dealt with? Let me handle it. Until Ethniu is put down, Corb can only be a diversion of your resources. Right?"

Mab narrowed her eyes and tilted her head. Then she said, her lips stiff, "From the mouths of babes." A gesture toward the Redcap was apparently enough to convey the order to stand the malks down, at least for the time being.

"For the sake of your health and happiness, my Knight, it is an excellent thing that you are necessary to my design. But there will be more of these attacks. See to the matter your way, or I will do so in mine." Then she stepped back and inclined her head slightly to Ebenezar. "Excuse me. I must coordinate with my sister's forces. Brief him on the plan, if you please."

The old man clenched his jaw, but he gave Mab a respectful nod nonetheless. The Queen of Winter turned away from us as though we were of no more concern, and approached a table where Vadderung and one of Mab's highest vassals, the Faerie huntsman known as the Erlking, lord of the goblins and master of the Wild Hunt, were poring over a map of Chicago.

The Erlking wore his helmet, and its shadows hid his face, but he was taller than human and lean in his hunting leathers and mail. Vadderung looked like an ancient seafaring pirate gone corporate, with his scarred, lean face and his roguish black eyepatch paired with his excellent double-breasted suit. Both were there to fight.

I swallowed and looked around the roof. River Shoulders came swarming up the outside of the castle wall and flipped himself onto the roof. The Sasquatch must have weighed a thousand pounds, but he landed with hardly a thump. His Victorian-era tuxedo had taken a bit of a beating during the climb—his calves had flexed and split the lower legs of his trousers at the seams. The Forest Person straightened, lifting his shovel-sized hands to carefully straighten the little spectacles he wore across his nose, and nodded down to Listens-to-Wind. The old Native American's hair looked a little more rumpled than usual in its long braid—the old man was the most skilled shapeshifter on the White Council, and he'd probably been out and about while I'd run to the island and back.

The Sasquatch dropped casually to his haunches near the shaman and the two began speaking in quiet, earnest tones while Wild Bill drew back an apprehensive step from River's sheer mass.

Even as I watched, a troop of svartalves simply melded out of the stones of the castle's roof, carrying tools and poles and spools of wire. They began setting down their burdens, looking up at the sky and muttering darkly as they began measuring out distances on the roof, displacing high nobility and supernatural royalty alike without apology as they worked—and all of them, Mab included, moved when necessary without complaint.

Rapidly and efficiently, metal base plates were screwed into the stone of the roof, poles erected, and razor wire strung overhead in a canopy maybe ten feet high. Ah. The svartalves had recognized the danger of Corb's flying assassin creatures and were taking steps to limit their avenues of approach.

Sharp bunch, those svartalves. No wonder even Mab herself didn't complain. Doesn't matter where you go in the world—if you're good at your job, people who are good enough at theirs to see it will respect you for it.

Though it would also seem to be an indicator of how much trouble we were in.

"How you doing, Hoss?" Ebenezar asked me in a gentler tone.

"Um," I said, and licked my lips. "I'm not sure I've been involved in anything quite this . . . overblown, before."

The old man grunted. "You figure Chichén Itzá was a quiet little tea party, I guess."

"Hey, that was just the Council and the Red Court." I had to take a step back to let a ghoul walk past me. The thing was half-shifted into its feral form and was struggling to fit into mail it must have acquired from Marcone's people. I felt a familiar stab of hatred go through me at the sight of the thing. I set it carefully on the back burner. "This is everybody."

Ebenezar snorted out a quick laugh. "Not everybody, boy. Not even close." He looked around the rooftop and nodded. "But I'll allow as it's been a while since there was a dustup quite this big."

I couldn't just stand there talking shop with the old man. "Sir," I blurted, "when this is over, you and I should probably talk about some things."

Ebenezar glanced up at me. His eyes were like granite. "We got to the end of talking, boy. Remember?"

I glowered at him and we both kept walking along grumpily, our staves hitting the ground at the same time.

We reached the map table, and Vadderung and the Erlking both looked up at us. Vadderung was still wearing his business suit. The Erlking was dressed in hunting leathers from somewhere before the Renaissance, under a suit of dark mail. He wore a hunting sword at his hip, and his usual horned helmet had been set aside. The king of the goblins, one of Mab's major vassals, he had an asymmetric, scarred face that somehow managed to be roguishly handsome. The past few times I'd seen him, he'd been really big and really scary. Now he was more like regular human size: He could have passed for a particularly large and graceful professional athlete.

"Ah, the young wolf," the Erlking said in a resonant basso as I approached. "I had not realized he was your pupil, Blackstaff."

The old man nodded to the Erlking. "Oh, he was mostly a hired hand for a little while. Just had to learn a few things before he went off on his own."

The Erlking tilted his head, frowning. "He wears the amulet of Margaret LeFay."

"My mother," I said.

Ebenezar gave me a sharp glance. The old man didn't believe in giving away information for nothing, at least not between the nations. Which was probably going to make that talk with him a little more difficult to arrange and frustrating to attempt. Super.

The current master of the Wild Hunt lifted his eyebrows. He looked back and forth between us before he said, "Margaret's child? Much is explained." He shook his head wryly. "You've no idea how many headaches your mother caused me in her day. Your . . . visit to my realm makes a great deal more sense now."

Vadderung had never looked up from the map. He cleared his throat and said, diffidently, "Gentlemen, to business?"

I bellied up to the table and squinted down at the map. It was well illuminated by chemical light sticks holding down its edges. It had been done on heavy yellowed vellum in sepia inks, all of it in the style of the old Scandinavian mapmakers, complete with Norse runic letters.

And it was moving. Even as I watched, several tiny blue blocks marked with an X glided slowly down streets marked on the map. They stood out against the old-timey artistry as sharply as if they'd been some kind of video game.

"A tactical map," I noted. "Of my town."

Vadderung glanced up at me with his one eye and then back down. "What of it?"

"Takes a lot of effort to make a construct like this," I said. "And a lot of being in the place you're making the map of."

"I've had more time than most to be more places than most," he said.

Ebenezar thumped a thick finger down on the map. "What does this represent?"

"Light infantry," Vadderung replied. "Mostly what we have available to us. Marcone's people here. The White Court's people are there. The local Fae forces are there."

They were spread out in three defensive positions along Lake Shore Drive so that they'd be able to respond to the enemy wherever they came ashore. Two large blue circles marked the map inland of them—one here, atop the castle, and the second hovering over the svartalf embassy.

"Our reserve positions," Vadderung noted. "Heavy response forces have been positioned at each of these points, and they both stand as defensive positions."

"You need to mark a couple more defensive emplacements," I said. I pointed them out on the map. "There. St. Mary of the Angels."

"A church?" the Erlking asked skeptically.

"*The* church," I said. "At least here in Chicago. There's real faith there. Believe it. If we need to fall back to it, they'll open the doors."

"And the second?" Vadderung asked.

I put my finger on the map. "Michael Carpenter's house. The Knights of Hope and Faith are there. Both of them."

"Two doughty foes," the Erlking noted. "And armed with fell blades. But only two."

"There's a dozen guardian angels on duty there at any given time," I said. "Part of Sir Michael's retirement package."

"We will not plan to use them," Vadderung said in a tone of absolute certainty. "Not the angels, and not the Knights. Not in any way. The being you call Mister Sunshine would be quite annoyed at the intrusion."

I arched an eyebrow at Vadderung. I was pretty sure I hadn't ever mentioned my nickname for Uriel to him.

Vadderung gave me a very bland look. "We have lunch once a year."

"Ah," I said. "Well. If some bad guys just happened to walk a little too close, I'm pretty sure they're going to get incinerated. Course, Mister Sunshine thinks a lot of the Accorded folks are bad guys, too." And I agreed with him.

And might have been one of them. I glowered in the direction of the ghouls. "But if we need to move people in a direction, we can send them that way and be pretty sure that the frogs are going to be real slow to chase them."

Vadderung looked up at me sharply. A small, grim smile hit his face for an instant and was gone. "The frogs?"

"Fomor, whatever," I said. "I mean, we can stop being diplomatic with these assholes now, right?"

The other men at the table huffed out low, nervous laughs.

"Frogs," Ebenezar agreed.

"Frogs," echoed the Erlking.

Vadderung's eye gleamed. He shook his head but muttered something and touched the edge of the map, and blue circles blossomed around both indicated positions.

"Our main problem," he noted, "is Ethniu. While she is not the only problem, so long as she stands, no victory is possible."

"She wears Titanic bronze," the Erlking said in a tone that suggested he had said it several times in the past couple of hours.

I held up a hand. "Question from the classroom floor. What is that, exactly?"

"A unique alloy of Olympian bronze and mordite," Vadderung replied. "Kinetic weapons will be of very little use against her. Elemental energies will do little more. It will take a being of divine status to physically penetrate the armor."

"Divine status," I said. "Meaning what?"

"Your Knights, perhaps," the Erlking mused. "Their power would seem to be of the proper origins."

"Those angels you mentioned could do it," Ebenezar said. "Mordite is condensed from the darkest, most evil stuff of the Outside. Once it's alloyed, instead of devouring life it devours energy. Heat, force, lightning, what have you, all backed by the will of the being wearing it. Getting through that takes more than simple power."

"It has to come from the proper source," Vadderung agreed. "And be used for the proper reasons."

Mab glided up to the table. "Sufficiently infernal power could manage the task as well," she murmured. "I daresay Nicodemus Archleone might strike through Titanic bronze."

"Assuming she just stands there and lets any of those beings attack her," the Erlking pointed out. "In the first place, those assets are not under our command. In the second place, she won't. She'll do battle, and most likely kill them."

Vadderung scowled up at the Erlking for a full five seconds before he said, "You're gloomy."

"Merely realistic," the Erlking said.

"You're saying that to get to her, we'd need a sponsor," I said. "And that basically no one around here is strong enough or on the right frequency enough to sponsor that kind of thing."

"Precisely," Mab said.

Gulp.

"So we don't have a tool that can break the armor," I said.

"Probably not," Ebenezar said. "This has to be done the hard way."

Mab nodded. "We must find her if possible, or wait for her to reveal herself if not."

"That means we have to react to her," the Erlking objected.

"Yes," Mab said. "We must be adaptable, above all. Then we must confront her and force her to expend power against us."

"Uh," I said. "That's . . . going to hurt, isn't it?"

"I expect many to die," Mab said. "Once we have engaged her we must grind her down and, when we have weakened her as much as possible, drive her to the water." Her huge, luminous green-grey eyes turned up toward me. "Where we must hope that the will of my Knight is sufficient to contend with hers."

I swallowed. "Yeah. What happens if I miss?"

Mab regarded me steadily. "I should think that the Last Titan will laugh and do precisely what she said she would do. Destroy this city and anyone who stands in her way."

Hoo boy.

"So it's all resting on me," I said.

"We'll do the heavy lifting for you, Hoss," Ebenezar promised. "You just finish the job."

"Yes," Mab said. "Do not fail."

I looked down at the map.

In one of those little blue circles, there was a little girl who was probably asleep by now, watched over by Knights and angels.

And by me.

My chest hurt a little and I carefully packed the feeling away, bottling it, ready to be used later. My terror for my child would not make me better able to defend her. Storing it up and using it to power spells that would destroy the things trying to hurt her would.

Damn right, Harry.

Do. Not. Fail.

"First things first," I said. "I'm going to need pizza."

Chapter

Seven

Getting pizza wasn't as hard as I thought it would be. There was plenty of frozen stuff in the freezers in Castle Marcone's kitchens to feed hungry Einherjaren, and the gas was still working fine. So, in a little less than half an hour, I had several pizzas delivered to the roof.

In that time, twenty more assassin squid streaked across the sky. With the razor-wire canopy, they couldn't dive straight down, so their runs weren't as fast—but they were determined. One of them went for Childs, and one of Marcone's people dived in the way to intercept. He took a tentacle across the throat and went down screaming.

An Einherjar with a medical kit came sprinting, but there was nothing to be done. Marcone's gunman thrashed and flailed so hard that I could hear the snap and crackle of breaking bone and tearing cartilage. He emitted a single-tone, high-pitched scream that went on and on, growing rougher and rougher—until the venom in the myriad tiny wounds just dissolved the flesh of his throat and it erupted into a small fountain of gore.

And that was the first death of the night.

The Redcap proved handiest for this work. He stood by with a suppressed nine-millimeter, cat-pupiled eyes half-closed, standing in a perfectly relaxed posture, and waited. Rather casually, he brought down fourteen of the twenty or so assassin-beasts. The last squidward before the pizza came up slammed into Cristos's back and clubbed him to the roof, but his suit was at least as heavily enchanted with defenses as my own—and Yoshimo's sword cut the squid in half before it had bounced off Cristos and fallen to the floor. He hadn't taken any of the venom, so he would still be in the fight.

Once the pizza got there, I had them take it to the far side of the battlements from where the White Council had set up shop. Then I strode over to Molly and tapped her on the shoulder.

Molly hadn't changed into mail and was still wearing the dive suit she'd had on at the kraken fight. She sat cross-legged, her back straight, her palms resting on her knees. Winter Fae, pixie-sized, but more savage and vicious-looking than my crew, hovered in a cloud around her, darting in and away with messages as she coordinated the movement of troops, I assumed.

She turned to look at me and I froze in place for a moment. It took her a couple of seconds to focus on me, her expression settled in the liquid serenity of deep focus. She spoke, her voice rich and sleepy-sensual. "What is it, my Knight?"

Her eyes had changed.

They were a deep, glacial blue-green. And her pupils had changed shape. They had become feline, like most of the Sidhe.

She blinked several times, focusing on me by degrees, coming up out of the state of concentration she'd been in, and as she did her eyes changed color again, lightening to their natural sky blue, pupils shifting back to circles. "Give me a second, Harry. I'm . . . tracking about two dozen conversations. . . ." Then she exhaled, sighed, scratched at the end of her nose, and said, "What can I do you for?"

I hooked a thumb at the Redcap. "Need to borrow him for a few minutes. I'm going to do something about these squid things and I figure they might object."

Molly arched an eyebrow. "You'd trust him?"

"I'd trust you."

Molly eyed me and then nodded. "Sure. Go with him, Red. Guard him as you would me."

The Redcap bowed his head deeply toward Molly and said, "My lady." Then he turned to me, smiling diffidently. "Sir Knight, I am at your disposal."

"If you were," I said, "I would."

"Bold words for a man about to trust me with his life," the Redcap mused.

"Just making it clear where we stand," I said.

The Redcap smirked. He . . . reminded me considerably of Thomas, now that I thought about it. Six feet and a little lean, dark-haired, and beautiful in the alien way of the Sidhe that would only have let him blend into the oddest of crowds. He was pantherine, slim with hard muscle, relaxed and flowing in his movements, and capable of tremendous speed and the effortless grace that I had witnessed nowhere so much as in the Sidhe at war.

Legend had it that his hat was red because he constantly dipped it in the blood of his victims to keep it nice and bright. He was one of the more prolific killers in the Winter Court, and his star had been in bloody ascendance ever since the death of the last Winter Lady.

I stared at him for a second and said, "Considering you were helping Maeve screw up the world the last time I saw you, you've done pretty well in your career path."

"Is that what I was doing?" the Redcap asked, his tone guileless.

I stopped and stared at him for a second. Then I said, "Hell's bells."

"Ah," the Redcap said, grinning. "The ape finally works it out."

"You weren't working for Maeve at all, were you?"

"Years late to the party," the Redcap said, "but I suppose you got there eventually." He tapped his pistol against his leg. "Mab had positioned me in Maeve's court about thirty years before. I'd been feeding her information while I served her daughter."

"And everything you did to me was meant to assist me."

"Or keep my cover with Maeve, yes," the Redcap said. "Or because it was amusing. I'd apologize for the wound, but hurting you at that time was all three. Honestly, we all thought you would realize the script and play along. But you bumbled your way through it more or less, I suppose."

I just stared at him for a second. Then I said, "I don't suppose it occurred to anyone to just talk to me."

"How many feet higher do the letters need to be in order to spell it out for you, wizard?" the Redcap asked, amused. "Best you learn to read the subtext, if you wish to continue in this business. Besides. It's not as if Mab can just *hand* the Wild Hunt to a mortal to play with." He shook his head. "Strife between queens is a terrible thing for the rest of us. Each can lay commands upon us that we cannot refuse. If one is to hold to one's loyalties, it requires a great deal of careful negotiation of circumstance and conversation to function at all."

"So you were bodyguarding Maeve," I said. "And you more or less betrayed her to her death."

"It was necessary."

"And now you're bodyguarding Molly."

"That is my privilege."

"And if it becomes necessary to betray the Winter Lady again?"

"I should do so without hesitation," he replied calmly.

"If you do," I said, "there will be stories about what happens to you."

The Redcap tilted his head and regarded me quizzically. "I don't think you understand my position, wizard. The lady I now serve meets the highest criteria for my approval that I could reasonably expect from someone still so . . . mortal. She is attentive to her duty, efficient in her execution, and deals appropriately with her enemies. So long as she continues so, she will have my support."

"And the moment she weakens?"

The Redcap gave me a small smile that showed sharp canines. "This *is* the Winter Court. One shudders to think what would happen to her." His smile sharpened slightly. "Or you."

I glowered at him.

"Just making it clear where we stand," he said, in the most annoying way possible. "Honestly, I have no feelings for you personally either way. Excuse me."

And he lifted his gun and sent a bullet about six inches past my left ear.

By the time I flinched, there was a splattering sound and one of the squid things flopped and contorted on the floor, coming to a halt and dying a leaking, broken little monstrosity, ichor making the stones of the castle spark and sizzle.

I rubbed furiously at my ear, which itched tremendously for no good reason at all, and scowled at the Redcap.

He lifted his pistol, smiled, and said, "As my lady commands. Proceed, wizard."

I grimaced at him. Then I trudged over to the battlements where the pizza had been set up and crouched down in the corner, where I'd have cover from assassin squid from a couple of directions at least. The Redcap followed, coming to a halt about ten feet away from me and simply standing there, gun in hand, waiting.

I got down to business. A stick of chalk from my pocket and the pizza were all I really needed. Summonings were pretty straightforward affairs, magically speaking. It was the *consequences* of summonings that got complicated.

For example, I was about to attempt a summoning using a being's true name, right here in front of half of the world. Dammit. I'd have to go nonverbal on this one. It was a low-powered-enough spell that, with any luck, wouldn't hurt too much to perform silently.

Words and magic go hand in hand. Hell, half the words to describe magic practitioners go back to root sources that basically mean *speaker*. There's a reason for that. Magic happens mainly in your head, fueled by emotion and shaped by concentration, reason, and raw will. There's an awful lot of juice going through your brain at any given moment while performing real magic, enough to actually do damage to it.

Part of what keeps your brain insulated from damage is "wrapping" the concept of a given spell up in verbalized phonemes—and it's got to be done in a language that you're not really familiar with, if it's going to do you any good. It provides a kind of insulation for your mind and thoughts. You can do magic without using words all you like—but it has consequences that begin with twitches and disorientation and eventually result in violent seizures and death. No wizard with an ounce of sense makes a practice of doing his magic silently.

But that doesn't mean we can't cheat now and then.

The circle trap with the pizza bait was purely pro forma at this point. I'd been working with this particular being too long and too closely to really require it. So, once things were set up, I settled down on my knees, closed my eyes, and created a mental image of myself in my head, positioned just as I was in life and softly chanting a Name. I poured a whisper of energy into it and held the image, silently kneeling and waiting.

It took less than a long moment. There was a burring sound in the air, and I saw the Redcap tense and raise his gun. I held up my palm toward him sharply and gave my head a single firm shake. He stared hard at me for a second before lowering the gun, and then my only actual vassal arrived.

Major General Toot-Toot Minimus resembled a glowing violet comet more than anything else as he approached
in a low-pitched buzz of dragonfly wings. It wasn't until
he got closer that the nimbus around him resolved into
the shape of an athletic young man crowned with a shock
of dandelion-silk hair in shades of lavender and violet. He
might have cut a very impressive figure if he'd been more
than about thirty inches tall.

Toot . . . was not dressed properly. I'd grown used to
his little outfits made of cast-off doll clothing and repur-
posed human refuse, which had served him well for weapons and armor over the years. But now Toot-Toot had
been upgraded.

He wore a full suit of gothic plate armor, made of some
weird-looking alloy colored a deep, almost black shade of
purple. It came complete with a small black cape embla-
zoned with the corporate logo of Pizza 'Spress, a local
delivery chain, in gold embroidery, surrounded by letters
in the logo, FOR THE ZA LORD.

Instead of his usual utility blade or X-Acto knife, he
bore in his hands a spear as long as he was with a broad
head suitable for stabbing or slashing, made from the same
metal as his armor. Upon his back, between his wings, was
a pair of short blades hanging from a harness, also in the
same kind of metal.

Toot deftly avoided a clutch of darting pixie messengers
and came streaking directly toward me—ignoring the circle completely and coming to a screeching halt in midair
in front of the Redcap at eye level.

"Avaunt, scoundrel!" he piped at the Sidhe warrior. For

a pixie, Toot had an absolutely roaring basso of a voice. For everyone else, he sounded like a cute cartoon character. "I saw you giving my lord dirty looks!"

The Redcap narrowed his eyes and showed his teeth in a lazy smile. "Care, little one. I'd prefer not to waste a bullet on you when there's so much more interesting game in the offing."

"I'd like to see you *try* it!" huffed Toot, buzzing in a little circle that sent motes of light exploding out from him like a cartoon figure's cloud of dust.

Even as I watched, there was a flitting shadow, and by the time the sound of a second set of buzzing wings was audible, a slender figure in black fae armor, almost Toot's size, was hovering just behind the Redcap, the tip of her little black lance touching the skin of the back of the Redcap's neck with delicate precision. The pixie holding the lance was female, pale of skin and dark of hair, and she had way too much makeup around her eyes.

"Think carefully, biggun," the pixie piped. "For though one day I will end his miserable life, while my durance continues I will lend my arm to the major general."

The Redcap's eyes shifted behind him. By the time they moved back to Toot, the pixie's distraction was over, and his lance was resting a hairsbreadth from the Redcap's eye.

"Lacuna *adores* me!" Toot shrilled.

"We are comrades in arms," Lacuna said. "Then I will kill you."

"It is *love*!" Toot insisted.

"When you're dead," Lacuna said, "I get your teeth."

Toot beamed broadly. "See? She loves me for *me*!"

The Redcap took a deep breath and said, "Boo!"

Both pixies fluttered back a dozen feet before the sound was done leaving his mouth.

"Dresden," the Redcap said, a touch plaintively.

"Major General," I said, "Lacuna, stand down. Tonight, he is the enemy of my enemy."

Toot gasped and gripped his spear more tightly. "A double enemy!"

Lacuna buzzed over to hover near Toot. "No, idiot. It means he is an ally right now."

Toot gripped his lance in both hands, his arms extended to full length, and buzzed in a happy circle. "My girlfriend is so smart!"

"I am not your girlfriend," Lacuna said sullenly. "I am a prisoner of war."

"Harry, I must say," Toot-Toot said, dropping his voice to a stage sotto voce, "that's *frozen* pizza. What are you doing?"

"It's symbolic pizza," I said.

"Symbolic pizza sucks!" Toot shouted.

"None of it is good for you," Lacuna insisted.

"Guys!" I said. "The pizza—*all* the pizza—is in danger!" That got their attention.

Toot-Toot whirled to face me in horror. "What?!"

Lacuna's face suffused with joy. "What!?"

I gave them the kindergarten-level, probably cheaply animated rundown on who Ethniu was. "And now," I concluded, "she's coming here to kill all the people."

"Uh-huh," Toot said, nodding, listening, completely supportive.

"And me," I said.

"Uh-huh," Toot said brightly, waiting.

"And all the pizza shops," I said.

"Oh no!" Toot wailed. He buzzed in a vertical circle. "Oh no, oh no, oh no!"

"That will definitely be better for your teeth," Lacuna said.

"The stars take my teeth, woman!" Toot bellowed.

Lacuna gasped, shocked.

"This cannot be borne!" Toot trumpeted. "It cannot be endured! We must fight!" He shot out into the open air above the street, spinning as he went, so filled with fury was his tiny form, glowing brighter and brighter. "We must fight!" he called, and his shrill voice rattled from the stones of the castle. *"WE MUST FIGHT!"* came his tiny roar, echoing down the streets.

And something happened that I had not expected.

The stars fell on Castle Marcone.

One moment, the bustle of the command center was proceeding along. The next, glowing lights, some as tiny as the little elements inside Christmas lights, some as large as beach balls, all began descending from overhead, emerging from corners and crevices of houses, rising from gardens and bushes and gliding from trees. In moments, the torch-lit night, full of shadows and uncertainty, had become filled with an ambient aurora that bathed entire blocks around the little castle in multicolored radiance. They weren't coming by the handful or by the dozen, but by the hundreds and *thousands*, with more gathering from every direction.

In a particular circle around Toot-Toot, thirty or so of the largest and fiercest of the pixie warriors had gathered, each of them armed and armored like their leader, in finely made fae plate, bearing small and wickedly sharp weaponry. The Za Lord's Guard had turned out for battle, but it was more than that.

I realized that I was watching something that I had never seen or even much heard of before.

The Little Folk were mobilizing for war.

For pizza.

Hell's bells.

Well.

You always find support for your causes by making them relatable to people where they live, I guess.

"Idiots," Lacuna breathed. "We could just hide and then take all the teeth we wanted from the dead."

"You are a highly creepy little person," I said.

"Thank you," Lacuna said gravely.

"Where'd they get the armor?" I asked.

"Lady Molly had it and the new weapons delivered with the pizza, at the solstice," she said.

I eyed her armor. "What happened to all the barbed fishhooks that were welded on yours?"

She sniffed and gave me a haughty, disgusted look. "The general kept cutting himself. Because he knew I would be honor bound to nurse him back to health after. It was necessary."

"Toot and Lacuna, sitting in a tree," I chanted, grinning. "K-I-S-S—"

The tip of Lacuna's lance landed firmly in the space between my two front teeth.

"Attempt to complete that enchantment, wizard," she said, "and I will ram this lance through your uvula."

I couldn't stop smiling without the blade of the lance cutting my lips. So I stood there carefully with my teeth together and my lips lifted away from them and said, "Okay."

There wasn't a visible signal, but Lacuna looped up into the air, joining the Za Lord's Guard, and then, in a coordinated streak of light, all thirty of them came zipping down to the roof of the castle and hit the ground in formation, in unison—in the classic superhero landing—before straightening to slam tiny fists to tiny breastplates, the faemetal ringing like a chorus of wind chimes.

"My lord!" Toot shrilled. "Your Guard stands ready to serve and to lead our people in defense of the pizza!"

I looked up and . . . the sky was full of a wheel of tiny lights, tens of thousands, maybe *hundreds* of thousands of the Little Folk, in an aerial field half a mile across and slowly rotating, as if that entire circle, that entire . . . pizza of tiny fae, was deliberately, precisely centered.

Above me.

The talk and chatter died away as light bathed the grim, dark little castle. Silence spread across the rooftop. I looked down to see Mab and the Ladies regarding me with small, knowing smiles. Everyone else, from ghouls to White Council to svartalves to Sasquatch, just stared up at the sky and then at the focus of the whirling mandala of Little Folk, at the kneeling formation of warriors, awaiting my word.

They all stared at me.

Mab's eyes glittered with fierce, bright pride.

I didn't really know what else to do. So I just got to work.

I dropped to one knee to address my little fighters, like a football captain in a huddle. I pointed at the body of the dead assassin squid and said, "See those things?"

Toot growled, and the Guard followed suit. It was kind of adorable.

"The bad guys are sending those things to kill the big people trying to protect the pizza," I said. "They fly and they're under a veil. We need your help. Only the Little Folk can protect us against them. I want a cohort stationed here and at the svartalf embassy to intercept any of these creatures coming in. Everyone else should hunt them down wherever they can be found. The littlest of your folk can help us by watching out for veils. If they see any bad guys moving around under veils or being sneaky, they should swarm them and make sure the big folk can see them and fight them."

"Kill these things," Toot said, gesturing at the fallen assassin squid. "Guard this house and the svartalf house. And point out any sneaky bad guys to the poor, stupid bigguns."

"Exactly, General," I said. "Can you do it?"

Toot shot to his feet and up to my eye level, and the rest of the Guard came with him. He shouldered his lance and slammed a little fist over his heart, making the faemetal chime again, and whirled to begin giving orders. He pointed and gesticulated wildly, speaking in too rapid and high-pitched a tone for my poor biggun ears to clearly understand. Individual members of the Guard sped out into the night, up to the cloud of Little Folk above, to gather a constellation of glowing lights around them and speed off in different directions.

Within minutes, the effects could be seen. Clouds of determined Little Folk, too small to fight individually, would zip around darting assassin squid in little swarms, creating streaks of light across the sky. When the first one was sighted, Toot himself zipped out with his lance gripped tight, Lacuna on his wing. Within a moment, the pair of them flew a dead squid back to the roof and dropped it proudly at my feet. Their armor and lances were stained with ichor, their little faces satisfied and proud. "Like that?" Toot asked.

"Good work, General," I said firmly. "Carry on until we've driven them all away or the battle is lost."

"We will *not* lose the pizza," Toot-Toot said grimly.

Lacuna sighed.

Then the pair of them zipped off into the night.

"Impressive," the Redcap said, once they were gone. He glanced at his pistol with a faint expression of disappointment and then slipped it into his waistband at the small of his back. "How did you manage to bind them all?"

"Trade secrets," I said. I tried not to think about how much pizza it would take to pay off *that* many of the Little Folk. Maybe I'd send Marcone the bill. It was technically his stupid territory we were defending. "I'm done with you."

The Redcap narrowed his eyes but nodded at me politely and went back over to Molly, who had returned to running her own communications through her own Little Folk crew.

Mab approached and stood beside me for a moment, looking out at the night. You could see a squid being taken down every minute or so. It was a bit like watching for falling stars at the right time of year.

"Mortals ask a question," she said after a moment. "Is it better to be feared or loved?"

"I can guess your answer," I said.

"And I yours. Yet they do not love *you*, per se," she mused.

"Not exactly, no," I said. "But I found something they do love. Something that unites them."

Mab looked at me blankly.

"When a group comes together around something they love," I said, "it changes things. It changes how they see one another. It becomes a community. Something greater than the sum of its parts."

Mab did not seem enlightened.

I tried to explain another way. "The creation of the community encourages investment in that community," I said. "Once they've invested, they'll fight to protect it."

Mab's eyebrows went up in comprehension. "Ah. You found a weakness in their psychology and manipulated it. You provided them with a resource and incurred their debt."

"I made them see themselves differently."

"Neuromancy? You? I shudder to think of the results of that."

I sighed. "Look. Maybe you'll just have to trust me. It's a mortal thing."

"Ah," Mab said dismissively. "Still. An impressive display. You frightened several very confident beings tonight. I found it entertaining."

"Yeah, it just . . . sort of happened," I said. I leaned tiredly on the battlements. I wished I had a sandwich.

I sneezed out of nowhere, so hard that I nearly slammed my head into the merlon I was leaning on. By this time, I was getting used to it. I felt the surge of wearying energy leave me, felt where the conjuration point drew matter from the Nevernever into the mortal world and shaped it. I managed to get my hands into the air above my head in time to deflect a falling club sandwich. It bounced off one of my forearms, splattered partly on one shoulder and partly on the ground—before promptly turning to gooey ectoplasm.

Mab stared at me as though I had just begun dissecting a fetal pig at the dinner table. She shook her head slowly, once, and said, "Just as you begin to impress me."

"Oh bide be," I muttered, and fished out a handkerchief to blow my nose.

Stupid conjuritis.

I was exhaling when the first explosion thudded through the night air.

Everyone froze.

To the east and a little south of us, a column of flames rose into the air, flaring out in the night. The shock wave of the explosion was tangible, even where we stood on the roof, something I felt push through my chest.

"Was that . . . ?" I breathed.

Mab drew herself upright, cold light gathering around her brow in a coronet of glittering motes that trailed a veil of tiny snowflakes behind it. Every eye on the roof turned to her, as the Queen of Air and Darkness lifted her face to the night sky and spoke in a voice that did not so much thunder through the air as glide into the earth itself and resonate in gentle music from every solid surface in sight.

"Accorded nations," Mab said calmly. "Stand to arms. Mortal men of Chicago, remain in the homes that offer you your only safety. The enemy has come for the city."

Chapter Eight

My stomach did a little twisty flip.

Somewhere in my head, I'd been processing it all night, that events this large could not go by unnoticed. That destruction on this scale simply could not be brushed under the rug, that this many witnesses could not be silenced. Whatever happened in the battle, whoever prevailed, one fact was clear.

Things were going to change.

The mortal world couldn't take something like this in stride.

I'd known that on an instinctual level for a while, I thought, but I hadn't consciously processed it until I'd heard Mab addressing the mortal population of Chicago by means entirely and self-evidently magical.

She wasn't even trying to keep things subtle.

God, that had the potential to be the greatest nightmare I could imagine—the mortal world, turned against the supernatural. The war that would be born from that conflict would redefine barbarism—and it could already be lurching into motion, right here in front of my eyes.

Of course, if Ethniu had her way, it was an absolute certainty. So we'd have to stop her here and now and as quickly as freaking possible.

But whatever happened, after tonight there would be walls coming down between the mortal world and the supernatural one that had stood solidly for centuries. Stars and stones, I didn't think anyone knew what that might mean.

Focus, Harry.

Save the city.

Stop the Titan.

Don't mess it up.

While I was busy trying to screw my courage to the sticking place, Mab was already moving. She spoke quietly to Listens-to-Wind and the two had a brief exchange before the old shaman inclined his head to her, murmured to Wild Bill, and then simply leaned and fell off the edge of the building and out of sight.

A heartbeat later, the gliding, silent form of a great owl swept up from below the battlements and soared in the direction of the explosion.

Out in the distance, I heard the sound of gunfire. Not the usual stuff, the kind of thing you might hear from time to time, that could maybe be a car backfiring. This sounded like a war movie, a crackling like deadly popcorn.

Mab listened to the gunfire for a moment. Then she stopped outside Martha Liberty's circle, speaking quietly, and listened to what one of the poppets had to say. From there she stopped in with Lara Raith, holding a brief conversation that featured several nods from each of them.

Ebenezar stumped over to stand next to me. There was

a long moment of strained silence. Then he cleared his throat and said, "How you doing, Hoss?"

"I feel like I should be moving," I said. "Explosion, gunfire." I nodded in the direction in which Listens-to-Wind had vanished. "I should be running toward that."

The old man grunted. "Do you remember the hardest lesson of power?"

"Knowing when *not* to use it?"

"Aye," he said, his voice rough. He leaned on a merlon and stared out at the night. Firelight from a circle of road flares several blocks away reflected in his spectacles. He watched the Little Folk take down another assassin squid. "Well. In this fight, you've got to be in the right place at the right time. That means hanging back until you know where to throw your weight."

I clenched my fists. He was right. I knew that. That didn't mean I had to like it.

"I hate it, Hoss," he said in a very quiet voice.

I turned toward him and listened.

"Seeing you like this, all the time. In the worst of the cross fire. It was like this with your mother. Getting more and more isolated from other wizards." He glowered at Lara and Mab. "Getting caught up with a bad crowd. And I didn't know what the hell to do. What to say to her. Either." He coughed and blinked his eyes. "Dammit, Hoss. You keep getting hurt. And I can't stop it."

I might have blinked my eyes once or twice, too. Then I leaned on the merlon beside him and said, "Well. Could be that I get myself involved in things sometimes."

His eyes wrinkled at the corners. "You don't know how to sit things out, and that's a fact."

"Maybe I should have had a better teacher."

He puffed out a breath and glowered at me briefly. "Wiseass."

I sighed. "You think I've made the wrong calls."

"I think I don't know anyone who gets into bed with Mab without regretting it," the old man said, without any heat. "You're keeping real dangerous company, Hoss."

"She's played it pretty straight with me so far," I said.

"Aye. And it's making you lower your guard. Like it's supposed to." He shook his head. "She's immortal. She can take her time. Entangle you one strand of web at a time. You and your apprentice, too."

I thought about Molly's eyes. Or maybe not-Molly's eyes, cat-pupiled and alien.

"It's dangerous," I said. "I know that. I went in with my eyes open. If Mab compromises my free will, she loses what makes me an effective weapon. It's still me, sir."

The old man glanced at me from under his shaggy silver brows. His voice softened slightly.

"You're betting an awful lot on that," he said.

"Am I wrong?" I asked.

His jaw muscles tensed and relaxed several times. "There's falling from grace," he said, finally. "And there's being pushed. And you're standing pretty far out on a ledge, Hoss."

"My choice," I said. "Eyes open."

The old man snorted. "Aye. Don't mean I got to like it."

"Neither do I," I said candidly. "But it's what I've got."

His eyes glittered brightly behind his spectacles as he stared at Mab. "You should get out."

"Not without Molly," I said.

He sighed. "Why do you think Mab roped her in, boy?"

"Not without Molly," I said, in exactly the same tone.

"Dammit," he said. But he stopped pressing. "Her next move will be to start putting the nails in. Get you pegged down the way she wants."

"Like what?"

"God Almighty knows, boy. Responsibility, maybe. God knows you collect enough of that. She would use wealth to weigh you down, if you cared about that kind of thing much. Power, maybe, influence. Maybe she'll throw some honey on top. But whatever it is, it'll look good at first glance, and it'll put you on a tighter leash."

"Sir," I said, "how well does history suggest that leashes will work out with me? For anybody at all."

He snorted quietly. "Mab ain't a high school gym teacher, Hoss. Or a batch of worried, cautious old fools." He coughed. "Or a worn-out farmer who cares too much about you."

I put my hand on his shoulder and squeezed.

He nodded at me.

"You understand," he said. "I'm going to do what I think is right for you, Hoss. I have to. How can I do any less?"

"You are a stubborn old pain in the ass, sir," I said, warmly and sadly. "Who ought to know better."

"Well. I was never much good at learning my own lessons," he said.

Another explosion happened, only to the other side, farther north. This one was softer and broader, somehow. It didn't go *kapow* so much as it went *whoomph*. Light flared out and showed us the shadows of buildings in a city block for a quarter of a minute, though we couldn't see the source of the light.

My stomach quivered again, uneasiness going through me. Fire. Gunshots continued.

We weren't close enough to hear any screams.

Not yet.

My heart started beating faster.

"Gas tank went up, maybe," I said. My throat felt tight. My voice came out scratchy.

"Aye," agreed the old man. He eyed me. Then, without a word, reached a hand into his overall pocket and came out with a flask. He offered it to me.

I opened it and sniffed, then sipped. Water. I wetted my whistle gratefully. "That came from up by the svartalf embassy," I said.

He grunted. "Etri and his svartalves are set up in that area. He and the Archive are commanding from there."

"Ivy, huh?" I asked. "I thought she was neutral."

"She was, until Ethniu included her in her threat with the rest of us," Ebenezar said. "The Archive realizes the need for self-preservation—and if the Titan truly wishes to subjugate humanity, she must destroy literacy as part of the process."

"Huh. It's not so much that, I think," I said thoughtfully.

The old man looked at me.

I shrugged. "Ivy . . . she's on our side. On the side of people. On a fundamental level."

"How do you figure?"

"She's made to record and preserve knowledge," I said.

"No people, no knowledge. Nothing to record and preserve, and no reason to record or preserve it. Her existential purpose requires . . . us."

"Wouldn't get my hopes up too far about that one," Ebenezar said. "But you might be onto something."

The Redcap must have vanished from the rooftop for a while, because I saw him come back up from below with a big black nylon equipment bag. He took it over to Molly, who looked up, waved away several of the Little Folk playing messenger around her, and rose to her feet. She took the bag from him, carried it over to us, and tossed it down at my feet.

"There," she said. She eyed me. "I'm just not feeling the suit for this kind of work. Go change."

I arched an eyebrow at her. Then I leaned down and opened the bag.

It had my stuff in it, from the apartment. A pair of jeans, a T-shirt, and my ensorcelled leather duster. My gun belt was in there, too, with my big old monster-shooting revolver, as well as a short-barreled coach gun in a scabbard on a bandolier loaded with various-colored shells.

"Suit up, Sir Knight," Molly said, and winked at me.

"Hell's bells," I muttered. "I'm just a great big Ken doll for you people to dress up, aren't I?"

"You're lucky the Leanansidhe is commanding the outer defenses," Molly said. "Auntie Lea would have insisted you be properly attired." Her smile faded. Her eyes searched for words for a moment, and when she spoke, she was choosing them carefully. "Harry. I won't be here for you tonight."

I paused and stared at her. "What? Why?"

"I can't tell you." She grimaced, frustration in her eyes for a moment. "But it's necessary. And it's got to be me."

I drew a deep breath. I'd been counting on having the grasshopper to back me up. The now-immortal grasshopper, for crying out loud.

On the other hand, this was Molly.

I stared at her eyes for a while. She and I had taken each other's measure already. And what I had seen in her was a dark and terrible potential, power that could be used for weal or woe, based upon her choices. I guess the real question was whether it was really Molly making the choices any longer. If it was still the young woman I'd known.

I knew where I stood on that one.

If my Molly said she had to leave, she had a damned good reason.

"Okay," I said. I winked at her. "I mean, dammit, but okay."

She lifted both her eyebrows in surprise for a moment. Then she clasped my hands and gave me a brief luminous smile. She nodded to Ebenezar and turned away, beckoning with a finger and collecting the Redcap like a well-trained hound. The pair of them hurried from the command center and vanished below, presumably to leave the castle.

And I felt a little more alone than I had a moment before.

My stomach wasn't quite cramping, but . . . the tension was getting higher. The quivering unrest inside me would not cease. We stood there waiting and doing nothing while a war began around us.

Another car went up, this time farther to the south. An

assassin squid made it all the way to the roof before Lacuna rammed her spear through it and pinned it to the map table six inches from Vadderung's hand. The one-eyed man grunted without looking up from the map, unstuck the spear absently, flicked the squid over the side of the building, and offered the weapon back to the small fae.

Wizard Cristos came over, looking dignified and severe in his suit and robes, and spoke quietly in Ebenezar's ear. The old man nodded, thumped my shoulder with his fist, and walked off to one corner of the rooftop, speaking quietly to the other Senior Councilman.

I couldn't stand there doing nothing all by myself. I grabbed the nylon bag and took it down to the locker room next to the gym. Then I started doing what you do in locker rooms, and changed clothes. It was a busy place; the Einherjaren who were still coming in from the blacked-out city surrounding the castle would rush in to suit up and arm themselves from the weapons locker.

I was down to my underwear when a man the size of a small polar bear slammed his locker and departed, still buckling a vambrace onto one arm, and abruptly left me alone in the locker bay with Gentleman John Marcone.

The robber baron of Chicago had undressed down to his undershirt and slacks and was currently fastening the fittings on a vest of overlapping scales of some advanced-looking material that covered his torso closely enough to be custom fit. I'd seen him out of a suit only once before, and he'd been in rough shape at the time. Despite his age, Marcone was built like a light-heavyweight boxer. The muscles moving under his forearms were made of lean steel cable. As I watched, he shrugged into his suit shirt and began buttoning it up.

"Did you forget the next step in the dressing process, Dresden?" he asked, without looking up at me. "Or is this some sort of awkward sexual reconnaissance?"

With massive dignity, I put on my pants one leg at a time. "Locker room talk? Really?"

"It seemed something you would be capable of appreciating."

I snorted and kept getting dressed. Marcone put on a gun belt and hung a pistol under each arm.

"I saw you earlier," I said. "Facing Ethniu."

He eyed me without actually looking at me.

The words tasted bitter and tainted in my mouth, but I said, "That took guts."

His mouth twisted at one corner. "Ouch. That must have hurt."

I nodded and spat into a trash can. "No idea."

Marcone took up his suit jacket and shrugged into it. He adjusted it until the cloth fell without revealing the guns. "Do you know the difference between courage and foolhardiness, Dresden?"

"Any insurance adjuster would say no."

He waved a hand at my banter, as though that was all the acknowledgment it deserved. "Hindsight," he said. "Until the extended consequences of any action are known, it is both courageous and foolish. And neither."

"Well," I said, "tonight you earned yourself a Schrödinger's Medal, I guess."

He seemed to muse on that for a moment. "Yes," he

said, fastening one button. "I suppose I did." He paused and glanced at me. "I notice you kept quiet."

"Maybe I'm finally learning my lesson."

"*That's* not it." Marcone tilted his head, frowning. "The only way that would have happened is, frankly . . . if you had not been present."

Okay, well. Sometimes even the bad guys are right, more or less. I kept my mouth shut and finished getting dressed.

"Dresden," Marcone said, "while I have enjoyed working with your queen, and find her business practices admirable, do not presume any sort of personal amity between us. At all."

"Oh. I don't."

"Excellent," Marcone said. "Then I will not need to explain how severely I will be obliged to react to you should you engage in any of your . . . typical shenanigans in violation of my territory or my sovereign rights under the Accords."

"Really?" I said. "Right now, you're comparing testosterone size?"

"I have no intention of dying tonight, Dresden," Marcone said. "Nor of losing what I have fought to claim. I am a survivor. As, improbably, are you." He nodded to me politely and spoke in a very quiet, reasonable tone that was all the more chilling for the absolute granite rumbling beneath the surface. "I only wish you to be aware that I mean to continue as I have begun. After tonight, I will still be here—and you, by God, will show respect."

"Or what?" I asked him, lightly.

Marcone's stare was not a matter for lightness. "I will

pursue my rights under Mab's Accords. And she will not protect you."

I felt a little cold chill go through my guts, way down low. Marcone had me dead to rights there. I *had* violated his territory under the Accords, more than once. He'd just never wanted to shove it in the face of the White Council, who would have had no interest in bowing to a lesser power. Offhand, I wasn't sure what the penalty would be for that kind of lawbreaking, but Mab's idea of justice wasn't exactly a progressive one. More to the point, her idea of justice was damned near an absolute: If I had broken her laws, I would deserve to be punished under them. My status as the Winter Knight would not matter to her in the least, except that she might be that much more annoyed before she executed me.

Dammit, Thomas. Why in the hell do you get me into messes like this?

"As long as we're being honest," I said, "you should probably know that I still think you're a prick. I still think you're responsible for a lot of good people getting hurt. And I'm going to tear you down one day."

Marcone stared hard at me for a moment. He wasn't afraid of my eyes. He'd taken my measure, too, and I remembered the cold, fearless core of him, of an apex predator who happened to wear a human form. Then he, too, did something eerie.

He smiled.

A wolf would have been jealous.

"Excellent," he said.

Then he left.

*   *   *

I walked back out onto the roof, the heat of the summer night wet and heavy against my face. My duster hung heavy over my shoulders, too hot for the night, the spell-infused leather a comforting weight around me. I gripped my staff in my left hand. From one hip hung my big .50-caliber revolver. The scabbard for the short coach gun, loaded with Dragon's Breath rounds, hung from the other. My Warden's cloak was fastened over one shoulder, where it would be adding the least to my discomfort in the sultry air, yet still declare my allegiance to the Council.

Over on the eastern edge of the roof, Mab, Lara, the Senior Council, Vadderung, the Erlking, and the Summer Lady had gathered together in a silent group, with River Shoulders looming over them in the back. They were staring out at the night, now lit by more fires, and the wind coming off the lake brought us the distant scent of burning rubber and black smoke.

I looked down at the shadow being cast in front of me. The long, billowing outline of the duster. The slender length of my staff. The outline of my head, with my ears sticking out a little, my hair a mussed mess.

I'd been doing this for a while. The duster and the staff and the attitude. I mean, you'd think I'd have grown up at some point. But I was, in a lot of ways, still that dumb kid opening up his own private investigations business, all those years ago.

Across that roof stood some of the greatest monsters, legends, even gods of our world. They were staring out at the night, standing together.

They were frightened.

Underneath the calm, the steady action, the relentless calculation, the superhuman power—they were frightened. Them.

And I was just me.

I took a deep breath.

My sneakers squeaked as I paced across the roof and joined them.

The Erlking nodded to me as I stopped by his elbow. "They're moving now," he reported. He nodded out toward the original explosion. "Hear that?"

The gunfire had increased to a frantic pace. Heavier ordnance was going off from time to time. Maybe grenades or something? I wasn't all that familiar with the practicalities of military weapons in action.

The Erlking directed my attention to the north and south. "There, that dark space, that's where my troops are. They're forcing the Fomor to move around them, to the north and south. See the fires?"

I looked. He was right. Fires had begun to burn in a path around the embattled position.

"There's too many of them," I breathed.

The Erlking nodded. "For the time being. Do not be distracted. This battle is not about Corb or his forces. It is about Ethniu."

"Right," I said, watching the fires spread through my city, lighting more and more of it, and bringing with them a pall of smoke. "Right. Be cool."

My stomach hurt, and I realized, dimly, that somewhere deep down I was furious. Foes had come to harm my neighbors, my city, my home. There could be no fires too hot to devour them. And I was just standing there, doing nothing.

My knuckles ached as I gripped my staff.

"Contact!" shouted one of the Einherjaren.

Without hesitation, Vadderung pointed at another of the eternal soldiers, standing near him. The man lifted one of those grenade launchers with the big cylinder like a giant revolver to his shoulder and aimed it up. He fired three times, *phoont, phoont, phoont,* and within a few seconds a number of flares were falling from high above, showering light onto the neighborhood around the castle.

There were bipedal forms out there, shadows really, stalking down the streets, sidewalks, yards, moving stealthily—freezing in place where the light fell on them, while the shapes moving in the deeper shadows seemed to become that much more furtive and agitated.

"Ready stations," called Marcone's voice. "Prepare to fire."

I turned to see the Baron of Chicago walk briskly onto the roof, flanked by Gard and Hendricks. He ignored me as he walked past to stand beside Vadderung. "An assault force?"

"Light infantry, I think, Baron," Vadderung said, squinting his eye out at the night. "Their forward elements. Scouts. They haven't shown us their strength yet."

Marcone nodded. "Hold fire unless the enemy engages us," he said to the nearest of the Einherjaren, and one of the tallest. The man nodded and passed the order down the line.

"Wait," I said. "What?"

From down the street, my street, I heard the sound of shattering glass.

Someone screamed. I couldn't tell if it was a man or a woman. It was high-pitched and desperate. The human voice rang out surprisingly loud in the stillness of the night.

That was a person. Terrified.

Someone who lived on my street.

I heard the frantic panic fire from a pistol, maybe some-one's revolver. A scream, something that sounded too harsh and brassy to be human. There was a long, drawn-out howl, then a flash of light, and I saw something red and flickering hit a car about a hundred yards down the street. There was a breathless quarter second, and then the car went up in a fireball as its gas tank exploded.

I could see figures, furry or fur-clad, rushing toward the open front doors of one of a row of rental houses. There were few supernaturally significant thresholds to speak of on such properties, little protection from the powers of darkness.

My stomach twisted in fear and rage. Every instinct in my body urged me forward. The predator's territoriality within the Winter Knight's mantle was in complete ac-cord, the need for violence, to defend my territory, to rend my foes, pulsing through my veins with every heartbeat.

"There," I said, and pointed a shaking hand. "We have to help them."

"That is not our role in this fight," said Vadderung.

Another scream came down the street. This time there was no mistaking it.

It was a child's voice, a single high-pitched note.

"Hoss," said Ebenezar warningly.

I couldn't see. My vision was narrowing to a tunnel. My chest heaved.

I looked to my left. In the tunnel of my vision, Mab was a slender, pale white light, her eyes bright, feline, narrowed. She watched me.

"We have to help them," I said, louder and harder.

Mab's teeth showed.

"We can't," Ebenezar said. "Hoss, there's too many of them. We can't commit until we know."

I stared around the rooftop. Then I said, "To hell with all of you."

And I did something I'd been working every day for months *not* to do.

I let the Winter mantle do its thing.

I went off the roof in a leap, windmilling my arms and legs. I hit the ground, let my body break my fall at its natural bending points, dropped into a forward roll, and came up running, moving as quick and sure as any creature of the wild.

There was a heavy thud, and a thousand pounds of River Shoulders landed next to me, an eager growl bubbling in his chest that sounded freaking tectonic. Ahead of me, another car exploded, part of the fireball catching one end of the rental house and enveloping it in flames. Indistinct inhuman figures leapt in through the front door.

And me and a genuine, honest-to-God Bigfoot let out simultaneous roars of rage, one way more impressive than the other, and launched ourselves at the invaders.

Chapter

Nine

caught their scent at about sixty feet.

It was a wild, fierce smell, something that hit my hindbrain and set the hairs all along my spine up straight. Ever smelled a predator's den? There's the musk of the creature's odor, mixed in with the scent of urine, a little bit of rotten meat, and the faint sweetness of marrow with the rasping dryness of cracked bone.

That same predator reek hit me as we closed in on the invaders—figures with massive, fur-outlined bodies and gnarled, muscular limbs. I got a good look at the first of them as we hit the sidewalk outside the embattled home.

It looked almost human. Skin the color of wet ashes. Six and a half feet tall, maybe, with the lean, ropy muscle of someone who can cover a lot of ground in a hurry. Its hair was a mane, ferocious and long, with feathers and claws bound in among it. The horns of a stag either grew from its skull or had been bound there somehow. A heavy mantle of furs over a long cloak of the same gave its lean torso some kind of protection, and it carried a long spear of some blackened metal in its hands.

Even as we closed, the creature had whirled toward us, bringing the tip of the spear up. There was a low howling sound, and a flicker of reddish light gathered around the creature's hands. The light flashed up the shaft of the spear, hitting a number of pictographs etched into the metal along the way, each exploding in a sequential flash. I had about enough time to realize that a projectile was coming my way, and then the tip of the spear glared scarlet and I flung myself to the side.

There was a shrieking, howling sound, and a chunk of asphalt half the size of a garbage can flew up into a spray of scorched, blobby, flaming road material ten yards behind me.

I hit the ground at a roll, tried to come up running, and tripped on the damned Warden's cape. I half strangled myself and fell.

River Shoulders had me covered. Even as the creature's spear tracked toward me, the Sasquatch simply took a bounding stride, lowered a shoulder the size of an off-road tire, and ran into the thing.

If the creature had been standing in front of a train, it might have been better off. About half a ton of supernaturally powerful muscle hit the creature in a concentrated burst of precisely aimed energy as focused and directed as that of any martial artist. The creature's body went rag doll, flying back from the impact in an explosive crackling of breaking bone—only to hit against a large old oak standing stolidly in the house's front yard despite severe trimming to allow for power lines.

The shape that fell to the ground at the base of the tree was kind of . . . amorphous.

River Shoulders turned toward the front of the house and let out a roar that literally shattered the first-floor windows, a primal scream—and, the Winter mantle told me, a challenge that could not be ignored, not by foes as primally bound as these.

There was a faint sound to one side, and my eyes snapped forward to see a second of the creatures, this one larger and better-muscled than the first, ease around the corner of the house, outside River Shoulders' view, and raise its spear to aim at the Sasquatch's back.

I drew without thinking, from a prostrated position, tightening my abs and aiming slightly to the right of my right foot. I had a great sight picture and lined up the dots of the big .50-caliber revolver and squeezed the trigger without once thinking a single thought. The bullet went through the creature's right cheekbone, holy crap, and came out somewhere behind where its right ear would have been . . .

. . . and the thing whirled toward me, shrieking in fury, lips peeling back from a row of nightmare needle teeth, and leapt at me, its black spear lashing toward me.

Hell's bells.

That should have been terrifying.

But the Winter mantle didn't really do fear. Instead, I felt myself noting that the thing was damned stupid to leap in the air and go ballistic like that. Had it come toward me low to the ground, serpentine, I might have had a hard time shooting it, since it could have changed direction unpredictably. Up in the air like that, it was at the mercy of Newtonian physics, and it was a simple matter to predict where it would be at any given time.

I put the second round through its upper neck at ten feet, and rolled to the side. It crashed heavily to the grass where I'd been, and kind of flopped onto the sidewalk in front of the house, twitching in hideous spasms and making gurgling sounds as it died.

I came to my feet, regained my staff, and staggered as River Shoulders' scream was answered by multiple throats from inside the house—brassy cries that could not possibly be entirely human ones.

Wooden window frames and the pieces of glass that still hung in them exploded outward from the house as somewhere between six and ten creatures came screaming out at us. We had, apparently, been fighting the skinny little ones so far, because these things must have massed twenty percent more than either of the first two and looked taller and stronger to boot.

"Dresden! These are Huntsmen! Kill them quickly!" River shouted. He bounded toward a figure as it came screaming out the front door of the house. One of his huge hands slapped the head of the Huntsman's spear aside. The other seized the Huntsman's furry neck and squeezed.

Imagine a toddler having fun with his banana. It was like that, but redder.

"I don't know what that means!" I screamed. I barely had time to clear my shield bracelet and raise a shield before three of them opened up on me with the howling, flaming thunder of those black spears. Fire and force enveloped my shield and made the air hot and too full of smoke and choking gas to breathe. I had to stagger back out of it. The Huntsmen didn't let being blinded by a cloud of smoke slow them down. Those spears howled and sent concussive force and fire splashing against my shield— or missing me completely, and hitting the houses across the street.

River came sailing through the air and landed behind my shield in a crouch to be able to keep his head at the same level as mine. He dropped something messy out of his right hand—the Huntsman's grey corpse, minus its head. "Look," he said.

I did. Right before my eyes, the corpse withered and shrank away, deflating as if it had been a skin filled with air. I could sense energy rushing out of it, something moving almost too quickly to be sensed at all.

And the other Huntsmen screamed again, in primal fury. Louder.

"Each that falls gives its strength to its packmates," River Shoulders snarled. "Quickly!"

He turned to one side and leapt, fifty freaking feet in a single bound, both huge fists coming down on a Huntsman better than seven feet tall. He didn't strike twice. When River Shoulders hit something, it went down and it stayed there. Without slowing, he bounded forward into the smoke, even as the pack howled again.

A Huntsman emerged from the smoke and leapt over my shield like it was on wires. I kept the shield held out toward its packmates back in the smoke, tracked it with the big Smith & Wesson, and started pulling the trigger as it landed and whirled with its spear.

The first round hit it center mass, and the big, slow bullet staggered it, even if it didn't make it blink. It snarled and thrust the spear at me, but I'd gained enough time to shoot again, and before it could commit its weight to the thrust, the second round hit it lower and must have gotten its spine, because it dropped limp to the ground—

—and sank the fingers of one hand into the dirt and drove the spear at my face with the other, screaming.

I ducked and slapped the head of the spear with the barrel of the revolver, throwing up sparks. Then I recovered my aim and sent my last round through its forehead from five feet away. Its head snapped back and then flopped limply into the dust, its body already desiccating and draining away.

And the pack screamed. Louder. Deeper. Harder.

I holstered the gun and darted to one side, dropping the shield and trying not to gag and choke in the smoke. I tripped over a bundle of furs and loose skin, the remains of a Huntsman that River had apparently gotten. I recovered my balance in time to see a freaking icon of a Huntsman, nearly a foot taller than me and rippling with muscle, emerge from the smoke, whirling its heavy metal spear like it was a parade marshal's baton and swinging it at my head.

There was no blocking that kind of force. It would have shattered my staff if I'd tried. I ducked and backpedaled and barely sensed the second Huntsman close in on my flank in time to fling myself out of the way. Its spear came down close enough to slice through the bottom hem of one of the legs of my jeans and to leave a cut in the side of the sole of my shoe.

Two more Huntsmen emerged from the smoke, enormous and terrifying. One hefted its black spear and hurled it at me. The other simply lunged, hands outstretched, filthy nails like talons spreading wide.

The spear hit me in the left shoulder. When its tip met the ensorcelled leather of my duster, there was a sudden shower of sparks as the energies in the weapon and the garment met and clashed. The impact was vicious, like getting slugged with a weighted bat, and it spun me to one side in an explosion of neutral white-noise sensation that the Winter mantle substituted for pain.

One of the Huntsmen flung itself at me in a human-spear attack and hit me in the right biceps. Right about the same time, the one with the bad nails came flying at me from not quite the opposite angle. Only it hit me in the shins.

I went down, hard.

There was an explosion of sensation that would have left me stunned and breathless without the Winter mantle's influence. As it was, I kept enough awareness to twist on the way down and keep from getting any broken bones—and once I'd hit, kept my breath, drew in my will, and shouted, *"Repellere!"*

Naked, unseen force exploded out of me in a half sphere, a wave of thick, heavy energy that lifted the Huntsmen from their feet and flung them a dozen feet back through the air. They twisted and bent in graceful arcs as they went, and every damned one of them landed on all fours like some kind of big ugly cat.

I was on my feet by the time they were, but my shoulder wasn't working so good. I was pretty sure it had been dislocated.

One of the Huntsmen made a sound like a wild boar, and the others moved, clearing to one side as it lowered its spear and readied another blast.

I cross-drew the coach gun from its scabbard, thumbed back the hammers as I raised it; and let him have it with both barrels of Dragon's Breath.

Dragon's Breath is a specialty shotgun ammunition. It normally consists mainly of hard pellets of magnesium.

But Molly's people had added white phosphorus into these rounds.

Twin fireballs bellowed from the coach gun and splattered the top half of the lead Huntsman in a cloud of white-hot pellets of burning magnesium and white phosphorous.

The burning metal didn't stop burning just because it had been buried deep in the thing's flesh, and the Huntsman and a five-foot circle of grass around it burst into flame, sending up a squealing scream from the creature that felt like it could burst my eardrums. It thrashed horribly, staggering in a small circle before falling to its hands and knees.

I dropped the coach gun, turned toward the other three, and started to bring up my shield again—but one of them had rolled a higher initiative this round, and a little horn-handled knife tumbled past the hem of my duster and sank into my thigh.

Agony seared through me as if the knife had been white-hot. Pain had been a long-absent visitor in my daily experience, and its sudden arrival sucked the wind out of my lungs. Fire pierced my leg like a bar of red-hot metal. I could feel it searing me to the very marrow of my bones.

At the same time, my shoulder exploded in silver threads of nerve-rending torment as my rotator cuff screamed in protest at the damage.

Iron. The bane of the Fae and their magics.

The Winter mantle screamed.

I staggered and fell to a knee as I seized the bone handle of the little knife and wrenched it out of my leg—just in time to catch a stomping kick to the sternum that knocked me back in a short, brutal arc to the ground. Stars exploded in my vision and something in my head felt loose and hot. The breath was gone from my lungs. I tried to gather my will again, but they piled onto me, tearing with nails and *biting*, for crying out loud.

And then there was the sound of a dinosaur's footsteps shaking the ground, and River Shoulders tackled all three of them, swept them into the circle of arms thicker than a horse's neck, and squeezed. There was a quick series of wet, crunching sounds. River stood up with a contemptuous shake of his arms and dropped the Huntsmen.

What was left was . . . sort of smushed together. Ever seen *The Thing?* Think in that direction, only more slippery.

With the little knife gone from my flesh, the Winter mantle recovered itself pretty rapidly. I took a couple of breaths and then pushed myself to my feet, the pain once more vanishing into a vague haze. That was the great weakness of the fae, their bane. And mine, I supposed. Iron. Wow, that had hurt.

"How many?" River demanded. "How many did you kill?"

"Three," I said. "You?"

"Nine," he said.

Well.

Okay, then.

"Smoke," River spat in the tone of a swear. "We missed one."

"What?" I said.

"There are always thirteen."

The burning corpse and the smushed ones abruptly deflated.

And there was a sudden crashing sound as a Huntsman half a head taller than River Shoulders just shrugged its way out through the front wall of the house, taking maybe half of the front of the house down. It raised its spear and let out a bestial roar that would have set off car alarms had any of them been working.

It leapt toward River Shoulders, its heavy iron spear held in one hand like an assegai, and thrust it at the Sasquatch. River took a pair of quick pivoting steps that I had seen Murphy do before, guiding the spear's tip past him with one hand and getting in close to the Huntsman where he could seize the weapon's haft and try to wrench it from his foe.

The Huntsman roared its defiance and fought.

The heavy iron bent and snapped like cheap plastic before the application of that much raw physical power. The Huntsman promptly rammed the snapped end of the spear in its hand into River Shoulders' neck.

If River had been human, the blow would have killed him. But the Sasquatch had layers of muscle mounded up around his neck. His trapezius muscles went all the way to the bottom of his ears, and the shard of the weapon was ineffective at penetrating that much meat. Even so, the Huntsman got its other arm around River Shoulders' waist and lifted the Sasquatch off the ground, charging forward to ram him into the old tree.

I lunged, seized the thirteenth Huntsman's leg with both arms, summoned my will, and screamed, *"Arctis!"*

Cold, the pure supernatural cold of true Winter, flooded out of my hands and into the Huntsman. There was a horrible crackling sound as the temperature of the flesh I was touching sank to single digits on the Kelvin scale.

The Huntsman shrieked in pain and kicked its leg in an attempt to dislodge me.

I hung on.

There was a crackling sound, and I took the leg from the knee down with me.

The Huntsman screamed and fell in a shower of ice chips and a gout of blood.

Without hesitating an instant, River Shoulders seized the frame of the sedan in the driveway, picked it up with a tectonic knotting of massive muscles, swung it overhead like a man using a sledgehammer, and brought the engine block down on top of the thirteenth Huntsman in a massive swing.

Though it was crushed flat, there was still a horrible vitality in the Huntsman. It let out a burbling, hissing sound that somehow conveyed the same impotent fury as a shriek.

And then it spasmed and died. The car rocked and snapped and groaned in the Huntsman's death throes.

I pushed the frozen leg away from me and got slowly to my feet. I'd lost my staff at some point. I recovered it. While I did that, River pulled the iron bar from his neck. He let it fall by the last Huntsman. The body began deflating just like the others, and as it went, the shard of the iron spear crumbled with it.

"What," I breathed, "in the hell was that?"

River poked the spear. "Welsh creatures. The Huntsmen of the Land of the Dead. Whole pack makes their spears from their blended blood over years. Forges them together." He shook his head. "Bad news. Very bad."

"These things are the *scouts*?" I demanded. "That's not fair."

We heard bestial screams coming from the east and south. "Hell's bells," I muttered. I coughed, gagging on the smoke. There was enough of it. More houses were on fire now. People were running out. "Come on. We can't leave them out here."

I strode up to the door of the house, shield bracelet raised and ready. Someone had been shooting here, after all. I didn't plan on getting cooked by some panicked normie.

"Hello, the house!" I said. "My name is Dresden! I used to live down the block in Mrs. Spunkelcrief's old place."

There was a pause. Then a male voice with a Hispanic accent asked, "With the dog?"

"Yeah," I said. "The big grey dog."

"Mouse," the man said.

I couldn't ever remember actually doing more than waving at this guy as I went past. I was pretty sure I hadn't ever introduced my dog. How did he know Mouse's name?

Damned pooch is more of a people person than I'll ever be.

There was a clattering sound and then a slim, medium-height man in his late thirties emerged from a back room of the house. Behind him came a woman who matched him well, and a little girl holding a stuffed animal of some indeterminate but well-loved kind.

"It is you," he said.

"Hey, man," I said, lifting my chin. "Things are crazy, huh?"

He stared out at the night and the flames and the smoke, and at the remains on his front lawn. He nodded numbly.

"Okay," I said. "Come on. I need your help. We're gonna get all these people into the castle they built at the old place. There're people sitting on their asses there with nothing better to do than protect you guys. Okay?"

The man looked numbly at the street, then at me. There was shock happening. He stared for a blank second and then nodded jerkily. "Castle. Get everyone in the castle."

"And hurry," I said. "Oh, and never mind the Sasquatch. He's with me."

"¿Qué?" said my neighbor.

"Just roll with it," I said. "Get them rounded up. Go!"

He staggered toward a man who had emerged from the house across the street and was watching it burn. The two talked, then grabbed another neighbor. People started getting herded toward the castle.

"Come on," I said, "before Marcone does something stupid."

I strode forward, back to the castle, several yards ahead of the first stragglers to stumble that way. I marched up to the base of the wall where everyone had been observing things and shouted, "Marcone!"

There was a muttered conversation above. Marcone leaned out and peered down at me a moment later. "What?"

"These people need shelter," I said. "Let 'em in."

Marcone glowered at me. His pale green eyes tracked past me to the stragglers coming in.

"I am not a charitable organization," he replied.

"You want to be Lord of Chicago?" I spat, contempt in my voice. "Talk is cheap. Act like it."

Up on the wall, I saw Mab put a hand on Marcone's arm in restraint and say something.

Marcone locked eyes.

With *Mab*.

Then he simply looked at her hand and arched an eyebrow.

Mab withdrew it, her eyes narrowed.

Marcone inclined his head to her in a small bow and turned back to me.

More Huntsmen let out shrieks. They were not in the distance. More of those howling blasts from their spears lanced through the night. I heard someone else scream, maybe a couple of blocks away.

"Dammit, man!" I snarled.

Marcone leaned an elbow on a merlon and considered me for a moment. Then the people again. He nodded his chin once.

"Talk *is* cheap," he confirmed. "Send them in."

I blinked.

Marcone glared out at the smoking, howl-haunted, firelit night and clenched his jaw. The granite of the castle seemed less substantial. "Hendricks. Gard. With me."

Then the Lord of Chicago spun on his heel and went to see to his people.

Chapter

Ten

So, I and River Shoulders and the Einherjaren and Marcone's troubleshooters started clearing the way for people to get to the castle. There were a number of short, vicious clashes with the enemy's Huntsmen, and Marcone's people acquitted themselves like professionals—which is to say that the fight never even came close to being fair.

Even so, they had a couple of their people taken out with injuries, and the foe just kept coming—until one of the Einherjaren matter-of-factly started hanging up the flapping empty skins of the fallen foe across the street on a ghastly improvised clothesline.

Once that gruesome warning marker was up on the streets surrounding the castle, the foe started giving the area a wider berth. Marcone got snipers onto the rooftops to handle anything that approached along the street, and they taught the enemy to keep back. It was all accomplished pretty much by the numbers.

Of course, I noted, that was the point of sending out disposable light troops to attack the city: have them go everywhere, causing havoc, until someone started killing them. Then all Ethniu would have to do would be to go to wherever the bodies were piling up and engage the enemy—or she could *avoid* those areas and wreak havoc unopposed, throwing more and more troops between her and us while she smashed the place.

It was a bloody price to pay for the map of the town's defenses. Apparently they thought they could afford it.

The Erlking himself came down to oversee the downing of a last towering Huntsman. A couple of the largest Einherjaren fought the thing with six-foot claymores and made a bloody mess of the street, laughing uproariously the entire time.

I'm not kidding. Laughing. The freaking eternal soldiers were having a ball tonight. That poor lunkhead Lara had left unconscious in the basement was missing Viking Christmas.

"So what's the name of the place the Huntsmen are from again?" I asked.

"Annuvin," River Shoulders said. "Welsh Land of the Dead, ruled by Arawn, once upon a time. But the Tuatha settled his hash back in the day, just like Ethniu did poor Gwyn ap Nudd."

I had picked up one of their black metal spears. They felt cold and greasy to the touch, and just holding one made my joints ache a little. They quivered with a kind of stone-flake, primitive enchantment that had been shaped into them with hours of throbbing drumbeat and primal screams. "Some kind of iron alloy. I think the damned thing runs on hate. That's how you shoot it. You've just got to hate hard enough."

"Seems about right," River Shoulders rumbled. He had one hand wrapped around my forearm, my entire freaking forearm, gently. The other was braced against my chest—my entire chest. "Okay, on three. One," he said, and he put my arm back into its socket.

There was an explosion of static and then a bunch of the white noise cleared away. River Shoulders released me carefully and arched an eyebrow. I tried my shoulder. It functioned much more smoothly, and I nodded my thanks at him.

"Yes," agreed the Erlking, turning from the last throes of the fallen Huntsman. "It makes them easy to lure forward and impossible to drive away." He paused to nudge the deflated remains of a Huntsman with the toe of one boot. "It is not possible to contain more than a handful of such creatures for any length of time. The enemy has been breeding this batch up of late."

I grimaced. "Yeah. They've been taking people since the Red Court fell."

"Now we know why," River Shoulders said.

"Wait," I said, feeling sick. "They . . . breed more of these things from people? Or they *make* more of them from people?"

"The process is . . . somewhat distasteful," began the Erlking.

"Wait," I said again. "Stop. Just stop. I don't want to know."

"This," he said, "will not be the worst of it."

"Cheerful," I said.

He shrugged, hunting leathers creaking. "Incoming," he noted calmly.

A great grey owl swooped quickly down from the night air, backwinged in a thunder of feathers, and landed in a heap. The heap kind of quivered and then resolved itself into the shape of Listens-to-Wind. The old man shimmied his shoulders a little, then winced and rolled one arm while grasping at his shoulder with the other hand.

"Need to do more yoga," the old man muttered with a grimace. "Hey, River."

"Mobility routines are important for a human your age," River Shoulders said, his tone clearly worried.

Listens-to-Wind broke out into a boyish grin that took a couple of centuries off the old man's weathered face. "Ain't been your apprentice in a long time now, *tanka*."

"Never listened when you were."

"What of the enemy?" the Erlking asked.

"Our boys getting hit pretty hard," Listens-to-Wind said. "They got these gorilla-squid things—"

"Octokongs," I interjected.

Everyone stopped to eye me.

"Hey, it's important to have specific language, isn't it?" I complained. "I went to all the trouble to give them a usable nomenclature."

"And," River Shoulders rumbled, "you named 'em octokongs, huh."

"It fits," I said.

"Fits," Listens-to-Wind acknowledged.

"Goofy-looking, right?" I said.

"Goofy-looking and they can carry rifles and crawl on the sides of buildings," Listens-to-Wind replied. "Hell of an advantage in a city. Things can't shoot much, but if you get enough of them, they don't have to be good. Plus, some teams of them fellas in turtlenecks are back there providing fire support. They're sniping at anyone with a radio, trying to kill communications."

"That'll be Listen," I said. "King Turtleneck. Way I hear it, the enemy got good help."

"Annoying when they do that," the Erlking noted.

"About time we thought about going to help our people, if we're going to go at all," the old man said. "They'll get cut off soon."

The Erlking nodded sharply and started walking. "Let us tell One-Eye." Listens-to-Wind fell into pace beside the Erlking, who paused and then added, sotto voce, "If we go without him, you know how he gets."

"Lot of guys like that got control issues," the old man opined. "To be expected."

"Kringle suits him better," the Erlking muttered.

"Kringle would suit anyone better. Even you."

The Erlking looked shocked.

The two of them vanished back into the castle.

A fire team of Einherjaren went by, escorting a stunned-looking group of civilians inside, where they would be waved through by the various sentries to the castle's interior. Out in the night, there was a constant background of crackling gunfire and shrieks and the howling screams of those dark metal spears like the one I held—at least until it started flaking and turning to rust right in front of my eyes.

There was more ambient light now. And more smoke.

Chicago was burning.

"How many can we fit in there, do you think?" River Shoulders asked me.

"Well. We aren't exactly worrying about fire codes right

now," I said. "Maybe three or four hundred if we pack them in?"

"How many of your people, in this city?"

"Eight million, all told," I said heavily. "Give or take."

"Not much difference," he said.

I pointed at a couple of half-dressed parents with half a dozen kids in various stages of pajamas hurrying inside the squatting stone solidity of the castle. "Makes a pretty big difference to them."

The Sasquatch flashed a sudden, very wide, very white grin. It might have been charming from a safe distance. From right there, it was imposing as hell. "Yes," he said. "That's right."

"Stars and stones, River," I said. "I'm glad you're on my side."

"Means you got good taste," the Sasquatch said. "Besides. You stood with me when I needed it."

"Yeah," I said. "Those situations weren't ever exactly of this magnitude."

"Be kind of a lousy friend, I counted the beans between us that close," the Sasquatch said.

I blinked at that. "Friend, huh."

"Helped me with my kid," River Shoulders said. "With family. You been my friend. Now it's my turn." Again he showed me the terrifying smile. "Besides. This is kinda fun, eh?"

I started to sputter. But instead I found myself just grinning back at him.

Taking out a bunch of monsters and saving a bunch of people had damned right been fun. Terrifying and night-mare inducing and fun—and *right*.

Hell's bells, it felt good to be doing something I knew was right.

I held up a fist.

He eyed me for a moment. Then he made a fist and, carefully, bumped knuckles with me. The shock of it threatened to dislocate my shoulder again, but being all manly I didn't make any high-pitched noises or anything. And you can't prove otherwise.

The battle was a hell of a thing. I could hear it happening around me. I could still smell blood and death. I knew it was going on—but here, where we were strong, the enemy was keeping his distance for the time being. Occasionally, one of the snipers would fire a shot, generally to the sound of squealing screams in the distance.

I wanted to be fighting. But that battle with the Huntsmen had convinced me that charging out there all blind and righteous would probably get me killed within half a dozen blocks or so, at best. Even with River Shoulders next to me, that had been a close one. What if a second pack had crashed in during that? Maybe it would have been my skin hanging up on a clothesline—and the plan to stop Ethniu would officially be over.

I checked the coach gun. I'd recovered it and my revolver. I'd reloaded the trusty hogleg and strapped it back on. Dragon's Breath rounds were rough on the weapons you fired them through, but the coach gun was as solid and simple a piece of American steel as you could find, and the barrels were short enough to make eventual heat warping a nonissue. It would serve me a while yet. I reloaded the weapon with a couple more Dragon's Breath shells and slid it into its scabbard.

There was the tromp of boots from the castle, and then Marcone came out, flanked by Gard and Hendricks and trailed by a column of heavily armed and armored Einherjaren, who immediately assembled in the street. A dozen ghouls came gamboling into the night after them, transformed into their half-bestial state, and armed and armored from the castle's stores, blades and guns, mail and Kevlar, as they had chosen. They immediately loped into the night toward the lake, muzzles wide, tongues lolling and drooling.

Our scouts. Ick.

Lara came out next, dressed in a loose-fitting white garment of some kind, trailed by Riley and half a dozen of his professional shooters, and another half a dozen members of House Raith—which is to say a sort of dizzying vision of dark-haired and pale-skinned women who wore the same loose-fitting white garments, moved like leopards, and carried a variety of instruments of death. Lara went by with a glance and a smirk—and she and her people ghosted out into the shadows as our vanguard.

The White Council emerged last, Ebenezar, Listens-to-Wind, and Cristos backed up by Ramirez and his squad, all in grey cloaks now, staves in hand, weapons strapped, ready for action. The old man headed straight for me and I rose to meet them.

"Okay, Hoss," he said. "Remember we've got three positions between here and the lake?"

"Yeah," I said.

"Well, we're heading for the opening between the northernmost two," he said. "And Etri and his people, along with the Summer Lady and the rest of her gang, are heading for the gap on the south side. The idea is to force the Fomor to a stop so that they have to bring up their heavy troops if they want to advance."

I frowned. "I thought the idea was to wait until Ethniu revealed herself."

The old man grimaced. "If we don't stop the advance," he said, "the battle won't get that far. It won't need to. She'll have won already." He shook his head. "We have to force her to use the Eye to get through us."

"If they've got that many troops," I said, "why should she? She can just grind us away."

"She doesn't have time," the old man said, his eyes glinting. "Mortal emergency response systems are already in motion. The National Guard is already mobilizing and on its way. They've got to bring up heavy equipment to clear the roads so they can get through, but they'll be here by dawn. Maybe sooner."

"So," I clarified, finding myself grinning irrationally, "we're going to charge into the meat grinder as fast as we can to force her to hit us as hard as she can, and then hope that we can punch her lights out before the army gets here and starts killing everybody in sight."

"We . . ." Ebenezar sighed. "Aye, fair enough."

"Yippee," I said. "That sounds like fun."

"Heh," rumbled River Shoulders. "Heh, heh, heh."

The White Council suddenly looked very cautious to be standing in the proximity of the Sasquatch's rumbling laugh.

"Well," I said to River Shoulders. "Shall we?"

My grandfather lifted his eyebrows.

"Sure," River Shoulders said, and climbed to his feet, lightly for all his enormity. "Be good fun. Bigfoot versus octokongs."

"What?" asked Cristos, his handsome face confused.

"You heard him," I said. "Let's go."

Chapter

Eleven

So we moved out, into the smoke and the dark and the chaos, and the enemy did what the enemy always does. They showed up without calling ahead and screwed with our nice plan.

We'd marched down to Montrose and turned east, heading down the streets at a trot. I found myself moving next to Ramirez, who grimaced and clenched his jaw and kept the pace with silent, pained determination until we got to Welles Park. The darkened buildings and looming shadows of the park could hold hundreds of enemies. We pulled up to wait for a moment while Lara's people swept the place.

Ramirez found a bench and eased onto it, gasping. I knelt next to him. We watched as people fleeing the chaos between here and the lake paced silently past us, eyes wide and haunted. They crossed to the other side of the street as they approached and realized that we were a large, armed group. I didn't blame them. There was a god-damned Bigfoot standing on the corner, apparently examining a crosswalk pedestrian button in fascination.

Chandler, Wild Bill, and Yoshimo joined us as a factor of natural gravity, and I watched Ramirez will the pain and weariness away before he addressed them.

"So," Ramirez said, without pausing, "the enemy's northern arm came ashore at Montrose Beach. Lara's mercenaries are to the north of us in Uptown. They were holding the line at Lake Shore Drive but they got pushed back to Sheridan. Marcone's people are down south of us and they're dug in around Wrigley. They're holding. That's funneling the enemy right into the space in the middle as they try to get around them. McCoy and the Senior Council are going to go stop them from doing that, and we're going to swat any flies that bother them while they do."

"How's your leg there, boss?" Wild Bill asked casually.

"I can't feel it," Ramirez lied. "It'll last the night."

"You are hurt," Yoshimo said. That she had spoken at all was remarkable. Her Latin was flawless, her English only so-so, and she wasn't the chatty type. "It is not appropriate for you to be entering battle."

"It is not ideal," Ramirez agreed, still struggling to control his breathing. "But we need every hand on this one."

"If this don't go so good and we have to skedaddle," Wild Bill said, "you're gonna be a little slow, Pancho. It could get dicey."

That was putting it mildly. Come time to run from a battle, the slow and wounded die. That's just how it works.

Ramirez just looked at Wild Bill and said, with weary amusement, "I'm Spanish, not Mexican. You damned Texan."

Wild Bill put a hand on Ramirez's shoulder and flashed him a wolfish grin.

River Shoulders came over and dropped to his haunches next to me. That put him on an eye level with Chandler, standing. The dapper Brit eyed the Sasquatch with a bland expression and did not flinch. Much.

"How do you do?" rumbled River Shoulders.

"Well, thank you," said Chandler, with the flawless, reflexive courtesy you only get from a finishing school. "I understand you and Harry have worked together before?"

"Nah," River Shoulders said. "He come and bailed me out a few times when I needed help." He grinned. His teeth were very white. They stood out against the spatters of dark blood still on his fur. "But we did some good work tonight."

Chandler was too refined to take an intimidated step back. But he leaned.

I had just retied one of my shoes when the order came back down the line from Ebenezar, who seemed to have de facto command of the group. Time to move ahead. I had just gotten moving again when there was a flash of violet light that streaked down the road, swept high over the group's line, and plunged down toward me.

"My lord!" piped Major General Toot-Toot. The little fae came to a wavering hover in the air before me and saluted, grinning fiercely at me. "There is knavery afoot!"

"Talk to me, Major General," I said, even as I broke into a jog to keep pace.

"We didn't see them until they got there! The foe has sneakily snucked a sneak attack behind our lines, like a sneaky sneak!"

"What kind of sneak attack?"

"The sneaky kind!" Toot-Toot shouted. "They used veils and got around behind the lines and now they're in the park, and they are Up To Something!"

I frowned. "What park?"

"Up ahead!" Toot-Toot said. "On this road! You'll go right past it!"

My already quivery stomach got cold.

"Toot," I said, thinking furiously and drawing out the word. "That's . . . not a park. That's Graceland Cemetery."

And, dimly over the sound of all the footsteps in motion, I heard the thrumming thud of a large drum in the distance.

My eyes widened.

Hell's bells.

I broke out of line and sprinted ahead until I reached the old man's side. "Hey," I said. "You hear that?"

Ebenezar glanced at me, frowning, but then turned his attention to the distance. "War drum?"

"No," I said grimly. "That's coming from Chicago's most notorious graveyard. Toot says they slipped in under veils."

"Necromancy," he spat. "Stars and stones. How many zombies could they get out of it?"

"About fifty hectares' worth of zombies?" I said, a little exasperated. "A *lot*. And they'd swarm Marcone's people in minutes."

The old man snarled. Necromancy is the gift that keeps on giving. The same spell that animated corpses could be expanded to sweep up freshly made bodies as well. New corpses weren't as good for the work, but they'd be more than a match for the citizenry. It would mean death in a geometric progression.

The old man scowled furiously for maybe half a minute. I let him think. It's important to think when things are going crazy, if you want to take the smartest action to get them sane again.

"Okay, Hoss," he said heavily. "We don't know how strong these practitioners are. But we know what's going to happen to our allies if we don't support them. So I'm taking the big guns ahead to relieve the pressure on the troops."

"Got it," I said.

He spoke in the slightly heavy tones of someone who is thinking through a problem as he speaks about it. "Practitioners means the Council needs to counter them. You've fought necromancers before. You've fought in that grave-yard before. You're the best person here for the work." He grimaced and spat. "Dammit. You've got the job."

"Okay," I said.

"Take the Wardens and the Sasquatch."

There was a huge fluttering sound, and I let out a little shriek and flinched, and it took me a second to sort out that an absolutely enormous, shaggy old raven had swooped down and landed firmly on my shoulder.

"Um," I said.

"Caw," said the raven.

Ebenezar scowled. "You are just damned useless in a military situation," he said to the raven. "No discipline at all."

"Redneck!" cried the raven. "Caw!"

Ebenezar waved a grumpy hand at the raven. "Fine.

Take the Indian, too. Silence that drum." He put a hand on my arm and met my eyes. "Hoss. Do not pull your punches tonight."

"That's always been my biggest problem," I said, spreading my hands. "All this restraint."

I broke away from him and dropped back to the rear, where Ramirez was laboring along while the other Wardens flanked him and kept worried expressions when he wasn't looking.

"Okay, kids," I said. "We've got problems."

I explained the situation.

"Yes!" Wild Bill said. "Necromancers!"

I eyed him. "Seriously?"

"I like shooting zombies," he drawled. "That's all. I got a patch and everything."

"Well, the idea is to stop them before they get the zombie horde rolling," I said.

"Aw," he said, disappointed, "that ain't half as much fun."

"Dammit, Bill."

"Yeah, yeah," he said. "We'll get it done."

"River," I said.

The Sasquatch nodded. "Can't stand necromancers. Make the earth scream."

"We gotta move fast." I nodded at Ramirez and winced. "Sorry about this, man."

Carlos looked from me to the Bigfoot. He was having enough trouble keeping up that he spoke in a gasp. "Dammit. Do it."

"Give him a hand?" I asked River.

The Sasquatch promptly scooped Ramirez up. He could

carry the man sitting on his palm under one arm with no more effort than a farmwife toting a basket of eggs.

The raven on my shoulder squawked and took off into the night air.

"All right, Toot," I said. "Show me."

Graceland is, in many ways, Chicago's memory. The graves there mark the resting places of titans of industry, holy men, gangsters, politicians, near saints, and madmen and murderers. Tales of tragedy, of vast hubris, of bitter greed and steadfast love, are represented in the markers that stand over the graves of thousands. Statuary, mausoleums, even a small replica of an ancient Greek temple stand in stately silence over the lush green grass.

And yet the walls around the cemetery are there for a reason. The shades of many of those folk walk the grave-yard at night and are the source of thousands of whispered tales that make skin creep and flesh crawl.

I'd been one of them once. I had a grave waiting for me in Graceland, kept open by force of whatever contract a deceased foe had prepared for me.

There was no time to go around to the gates. We went over the wall of rough stone behind a large mausoleum and gathered in the sheltering darkness behind it. Toot descended to the ground, something I'd seen him do only occasionally, and the aura of light around him dimmed and went out.

"This way, my lord!" Toot rasped in a low, dramatic tone. "They are near Inez's statue."

I grunted. The statue was a local legend. It went miss-ing from time to time, and it came back just as mysteriously. There were often sightings of a little girl in Victorian dress skipping among the headstones when the statue was gone. And I knew it had once been used as a conduit by Queen Mab, when her physical form had been busy keeping mine alive, just as the spirit of Demonreach had inhabited a statue of Death that dwelt not far away.

Graceland is the repository of Chicago's greatest dreams and darkest nightmares. There is a power there, dark and potent—and I could feel it stirring and swirling in the air, like oil being heated over a fire and becoming steadily more liquid, quicker to move, to shape. The sound of the drum continued, a stalwart tempo. It would do a lot to mask the sounds of our approach, especially if we stepped in time to the beat.

I dropped low and followed Toot into the darkness among the tombstones. I knew the place well enough to get around generally. Toot led me to a position a little uphill from Incz's spot, and I stepped on one headstone to belly crawl up onto a mausoleum and peer ahead.

Spread in a circle near Incz's grave were seven cloaked figures, speaking in whispering voices in a breathy chant. One of them held a large drum on a shoulder strap and steadily struck it with a thick-headed drumstick in one hand. From there, I could sense the power of the circle around them, but they were making an effort to work magical forces without any sloppy inefficiencies of energy transfer, which generally manifested themselves as visible light. This was a stealthy working.

There was a lump on the ground in the center of the circle. I couldn't see who it was, but it was human-shaped, if you allowed for some ropes for immobility. A human sacrifice, doubtless, for the ceremony's finale. It remained the single most effective way to turbocharge black magic.

Hell's bells. Seven necromancers could wreck Chicago all by themselves. Four of them nearly *had* done it, once. Five, if you counted me, which I didn't, even though my entry in that evening's animation festival had taken best in show. I could feel the intensity of the working they had underway. I didn't know who they were, but they were pros. If they were allowed to finish, they could wreck the town without the help of any army of improbably conceived monsters.

And if Toot and his people hadn't warned me, we would never have seen it coming. I wonder what it says about me that pizza has been one of the better long-term investments in my career.

I slipped back down and away, unseen by the baddies. I returned to my allies and spoke in harsh, quick terms. "Seven. Six casters and a drummer. Cloaked, dark. I don't know who or what they are. They're with the Fomor, so they're probably bad-guy leftovers from somewhere. They're in a circle. They've got a prisoner."

River Shoulders growled. It was a sound so low that I couldn't hear it so much as feel it vibrating the bones of my skull. "Where you want me?"

"No time to get fancy," I said. "Get behind them. You get two minutes. Then we'll go right at them from this side, make plenty of noise, and draw their fire. Once we have their attention, you get in, get their sacrifice out. Then . . ." I brought my hands together in a silent clap.

"Simple is good," River Shoulders said.

Then he gave himself a little shake, bounded maybe

four feet into the air off one massive foot, shimmered, and turned into a goddamned owl with a wingspan as long as a freaking car. The massive owl glided out over the tombstones, arcing to one side, and vanished into the night.

"Jesus Remington Winchester Christ," Wild Bill blurted in a strangled voice. "He's a *wizard*?"

"Yeah," I said. "Taught old Listens-to-Wind, the way I hear it."

"Huh," Bill said. "Now, that just ain't fair."

"Don't complain. He's on our side."

"I'll take two," Wild Bill said.

I'd been counting in my head. When I got to a hundred, I said, "Okay, folks. Just like the old days. Chandler, you know the drill?"

"I may have been in the field once or twice," Chandler said.

"Groovy."

The team of young Wardens stacked up behind me, walking in close order, hands on shoulders in the dark to guide one another, and I headed out.

Warden fire teams work much like any soldiers. Any one of us can put out enough firepower to kill every one of us if we're careless or stupid, and working together means developing trust and respect in one another's skills. I'd go first and make the call about when the fight started. If necessary, my shield would cover the entire team—who could then fan out, Hydra-like, and take out the source of any threat.

Granted, if I stepped on a land mine or something on the way there, we were all dead together. But that wasn't how most supernatural types tended to think.

I took long, striding steps in time with the drum, and as we approached the necromancers' position, I felt Ramirez's veil wrap us in a cloak of less-than-visibility. Yoshimo did something to the air that made us less-than-audible. They'd cover us until we got into place.

Wild Bill whispered something to the lever-action rifle he carried instead of a staff these days and plucked a rune-inscribed brass shell from his belt and slid it carefully into the rifle's loading port before closing the action with a cautious, precise movement. My leather coat creaked, and I sweltered in the summer heat, within its smothering protection.

My shield was by far the noisiest and most obvious active spell we had among us, magically speaking, and would be the last to go up. I waited until we rounded the corner of the last mausoleum blocking our line of sight to shake out the bracelet and ready my defenses.

But first things first. We had two major problems to overcome.

One, the bad guys were standing inside a ritual circle. We could throw as much power as we wanted at them—it would splash uselessly on that thing until someone took the circle down. So we'd have to do that before we could really come to grips with them.

Second, if you want to control the dead, you've got to drop a beat on them. End that beat, end any possibility of summoning and controlling the undead. I drew my revolver, with its boring old regular, entirely mundane rounds, stepped around the corner, and raised the pistol, sighting on the drummer.

Swear to God, on a normal day, I barely shoot competently. But with the Winter mantle guiding my hand, I lifted my arm and made a one-handed shot in the dark at maybe twenty yards that drilled the drummer in the back with a thunderous report.

Two things happened immediately.

First, the round passing through the plane of the circle, sent there by my hand and will, disrupted the essential magical screen of the ritual circle. Stealthy the working might have been, but nothing works right when it's falling to pieces, and it shattered away in flickers and shards of scarlet light.

Second, the round tore right through where the drummer's liver should have been.

The hooded head whipped around, owl-like, nearly one hundred and eighty degrees, with such unnatural speed that the hood was flung back.

In the scarlet light of the disintegrating circle, I could see a ruined, desiccated face. The skin was drawn tight over the bones of the drummer's face, withered and weathered like a corpse exposed to the sky. The eyes were milky white; the lips were leathery strips of jerky partly covering yellowed old teeth. Hair hung on to the scalp in clumps of soiled tangles, but much of it was bald and grey-white.

A vampire of the Black Court. And I knew her.

"Mavra of the Black Court!" I snarled. "You got a permit for raising zombies in my town?"

"Oh," Mavra said. Her body turned to match the facing of her head, the motion weirdly liquid and mechanical at the same time. "It's you."

Five of the other six figures turned to face us, hoods coming down.

Black Court vampires. All of them. I didn't recognize any of the others—but it seemed pretty clear that Mavra, as the drummer, was the least among them. The Black Court had been all but exterminated, thanks to a really underhanded move by Lara's people a century and change back. The only ones who were still alive—well, who continued to exist—were the oldest, wiliest, most vicious, and most powerful of their kind.

These vampires were old-school, the real deal, nightmares of the Old World. A Black Court vampire was a match for any dozen counterparts in the Red or White Court.

And we had seven of them.

"My lord," Mavra said. "May I suggest violence."

The last and tallest of the hooded figures straightened his shoulders, turned, and lowered his hood with one hand. In the other, he held a ritual athame, an ancient knife of rough iron. He stood over the bound figure on the ground. His face was not like those of the other vampires present. No rotted corpse he; his face had the severe, angular regularity of a marble statue's, beautiful in the severe fashion of frozen mountains and crackling ice. Thick black hair swept back from his face and down his back. His hands were long and white, the fingers fine like an artist's.

But his eyes.

Dark.

Black.

Empty as the soul of hell.

I had just looked *toward* them, and they'd nearly sucked me in. Hell's bells. I shored up my mental defenses with as much focus as I dared spare from my environment and kept my eyes away from his face.

"So," he said. His voice was . . . pure, smooth whiskey, touched with a soft, throaty accent. "This is the city's wizard."

"I'm in the phone book and everything," I said. "In the name of the city of Chicago, and by the authority of Cook County and the state of Illinois," I said, loudly, hoping to give River that much more of a distraction, "I order you to cease any and all supernatural activity and return forthwith to your place of origin or to the next convenient parallel dimension."

Ramirez choked.

"Welp," Wild Bill drawled. "That oughta do it. Thanks, Harry."

"Who *is* that?" breathed Yoshimo.

"That," said Chandler in a low, shaking voice, "is Drakul."

Okay.

My eyes might have gotten a little wider.

I might have had trouble swallowing.

"Oh boy," I breathed

And Drakul smiled, as if genuinely delighted, and said, "Wise enough to know, but not wise enough to run. Wizards. Arrogant. Take them, my children."

Chapter

Twelve

Elders of the Black Court do not screw around.

Before Drakul had entirely finished his sentence, the air sizzled and spat with magical energy, as five elders of the Black Court unleashed a tsunami of sorcery.

I lifted my shield bracelet and stepped forward to meet it.

Once upon a time, that gesture would have been futile. Defensive shields were a fairly standard working of magic, but they had limits. The more kinds of energy you want to defend against, the more layers of shielding it takes—and the more power you have to put into it. Back when, my shield had been handy for stopping objects that were moving very quickly and not much more.

But times had changed. I was older now. I'd learned lessons the hard way and had the scars to prove it.

So five heavyweights hit me all at once: A couple of lances of white-hot energy, a sputtering globule of some kind of horrible-smelling acid, a crackling bolt of lightning, and what looked like a ghostly tentacle made of translucent green mist hit the shield like five separate speeding automobiles. My rough shield bracelet dribbled green-gold sparks and grew uncomfortably hot in seconds. The shield itself flared out in a quarter dome of blue-white, nearly coherent light, a barrier of raw, stubborn will.

Maybe if it had happened somewhere else, at a different time, I might not have been able to stop them all. Maybe if it had just been me, it would have gone badly. But tonight, my city was under siege. Tonight, millions of terrified people were going to die unless they got help from people like me. Tonight, their fear rode the air, an inflammable mist that needed only a magical spark to roar into reality.

Tonight, Chicago fought for its life.

And my shield held against them all. Though it scorched my wrist, though my feet were driven six inches back across the green grass, I stopped them.

All of them.

Meanwhile, my companions had not been standing around with their fingers up their anatomies. Yoshimo's arms swept out and whirled in circles, and within a second she sent a slender column of whirling air arcing up over my shield and down among the Black Court. When the white column touched the earth, it roared up into a whirling dervish of dirt and flying grass, blinding the foe and disrupting their evocations.

Ramirez's hand came down on my shoulder and he said, "Now!"

I dropped the shield.

Now, don't get me wrong. What the elders of the Black Court had dished out at us was enough energy to put us all in the ground and then some. But on the White Council, we call people with talent like that "sorcerers." And we sneer when we say it, for a reason. Yeah, maybe they can throw the raw magical strength around. But magic is about a hell of a lot more than simply power—and though they might have been young, the people backing me up were wizards of the White Council, and each and every one of them had cut their teeth on war.

I checked over my shoulder to see Chandler standing calmly with both hands planted on the handle of his cane. A dozen stones the size of my head floated in a small cloud around his shoulders, and as my shield came down, the stones began to leap forward as if fired from a cannon, hissing toward their targets. Not to be outdone, Wild Bill murmured something to his old lever-action rifle and the old steel of the weapon suddenly pulsed with threads of scarlet fire in the shape of some kind of primitive pictograms. As my shield dropped, he raised the rifle to his shoulder, sighted on the nearest vampire, and with a word sent a rod of semisolid fire the thickness of my wrist right through the vampire's belly and one of the huge headstones behind it alike, splitting the air with the thunder of sundered stone.

The vampire let out a scream that ripped and slashed the air it passed through and . . . was apparently pulled back and away from us by some unseen, horribly fast force.

Ramirez cast a beam of pale light at the vampire whose strike had gone all hentai on us. That one was a large male, or what was left of one, and he swung both arms dramatically and sent his ghostly tentacle smashing into Ramirez's disintegration ray. The collision of forces was enough to turn the whole thing into a thrashing mess that spewed ectoplasm in every direction.

Two of the vampires who might have been twins, or similarly sized siblings, before all the decay had set in, blurred and became a pair of great, greasy-furred grey wolves the size of ponies. Both shot in opposite directions in great, bounding leaps.

"Flankers!" I shouted. "Yoshimo, Bill!"

Yoshimo bounded a step into the air, and the wind itself seemed to gather beneath her feet and springboard her with silent grace to the top of the nearest mausoleum. She began to bound in twenty-foot steps, her toes barely coming down to touch the tops of grave markers, statues, and marble tombs, moving as if weightless to intercept one of the great wolves.

Bill immediately swung away from his target—a move that took no small amount of discipline—to begin tracking the second wolf with his rifle as it swung wide around us, a flicker among the smoke and shadows. Bill was an old-school shooter. He welded his cheek to the stock of the weapon, sighting carefully, and went almost entirely still as the barrel tracked the enemy and Wild Bill waited for his shot.

I was keeping my eyes on Drakul.

The pale figure watched the fight with keen interest, eyes like a pair of black holes, drawing in everything and giving nothing in return. He watched the opening exchange with the interest of a general observing children at chess, lips pursed thoughtfully. Then he took a step to the left and . . .

. . . and just freaking vanished. I don't mean that he went behind a veil, or teleported, or opened a portal to the Nevernever. *I* can do those things, if I have to. This guy took a step and just up and up went *away*, as if stepping behind a telephone pole and never appearing on the other side. Gone. Just gone.

Except that in this case, "gone" turned out to be six inches behind me.

My ears suddenly twinged hard, like when the pressure shifts in an airplane, and the empty space behind me wasn't empty anymore. I whirled, drawing my revolver, raising it—

—too late. Drakul caught the weapon's barrel in the pale fingers of one hand and simply crushed it shut.

His other arm swept out and clubbed Ramirez into a tombstone and to the ground as if Drakul's flesh had been made from cold, heavy marble. Drakul whirled toward Wild Bill, who flung himself into an evasive dive without ever looking back from his gun. It wouldn't have been fast enough to save him, except that Chandler sent a quick trio of stones zipping into Drakul's kidneys, *wham*, *pow*, *crunch*, with each stone exploding into gravel from the force of its impact.

Drakul turned to Chandler, muttered a word, and flicked an annoyed wrist.

The air behind the young Warden split with a howl of frozen wind, and a circle of pitch-black absence of light maybe four feet across appeared behind him. A stone seemed to turn beneath his foot. Chandler's balance wavered and he stumbled a step back, into the circle.

The air somehow *un*screamed, and the void black circle vanished.

Chandler went with it.

Drakul's black-hole eyes swept back to me, and suddenly I was being crushed to the ground by the weight of the universe itself. The very thought that I could have done something against a power like that was laughable—but I'd felt this kind of raw, universe-bending will before, in Chichén Itzá. Drakul, whatever he was, had considerably more personal power than the Lords of Outer Night had ever managed to show me.

But I had hoisted those Red Court losers on their own petard, when everything was said and done. I would be damned if I rolled over for Dracula's less famous dad.

I ground my teeth and fought back against the power crushing me, not with my muscles but with my mind. I pictured Drakul's will as a great, dark hand pressing me down—and mine as my own hand, rising to force it away. I poured my will into the image, a couple of decades of discipline, experience, and focus, investing it with power, with reality, with life.

Gasping, one inch at a time, I lifted my hand until my right palm faced Drakul and steadied. I couldn't stand—but I got an elbow underneath me and snarled silent defiance up at him, my right hand raised against his power.

An expression touched Drakul's face for the first time—a small smile that showed cruelly curved, sharpened canine teeth.

"Ah," he said, raising the knife he'd been planning to use for a blood sacrifice. "If only my own heir had been possessed of such determination."

It took a lot of concentration to free up enough mental cycles to make word sounds with my mouth, but I wasn't going to sit there and take it quietly. "Guess you're Ethniu's bitch now," I gasped.

The smile again. "It cost little enough to support her.

Minor squabbles like this are a good place to take stock of the field."

"Field?"

"Oh, wizard," Drakul chided me. "Their immaculate beardlinesses have you in the dark even now? As one star-born to another, I must say it seems unseemly in the extreme."

I stared at him hard. "What does it mean?"

Drakul's smile widened into something genuinely merry. Except for those empty eyes. Any expression that had those eyes in it could be nothing but a mask. "You'll never value information that comes to you easily."

"Thanks, Dad."

Something ugly flickered in that smile for a few beats. Then Drakul shook his head. "I would tell you to ask of your own White Council what they aren't telling you, what they bred you for, and what they expect you to do." He considered. "Well. Except that it seems unlikely you'll have the chance on this side of the veil, I'm afraid."

"Chump like you?" I gasped. "Tonight, you're the warm-up act."

Drakul regarded me for a second. Then he made an exasperated little sound and put one hand on his hip. "I'll be open with you, starborn. At this point of conversations like this one, I often offer the dark gift of immortality to someone in your position. It's occasionally a way to obtain a useful tool, but mostly I just want to see how they react. One sees people for who they truly are when they face death . . . but, honestly, five minutes of you in my life has been quite enough. You've no . . . gravitas. No decorum. No style at all." He knelt over me and lifted the knife toward my throat. "But I suppose your blood will call to the dead as well as anyone's."

"Knock-knock," I said.

Drakul frowned down at me and arched an eyebrow.

"Oh, come on," I said. "Here I am facing death and telling you a knock-knock joke. Why would I do such a thing?" I gave him the best grin I could while clenching my teeth. "Eternity is a long time to wonder about a punch line. Knock-knock."

"Who," said Drakul, in his mellifluous accent, his eyes narrowed, "is there?"

"Thousand-pound gorilla," I rasped.

"Thousand-pound gorilla *who?*" asked Drakul.

And River Shoulders roared and hit him with a twelve-foot-long concrete obelisk.

One second, Drakul loomed over me. The next there was an enormous sound and an explosion of shattering concrete that left half a dozen little cuts on my face, and Drakul was nowhere to be seen. The weight vanished from me so abruptly that for a second I thought I was levitating off the ground. I was suddenly dizzy, and my vision narrowed to a tunnel.

"Now, *that*," I gasped, "is comedy."

River Shoulders roared and bounded after Drakul, jumping with all four limbs.

Drakul, for his part, tumbled calmly, and if his shoes had cost more than some vehicles I had driven, they held up well enough as he dug them into the grass to arrest his momentum and bring himself to a controlled halt among tumbling fragments of concrete. He was wearing, I kid you not, a tuxedo under the long black cloak.

And he looked annoyed.

River Shoulders lowered his shoulder to slam into Drakul, but the big guy might as well have been trying to ram water. Drakul took a step and vanished, out from in front of the charging Sasquatch and to one side—where he crouched and swept his arm out at shin height to the Sasquatch, catching River Shoulders' enormous leg in the crook of his elbow and arresting its momentum as Drakul rose to his feet. The Sasquatch went forward in a sprawl, which he could not turn into a controlled roll before crashing through two enormous side-by-side tombstones.

River Shoulders began to rise and then sank back to the earth with a groan.

Hell's bells.

Drakul turned toward River Shoulders with his knife, and I saw what was coming in my head as clearly and sharply as if I was remembering it. The Forest People aren't exactly wizards. They just sort of live their lives so steeped in the world of magic that they just *do it*, the way a fish swims or a bird flies. Their aura of life energy is especially dense and potent, constantly absorbing power from the natural world around them.

Which would make the big guy a great big tank of nitrous for Drakul's necromantic summoning, if the master of the Black Court could spill River's blood to fuel the spell.

I grabbed my staff and brought it to bear, feeling the seething energy stored within its runes and sigils vibrate to life. The staff began to glow with green-gold light, even as I reached out to a portion of the energy stored within it, stirring it, urging it to glow even more brightly. I wanted him to see this one coming.

"Hey!" I shouted. "You! Ugly!"

Yeah, yeah. Not my best insult work. But you know. It's the thought that counts.

Drakul turned to look at me and froze for a second as if in surprise, presenting a fleeting instant of vulnerability.

"Forzare!" I shouted.

As I began the word, Drakul took a step to one side and vanished.

I whipped my still-glowing staff toward River Shoulders and this time unleashed *my will* along with the word. *"Forzare!"*

A glowing column of green-gold light, flickering and ephemeral as the aurora borealis, lashed across the ground between me and River Shoulders—

—and caught Drakul right in the breadbasket as he reappeared standing over River Shoulders' head with his knife.

The column of power hit Drakul with the energy of a speeding train engine. It blew back his hair and his clothing, ripping the latter to tatters, and sent him hurtling into the side of a marble mausoleum with such force that it sent a spiderweb of cracks through the stone.

Then there was the cry of an eagle from somewhere up above us, defiant and mocking, and the sweltering summer air was split by a sound so loud and a light so bright that it robbed me of my breath. The image of a bolt of blue-white lightning coming down in a nearly vertical column was burned onto the backs of my eyelids. It hit Drakul like a giant's sledgehammer, pounding him to the ground—and a second later, a bear, a goddamned Kodiak grizzly, just plummeted out of the sky, landed on Drakul, and started slamming sledgehammer paws down onto the pale being's skull.

Elders of the White Council don't screw around, either, and Listens-to-Wind knew how to make an entrance.

I staggered, catching my balance on my staff. The lightning had left my eyes dazzled. The thunder had left my ears ringing. I couldn't hear, couldn't see any of my companions except for River Shoulders. I hurried to his side, and even as I did, River shook his head groggily and began to push himself up.

"That's cheating," the Sasquatch rumbled, and his voice was angry, terrifying. River came to his feet in a single fluid motion, gathering with him a small tidal wave of magical energy that suddenly crackled and sparkled with static in the air around him. He screamed and slammed both fists down onto the earth, sending out a wave of raw power that I couldn't have matched at my best—just as the Kodiak bear let out a roar of pain and went flying away and to one side.

Drakul came to his feet, a marble statue clad in scorched shreds of black and white. He whirled toward River Shoulders, smiled, took a step to one side—

—and collided with empty air with an audible sound of impact.

Drakul blinked, this time clearly surprised, and recoiled in the other direction—only to rebound again, as if from the surface of a fun-house mirror maze. He turned toward the Sasquatch, dark eyes narrowing.

"Okay, Mister Dancy Pants," growled River Shoulders. "Now let's see how tough you are."

Drakul's black eyes glittered with an almost sexual intensity, and his sudden, wide smile was utterly unnerving. "I like this game much better," he said in something like a purr. And he laughed, taking slow steps back. As he did, without a whisper of power evident in the air, the grave-yard began to fill with fog, as swiftly and rapidly as if he'd pulled down a cloud on top of us. The laughter lingered behind him like the Cheshire cat's smile.

The Kodiak rolled to its feet and padded over to us. Some-where along the way, in the sudden fog, Listens-to-Wind took its place. The old man padded to us and put his back to ours, his eyes and senses clearly focused outward, over the rims of his spectacles. Listens-to-Wind never looked excited, but tonight his dark eyes glittered brightly.

"Mister Dancy Pants?" I asked River Shoulders.

The Sasquatch shrugged. "Better than 'Hey, you, ugly.'"

Listens-to-Wind made a soft hissing sound that com-manded silence. River Shoulders listened to him, so it seemed like maybe it would be wise for me to do it, too.

So I heard the last few deep thuds of heavy paws strik-ing the ground, and a great black nightmare wolf, a crea-ture out of prehistoric nightmares, taller than me at the shoulders and weighing more than many cars, plunged into our group.

I dove out of the great wolf's path and only got my ankles clipped as I went. It spun me a hundred and eighty degrees before I hit the ground, still spinning.

I looked back over my shoulder to see the form of the vast wolf overbear River Shoulders and ride him to the ground. The Sasquatch roared and slammed his fists into the Drakul-wolf, but the beast shrugged the blows off, fangs seeking River's throat.

I twisted and lifted my staff, preparing a blast of force that would push the wolf off River Shoulders.

And an arm like a bar of cold iron slipped around my throat, as swift and lithe as a young serpent.

My air was cut off immediately. I couldn't make a sound. I struggled, but I felt like a child trying to fight an adult. Within seconds, I was off-balance and being dragged silently away among the tombstones.

I saw Listens-to-Wind turn into a friggin' bison and charge the great wolf's flank before the fog swallowed them all, and I had time to realize that *neither of them had seen me being taken*.

And, in all the fog, *neither had anyone else*.

I was alone.

"Dresden," Mavra hissed. Her voice sounded almost as pleasant as beetles devouring desiccated flesh. "I have *so* been looking forward to seeing you again."

Chapter
Thirteen

Thanks to the Winter mantle, I am stronger than most, by which I mean, most professional wrestlers. Strong as I am, though, my strength still falls within the normal parameters of humanity. I might be pretty far along that bell curve, but I'm still on the same graph.

Black Court vampire strength is on the same graph as military vehicles and construction equipment.

Mavra dragged me as effortlessly as if I'd been leashed to a bulldozer, and the arm around my neck might as well have been made of carbon steel. I thrashed and kicked, and not only was it futile; she didn't even take *notice* of it. I was able to gasp in a few precious wisps of air during the struggles, but probably not enough to make up for the loss of the struggle itself.

I wanted to panic. But panic wouldn't help me survive.

So I fastened my grip on that implacable arm and held on tight, trying to take the pressure off my neck, and otherwise ceased doing anything but fighting for air. The struggle behind me was a nearly silent one, broken only by the sounds of impacts, weight scrambling on the grass, and harsh exhalations.

Mavra dragged me silently through the graveyard in the fog until we found other dark, silent forms beneath the branches of a spreading tree.

And on the ground at their feet were more figures.

Wild Bill. Yoshimo. Ramirez.

Wild Bill and Yoshimo were a mess of blood that looked wet and black in the dim light.

Ramirez was still alive. He was on his knees, and one of the Black Court elders, the one with the tentacle spell, held Carlos's wrists pinned behind his back.

"Where is the drum?" demanded Tentacles Guy as Mavra approached.

"Welcome, Mavra," Mavra said in a light, mocking rasp. "You were right about how they would respond to the threat, Mavra. The Master was wise to trust you, Mavra."

Yoshimo had died with her eyes partly open. They stared. She didn't look like a young woman anymore. She looked like a broken, discarded machine.

Tentacles Guy bared bloodied teeth and hissed. "We must finish preparing these and go to the Master's aid."

Mavra hissed a little laugh. "If you wish to disturb his recreation, by all means."

One of the two twin corpse-vampires was on the ground. It looked like a chunk of mass that might have weighed thirty pounds in a living being was just missing from one of the twins' abdomens. Ramirez's blasts, probably. Its mouth was covered in fresh blood, and there were slurping, sucking sounds coming from the open wound, as blood and matter shifted and slowly renewed the missing mass. It was staring steadily, hungrily, at Ramirez.

The other twin pointed at me. "Give it to my sister. She must restore herself."

"His blood is not for the likes of you or me," Mavra replied calmly. "Starborn are for the Master."

Both twins hissed at Mavra, who appeared to take no notice of them.

Wild Bill had gone down fighting. His rifle and sidearm were both gone. So was his trademark knife. The skin was gone from his knuckles, and there was something black and sludgy on his open mouth. He'd gone down swinging, with bits of his enemy literally between his teeth.

"The drum!" Tentacles Guy insisted.

"This was never about raising an army, fool," Mavra hissed. "It was about acquiring new blood for the stars and stones. Let Corb and Ethniu thrash about and draw the ire of the mortals upon themselves. We will be well positioned to rule the rubble." She pointed a finger at Ramirez. "Give her that one to eat."

Tentacles Guy stared at Mavra harshly. Then he dragged Ramirez over to the wounded twin. Ramirez fought against Tentacles Guy, with just as much to show for it as I had with Mavra. The other twin stretched out Ramirez's arm and raked rotten nails across his wrists, tearing open flesh and veins with all the precision and subtlety of an ox-driven plow.

Ramirez screamed.

The downed twin fastened her rotting lips over the wound in his arm.

My friends were dead and dying.

And these . . . things . . . wanted to make of their remains a home for more monsters.

Sickness and rage filled me.

Power rushed in with them.

Mavra's grip on my neck tightened like something driven by hydraulics, and suddenly there was nothing but blind, furious sensation filtered through the Winter mantle in a tsunami of confusing sensory input that became its own agonizing analogue of prosaic pain.

"The Master won't mind drinking you at room temperature, Dresden," she chided me. The universe blurred, and suddenly the floor rose to give me a full-body hug. It blew the wind out of me in an exhalation not even Mavra's strength could shut off entirely and left me lying stunned.

"Pendejos," Ramirez snarled. I could feel the air tighten as he drew in power.

The other twin's hands shot out as he did, dragging his face to hers. Her milky-white eyes widened as she locked gazes with Ramirez. My friend let out a furious, despairing scream as her psychic assault began. Yeah. The Black Court had a method for dealing with the potential devastation of a wizard's death curse—tough to put together a spell when someone is trying to climb into your brain and redecorate.

The vampires watched the dying man intently, slipping into a corpselike, absolute stillness as they did.

Carlos tried to scream again. It came out weaker.

There was nothing I could do.

And then something wispy and violet poked out from behind a tombstone twenty feet away.

Someone *had* seen me.

The major general was still on the job.

Toot-Toot scanned the scene quickly, flashed me a manic grin and a wink, and slid back behind the tombstone. When he emerged a moment later, he held a short sword the size of a small hunting knife in one hand.

And in the other, gripped like a severed head, was an open packet of chopped garlic from Pizza 'Spress.

Toot crouched, still grinning, and a nimbus of blue and violet energy surrounded him—and then he shot like an arrow from a bow at Mavra's back.

There was a streak of light as Toot flew at her, slashing down with his knife at the dead-tough flesh of her back, the scalpel-sharp blade opening a deep cut.

Into which my little ally plunged his packet of garlic.

Black Court vampires are very, very tough customers. But they pay for it, in some really inconvenient vulnerabilities. You can read about them in Stoker's book. It's basically a field guide on how to kill Black Court vampires.

Turns out there's a pretty good reason vampires are repelled by garlic.

Mavra's dead flesh burst into silver-white flame.

I mean, it was awkward to see from my angle, but a freaking jet of argent fire shot out of the wound, and the sound of her shriek of agony became the entire world for a few seconds. I guess being set on fire is kind of distracting. I fought the headlock with all my strength and exploded out of it, drawing in a deep gasp of sweet, sweet air.

Which, instead of turning into the words of an immediate spell, got locked into the helpless autonomic cycle of an oncoming sneeze.

Of all the times, stupid conjuritis, *now*!?

Mavra thrashed out with one arm, hit me in the back, and clubbed me ten feet. Only the protective spells on my duster kept me from getting broken bones. I got my arms between my skull and the oncoming tombstone or I would have checked out right then and there, bounced, and hit the ground.

I focused, bringing power and image to my thoughts, rapidly gathering energy to put behind the oncoming sneeze.

The unwounded twin whirled her head toward me and hissed.

My chest convulsed into a sneeze that might have torn some muscles somewhere.

I sent power and image out along with it.

And an anvil, black and funny-shaped and half as long as a freaking car, plunged out of the night air and right onto the back half of Tentacles Guy's noggin.

The plummeting anvil had to have weighed at least a ton. And while you could whale on a Black Court vampire with a baseball bat all day and inflict nothing more than annoyance, that much weight moving at that rate of speed was an entirely different ball game.

Imagine holding up a fully hung suit and dropping it to the floor.

Now add a spray pattern of ink black, ichorous splatter. Plus a big freaking anvil.

Get the picture?

Mavra vanished, screaming into the night, the fog lit weirdly by argent fire in her wake. The healthy twin stared in shock at the anvil—which suddenly collapsed into gelatinous ectoplasm, mixing with whatever was left of Tentacles Guy, who was still, somehow, thrashing. It looked kind of like the inside of a blender.

I swiped a shaking arm over my running nose and wheezed drunkenly, "I told you, you Black Court bastards! Next time, anvils!"

Ramirez, his arms freed, whipped toward the creature mindlessly feeding upon his wounded arm, snarled a word, flicked his other wrist, and suddenly her *head* just turned into a slurry of water and powder. The remainder of the body started thrashing around silently, spewing ichor everywhere. Carlos gasped as bones in his forearm snapped in the grip of superhumanly powerful hands.

The other twin seized a tombstone, ripped it out of the ground as if it had been a damned dandelion, and flung it at my head.

There was just time to get my shield up, and the tombstone exploded into gravel against it.

By the time I lowered my hand and looked around again, shield bracelet still dribbling green-gold sparks, the twin was gone. So were the bodies of Yoshimo and Wild Bill.

I stumbled over to Ramirez's side. We wrestled the stupidly powerful strength still left in the dead vampire's hands, until I finally had to pit what felt like the strength of my whole body against the vampire's fingers, one at a time. It wasn't easy on Ramirez, who must have been suffering agonies, but we got it done.

I pulled him back as he cradled his shattered arm, and we watched the corpse thrash itself across the ground.

"They took them," Ramirez muttered. "They're going to . . ."

"Nothing we can do for them this second," I said. I got into the first-aid pack on his belt. In the dark it was a sloppy mess, but I got a pressure bandage over his wrist and got it tightly covered. It had to have hurt like hell on the broken arm, but we had to stop the bleeding. Ramirez clenched his jaw and hissed but gave no other sign of discomfort. I finished and rose. "Come on. We need to back up River and Listens-to-Wind."

He looked up at me, his face pale, his eyes too shiny and hard. But he grimaced and nodded and lifted his good hand.

I hauled him up, and the two of us had just turned toward where I'd last seen the Senior Councilman and River Shoulders when the same pair walked out of the fog. River's chest was rising and falling harshly. He sounded like a racehorse and moved as if his entire body was one enormous bruise. He was carrying an unconscious teenage girl in the crook of one arm like an infant—the victim Drakul and company had been preparing to sacrifice. Listens-to-Wind looked unutterably weary, but unhurt.

"What happened?" I asked.

"He left before we could get hurt too bad," River Shoulders said, his voice pained.

Listens-to-Wind grimaced and reached way, way up to thump a hand against River Shoulders' shoulder. "Creature like that, you don't beat it. You win by surviving. We won."

"Not all of us," Ramirez said in a harsh voice.

"Drakul sent Chandler through some kind of gate," I said. "It didn't look like the usual passage to the Nevernever. It was all neat and symmetrical." Which meant that Chandler could have wound up anywhere. Or, worse, nowhere. I leaned into the Winter. My voice sounded steady and rational. "No idea of his status. Meyers and Yoshimo are dead. Probably turned."

The pain was still there. Shock and the Winter mantle might have been numbing it. I didn't have a whole ton of friends. Losing three of them at once was going to hurt like hell, later. Even thinking about that made my guts quiver and my heart burn with rage.

Listens-to-Wind seemed to shrink a little and closed his eyes. "I think . . . Ah. This wasn't an alliance for Drakul. Merely a profitable ploy. If we did not arrive in sufficient strength to stop the sacrifice, the enemy has an army at our backs, the city is overrun, and I daresay Drakul would have his choice of potential recruits in the chaos. If we did send those of sufficient power to stop him, Drakul need not go hunting for potent new servants—they have voluntarily identified themselves."

"He left because he'd gotten what he'd come for," I said.

Listens-to-Wind opened his eyes and nodded. "And because he doesn't care about what's happening here today."

"What's happening here today is going to affect *everyone*," I said.

"Not him," the old wizard said, his voice certain. "He's got a different set of priorities."

"Because he's starborn," I guessed.

Listens-to-Wind looked at me sharply.

"Hey," I said brightly. "What are the stars and stones?"

The old man's eyes narrowed. He traded a long look with River Shoulders.

"We should get back to the others," Listens-to-Wind said, and turned to start walking back the way we'd come.

I took a long step and got in his way.

"I asked you a question, Senior Councilman," I said quietly but firmly.

River Shoulders shook his head tiredly. "Hoss Dresden. We got a lot on our plates right now. There's plenty that you don't know yet. And maybe this story isn't mine to tell."

"Seriously?" I asked. "That's your excuse? You don't want to spoiler me?"

He regarded me levelly. "I've said what I'm going to, Hoss Dresden. It ain't time yet."

I shook my head impatiently. "I'm getting some damned answers. My whole life I've . . . No. Since my parents died, my life has been one person after another trying to get something out of me. Wanting me to make deals. Give them my loyalty. And there's this whole starborn thing." My voice dropped. "My whole life, I've had to figure it out on my own. I'm getting a damned answer. I've put myself at risk over and over for the Council. I've lost fr—" I swallowed. "I've paid for it. You owe me."

The old man looked away and wouldn't meet my eyes.

"We owe you," he confirmed. "But it ain't about debt. There's some secrets that do worse than get you killed. A whole hell of a lot worse." He eyed me. "You need to trust us."

I barked out a laugh. It sounded weird in the graveyard. "Pull the other one."

The old man sighed. Then he said, "Make you a deal."

"What?"

"You get through tonight," Listens-to-Wind said, "you give me a little time. I'll be your advocate. I'll speak on your behalf to the others."

"Or you could just tell me yourself."

"I'm a wizard, Hoss. Which means I'm arrogant." He smiled a little. "But not *that* arrogant. That's how big this is, boy. I, a senior wizard of the White Council, don't think I'm smart enough to make this call alone."

I blinked.

That was not a sentiment I'd ever thought I might hear from a Senior Councilman.

"Oh," I said. "Wow."

"Best I can do," he said.

"I'll wait a month."

He snorted through his nose. "The people I need to talk to? Make it a year."

"Fuck that," I said.

"Oh?" he asked. "Tell me. What's your next best offer?"

The old man lifted his eyebrows and waited, visibly and politely.

"Fine," I said sourly. "A year."

He nodded. "Done."

The would-be sacrificial girl on River Shoulders' shoulder stirred, looked around at the Sasquatch, opened her mouth to scream in horror—and almost immediately fainted again.

River Shoulders looked mournful. "I lost my glasses in the fighting."

"Not your fault, big guy," I said. "Some people just don't know good company when they see it. We'd better drop her off with the next group of cops we pass."

"Agreed," Listens-to-Wind said.

"You're just going to keep going," Ramirez said. His voice shook with intensity. "Those things took our people. They're *profaning* them."

Cold rage suffused me and I whirled on Carlos. "And they're going to get theirs. But not now. There are eight million people who have no one else to defend them. Just us. So we're going to take care of business. And once we're done here, we're going to settle up with Drakul and his peeps. Right now, there are more important things to handle. But they're on our list, and we will check them off. Bank on it."

Ramirez stared hard at me for a second. Then he raised his fist.

I answered.

We bumped knuckles, hard enough to draw blood.

Chapter
Fourteen

If there is anything "good" about a fight, it's that they don't tend to last very long. Especially not fights between a terror as absolute as vampires of the Black Court and people slinging around the power of Creation itself. If we hurried, we might catch up with the rest of the group before they got to the front.

It's easier to move faster with fewer people.

We left the cemetery behind and kept heading east, toward the shores of Lake Michigan. There were more people fleeing now, screams and shouts and hushed, forced whispers. River Shoulders strode openly down the street, carrying the unconscious young woman in one arm and Ramirez in the other. I jogged along, and Listens-to-Wind shook himself into the shape of a rangy old hound and loped easily along beside me.

At the junction of Montrose and Hazel, there was a large group of police officers waving people past them and instructing them to head west at their best speed. There was a little pub there that had a courtyard that had only one entrance, where customers could park their cars. Several cars had been pushed across that entrance as an improvised barricade, and police officers with assault rifles stood at the barricade, looking nervously out into the darkness.

Behind them was a triage area, where several EMTs were working frantically in battlefield conditions to save lives. There were maybe a dozen people back there. Several looked like refugees who had fallen or been hit by some kind of debris. But three of them were Einherjaren—trust me, they stand out like a biker at the Vatican—and they were clearly the worst off.

It was well lit enough by a large fire in a steel barrel and dozens of flares that you could see the walls around the courtyard all the way up to the roof. Three officers had positioned themselves to watch the roof at the head of each wall.

There were bloodstains up there. Something had evidently tried to come over it and been fought back. The light was a problem, really, in this situation. Standing in it meant that you had to stay in it, or else work blind in the dark while your eyes slowly adjusted. Of course, without the light the EMTs couldn't do their work. It's an imperfect world.

The gunfire was closer and heavier now. I could make out individual shots. And hear screams. Screams on a battlefield aren't like the ones you hear on TV. They're high-pitched, falsetto shrieks and choked, gasping exhalations. Not all of them could have been human, but from where I was standing, they all sounded pretty much the same.

I stopped before we walked into the radius of the light around the defensive position and said, "River, maybe instead of walking up to all the nice frightened officers holding assault rifles, you should let me take the girl over there."

"Huh," the Sasquatch said. "Well. I did lose my glasses. Might be simpler."

I took the girl from him, carrying her in both arms. The old hound paced along lightly at my side, moving with the spring of a much younger creature. I walked forward into the light, holding the girl, and said, "Hey! CPD! I need to get this girl some help!"

Rifles swung to cover me, and I prayed that the officers had decent trigger discipline. I'd have hated to get accidentally shot.

"Don't move!" shouted several cops at the barricades. I didn't.

"Keep moving west, sir!" shouted several others at the same time.

"Which is it, guys?" I called back to them. "I can't not move *and* go west."

There was a commotion at the barricade. One of the officers stepped back, and a dark, scowling face under a tight cut of silver hair peered out at me. "Dresden?" he called. "That you?"

"Rawlins!" I said.

The old detective had spent a lot of time in Special Investigations. We'd worked together before. He was a burly man with a particularly expressive face, and his knuckles were lumpy with ancient scars. He carried a shotgun like it was an additional limb, and I trusted him.

"What the hell, man?" I called. "I thought you retired."

He grimaced and nodded toward the sound of gunfire. "Two more weeks."

I nodded toward the girl. "I need to drop her off with someone. I got stuff to do. Can I come in?"

"Depends, man. What was the name you knew me by the first time we met?"

"An Authority Figure," I replied.

"Good enough for me," he said. He nodded to the officers on the barricade. "Let him in."

I carried the girl across the street and through a narrow gap in the cars that I had to turn sideways to navigate. Rawlins met me inside and led me back to the triage area.

It took me a second to realize that practically every cop there was staring at me. I overheard them speaking to one another. They must have fired enough rounds to make their ears ring, because their mutters were coming out at conversational volume.

"Is that him?" someone asked.

"The wizard, Dresden, yeah."

"Is he for real?"

"Sure as hell hope so. Did you *see* those things?"

"Bullshit. He's just a con man."

"Eyes out!" Rawlins snapped, to all of them. "You think this is a goddamned circus?"

That did it, and they piped down and went back to watching the darkness.

Rawlins led me to an improvised bed made out of a folding table laid flat on the ground, with a layer of soft packing foam on top. I laid the girl down on it, and an EMT, his skin nearly as dark as Rawlins's, bent over to examine her.

"Lamar," I said. "Long time no see."

"That's because I don't want nothing to do with you and your weird shit, Dresden," Lamar said.

Lamar is one of the more sensible people I've ever met.

"Then what are you doing here?" I asked.

Lamar shrugged. "What I do." He peeled back an eyelid on the girl, checked her pulse with a stethoscope, and rummaged in a medical kit beside him. "This your fault?"

"Not this time," I said. "Honest."

"Uh-huh," he drawled, infusing both syllables with skepticism.

"It's not *always* my fault," I said.

"Sure," he said. With even denser skepticism. He took out a small paper tube from the kit. He snapped it in half and waved the broken ends under the young woman's nose. She shuddered and abruptly lurched, her eyes flying wide open. She started screaming.

"Back off, both of you," Lamar said. "Let me work."

I traded a glance with Rawlins and we backed off. He beckoned and walked over to an empty corner of the courtyard. I followed.

"The hell is happening?" Rawlins asked me intently under his breath once we were out of earshot. "Monsters on the walls with guns, guys with spears that shoot explosions, goddamned mercenaries with military-grade gear. What the *hell* is going on?"

I took a breath to try to think how best to condense it. "Bad guys from my side of the street have decided to destroy Chicago. And every monster and weirdo in Chicago has turned out to fight them."

Rawlins stared at me for a moment before he said, "Shit."

Rawlins was even better at condensing than me.

I glanced over at Lamar, who had gotten the girl to sit up. She was weeping and shuddering uncontrollably, and he was trying to get her to drink some water. "I gotta go, man," I said. "Every minute I'm here is costing lives."

"Where's Karrie?"

Rawlins had been friends with Murphy's dad, back in the day. He was the only person I knew who dared to call her by a diminutive nickname. "As safe as I could make her."

He pursed his lips. "Oh. Bet she loved that." He leaned over to ruffle the hound's ears affectionately and glanced down at my hip as he did. "That coach gun legal?"

"No."

He nodded. "Didn't think so. You got enough ammo?"

"Tonight, there's no such thing as enough ammo."

Rawlins snorted. "Ain't that the truth." He leaned a little closer and said, very quietly, "Rudolph and his partner were in the middle of putting out an APB on you when the grid blew out. Once it's up again, I figure they're gonna have the entire CPD looking for you."

"Oh," I sighed. "Joy." I eyed him. "Why tell me?"

"Karrie likes you. And Rudolph is a prick."

"Tough to argue with that."

His teeth flashed very white when he smiled. "Good hunting, Dresden."

I clasped his shoulder wordlessly for a second, then spun and headed back out of the courtyard to rejoin River and Ramirez.

"Two weeks," Rawlins muttered as I left. "Gonna die of cliché poisoning."

I walked back into the darkness and was promptly blinded to anything in it. I stumbled and faltered, but the hound stayed at my side, his shoulder against my leg, guiding me. I kept walking in the direction I knew they were, and tried not to gibber as I walked sightlessly forward.

"I'm just saying," River Shoulders' rumbling voice said, "you just draw two little lines from the corner of your mouth and then we have a public relations act. Humans love ventriloquists."

Ramirez replied in an exhausted, bemused voice. "It might take more than that to establish relations between the Forest People and humanity at large."

"Gotta start somewhere," River Shoulders said.

"And the first place you went was a ventriloquist act?" Ramirez asked. "Maybe we should live through the night first. Then think it through for a while."

"Mmmmm," River Shoulders rumbled. "Probably smart."

My eyes adjusted enough to make out dim shapes, and I said, "All right, folks. Let's get a move on."

The hound ran forward and leapt into the air, and a hawk soared away.

Man. I needed to learn how to do stuff like that one of these days.

"All right," I said, "we—"

River Shoulders scooped me up in his other arm and bounded forward.

Now, I don't know if you've ever been scooped up by a

Sasquatch or not, but it isn't the sort of thing you forget. I'm a pretty big guy. River lifted me as if I were a toddler. And when he ran . . .

It wasn't running, really, in any typical sense. It was more like a series of alternating single-leg broad jumps, covering thirty feet at a stride. River went from zero to maybe fifty miles an hour in three steps, and damned near gave me whiplash doing it.

The gunfire swelled rapidly as we reached Montrose and Clarendon.

On the left side of Montrose was a large art deco office building, shining glass and steel. The first two levels of the structure were an open-sided parking garage. The Einherjaren had taken it and gunfire roared out of the garage on both levels, flashes of light and bursts of thunder, all directed toward Clarendon Park. On the right side of the street was another office building, nearly the size of its opposite, and I could see teams on the roof firing big, big single rounds down toward the park with those huge sniper rifles Barrett makes.

Shadow and motion filled the park. Huntsmen and octokongs rushed forward in swift dashes—faster than any human could have done it. The city's defenders concentrated their fire on the Huntsmen, and with good reason—there were several large holes blown in the low walls of the parking garage, and ugly scorched remains were visible. Assault rifles did an excellent job on the first several Huntsmen of any given pack—but by the time the last few of them had gone all Hulk, it was up to the Barretts.

The octokongs weren't as much of a threat—until they

got closer. The ape-squid things had the upper body of a gorilla mounted on the lower chassis of an octopus, hence *octokong*. Good thing they hadn't used chimps, or I'd have had to call them *octopongs*. And that just sounds silly.

The octokongs could slither along the ground at great speed, and when they climbed, tentacles flailing, they didn't really slow down. Each bore a large, crude-looking weapon that made me think of those old blunderbusses, but they were fed by a magazine of some kind. The octokongs weren't exactly snipers. They didn't really aim. They just pointed the weapons in a general direction and pulled the trigger, sending out sprays of what must have been buckshot, if the chewed concrete around the parking garage was any indicator.

"Dresden!" River said sharply. The Sasquatch set me roughly on my feet and pointed.

I looked. The building on the south side of the street, where the Einherjaren snipers were set up, was mostly shrouded in darkness, but I could see well enough to glimpse the shapes of dozens of octokongs that had somehow circled the brick building and were climbing toward the roof, from the rear side, their tentacles probably leaving giant sucker marks on all the windows.

"Think you can handle them?" I asked him.

River set Ramirez down more carefully, his dark eyes just a ferocious gleam beneath his heavy brows, and bounded off in that direction, vanishing behind a veil as he went. A minute later, something grabbed one of the lowest octokongs, whirled it in a circle, and smashed it like a water balloon against the ground. I could see the blur of a form as it leapt a good fifteen feet up the side of the building, and dust exploded from the bricks, presumably from River Shoulders digging his fingers into them to get a good grip. He started climbing the building, seizing octokongs from behind and either smashing their skulls against the bricks or simply throwing them off and letting them fall to an ugly death.

Couldn't have happened to a nicer bunch.

"Hoss!" shouted Ebenezar's voice.

I turned to see my grandfather on the second level of the parking garage, waving at me. He beckoned, and I held up a fist in acknowledgment.

"Can you move?" I asked Carlos.

The young Warden gave me a sour look and started limping along at his best pace, clutching his broken arm to his body to keep it from swinging. I went with him.

By the time we reached the second level of the garage, the old man was at the front of the garage, facing the park. Shot rattled around him, but the Blackstaff was the White Council's dedicated killing machine. There were rumors among the Wardens that the old man's shield had completely held off a round from a German battleship's main guns in World War I. I didn't know if that was true or not, but buckshot scattered off it in little fluttery sparkles that had no chance, at all, of getting through.

The old man stared down at the park thoughtfully, heedless of the incoming fire, then nodded once, held out a fist, spoke a word, and gathered a sphere of white-hot light into the palm of his right hand. He flicked his wrist, and the sphere of light streaked over to the park and set the nearest tree there violently ablaze.

Octokongs screamed and poured out of it—to where they were well-lit by the fire on open ground.

The Einherjaren let out whoops of excitement and approval as their weapons roared, absolutely withering every octokong on the ground.

"Do it again, *seidrmadr*!"

"Let them have it, wizard!"

The old man obliged them, and another tree went up with similar results.

I heard the cry of a hawk, and then a bolt of lightning descended, crashing into several parked cars along the road, providing cover for the enemy. The cars exploded into flame with a number of whumping sounds.

Screeches of rage and pain rose from the park, but the enemy pressed closer and closer. One of the Einherjaren set down his rifle, picked up one of those grenade launchers with a rotary magazine, and quickly sent half a dozen grenades into the park, each with a report and a *phoont* sound. He had used white phosphorous rounds. The carnage was impressive, but the octokongs kept pouring mindlessly forward—

—and a sudden sound split the air.

It sounded like a call from a horn—if the horn was the size of a Buick. It was a deep, brassy, throaty sound. And it was loud. Loud as a thunderstorm. Loud enough to shake the concrete beneath my feet.

And then I saw him.

Striding forward, toward Lake Shore, his black hair soaked with lake water and clinging to his skull.

A giant.

A genuine, honest-to-God *giant*. A Jotun.

His features were crude, rough, his beard and hair were woven in enormous braids, and he wore the armor and kit of a Viking warrior—just on a much larger scale. In his hands he bore a horn made from God knows what kind of animal, and as I watched he lifted it to his lips and blew again, shaking the city.

I thought of footprints on the beach and started cackling.

And then . . .

More giants.

They came forward, in a straight line from the lake, two by two, each armored and tattooed and bearing swords and axes of enormous, rough design. One of the giants got caught up in the branches of a tree, and with a snarl he turned, and his twelve-foot-long sword burst into flame and swept clean through the tree, as if it had just been a weed in need of whacking. That not being enough, he turned to a car parked near him, split it in half with another swing of his sword, and kicked the separate pieces forty yards.

The first giant blew the horn again.

The others answered with a roar and began a basso chant, a war song, in some language that sounded thick and sludgy.

The gunfire had stopped.

I looked around me to see the Einherjaren staring at the incoming behemoths, mouths open, eyes bright.

Then the big guy with the grenade launcher screamed, in freaking *joy*, *"JOTNAR! JOTNAR OF MUSPEL-HEIM!"*

And the goddamned madmen roared their excitement and began their own war song in answer. The Jotnar focused on the parking garage and bellowed pure rage at the sound of that song.

Then they started sprinting right at us.

Chapter

Fifteen

From the top deck of the parking garage, we were at eye level with the Jotnar. It didn't make me feel any better. All it meant was that I could see the distinct expression of rage on each face as they either climbed and vaulted over the Lake Shore Drive bridge over Montrose, or else dropped under it, duckwalking under the bridge and rising as they emerged.

The scary part about it was that they were *fast*. Their walking speed would have been a fairly serious run for me. Running, they were moving at vehicle speeds.

I felt my hands shaking in pure, unadulterated fear. Doesn't matter how good you are in a fight—mass matters, and I had more sheer tonnage of angry bad guy coming at me than maybe ever before.

"Hoo boy," I said.

Ebenezar stumped forward to stand beside me, his eyes bright. Light from a flare shone off his bald, smooth-shaved pate. "Now, that, Hoss," he said, "is something you don't see every day."

All around me, Einherjaren were ditching their rifles.

Instead, they started pulling out axes and swords, laughing and singing as they did. A crew of several others came running in with crates made of heavy composite materials and opened them to reveal bricks of what I assumed to be explosive compounds of some sort. They started passing them out, along with small tubular detonators, which they clutched between their teeth as if they'd been passed a Cuban cigar.

"Okay," I said. "What the hell are these guys thinking?"

"They're thinking those giants are about to ram into this building and bring it down around us all," Ebenezar said.

"What are we gonna do about it?" I asked.

There was a soft set of footsteps and then Senior Councilman Cristos stood beside me, staring hard at the oncoming Jotnar. He was breathing hard, and his face looked grey and exhausted. "It's ready," he said to Ebenezar.

"Right," my grandfather said. He leaned forward, staring intently at the ground on the near side of the park. "Hoss, buy me a little time to work."

"Me?" I squeaked.

"Mmm. Or we'll die," he said calmly. "Those are fire giants. We don't stop these things here, they'll run right through us and turn the city into a kiln while the Titan sits back and laughs."

By this time, I could *feel* the shock when their feet, stumpier and wider than human feet would be, proportionately, struck the ground like an earthquake's vanguard.

"Carlos, shield me," I said. "I'm not going to have anything to spare."

Without a word, Ramirez lifted his left hand and the air in front of me quivered with a pale greenish disk of light that rippled like water. It wasn't more than a second before enemy fire struck it on one side, evidently with shot from the octokong weapons. The ball hit Ramirez's shield and in the act of passing through, it was ripped into a fine spray of metallic grit.

The Jotnar closed to two hundred yards.

I lifted my right hand, staff gripped in it, and gathered my power, reaching out to the cold, vicious core of Winter that now resided within me.

One hundred and fifty yards.

From deep within, I touched upon the reservoir of Soulfire that I'd been gifted with many moons before. Soulfire was the purest force of Creation in the universe, left over from the birth of the universe itself. Angels wielded Soulfire, and one of them had given me enough to last a lifetime. Soulfire didn't make magic more potent, precisely—but it made it more *real.* As the power of Creation itself, Soulfire was best used to create and protect, and what I had in mind was going to take a lot of it.

One hundred yards.

Cold blue light began to shine from me. That was enough to draw the fire of every octokong on the field, and Ramirez's shield glowed brighter and brighter. I struggled not to flinch as an increasing spray of fine grains of lead washed against my chest and face.

"Harry," Carlos gasped. "Hurry."

Fifty yards.

Within my thoughts, I merged the power from the heart of Winter with Soulfire.

My head exploded with raw agony as the energies met—and fed upon each other, growing into a thunderstorm in my thoughts. Frost formed over my fingernails and spread out along a couple of feet of my quarterstaff on either side of my gripping hand. Steam boiled off me in small clouds as Winter frost met the sultry summer night.

"Infriga!" I roared, pointing my staff at the ground to one side of the charging line of Jotnar.

Power coursed out of the heart of me, into the ancient oak of my wizard's staff, focused and concentrated within its length by the runes and sigils carved along it. The tool leapt in my hand like a firefighter's high-pressure hose, and I had to clamp both hands on it and strain every muscle just to hold steady, runes glowing the same bright green-gold as Alfred's eyes on Demonreach.

A howling lance of glacier-blue, coherent, observable, utter *cold* flooded into the night. The very summer air screamed in protest at the sudden, wild shift in temperature, with steam and mist boiling off me in a cloud. The beam struck the ground before the oncoming Jotnar—and where that beam struck, a wall of absolutely crystalline ice formed, twenty feet thick, thirty feet high, and curving forward like a breaking wave.

Howling in time with the wailing air, I slewed the beam from left to right across the path of the oncoming Jotnar—who collided with my barrier with all the power and momentum of a freight train. There was an enormous roar, a series of impacts, and cracks exploded through the clear ice in a spiderweb of crazed lines.

But the wall *held*.

I sagged as the last of the spell's energy washed out of

me and would have fallen if Ramirez hadn't steadied me. My vision blurred for a second, and I swiped a hand at my eyes, where frost crystals had frozen throughout my eyelashes and dragged them down in a wintry veil over my vision.

By the time I'd cleared it, Jotnar were roaring. Swords and axes exploded into flame as though they'd been coated in napalm and set alight. The flaming weapons were brought crashing down upon the Winter ice with echoing cracks like the bellow of cannons. Light rushed through the prism of the slowly shattering wall, dancing through hectic spectrums of color. Fragments of ice exploded outward in deadly showers. Screaming jets of steam erupted from each strike, some of them whistling like a haunted hell-bound train.

I dragged my gaze over to my grandfather, who stood with his legs planted solidly. Ebenezar held his hands at his sides, fingers wide, palms toward the ground, and the very air around him shivered with multiple forces of energy.

My wall of ice cracked and fell within seconds, the Jotnar hammering and hacking it down, heedless of the deadly jets of steam.

But a few seconds had been enough.

The old man abruptly opened his eyes, lifted his upper lip in a snarl, turned up his palms, and raised them, slow, shaking, as though they were carrying a weight too unthinkable to be readily quantified as he growled, *"Plimmyra."*

The Jotnar plunged ahead, screaming, their boots hammering the ground—

—and then the very earth *bubbled* and without ceremony simply swallowed them. Jotnar fell, with blaring
shouts of confusion and rage, thrashing in ground that
had a moment before been solid and was now, I could see,
so inundated with water that it had become something
very much like quicksand.

The giants thrashed and struggled, and I turned to see
the old man gasp and waver as the energy of the spell left
him. He braced a hand on the concrete edge of the parking garage, traded a look with Cristos, and then the pair
of them started cackling, half in exhaustion and half in
satisfaction.

The leader of the Einherjaren stared gleefully for a second, as the Jotnar thrashed and stumbled over one another, wallowing clumsily. Then he let out a howl of glee,
raised his axe, and just vaulted over the railing to the street
level twenty feet below him. The rest of the revenant warriors followed him in a wave of joyous howls. I thought I
could hear ankles breaking as they hit the ground.

They just didn't care.

What followed was . . . one of those things I still have
dreams about sometimes.

It was like looking at something straight out of mythology. Warriors with their axes and spears went screaming
for the Jotnar. Their weight was utterly insignificant compared to that of the giants, and they ran over the surface
of the inundated earth with no more difficulty than they
would a moderately muddy field.

Flaming Jotun weapons rose and fell, and if the giants
had been quick to cover ground, they were just too
damned big and too damned shackled in their movements

to respond with sufficient speed. The Norse warriors ducked and leapt and weaved as enormous weapons came scything toward them. Mostly, they were successful. But I saw one man crushed like an insect by a blow from the flat of a Jotun axe. Another was spitted like a damned pig, and the man screamed as the flaming sword lifted him high and burned his guts into a cloud of black ash. Still another was seized by a Jotun's meaty, thick-fingered hand, and the giant simply lifted the man's head and shoulders to his broad mouth—and bit them off with about as much effort as I would use on a chocolate bunny.

Dozens of the Einherjaren met horrible fates.

And then it was their turn.

Huge the Jotnar might have been, but the Einherjaren knew how to fight them. As some warriors engaged a Jotun's weaponry, sacrificing their lives to do so, others followed through the openings their companions' deaths had created. Their great swords and broadaxes began to swing and to hack the trapped Jotnar. Einherjaren thrust their blades between enormous links of mail where necessary and hacked at Jotun thighs and groins wherever possible. The giants were huge, but they were made of flesh and blood.

The fight became brutal beyond anything you could see in a movie theater. Small rivers of Jotun blood flowed. One gout caught the leader of the Einherjaren full in the face, and the man went up like the Human Torch—and as he burned, he continued hacking away with his axe until finally a charred black mannequin fell to the earth. A dozen Einherjaren together leapt against a Jotun's chest. Two of them were crushed to death on the way in, but the others overbore the giant, sending it crashing to its back in the quicksand, where they hacked at its face and neck with their weapons, screaming—until another Jotun's sword scythed across the ground at thigh level and ripped every single one of them in half.

Another Einherjar leapt up to sink a knife into that Jotun's thigh, held on, and with his other hand slammed the detonator into his brick of explosive compound. It went off with a great cough of sound that slammed against my chest—and severed the Jotun's leg at midthigh, sending it crashing and dying to the earth.

The Jotnar were killing the Einherjaren in job lots—and the Vikings just did not *care*.

They died, shouting and laughing and singing as they met fates more horrible than I want to think about or could easily describe.

And, by God, they took Jotnar with them.

The leader of the Jotnar, with his horn, thrashed his way to the edge of the quicksand and gained solid ground with one foot. A hawk shrieked defiance and plunged from the sky, sweeping along parallel to the ground in a burst of speed—and becoming a freaking fourteen-foot African elephant as it reached the Jotun.

Listens-to-Wind hit the Jotnar's leader with the speed of a hawk and the mass of a pachyderm, and tree-trunk-sized ribs snapped with cracks of miniature thunder. The Jotun fell back into the waterlogged earth, while the elephant's tusks ripped at his face and throat, gouging and tearing holes in flesh with raw strength and savage power.

Then octokongs and Huntsmen reached the fight, following in the wake of the Jotnar's charge. Massive fire poured down from the skyscraper across the street, but it couldn't stop them from coming forward. Momentum turned against the Einherjaren. Three more of them went up in explosions, laughing like madmen as the blasts took foes with them into death.

But there were more Fomor than there were Einherjaren.

The tide turned.

Just as it did, the world suddenly went silent, as if reality had taken a deep breath and held it. There was a low quiver in the concrete beneath my feet, a hideous pressure in the air, and then, from the direction of the lake, a column of red-white energy, pure power, hammered into the skyscraper where Marcone's fire teams were wreaking havoc on the enemy and slewed across it in a path of utter ruin.

The building shattered like a toy.

I stood staring in pure shock as the power of the Eye of Balor tore apart a modern skyscraper as if it had been built from balsa wood. Windows shattered. Steel melted and ran like water. The building groaned in agony and then simply collapsed in upon itself in a roar and a wash of fire and smoke and a vast storm of rising dust.

In seconds, an edifice that had required the hands and wills of thousands of men and women had been reduced to smoke and rubble.

Ethniu had taken the field.

The Last Titan had come for Chicago.

I staggered as the cloud of dust billowed over us, and then recoiled again as, seconds later, the broad, ugly form of a Jotun congealed out of the dust and let out a roar, raising its axe high over the parking garage in both hands.

"Run!" screamed the old man.

And then the vast flaming axe crashed down into the ceiling above us and shattered the world.

Chapter

Sixteen

There was no time.

I gave Ebenezar a push, getting him out of the way of falling stone. Ramirez had had the same idea, pulling from the other side, and had more momentum than I did. They got clear.

Several tons of concrete plus one Jotun-sized axe came crashing down toward me.

Someone hit me in the hip like a linebacker, legs driving. The impact lifted me off my feet and carried me to one side as the roof came down with a roar and a wash of dust and smoke. I covered my head with my arms and rolled in the direction that seemed away from all the falling stuff, dimly aware of someone else with me doing more or less the same thing.

By the time I had wits enough to look around me, I found myself at the edge of a ragged hole in the parking garage's floor leading to the level below.

Next to me, covered in grey dust and a white cloak, was Butters in his sports goggles. The wiry little guy wore tactical gear and one of Charity Carpenter's armored vests, this one made with titanium scales fixed to a Kevlar undergarment. His shock of black hair stood up every which way, dust coating it almost entirely.

"Holy smokes!" he said. "Was that a giant with a flaming axe?!"

"Butters!" I said.

The little guy blinked at me through the dust on his goggles and flashed me a huge and sudden grin. "Hey," he said, "I just straight up saved your life! That's Sir Waldo to you, buddy."

Outside the parking garage, the Jotun roared. Shadows shifted through the dust and smoke as the thing drew back that axe and swept it around in a horizontal arc. Both of us threw ourselves as flat as we could, still shielding our heads with our arms as the weapon smashed through the parking garage like a wrecking ball.

Chunks of concrete zinged around like shot from some unthinkably large cannon. One piece hit my thigh, through the spell-armored leather of my duster. It was like taking a glancing blow from a sledgehammer, and not even Winter's disregard for pain could block all of it, and I let out a shout that was at least fifty percent pure surprise.

"Fall back!" Ebenezar was roaring in the background. "Regroup at the next block!"

Butters bounced back to his feet. The little guy was never going to be physically intimidating, but the past few months of training with the Carpenters to be a Knight had made him quick and tough as nails. "Come on!"

One of my legs was just sort of hanging there uselessly, but I managed to struggle to the other one, holding on to my staff with both hands, coughing and choking on the dust in the air.

The world gasped and went scarlet again, red light flooding through the haze of war. The air screamed with unnatural power as the Eye of Balor unleashed raw destruction upon the city, and my heart took a terrified flutter. I had only once before witnessed destructive power on that order of magnitude, and that had been at the will of the Fallen Angel himself—and even then it had been carefully constrained, used for a purpose.

Ethniu had no such restraints.

The air and the ground shook as another building, out there in the haze, came crashing down.

Butters staggered over to me and got enough of himself under my arm to help me move forward. "What was *that*?"

"Magic superweapon," I gasped. We hurried for the ramp down to the first level. I couldn't tell who was left in the garage—the choking haze was just too damned thick. "Bunch of us came up here to back up Marcone's people. Guess we provided enough resistance that Ethniu had to break out the big guns." I coughed, spat, and said, "What are you doing here? Mister Sunshine arrange for you to be where you're needed?"

"Uh . . ." Butters said, drawing the sound out. "Now, don't be mad, Harry."

"What?" I asked, and I might have sounded a little grumpy.

"Me and Sanya kind of wound up by Mac's place," he said.

"Butters," I said warningly.

"We took a vote," he said.

We had just made it to the bottom of the ramp when I heard a sound behind me and I looked back to see a trio of octokongs come . . . sort of slurping across the ground, teeth bared in a furious mutant-gorilla grimace, weird weapons in hand.

I threw up my shield bracelet, rammed my will through it, and brought up a dome of sparkling green-gold light, easily seen in the haze and dust, just as their weapons began to fire.

I had been questioning the enemy's wisdom in handing all the octokongs what amounted to shotguns. But I hadn't been thinking. In the chaos of a city on fire, within the limited visibility of the smoke and darkness, nobody could see very well—and certainly not well enough for reliable precision shooting. "Firing thataway" with a shotgun was probably just about as close to accurate as it would be possible to get.

I dropped my staff, reached for my own coach gun in its scabbard, remembered that the staff had been helping support me, and fell hard against Butters, who grunted and crashed to a knee.

The octokongs kept relentless fire against my shield as I went down, and to my shock another dozen of the things came swarming along the walls and roof of the ramp, staying out of the line of fire of the original trio as they kept shooting.

Behind *them* came a sphere of wavery aqua light. In the haze, I could make out a tall, slender, frog-faced form at the center of the sphere. One of the Fomor themselves, then, driving his charges forward. The shape lifted a hand and sent a crackling bolt of green lightning crashing against my shield.

That one was some serious sorcery. I held it off, but it took a gasp of effort and energy to keep the shield in place.

My leg twitched when I tried to make it work, which was better than a moment before, but not good enough to get me out of this one. "Butters, get clear!" I screamed.

"Not yet!" he said. "Hold the shield!"

My ears picked out running footsteps from up the ramp—no, from the *opposite* ramp, the one leading up the other side of the parking garage.

I saw the shielded Fomor abruptly turn, just as an enormous, friendly voice boomed, "Hello!"

And the haze of battle vanished, burned away by an aurora of silver-white light around a curved, gleaming Sword. Sanya, Knight of the Cross, six and a half feet of muscle, dark-skinned and graceful, whipped the shining form of *Esperacchius* through an arc, and it was as if the Sword itself cleared and cleaned the air before it as it moved. It struck through the Fomor's arcane shields as if they had not existed, and before the foe could shriek, its head had jumped from its shoulders.

The big man's teeth shone white against his dark skin as he lobbed something calmly down among the octokongs and darted smoothly to one side in a sweep of white cloak.

"Grenade!" I screamed, and sent more power into the shield.

A second later, there was a sound you could chew, it was so thick, and a wash of power smashed against my shield, overloading what the bracelet could handle and scorching my wrist.

Octokongs tumbled from the walls, wounded, stunned, some of them dying.

Sanya let out a roar and reappeared, charging them, flanked on both sides by a pair of enormous wolves—Will Borden and the Alphas.

"Now, *you* stay down, Harry," Butters snarled.

And with a clarion shriek of choral fury, *Fidelacchius*'s blade of pure light sprang to life in his hands, and Butters zipped up the ramp, his cloak flying behind him.

Between the werewolves and the Knights, it took maybe ten seconds.

Then there was a low rumble behind me, and Karrin Murphy appeared, wearing her motorcycle jacket and riding her old Harley, sticking out her good leg to support it as she brought the bike to a growling halt.

I eyed the motorcycle. Then her. "How?"

"Like I don't keep this old baby behind wards," she said. "The Ordo Lebes did it for me years ago. And bikes are the only things that can get through the streets." She checked around her and then up the ramp. "Come on. There're more of them coming up from the lake." She drew a radio out of her pocket, turned it on, and said into it, "This is Valkryie. I've got Booster Gold."

"Hey," I objected.

"Roger that, Valkryie," came a calm voice over the radio. Marcone. "Be advised that Winter One has chosen her ground. All remaining forces in the north will rally at Wrigley. The enemy command has turned south. I recommend—"

The world went red again. Scarlet light flooded the

night and left us in deep shadow. Murphy's radio went up in a shower of sparks. The quivering roar that followed the blast of the Eye was less savage this time. Ethniu was farther away.

"Son of a bitch," Murphy swore in annoyance. She tossed the radio aside and reached into her coat pocket for a second. "My bike is old enough not to care much about magic, and our radios at command and control are shielded, but the field units aren't lasting long." She took a battery out of her other pocket and started popping it into the unit.

"I told you," Butters said. He shrugged out of a backpack that he'd been wearing under the cloak. "They don't have enough vacuum tubes."

"We can't stay here," Sanya said, nodding to the corpses of the octokongs and the Fomor.

Even as he did, I saw one of the dead octokong's wounds begin to . . . bubble. Its dark blood began to boil up out of the wounds with little hissing sounds, and a stench, dizzying in its intensity, began to fill the air of the ramp. The corpse actually quivered with the intensity of the chemical reaction, bits of flesh liquefying and sloughing off.

Murphy nodded, her nose wrinkling, and said to me, "Can you walk?"

"Kind of," I said. My leg muscles tightened when I told them to, but when I tried to stand on it, the limb still buckled limply.

She nodded and said, "Get on the bike. We can't stay here. CPD is bringing everyone they can get to the heart of the Loop and trying to evacuate."

I got to my feet and staggered to the Harley. I swung my hurt leg over in a burst of tactile white noise, and Murphy turned the bike around toward the exit on the back side of the parking garage, opposite the lake.

"Just curious. How long did you stay at Mac's?" I asked.

"Long enough to get everyone organized," she said. "There's no point discussing things with you once you get all chivalrous."

I opened my mouth in annoyance and then closed it again. "You shouldn't be here," I said.

"Yeah, well, tough."

I leaned my chin down onto her hair and closed my eyes. I felt her weight shift as she pressed her shoulder blades against my ribs. It was just for a moment, and for that moment I let myself feel. Intense relief at seeing her well. Intense fear at knowing that she was in danger. And pain. Loss. Terror. Confusion. Bewilderment. For a moment, I struggled against the sense that what was happening, all around me, could not *be* happening, could not be real.

But it was real.

Karrin found my hand and squeezed, hard.

I leaned my cheek against her hair and whispered, "Yoshimo and Wild Bill are dead. Probably Chandler, too. Black Court. And I don't know if Ramirez or my grandfather made it out of the garage."

She let out a breath and whispered back, "Oh, Harry."

My stomach quivered. My eyes burned with tears that could not be given form if I was to hold it together. Which I had to do. There was no time to break down, no time for tears.

War leaves you precious little time to be human. It's one of the more horrible realities about it.

I nodded, just enough so that she could feel my chin move, and the moment was over.

The four wolves loped easily forward, two taking places on our flanks, and two more ghosting silently out ahead of us, and Sanya and Butters came trotting along behind, keeping the pace, while I worked on preventing my hurt leg from just bouncing along the ground. It was recovering from the blow, stunned muscles sluggishly regaining sensibility, but for the moment I was pretty gimpy.

There was no way to ride the Harley at proper speed, not with all the dead cars as obstacles. I was surprised the thing kept on rumbling at all. Murphy rolled us slowly and carefully through the parking garage and didn't ease out of the building until one of the wolves appeared from the haze ahead of us, evidently signaling the all clear.

"Harry," called Butters from behind me.

I turned my head and took the backpack he offered me. It was light.

He nodded at the pack, grinning.

I opened it.

Inside was a human skull, bleached and ancient and battered—and an old friend.

The skull's empty eye sockets suddenly flooded with light the color of campfire embers, and the thing shook as though awakening from a sleep. Bob had been my assistant for most of my adult life. "Oh, hey there, Harry! Long time no see!"

"Bob!" I said. Despite everything that had happened, I grinned. "How the hell are you?"

"Terrified!" Bob piped up. "How's about we all pick a direction and run?"

"No can do," I said. "I'm working. What the hell is happening here?"

The world went red again. This time I saw the beam tear a building apart, farther south of us, bringing it crashing down like a sandcastle before the tide, and the light lingered in the air, tinging the haze an ugly shade of scarlet.

We all just stared at that for a second. No one made a sound.

"Big bad mojo," Bob said. His tone was . . . worried. "I haven't ever seen anything on this scale, boss. The amount of power flying around out there is more than it can handle."

"More than what can handle?" I demanded.

"*Reality,*" Bob said. "That's partly why the Tuatha fought the Fomor to begin with. Balor and his stupid Eye."

"Whoa, wait," I said. "Reality can break? That can happen?"

"Obviously it can happen," Bob said, annoyed. "There's . . . a structure to the universe, right? And like every structure it has limits. And a point of catastrophic failure."

"So when Ferrovax the dragon is bragging about cracking the world . . ."

"He's not kidding," Bob said, nodding vigorously. "And it's a process that feeds on itself. Like, you got about eight million terrified humans running around town right now, providing more and more energy for available use."

Murphy rolled out onto the street and turned west. I felt weirdly like the subject of a presidential motorcade, what with the Knights and werewolves running escort. "So what can we expect?" I asked.

"Chaos," Bob said.

"More specific?"

"Impossible! Widespread insanity for the mortals, maybe. Maybe *transmissible* insanity. Hallucinations, tulpas, and outright unintentional creation of things right out of people's imaginations. Animals and people changing form or nature. The breakdown of Newtonian physics. Hell, even the quantum-level rules might change, with consequences that are literally unimaginable. Two plus two might equal five. *Twilight Zone* stuff. I don't know. *No one* knows. You can't predict chaos because it's *chaos*, Harry."

The clear night sky suddenly rumbled with what sounded like perfectly natural thunder.

"See?" Bob demanded. "That's the boundary between the mortal world and the Nevernever. There's so much energy flying around that it's breaking down."

I felt my eyes widen. The barrier between the mortal world and the world of spirit was all that separated humanity from demons and devils and nightmarish creatures of literally every description. "Is it thin enough for anything to get through?"

"If it's not," Bob said ominously, "it will be. Right now, Ferrovax is holding that door closed. It's enormously inefficient to do it from the Nevernever side. He won't be able to keep it up forever without coming to this side, in his true form, and that would basically rip reality's nuts off."

"How long?" I asked. "Can he hold them out until dawn?"

"No one's seen a confrontation this big for thousands

of years, Harry," Bob said, and his tone was outright worried. "The Laws of Magic change over time. I don't know the answer to your question. I don't think anyone else knows, either."

Murphy looked back at me over her shoulder, then down at the bag, before turning her eyes back to the road. After a moment, she said, "My leg and arm don't hurt anymore."

Bob grunted. "Yeah. That's Mab."

I blinked. "What?"

"Mab. Preparing the field. What, you think she and Titania called up Tir na Nog and practiced against each other all those times for funsies? Mab's extending psychic power to those fighting on her side. And at the same time, she's making it more oppressive for her enemies." Bob jiggled his chin back toward the ground we had lost. "Everything coming in from that side *knows*, not in its head but deep down in its *guts*, that it is entering the lair of a predator and that it's never going home. Knows the odds are against it. Knows that every step forward brings it closer to death."

"How do you know that?" Murphy asked.

"Because I'm one of the beings Her Most Royal Frozen Naughtybits considers an enemy," Bob said brightly—but his voice had a brittle, tense undertone. "She's doing it to me as we speak."

Murphy glanced back, frowning. "And she's healing her allies?"

"Don't be ridiculous," Bob said. "She's just making it so you can't feel the pain. She'll blunt any non-useful terror you might feel, too. And she'll encourage your aggressive tendencies. Like maybe enough so that someone who is too physically screwed up to be involved in fighting instead convinces her friends to help her and heads out into the war."

Murphy snorted. "Yeah. There's just no way I would have done that otherwise."

I ran a quick mental inventory and found myself scowling. "How come she isn't doing any of that for *me*, then?"

Bob gave me a disgusted look. "You're the Winter freaking Knight. You get it all the time. Suck it up."

Again the sky turned red. Again metal and concrete screamed and rumbled. There was too much dust in the sky now. I couldn't see what had fallen—only the diffused glow of the power of the Eye and a slight thickening in the dusty cloud.

"Hell's bells," I complained. "How many shots does that thing have?"

"It's being fueled by the city's fear now, boss," Bob said seriously. "It'll run out when everyone's dead. Which was the general idea, when it was created. That's part of what Mab is trying to do, too. Dampen everyone's fear. Rob the enemy of power."

Butters leaned in to the conversation. "What happens if Mab keeps making things worse on the enemy?"

Bob let out a hysterical little cackle. "They go insane. I mean, obviously. It's a psychic assault."

Murphy gave me a sharp look. "So they have to stop her. If they don't, they can't meet their objective."

"Good luck finding her," I said.

Red light flashed again, staining the air with blood.

And, from the south, a sudden glaring column of blue

light, so intense and bright that it could readily be seen even through the haze, erupted cold and defiant into the sultry night.

"*Bozhe moi!*" Sanya blurted, lifting a hand to shield his eyes. "Is that . . ."

I knew power from the heart of Winter when I saw it. "Mab. Yeah." I thought furiously. "Crap."

"What?" Butters asked.

"Murphy's right," I said. "They've got to shut her down. And she's just told them where to find her."

"She's made herself bait," Murphy said. "They'll converge on her. From everywhere."

"Yeah, they will," I said, still thinking. "There's no way they'd pass up a chance to . . ." Mab's intent suddenly unfolded in my head. "Oh crap. We've got to turn south."

Murphy took a deep breath. "You sure?"

"I'm sure it will be worse if we don't," I said. "Follow that skybeam."

Chapter

Seventeen

We rode through pandemonium.

Pandemonium means "the place where all demons dwell."

And the demons were out tonight.

After a couple of blocks, someone in my head hit the pause button on whatever VCR recording my memory kept of the event. Things got blurry. Only pieces remained. Cuttings of memory.

. . . buildings were on fire. Black smoke poured out of them. An old woman stood in the street in her nightgown, screaming hysterically.

. . . a group of men had gathered around a policeman and were kicking his guts out. Sanya and Butters plunged into them and scattered them like a flock of chickens. The cop was already dead, but it took his body a minute to catch on. We had to leave his remains there.

. . . a Catholic priest at the door of a packed church, explaining to a crowd that there was only room for children.

. . . a dead neighborhood where the Huntsmen had

killed every man, woman, child, and pet. Had burned every plant and building. Destroyed every fire hydrant. Water two inches deep, most of it scarlet with spilled blood. Light and heat.

. . . a furtive group of men gathered around a beaten woman. The smell of propellant from Murphy's gun. Bloody fangs. Butters vomiting. Sanya, his eyes cold.

. . . a lot of cops, terrified and trying. Fire department guys with hopeless faces. Grim, quiet EMTs doing desperate battle with the Reaper himself. A lot of civilians, hard-faced and armed and determined, standing shoulder to shoulder with officers: the fighters. Veterans. Bikers. Parents. There were fewer people on the street now—those who could flee had already done so. Those who remained were the invalids, those determined to fight—and the dead.

So many dead.

The Fomor had spared no one. Not women. Not the elderly. And not children.

. . . flashes of red light. The roar of destruction that followed. Always, those flashes coloring the whole of the haze and sky in bloody scarlet, but for where that single column of icy defiance remained.

. . . a crib on its side on the street, the interior stained red.

God.

I would have nightmares for years about that one image.

Somewhere, inside my head, I knew that the events now transpiring were of historic proportions. That they were driven by forces and circumstances far beyond the scope or control of any one individual.

But when I asked whose fault this was, I could see only myself in the dim mirrors of the windows of broken buildings, staring in silent accusation. I knew it wasn't a rational position, and it didn't matter.

I had been given strength. A good man would use that strength to protect those who could not protect themselves.

Too many innocents had not been protected when they needed it most. I had failed them.

I saw Murphy's head track to one side as we passed that crib. I saw her face.

She felt exactly the same.

We were both wrong to feel that way. And it didn't make a damned bit of difference.

I looked around me. Butters walked with tears making grey streaks down his dusty face. The wolves slunk along, heads low, alert and miserable. Only Sanya, remote and calm, seemed to bear up under the horror with stoicism— but even Russians have limits. His face was tight with pain.

And we all felt it.

That we'd failed.

Winter called to me, the whole time. The cold would numb pain, swallow my sickness, leave everything calm and sharp-edged and rational and clear. I could lean into that power. Forget this pain, at least for a time.

But somewhere deep down inside my guts, there emerged a solid, unalterable realization of truth:

Some things *should* hurt.

Some things *should* leave you with scars.

Some things *should* haunt your nightmares.

Some things *should* be burned into memory.

Because that was the only way to make sure that they would be fought. It was the only way to face them. It was the only way to cast down the future agents of death and havoc before they could bring things to this.

The words *never again* mean more to some people than others.

So I rode behind Murphy and held Winter's cold comfort at arm's length. I knew that what I bore witness to would hurt me, permanently. I knew it would leave me scarred. Knew it would burn things into me that would never change.

I let it.

I faced it.

I remembered.

And wrath gathered around us.

I don't mean that in a metaphorical sense. Wrath *became* something real, a tangible presence in the air, as real and as observable as music, as the sharp, clean scent of ozone. The men and women we passed looked upon us and *knew* that we were on the way to deliver retribution upon those who had come to our city.

And those who felt it followed.

I looked back and saw a silent, grim, determined host of men and women. Some of them were cops. I saw a couple of military uniforms, donned in the emergency. Some were obviously from the rough side of the tracks. But most were just . . . people. Just folks.

Folks who'd had enough.

Folks who'd decided to take up arms and fight.

And above us, around us, the Little Folk marched behind my psychic banner. Always hidden, always flickers of motion in the corner of your eye, flittering shadows and whispers of sound—and the glitter of tiny weapons.

And there were other things out there in the night. The Winter Court included a vast array of nightmares and boogeymen and predators, any of whom might be roaming the underbelly of Chicago on a given evening. I could *feel* them responding to the banner of my will, feel them ghosting along the rooftops and alleys, gathering around the power of the Winter Knight, matching themselves to my thoughts and my purpose.

My allies began to take note as well. They saw the numbers gathering behind us. They saw the Little Folk, heard the occasionally manic, terrifying giggle that floated up from the shadows. They sensed the presence of horrible things, leashed to my will.

Will and the Alphas avoided making eye contact with me. Butters stared at me in awe and something like fear. Murphy looked at our forces, then at me, tensed her jaw, and gave me a single harsh nod before turning back to face the front.

This was what it was to be the Winter Knight. This was the purpose for which the office had been made.

"Bob," I said, and my voice sounded absolutely sepulchral. "What're we hearing on the radio bands?"

"Not much from in town," Bob replied in a meek tone. "The Eye keeps blowing out the field units. Scouts are having to observe and then report back to the command centers for any of this information to go out, and I'm not sure how many people are receiving it. Um. We're going to need new skyline pictures for the tourist postcards: Ethniu is apparently moving down Lake Shore Drive and mowing down buildings along the way."

"Mab's set up by the Bean, isn't she?"

"Looks that way, boss."

"Makes sense," I said.

"Why?" Murphy asked.

"In a lot of ways, it's the heart of Chicago. The city's energy will be most potent there. Lots of fuel for magic."

"Including the Eye, right?" Murphy asked.

"Exactly," I said. "What else can you tell me, Bob?"

The skull spoke in a nervous voice. "Um, good news, the cavalry is on the way. Bunch of National Guard units. Bad news—"

"This will be over before they get here," I said harshly.

"Don't kill me," Bob said quickly.

I blinked down at him. Then around me.

My friends were all staring at me as if I were . . . Darth Vader or somebody.

Murphy searched my face for a moment. There wasn't any fear in her expression. Only deep, pained concern.

I closed my eyes for a second and squeezed her gently with one arm. I tried to consciously make my voice sound calm and reasonable. Why did my throat hurt so much? "Okay. What's Mab got with her? And what's the enemy got with them?"

"Her personal guard," Bob said. "A cohort of warrior Sidhe. Sure as hell would be nice if she still had that elite troop of trolls right now. Lara's people are with her, and all the heavy hitters from the svartalf command post."

"All grouped up where they can be taken out at the same time," I said. All in the open in Millennium Park, no less. Mab was daring Ethniu to come at her, giving her a nice juicy group of enemies to target with the Eye.

Don't get me wrong: Mab was perfectly capable of kicking someone's teeth right down their throat. If she thought a slugfest with Ethniu would get things done, she wouldn't hesitate an instant. But if she decided it was time for podiatric dentistry, she wouldn't be waiting for Ethniu to come to her. Not Mab. Mab would be moving forward like Juggernaut, an inexorable force, not standing her ground.

So she was up to something else, and I was pretty sure I knew what.

My senses were suddenly filled with a harsh, swampy scent that wasn't being reported by my own nose. It took me a second to work out what the hell was happening, but it came to me as easily and instinctively as breathing.

A screen of half a dozen malks, savage feline creatures of Winter that bore as much resemblance to cats as serial killers did to kindergartners, had spread out in a skirmish line in front of my banner, and they'd found the enemy waiting for us. I could feel their eagerness and bloodlust rising, got just a hint of expended propellant and gun oil on a wind that never touched my physical nose. More turtlenecks, then. The other creatures of Winter sensed the enemy's presence, too, and a rising violent instinct spread among them—two shaggy, lurking ogres, seven or eight Black Dogs, a dozen psychotic gnomes with hooked knives, and a phobophage, a fear-eater, who had taken the form of a goddamned rake and whose shadowy profile, as it slipped past an open doorway, looked like a cross between a long-limbed Jack Skellington and Wolverine.

And tonight, in this battle, every single one of them was mine to command. I knew it the way I knew which way was down.

The enemy had taken an office building half a block down that would give them a good field of fire at an intersection and had evidently driven CPD away from the area. A number of silent uniformed figures on the ground testified to their deadliness.

But honestly.

Mab's "people" are the things the scary stories get written about.

"Stop," I said quietly.

Murphy brought the bike to a halt.

"This will just take a minute."

And as naturally as moving my own muscles, I sent the monsters for the Fomor.

The malks went in first, through the openings blasted into the building, silent as ghosts. The pony-sized Black Dogs followed, running right through the freaking walls, which I did not know they could do. The rake slithered up a power wire like a snake, and the ogres and gnomes leapt onto the roof. I saw only vague shapes moving in the scarlet haze. Mostly, I just *knew* where they were.

The building erupted in screams and gunfire. There were even a couple of crunching explosions.

And then there were only screams.

The creatures of Winter enjoy their killing. They think it's worth taking the time to do it right. And given the pain and suffering Listen and his turtlenecks had inflicted, it couldn't have happened to a nicer bunch.

"All right," I said. "Proceed."

"Jesus Christ," Murphy said, and she crossed herself, something I'd rarely seen her do.

But she took a deep breath and kept going. We passed the office building. It was largely glass. The creatures of Winter, at my will, had turned it into an abattoir, and it dripped with their enthusiasm.

"Did you do that, Harry?" she asked softly.

"Yeah," I said.

She looked at a dead cop as we went slowly by. Then her face hardened. She spoke very quietly. "Good."

"When we end this," I said, "I'm . . . We're going to need to get away. From all this. From everything. Some-place quiet. Just us. Get drunk for a month."

"God," she breathed, quiet longing in her voice. "I'm in."

"I hate that you're here with me," I said.

"I know."

"And I'm glad that you're here with me."

"I know."

I held her against me for a moment and whispered, "I'm scared. What's happening inside me. Stay close. Please."

Her hand clenched my wrist, fiercely, for a beat. "I'm here."

I shivered and leaned my chin against her hair and for a moment closed my eyes.

Then I straightened my spine and got my bearings. What was happening around me might be horrible, might be scraping away at whatever sanity I could legitimately lay claim to, but that didn't mean I could afford to check out.

I closed my eyes and pictured the city at Millennium Park. There was a lot of flat, open space, good for an old-school battlefield. There weren't a lot of places where you could have troops with rifles dig in, especially not in the vision-killing haze of dust and smoke. But Columbus Drive was a sunken road that divided Millennium Park from Daley Park, a natural obstacle that any troops coming in from the lake would have to overcome. Enough guns there would pile bodies in windrows.

I looked back at the men and women following me. If I put them there, they'd inflict the most damage on the enemy—for a while, anyway. Then they'd probably be overrun and slaughtered.

The question was whether or not that was still the right thing to do. The people marching behind me weren't children. They knew death was in the air. And if the enemy overcame us, the city was doomed. All of it.

But, hell, I wasn't even sure the people who were following me were actually doing it entirely of their own free will. The power of the Winter mantle and Mab's preparations could well be influencing their emotions to the degree that it wouldn't exactly be fair to call their willingness to fight a choice.

I knew how Mab would have called it. She had a battle to win.

Whereas I had people to protect.

"Sanya," I said.

"Da?"

"When we get to the park, I want you to take charge of these folks. The enemy will be coming in from the east and northeast. I want you to find a position where you can . . . What's the word where you get to shoot at them just fine, and they can't shoot back at you too good?"

The Russian smiled thinly. "I think you are trying to say 'defilade.'"

"Yeah. That. Defilade the crap out of them."

"No. *We* want to be in defilade. What you want to happen to *them* is to put them in enfilade."

"Whatever, you know what I'm after. Put them where they can do the most damage and take the least in reply."

"Visibility this low, might not be possible."

"Then guess," I said, exasperated. "I'm kind of counting on the Big Guy making things work out so that you're in the right place at the right time. Figure if I put these people with you, they'll be there, too." I looked back at the bleak, frightened, determined faces following me. "If God is going to be on anyone's side today, I want Him to be on theirs."

Sanya lifted both his eyebrows. "Faith? From you? *Bozhe moi.*"

"Less faith. More observation of operational patterns," I countered.

Sanya abruptly grinned and said, "*Da*, all right. Maybe the horse will sing."

"What?"

He waved a hand. "It is Russian thing."

"No, it isn't, Chekhov," Butters said, in the kind of pedantic tone of protest you only get from a confident nerd. "What about me, Harry?"

"Same deal," I said. "Only *I* want to be the one who's with you at the right place at the right time. Stick close to me."

The little Knight nodded. "Got it."

"And me?" Murphy asked.

"Keep driving," I said. "I need to stay mobile, and the

park is open ground. The bike should be able to move around pretty quick." I bumped my elbow on a black composite-material box that had been strapped to the back of the Harley. There was a printed label on it that read, CAMPING SUPPLIES.

"What's in here?" I asked her.

"My dancing shoes."

"Right." I looked over at Will, who was watching me with serious wolf eyes. "And I need you guys to run interference for me. When the enemy figures out what I'm doing, I'll"—I swallowed—"be target number one."

The wolf stared steadily at me for a moment and then nodded once, sharply. Will knew exactly what I was asking them to do: take bullets for me, of one kind or another.

"Bob," I said, "if anything useful comes over the airwaves, I want to know about it."

"Got it, boss," Bob said. "Um. But right now, there's a repeating message from the castle's command post, for any surviving forces to meet at Wrigley." He was quiet for a second and then said, "I don't think there's anybody left over there."

Somewhere in the distant haze ahead of us, a Jotun's horn blared out, a long and mournful wail, a sound that somehow encapsulated bleakness and rage, despair, the end of all things.

And, somewhere in the distance behind us, another horn answered.

I could feel uneasiness ripple through my friends, and through the crowd behind me. Not even the monsters of Winter could hear those horns without feeling a sense of slow, inevitable dread.

I didn't feel it, of course. I was a mighty wizard of the White Council, monarch of mental mastery, pharaoh of fickle fear.

I didn't pucker up at all.

So. The enemy was playing head games, too.

"Bozhe moi," Sanya murmured. "Are there enough of us?"

"Enough to do our country loss," I said. "Steady."

And we kept moving forward as the city once more turned the color of blood beneath the glare of the Eye.

Chapter

Eighteen

I don't know if you've ever seen the Bean. Probably you have, on a TV show or in a movie. It's this big silvery sculpture that's supposed to look like—I don't know—an air bubble underwater or something. It has an arch in the middle that you can pass under, and it was originally named the *Cloud Gate*, because from far overhead you can look down and see it reflecting the sky and the clouds.

But if you don't have that very privileged viewpoint, if you look at it from the perspective of everyday people, it looks like a big old bean lying on its side. So Chicagoans called it the Bean, much to the artist's apparent disgust. It casts a distorted reflection of the city skyline on one side, and of the concrete and trees of the park on the other.

Tonight, on one side of the Bean was a hazy reflection of a city on fire.

And the other side showed the backs of maybe a couple of hundred of Mab's soldiers, who were facing east, toward the lake, standing in their armored ranks, and waiting.

Before we rode into the hazy park, we heard a couple of sharp, high-pitched, twittering whistles. The Sidhe could communicate like that if they wished, in whistles and birdsong. They had a complex musical language, too, and for some reason the Winter Sidhe absolutely loved human music. No idea why, but it was a genuine thing with them. I'd rarely seen a gathering of Winter that didn't include mortal music, and mortal musicians where possible, though I had come away with the impression that one really, *really* didn't want to be chosen to perform for the Sidhe. Bad things tended to happen.

You know all those brilliant musicians who wound up dead way sooner than they should have? Call it maybe a fifty-fifty chance that the Sidhe were involved along the line. It was part of how my godmother had made her bones with Mab.

Mab stood behind them, in her battle mail, her pale hair glowing with starlight, mounted upon a freaking unicorn.

Don't get the wrong idea. The unicorns who serve Winter aren't like the ones you've maybe seen in books or movies or cartoons. These things aren't silver and white and pretty. They look like a unicorn as designed by H. R. Giger. They have exoskeletons in creepy variants of black that sort of nodded at other colors in the shining highlights. And they have no eyes. I'd seen exactly one of them, once before, and even that one had been only a glamour around a different creature.

This thing . . .

Power radiated from it. It was the size of a Budweiser horse, plus an extra few hundred pounds of armored chitin that looked black but shone deep purple wherever light reflected from it. Its smooth head and the blank spots where eye sockets should have been were eerie, and when it champed its jaws, it showed hard, serrated ridges of bone in a jaw that could open wider than it ought. Its ears swiveled about alertly, moving too smoothly, like exceedingly precise automation, and a flicker of insight made me realize why the Winter Sidhe respected their unicorns: They had no eyes to be deceived by glamour or beauty. It didn't have a horn. It had *horns*. Curling ram's horns as big across as a stop sign armored to either side of its skull, and the horn that arched from its forehead was more a spiked saber than a spiraling lance.

Mab's steed pounded a foot down against the concrete impatiently, and the energy that rippled out from that impact lifted a visible, expanding ring of dust from the ground and stirred the haze in the air. Mab laid a hand upon its neck, a soothing motion, and the unicorn stilled—but it didn't take a wizard to detect the rage and hatred seething off of the creature.

It wanted to fight. It wanted to kill.

I knew how it felt.

Ah, that was it, then. The horn. What had that Tim Curry character called it, an antenna pointing to heaven? Maybe he'd been half-right. After I focused my attention on the power surrounding the creature, I could feel Mab's subtle influence, the spirit of Winter in the air, pouring off the unicorn's horn, the energy buzzing like high-tension lines carrying current. The being was serving as a living focus for Mab's power, the way I'd use a staff or blasting rod—or the knife at my hip, the one I had carefully not touched, barely even with my thoughts, since coming ashore.

That artifact, taken from Hades' vault, continued to vibrate with a power all its own that remained unabated and uninfluenced by the terrible forces in the air around the city.

I kept on not touching it—and, after a moment of mental effort, not even thinking about it.

I touched a hand to Murphy's shoulder, and she brought the bike rumbling to a halt. I swung off and crossed fifty or sixty feet of concrete. A block of the Sidhe, each warrior armored in that faemetal they preferred to steel, shining in variegated shades of glacial green, winter blue, and deep, dark purples, whirled to face me as a single being, their boots stomping hard on the concrete as shields were raised and weapons came up.

I didn't so much as break stride. Lions do not lower their heads for jackals. Even jackals know they can kill what fears them.

The Winter Sidhe respected those who understood the law of the jungle, and I had demonstrated to them from the first that I wasn't putting up with any of their crap. They would test me—predators *always* test potential prey for weakness—but as long as I made them think it would be more trouble than amusement to push me, they would press no further.

The warrior Sidhe, male and female alike, each deadly skilled and experienced in the art and practice of war, yielded before me, melting as smoothly from my path as if they had never been there.

For today.

They would look for weakness again tomorrow. Assuming any of us survived to see it.

As I approached, I saw Mab staring hard at me, and then past me, at the uncertain form of the people who had followed my banner. Her eyes narrowed and then bored into mine, even as I walked the last few yards to her. For some reason, I felt . . . utterly naked, as if my clothing had vanished and a cold chill had swirled into damned uncomfortable places.

Then her expression changed. For a flickering portion of an instant, I thought I saw . . . something, in her eyes, some vague shadow of pain. Of . . . sympathy?

Then Mab was Mab again.

"My Knight," she murmured. "Half a dozen cohorts have come to your banner."

Eleven hundred and eighty-seven, I thought. I blinked. Because that's how many people had chosen to follow me. I didn't know how I knew that. It just . . . flew into my head. This had to be another instance of *intellectus*, a form of intelligence that bypassed standard human processes of rationality, just as I experienced on the island.

But this was different.

It was *people*.

Mab tilted her head to one side. "You did not embrace the cold."

"No," I said. My voice felt rough.

Her chin lifted, and her hard, cold eyes flickered in naked, unconcealed pride. "Never once in your life, my Knight, have you taken the easy road. I chose well."

"They're lightly armed. They need heavier weapons."

Mab's tone gained an icy edge. "They are not following *my* banner, O Knight."

I lowered my voice to a bare growl. "Then I'll send

them home," I said. "If you want me to fight for you, *quit making it more difficult to fight for you.* You and Marcone have been thick as thieves lately. I know you both. There are more weapons around here somewhere. I need them."

Slowly, slowly . . . the unicorn *noticed* me. Its head swiveled as smoothly as a gun turret, bringing that horn to point at me, and the power in the air around me made me feel like my hair should have been standing straight up. There were bits of bone still stuck in its serrated blade. Its breath smelled like rotten meat.

My scrotum attempted to travel back in time.

Mab suddenly threw back her head and let out a . . . sound. Imagine a witch's cackle, rolling up from her belly. Now imagine that at almost the exact instant said witch began it, she snapped a moldy scarf tight around her own throat. Then imagine the choked exhalation of what air remained above the point of strangulation.

Whatever the hell that sound was, it was *not* a laugh.

And it made the damned unicorn take a nervous side-step.

"Yes," Mab said, a wild fey light around her eyes, her head swaying as her mount shifted its weight nervously. "Oh yes. You'll do, child. Tell me, who takes out contracts in terms of a thousand years, these days?"

"Oh God," I said. I stared at her. Then at the Bean. "You're kidding."

Because that was the contract the artist of the Bean had with the city of Chicago. That the thing would stand for one thousand years. And when it had been finished, it had been encased in polished steel and enclosed, more or less permanently.

It was for all practical purposes a time capsule, out in plain sight, in front of God and everybody.

I stalked over to the *Cloud Gate*. I poked at polished panels of steel with my staff until one of them rang a little hollower than the others. I gave that one a series of solid thumps, and it popped off and clattered to the concrete. The red glare of the night was too dim to show me anything until I drew out my mother's pentacle amulet, sent a whisper of will into it, and set it aglow with azure wizard light.

The inside of the Bean isn't made of metal. It's all a wooden framework and looks more like the hold of an old pirate ship. The interior of the Bean was piled high with mil-spec weapons cases and boxes and boxes of ammunition, secure on a sturdy internal framework. Just right in the middle of Millennium Park.

"You've got a hell of a lot of nerve, Mab," I murmured.

And her voice whispered in my ear, as if she'd been standing flush against me, "Thank you, my Knight. It is a fine compliment."

I jumped and hit my head on the low opening and backed up enough to glower at her.

Mab turned her eyes away from me and said, "Do battle as you will, my Knight. Take command of your mortals and what few servants of Winter were near enough to join us." Her gaze returned to the northeast, where the red pulse of the Eye flashed again. "Make the Fomor bleed. You will know the time to come to me."

It was a clear dismissal, and Mab's tone made it obvious that she was done with my shenanigans.

But I'm not so much the kind who gets easily dismissed.

Not even by the Queen of Air and Darkness.

I went to her side, where I noticed that even the unicorn's *hooves* were set up like cruel, spiked maces, and said, "This . . . banner."

"Few Knights have had the strength to manifest it."

"You never spoke to me about it."

"Would you have listened?"

Well. Touché, I guess.

"I can feel them," I said. "The people following me."

Mab closed her eyes. Then she said, "Yes. Such is the rule of Winter."

"And when they die. I'll feel that, too."

"Obviously," Mab said, in a near whisper. "For all power there is a price."

I shuddered. My soul had already taken a beating in the past few days. I don't know that I needed to add on the psychic experience of living through hundreds of deaths to my list of mental scars.

I gritted my teeth. I could take a little more if I had to. And I had to. A lot more people were going to die if we didn't stop the enemy here.

I glanced aside at Mab and frowned.

Did she feel it, too? Her command of her subjects? Of . . . me?

Did she feel it when they died? Did she carry their pain, their rage, their terror, upon the back of her own soul, or whatever it was that passed for one now? Did she even have a soul anymore?

I was mortal once. . . .

I'd been waiting for Mab to lay into me with the magically enhanced temptation, the usual trappings and blandishments of corruption. I'd been expecting her, every time we met, to start putting me through Sith boot camp. *The Kurgan's Guide to Conflict Resolution.* Evil 101.

The whole time, I'd been wondering, *What happens when she does?*

The far more terrifying question had never once occurred to me: *What happens when she doesn't?*

Maybe the process of becoming something horrible wasn't about temptation to sin, forbidden delights, and bad impulse control.

Maybe it was about choosing to throw your soul into a meat grinder, over and over again. Until what remained couldn't even be seen as a soul any longer. Maybe the real monsters, the big bad monsters, aren't created.

They're forged. Hammered. One blow at a time.

I was mortal once. . . .

Mab opened her eyes again at last. The look she gave me was, for a second, very human: one weary, determined soldier staring at another. I had, in her eyes, passed some kind of test, some rite, that had changed my status.

And it terrified me.

The real battle for your own soul isn't about falling from a great height; it's about descending, or not, one choice at a time.

And sometimes, it's about choosing to pay a price so

someone else doesn't have to. I had rarely hesitated to hazard my body in the defense of those who needed it.

I looked back at the city behind us.

If more is required of me, so be it.

I offered my hand to Mab, plain soldier.

She took it.

Chapter
Nineteen

I put Sanya and Murphy on getting the arms out to our volunteers. Marcone had planned as if he'd intended a city block party's worth of amateurs to be kitted out with the one weapon that could do the most damage in their hands: shotguns. A hell of a lot of shotguns. And, given the haze over the city, it wasn't like anyone could see clearly more than thirty or forty yards anyway.

Not everybody took a shotgun. Dozens had heavier weapons of their own. But by the time we were done, everyone had a firearm of some type, and everyone had pockets full of shells.

I called Toot-Toot in and sent him with a message for Etri. Within five minutes of sending the little guy off, a squad of svartalf combat engineers had arrived, and I'd given them their instructions. They immediately turned to the open earth inside the pavilion and began shaping it into defensible earthworks beneath the enormous, arching trellis that supported the pavilion's sound system. People stared at that in awe. It's not often you see several hundred thousand tons of earth moving itself around thanks to the hand gestures of a crew of little grey guys.

"Defiladey enough for you?" I asked Sanya.

"*Da,*" the Russian replied. "Did not know this park was built on Styrofoam at bottom."

"Yeah, the whole place is technically kind of a rooftop garden," I said. "Can you hold?"

"Maybe, but then they go around us," Sanya said. "We leave one-third here. The rest, we go out and find them. Draw them back here if we have to fall back. They run across all this open space? Pow, pow, video-game easy."

"*If* you have to fall back, huh," I said.

The big man grinned. "*Da,* am Russian. We are a very positive people," Sanya said.

"No, you aren't!" came Butters's protest from somewhere off in the haze.

Sanya beamed. "I really like little Jedi man," he confided. "Here, look." He leaned down to scrape at loose earth with the tip of his knife. "Mab here. Us here. Enemy coming from there, there, there." He made marks to the north, east, and south. "See? Our people will hold against north threat from earthworks. Others go out, see if we can hit the east threat from flank once they engage Mab." He nodded toward the mark in the south. "That one, up to the Archive and Etri's people."

I nodded. "You'll just be wandering around blind out there."

"*Da,* but so are they. So it is fair."

"What kind of idiot wants to fight fair?" I complained.

"This is terrible fight," Sanya said. "But is only one we have. 'Fair' is many steps up ladder from where we are now."

"Good point," I said with a grimace. I frowned and checked. My contingent of wicked fae, who were lurking around out of sight of the mortals, had approximately tripled in size, mainly with malks. I knew there was a big colony of them in town, and now I had a good threescore of the vicious little killers slinking around in the haze and waiting for a chance to spill more blood. None of them were near the mortals who had followed me, which was what I had mostly worried about.

Hey, I thought, as loud as I could, in the direction of Winter. *The mortals of Chicago are off-limits. Cross me on this and I'll kill every last one of you.*

What came back to me from the creatures of Winter was a sensation of . . . Well, it wasn't compliance. It was deeper than that. My will *became* their will. I felt the adjustment of their very beings, their rising fury at the suffering inflicted upon . . . The closest thing I can come up with, to explain it, was that they felt the same rage a farmer does when something is after his livestock.

Maybe that's as close to being protective as Winter gets. But it was hard and cold and real.

The Winter Knight doesn't so much lead Winter's troops as command them as he would any other weapon in his grasp.

I sent the malks out in a circular screen around us. I wanted to know when the enemy got close, and the little killers were as silent and swift as any wraith.

Murphy was demonstrating to a group of volunteers how to load a shotgun. It's not real complicated. When it comes to firearms, shotguns are about as basic as it gets. She finished showing a number of drawn, determined faces how to handle the weapon.

"For what we're doing," she said to the volunteers, "you've got about the best weapon you can reasonably get. It'll shoot farther than you can see, and it will be hard to miss. Tuck it in tight to your shoulder and aim down the barrel. You have four rules. Never point your weapon at anything you don't want dead. Know your target so you don't shoot your neighbor. Know what's behind your target so you don't shoot your neighbor by accident. And for God's sake, keep your finger off the damned trigger until you've followed rules one through three." She held up her right forefinger. "You put this on the trigger, assume you are a deadly weapon and a threat to anything you're facing, period. Clear?"

There was a round of murmured affirmatives.

I walked up behind her and said, "I need your advice."

Murphy passed a shotgun to a nervous volunteer, a young man who said, "That's all we get?"

"Plenty of soldiers have gotten less," I said to him. "You want to run, head west. The enemy is coming in from all around us everywhere else."

The kid swallowed, nodded, and carefully kept his finger off the trigger.

Murphy clapped him on the shoulder, and then we turned to walk a little distance away.

"What do I do?" I asked her quietly. "How do I arrange this so that I don't get all these people killed?"

"Trust Sanya," she said frankly. "He's had some military experience. Neither of us does. That's the best we've got."

I looked over to where the Russian was talking to some guys in uniforms, laughing, his deep voice, the laughter itself, clear and somehow silvery. The air around him seemed less hazy than elsewhere, and I could read the faces of the people around him well enough to see that the Knight of the Sword's presence was combating the supernatural fear and frenzy in the air around them. They . . . just looked more like people, when they stood near Sanya.

"Right," I said.

I walked forward to stand next to Sanya, cleared my throat, and spoke out in what I hoped was a clear, firm voice. "All right, people. Gather in."

They did. I was tall enough for everyone to see. Hadn't ever really occurred to me why everyone thought military leaders should be tall. It simply offered a small practical advantage, for much of humanity's history.

They could see my face, my eyes. They could see me.

"This city has gone to hell in a handbasket," I declared. "And then a bunch of monsters showed up."

There was a rumble of nervous laughter. Chicagoans love their city, but they also have few illusions about how screwed up it can be. They live here.

"I know you're scared," I said. "I know you've all . . . seen things that nobody should have to see." I pushed the image of that damned crib out of my head. "I know you don't know who I am, and this is all weird. So, let me introduce myself. My name is Harry Dresden. I'm a wizard of the White Council. And I mean to fight to the death to defend this town."

"What?" came an incredulous voice from the crowd. "You think you're a what?"

I turned to that voice, identified the speaker through my link to the banner, and strode directly toward him.

People got out of my way. He was a skinny guy, late thirties, holding a hunting rifle. He drew back half a pace, apprehensively, as I approached.

"What's your name, man?" I asked.

"Uh . . . it's Randy."

"Okay, Randy. I'm only going to do this once."

I dropped my staff on the ground, held up my hands in front of me, palms facing each other, drew in a whisper of will, and murmured, *"Eggus Chennus."*

Green-gold lightning, not a ton of it, exploded from my palms, forming a current of energy that snapped and crackled in the sultry summer air, contained within the space between my hands.

I had thought through the spell before, but I'd never really tried it. It worked pretty well—except that rather than just going away, the power was cycling up one arm, around my shoulders, down the other arm, and then out between my hands again. It was a cycle that fed upon itself, and between that and the power-laden air of the terrified city, the energy built a whole hell of a lot faster than I would have liked. It had to go somewhere.

I picked a tree and unleashed a stroke of green lightning that smashed into the trunk about five feet up and brought the tree crashing down. It started burning with green flame, *green flame*—all hell was breaking loose. I could only attribute that to the breakdown in reality that Bob had warned me about.

My volunteers had fallen silent.

Randy looked like he'd swallowed multiple bugs.

"Wizard," I reiterated. "Any questions?"

"Are you on our side?" Randy asked.

"If you're here to defend the innocent, damned skippy I'm on your side," I said. I grabbed his shoulder and squeezed a little. Then I turned to look at everyone else.

"The monsters are coming," I said. "And they'll kill everyone in this town if they can. Unless we kill them first."

The crowd let out a sound that was a lot like a hungry growl.

I found myself smiling, more and more widely. Yeah, the world was full of monsters and demons. But it was a human world. It was our world because we were the cleverest, most resourceful, and most dangerous things in it. Maybe my little army wasn't the most martial representation of humanity, but people fighting for their homes had, historically, done incredible things.

Time for history to repeat itself.

"Sanya, raise your hand."

He did.

"This is Sanya. He's a Knight. He fights monsters for a living and he knows what he's talking about. Sanya is your commander. Sanya . . . hey, where the *hell* did you get a freaking Kalashnikov?"

Sanya shouldered his rifle by its strap, grinning. "Found it."

I waved a hand at him. "Whatever. Take charge, man."

"*Da*," Sanya said, and raised his voice to a bellow. "Hello. First of all, *da*, I am Russian. Cope. Second, you see these men and women in uniforms? Easy to recognize even in haze, *da*? They are your officers. I will make groups of about thirty. Each group get one officer. Officer tell you what to do, you do it."

Sanya turned to the uniformed men and women. "You

guys get to give one of three orders. Stand, retreat, and follow me. Keep it simple. Communications in battle are hard, even for professionals."

There was a round of nods. The military folks looked grim. They knew what a clusterfuck they were about to march into. And I knew about how hard it is to convey even simple ideas in a fight. We'd be lucky if the volunteers could follow even those limited orders reliably.

Sanya turned back to the crowd. "Everywhere we go tonight, assume that you have orders to kill the enemy on sight. If standing, and enemy comes, kill enemy. If retreating, kill enemy. If following officer and enemy comes, kill enemy." Sanya considered. "Basically tonight we are always killing enemy."

Another laugh at that. But he was playing to an easy room. People who are scared need to laugh, and the scarier things are, the more they need it.

"Okay!" Sanya called. "Officers will divide you into groups! Everyone keep quiet so you can hear them!"

Sanya and his officers started getting them sorted out.

I shivered a little and stepped over to one side, where I could close my eyes for a second and try to process everything that was happening.

I felt Murphy come up behind me and then lean against me. I leaned back.

"This is going to be ugly, isn't it," I said quietly.

"Yes," Murphy said simply. "Just remember whose fault it is."

There was a horrible shrieking sound, and the haze flared red. This time, I could hear the building falling again.

Ethniu was walking straight down Lake Shore, knocking down buildings like a kid kicking over anthills. She was coming for Mab.

Who was in essence using herself as bait to keep the Titan from noticing me.

I found Murphy's hand and squeezed gently. "What's going to happen after this, do you think?"

"I don't," she said. "Because I'm doing today first."

I snorted quietly.

Murphy squeezed back. "Harry. You can't fix tomorrow until it gets here."

"Which is weird, because you can screw it up from decades away."

I heard her laugh gently. "I got used to weird. It's not so bad."

"Flattery is unworthy of you," I said.

"It's definitely unworthy of one of us."

I opened my mouth to fire back like Sir Benedict would have wanted me to, but instead I had to deal with a sudden harsh, twisting feline voice radiating through my skull

Sir Knight, mewled the unsettling voice of a malk, *this is Grimalkin.*

Right. Grimalkin was Mab's . . . personal aide, in some ways. He was an Elder of the malks, which meant he was bigger and stronger and meaner than most, and had access to a number of powers, foremost of which was the ability to creep me out with his damned weird voice.

The enemy comes from the north, Sir Knight. I am also advised, by this irritating pixie, to inform you that there is a still-occupied child-care center in its path with a number of young mortals inside.

I clenched my jaw so hard that I chipped a tooth.

I looked around. Sanya was ordering the volunteers, but it would take time for him to get it done. If I shouted, "Follow me!" and started moving, I'd probably just walk them into a meat grinder. Sanya needed more time to get the volunteers organized.

"Harry?" Murph asked.

"Get the bike," I said.

She swung around and did. "Butters, Alphas, on me," I barked. "Sanya, incoming from the north. Get them organized first, then bring them after me. I'll try to slow the Fomor down."

"*Da*, go!" Sanya shouted. He turned and started bawling at the troops in a voice that could have been heard a quarter mile away.

Murphy rumbled up on her bike, and I swung a leg over. Will and Georgia loped out of the darkness and took up position on one side of the bike, and Andi and Marci took the other. Butters came trotting over. You'd never have guessed the little guy had been galloping all over the damned town all evening, from the spring in his step. I had to give it to him—Butters was never going to be a powerhouse, but the little guy didn't have an atom of quit anywhere in him.

From the north, maybe two or three blocks away, I heard the scream of Huntsmen's spear blasts, and a sudden sonic razor blade of ripping, tearing sound that was the simultaneous war cry of a dozen malks going into battle.

And then, flattening *that* sound was the bone-shaking blare of a Jotun's horn, the same one from before.

And my stomach fell out. Because shotguns were not

going to help against something *that* big, no matter how many of them we had. They'd only make it mad.

Hear me, Winter, I thought. *Converge on that engagement. Kill anything that tries to harm those children.*

The air was suddenly split with the screams and battle cries of ogres and gnomes, malks and Black Dogs, the wild ululations of a couple of Wyld Sidhe, the strangled moan of a freaking Rawhead, and the chittering screech of some of those damned big spiders that had been such a pain in my ass on several occasions, as they all leapt forward at their fastest pace to find and destroy the enemy.

Murphy gave me a wide-eyed look, glanced down and back, and then set her jaw.

"Go!" I shouted.

The Harley roared.

And with monsters as our vanguard, off we went to be Jotunslayers.

Chapter

Twenty

We heard the sound of gunfire ahead, a lone pistol firing measured shots. Its defiance sounded thin indeed against the shrieks of the Huntsmen's spear blasts.

"Cut the engine," I said.

Murphy goosed a little more power out of the throttle and then cut the Harley's engine. The heavy bike rolled forward almost silently on momentum and we had time to see what was happening.

A single man defended the doorway of a staircase that led up to the second level. A sign posted beside him read THIRD WATCH CHILD CARE. He wasn't terribly tall, was almost unbelievably stout, and with a shock I recognized Detective Bradley from Internal Affairs.

A howling blast from a spear blew an inch of stonework off the doorway next to Bradley, and though chips of stone cut into his scalp, he didn't flinch as he sighted down the barrel of his service pistol and squeezed off a shot.

One of the Huntsmen's heads jerked back and the creature fell to join three others on the ground—and those remaining screamed and swelled in size.

The slide of the pistol locked back, as the Huntsmen charged the doorway. Bradley calmly discarded the weapon, reached for his ankle, drew his backup, and put three rounds from a little revolver into the lead Huntsman's chest as it charged.

The thing staggered and thrust its spear at Bradley. The blocky man slapped the weapon aside with one hand, seized the haft in one thick fist, jammed the pistol up under the Huntsman's jaw, and emptied the little revolver, sending the thing crashing and thrashing to the ground.

Bradley, half his face masked in blood, dropped the empty revolver, took up the spear in a grip that showed he knew something about using one, faced the remaining Huntsmen, and screamed, "Come on!"

They roared back, the cries like a pack of beasts, none of them the same species.

Five dead Huntsmen. Bradley had picked a good position to fight from, surrounded in stone, slight elevation from the street, good cover. But he was out of ammo now, bleeding, and the remaining Huntsmen would only be that much stronger and more difficult to hurt.

And still he planted his feet. "Come on, you ugly bastards!"

"That son of a bitch beat me in every tournament I ever fought him," Murphy said. "Harry."

Winter, I thought. *Take the Huntsmen.*

The ogres went in first, simply leaping from adjacent rooftops, huge white-furred things like River Shoulders, if he'd been a smoker since childhood, after a heroin bender. Though lean and seedy-looking, they were still enormous, viciously strong, and unremittingly savage. One of them landed on a Huntsman with a three-story atomic elbow and crushed it with a great crackling of breaking bones. The other landed on a planted spear that went in its chest and burst through its back in a welter of gore and silver flame. The ogre shrieked like a demon as the Huntsman arced the spear to one side and brought the dying Winter fae crashing down to the street.

Malks yowled like a herd of chain saws and came bounding in from all angles. The Huntsmen's spears howled and sent some of the murderous beasts to whatever hell waited for them, but there were simply not enough of them to target the streaking forms of the malks. They overbore two of the Huntsmen and buried them in a mound of thick fur and frenzied claws sharper than X-Acto knives. The Huntsmen died screaming.

Beside them, the troop of gnomes had emerged from an alley and flung a dozen hatchets at another Huntsman, even as it swelled in size and power. The wickedly sharp weapons hit with savage effect, setting the Huntsman staggering, and Black Dogs flashed past, fangs raking, and tore through its hamstrings. Once it was at ground level, the gnomes, chestnut-skinned, white-haired little guys maybe two and a half or three feet high, had no problem reaching its vitals.

One of the remaining Huntsmen turned to flee—only to confront the Rawhead coming out of the alley. The fae beast, made of the bones of slaughtered animals and foes, was an enormous form under a great black cloak. The cloak flared out, and the bulky body of the Rawhead, made of hundreds of sharpened bones, began to contort and shriek in a sound uncomfortably like that of a meat grinder.

The Rawhead seized the Huntsman and dragged it beneath its cloak. Its bones rent and tore, where I couldn't see it, and the Huntsman screamed in fury. And then there was a lot of blood and sausage tumbling out from beneath the Rawhead's cloak and piling up on the Huntsman's feet and lower legs.

The last Huntsman roared, rearing up in size—and the second-largest malk I'd ever seen, the size of a mountain lion but far bulkier, flew like an arrow for the creature's face. Grimalkin's forepaws spread out to snowshoe proportions and sprouted two-inch claws that latched into the Huntsman's face. The Elder malk sank its jaws into one of the Huntsman's eyes, gripping on like a vise to the orbital bone beneath—and thus braced, the supernaturally powerful, swift cat began to rake with its rear claws.

In less than a second, the last Huntsman's throat looked like twenty or thirty pounds of pulled pork soaked in ketchup.

The Elder malk flung himself aside as the Huntsman, not even yet fully grown into the size of the ones we'd had to kill, dropped limply to the ground, gushing blood like a broken water main. Grimalkin landed not ten feet in front of the Harley, flicked each set of claws once, fastidiously, and said, in that utterly unnerving feline voice, "Sir Knight. Elder Grimalkin, reporting for duty."

"Jesus Mary Mother of God," Murphy breathed.

Grimalkin flattened his ears and gave Murphy a glower, then turned to me and said, "There are multiple warbands on the adjoining streets. My kin keep them occupied, for now. We are badly outnumbered, Sir Knight. Retreat would be ideal, before—"

The Jotun's horn blared. In the haze and among the buildings, it was impossible to tell where it was, other than . . .

"Close," Murphy breathed.

"Before *that*," Grimalkin said sourly.

"Well done, Elder," I said. "But we're getting those kids out."

The malk growled. "We cannot contest a Jotun, Sir Knight."

"Pussy," Murphy said.

I blinked at her.

She smirked. "Too good, couldn't resist."

Grimalkin's fur bristled and his weight shifted slightly.

Without breaking her smirk, Murphy swept her pistol out and covered the malk as quick as blinking. "Steel-jacketed rounds tonight, friend," she advised. "Play nice."

Grimalkin growled at Murphy, eyed me, then relaxed as if nothing had happened. He flexed the claws out of his right forepaw and regarded them idly, ignoring Murphy completely.

She put the gun away and returned the favor. But she never quite let the malk out of her sight.

They'd get on fine.

I swung off the bike. Murphy followed. I beckoned Butters and the Alphas. "We're getting those kids out first," I said, walking. "Grimalkin, you and Winter keep a corridor open for us, back to the defenses."

"We cannot hold it long," Grimalkin warned me.

"Do it," I said over my shoulder. "Go."

The Elder malk made a throaty, ugly sound and vanished before it could even complete turning away.

I came up on the entry to the day-care center stairwell to find Bradley gripping his spear and standing braced in the doorway, his eyes very, very wide. The spear was already degrading and flaking away. It'd be gone in a few more minutes.

"Hey, Detective Bradley. It's, uh, me. Harry Dresden. Remember?"

The blocky man stared at me. Then he jerked his head in a nod.

"Murph," I said.

She stepped past me, her hands out. "Hey, hey. Brian. You with me, buddy?"

Bradley stared at her for a second and then lowered the spear a little. "We aren't buddies, Sergeant. You kind of hate my guts."

Murphy looked from the liquefying forms of the slain Huntsmen to Bradley. "That was then. This is now."

He blinked. "What the hell are you talking about?" He twitched as the wolves and Butters brought up the rear. "What the hell is happening?"

"Hi," Butters said, and waved.

"Hi?" said Bradley. He blinked. "Doctor Butters?"

"You know all that stuff I told you in closed session that you thought was bullshit?" Murphy asked.

"And all that stuff I told you in closed session that you thought was bullshit?" Butters added brightly.

The blocky detective looked from the dead Huntsmen and the fallen fae back to Murphy and Butters. "Jesus Christ."

Bradley handled it pretty well. He got a little whiter around the eyes for a couple of seconds, and then he closed them firmly, set his jaw, and adjusted, visibly.

"Fuck it, I'll lose my mind later," he said, and when he opened his eyes again, he had his cop face on. "I got six kids, a nice old lady, and a Rudolph up there. How do we get them out?"

"Back to Millennium Park," I said. "We're keeping a corridor open. Send them west from there."

Shrieks and yowls burst out around us, as Winter launched an attack upon enemy forces. Huntsmen howled, and their spears wailed. In the background, but closer, came the thunder of the Eye claiming another building.

"Get the kids out now," Murphy said.

Bradley tensed his jaw, nodded, dropped the spear, and pounded up the stairway. He paused by the door, flattened himself against a wall, and called, "It's Bradley," before he opened it with one hand, staying well clear.

"Bradley?" came Rudolph's voice. It was panicky.

Rudolph had run into monsters a couple of times. Granted, both of those times had been bad. But he'd been like a lot of people who run into the supernatural—he just couldn't handle it. Maybe that was a personal shortcoming. Or maybe he'd just been born without the capacity to face that kind of terrifying reality. Either way, it made it harder to like him, especially at times like this.

"It's me," he said.

"Dammit, Bradley!" Rudolph screamed.

"It's me . . . sir . . ." Bradley said, his voice heavy with patience.

"Get in here! Get under cover!"

"We've got to get out of here while we can," Bradley said. "Get the kids—we've got to go."

"Are you crazy?" Rudolph demanded. "It's a war zone out there!"

I leaned in and shouted up the stairwell, "It's going to be a war zone right in there with you if you don't get moving, Rudolph!"

"Dresden!?"

"Yes, it's me, moron," I said, in my grumpiest wizard voice. "And we're not going to be able to get out for much longer, you knucklehead, so move it!"

"This is your doing!" Rudolph squealed. "More of your lies!"

Bradley got a peculiar expression on his face. I wasn't sure what it was, exactly, though you could probably have captioned the photo *How Could I Have Been So Blind?*

He held up a finger to me. Then he walked in through the door.

There was a thump, and a clatter.

Bradley emerged from the day care with Rudolph draped limply over one shoulder, and the man's pistol in his own shoulder holster. He was carrying a small child, maybe two years old, in the other arm.

Behind him came a woman with steely hair and a grandmother's clothing. She held an infant in the cradle of one arm and the hand of a small string of larger children who followed her, all holding hands.

Bradley led them down the stairs and onto the street. Butters immediately went to take the infant from the older woman, who surrendered the child with a grateful grimace and a twitch of her shoulder.

The wolves immediately took position around the children, without me telling them to. They wagged their tails and took little happy steps and generally performed the canine equivalent of pinching their cheeks and making a fuss over them. The kids were instantly enchanted by the group of doggies.

Who also did their best to keep their furry bodies between the children's eyes and the worst of the horrors around us.

They felt like I did. That no one should have to look at that kind of thing. And that those of us who already had? We were glad when we could spare someone else the same invisible wounds.

I fell in beside Bradley, who carried his own weight and that of two other souls without visible effort. "The wolves are great kids. They'll go with you, get you and the kids out. Two blocks south, to the park. There're volunteers holding out at the pavilion. Tell them that the wizard sent you to see Sanya. He's a big black Russian guy. Tell him I want him to give you an escort out."

"South, pavilion, Sanya, wizard sent me, get the kids out," Bradley confirmed. He eyed the wolves. "Friendlies?"

"Yeah," I said.

He heaved a breath. Then set his jaw, nodded, and said, "Got it."

"Good man," I said. "You're handling this well."

"I am *not*," Bradley said without slowing his steps. "I am *not*."

"Then you are freaking out in the most useful way possible," I said. "Keep it up."

Bradley stared at me for a second. Then he let out a bark of crack-voiced laughter. But it was a real laugh. He hoisted Rudolph into a slightly more comfortable position on one wide, thick shoulder—Rudolph let out a groan of protest neither of us listened to—and kept walking.

"Butters," I said, slowing my steps for a moment to drop even with the little Knight.

"It's kids, Harry," he said. He showed me the hilt of *Fidelacchius*, carried in the hand that wasn't holding a baby. "I'll take care of them."

I squeezed his shoulder.

And the ground shook.

We traded a wide-eyed look, and I said, "Get them out, go!"

"Harry!" Murphy shouted from behind me.

The ground shook again.

Bradley staggered and fell. He curled his body around the child to shield her, which meant that I'm afraid Rudolph took the brunt of it. The poor man. The gun hadn't been strapped into Bradley's holster and it clattered onto the street.

I whirled, feet spread wide for balance, as a pair of comets shot out of a side street half a block up, whirling in an evasive helix in the haze, as the damned Jotun from before, bruised and bloodied and furious, swiped its axe at them.

"My lord!" trumpeted Toot-Toot. "I have engaged the enemy!"

The axe nearly split my major general in twain, but the second glowing globe hit him at the last second, as Lacuna slammed a shoulder into his, causing them both to veer out of the weapon's way.

"Pay attention, fool!" she screamed.

The Jotun saw us and dropped into a low slide, legs spread wide like a surfer, slamming its axe into the street and dragging it behind like some berserk plow, rending the street with an enormous roar of breaking concrete and blacktop as it used the weapon to slow its enormous momentum.

So that it could turn toward *us*.

The ground shook under the violence of the Jotun's very presence.

I rubbernecked and saw Bradley struggling to rise. Butters was hurrying the nice old lady and the children along, but their best pace wasn't a fast walk, and they were all in plain sight of the Jotun, utterly vulnerable.

Right. That made my choice simple.

Suicidal, but simple.

I turned to fight.

Murphy sprinted past me and behind me as the Jotun roared and raised its axe from the street. As if in tandem with its rising fury, the axe burst into flame. The Jotun roared, flexed muscles the size of European automobiles, moved with the technique perfect to use the full force of its unthinkably powerful body—and flung the axe, spinning parallel to the ground like the blade of a lawn mower.

What must have been at least half a ton of hard, sharp, burning metal came whirling toward my freaking face.

Chapter

Twenty-one

It is often surprising to people to discover exactly how strong a human being can be if he knows what he's doing.

The Jotun knew what he was doing. Given the raw power behind that throw, there was no way I was going to stop it. I could put every inch of power I had into a shield and be unable to stop that axe's edge.

But I might be able to deflect it.

I summoned my will and rammed it into the shield bracelet on my left wrist. It hissed and popped with stray sparks of green-gold power as the energy of my magic met the inefficiencies in the material and spells carved into the copper bracelet, and the thing heated up almost immediately, as I brought a shimmering plane into being in front of me—and then I dropped to a knee and tilted the shield back, way back, into a slope of maybe twenty degrees.

The giant axe hit my shield in an explosion of kinetic and magical energy. Literally. There was an explosion centered where the shield and the axe met, and I realized with a belated shock that the Jotun had imbued considerable power of its own into the axe.

The world went white and silent.

I was flung a good fifteen feet back across the ground and wound up slamming into Bradley, who was only then getting moving again. Rudolph, tragically, got roughed up again as a result, oh no. I lay there for a second, stunned, and watched glass from hundreds of shattered windows fall with almost dreamy slowness toward the ground. My bracelet burned hot enough to scald skin, and the Winter mantle sent me pulses of weird tingly sensations to let me know what was going on.

I shook my head and looked around blearily. The axe had hit my shield at an odd angle and skittered off to my left and up. It was buried to the eye in what looked like an office building, as if an enormous lumberjack had sunk it in so that he could spit on his hands and get to work.

Oh right. The Jotun.

I drove my staff into the ground and shoved myself to my feet, shaking my head in an attempt to get the damned bells to stop ringing.

The ground shook as I did.

I looked up to find the Jotun standing maybe twenty yards away, scowling down at me. It tilted its enormous head and studied me for a few seconds. Then in a voice so deep I could barely understand the word, it rumbled, *"Seidrmadr."*

What the hell. I faced it and said, "Jotun."

Its brow furrowed with cold anger. His skin was ruddy, his features rough-hewn, and his eyes were an almost violent shade of grass green within the shadows of his helm.

From this close, I could see the enormous ugly scarring around his mouth, faded with time but lumpy and displeasing nonetheless. "Who are you and what have you done, that I might know whom I kill?"

Oh right. Old-school Viking. I had been recognized as someone worth fighting, and now it was time to boast, which suited me fine. I had people who needed time to escape.

I glanced back over my shoulder, to where Bradley was struggling to rise, cradling the child with great care and tenderness inside the circle of his torn and bleeding arms, and with a shock, I realized why he'd been at that day-care center in the first place.

The little girl was his.

Oh God.

If Maggie was on this street right now, I'd be losing my mind with terror for her.

Bradley staggered up drunkenly and then turned to Rudolph, who was stirring feebly.

"Get the girl out," I said in a low, intense voice. "She's more important. I'll take care of Rudy."

Bradley hesitated. Of course. No good cop leaves his partner behind. But Bradley had seen some awful things that night, and he made the choice most fathers would.

He picked up his little girl and ran to get her clear.

I turned back to the Jotun and drew myself up to my full height, which meant I was eye to lower quadriceps with him.

"I am Harry, son of Malcolm," I shouted back. "I have battled dark sorcerers and black knights! I have fought men and beasts in numbers too great for counting, invaded the heart of Winter, confronted necromancers and the living dead, vampires and ghouls and demons in their hordes endless! I have matched wits with the six Queens of Faerie and prevailed, and thwarted the combined will of the White Council! When they came for my child, I smote the Red Court of Vampires, and laid them in ruin for all the world to see. I am Harry, son of Malcolm, and I have entered the vaults of Tartarus, and stolen its treasures beneath the gaze of Hades himself! And I'm about to add giant slaying to my résumé."

That seemed to please the Jotun immensely. His smile grew wider and wider, showing more and more teeth the size of dinner plates. "Impressive claims."

"Damned right," I shouted back. "Who are you and what do you got?"

The Jotun lifted his hand. There was a groan of concrete and steel breaking, and then that damned huge axe just flew back into his hand as if it had been drawn by a cartoon magnet.

"I am Svangar, son of Svangi," the Jotun roared back. He used one hand to gesture toward his scarred mouth, infusing it with contempt. "I have fought the Odinson and lived to tell the tale."

I swallowed.

I didn't know much about Thor beyond what stories, comics, and movies tell. But from what I understood he was pretty much the Jotnar's boogeyman. If this particular Jotun had survived *that* boss fight, it was probably safe to assume he was no pushover.

Worse, I had hoped to keep his attention longer, while he bawled his boasts in my face. Just my luck, I had probably found the one Jotun in the universe who had a humblebrag of that magnitude. You couldn't *not* use that one to boast.

My mouth was pretty dry. I didn't reply. I just nodded.

Svangar nodded back.

Then he roared and came at me, axe whirling.

The thing about creatures as big as the Jotun is that they come without power steering. There was simply too much mass building too much momentum for them to be quick to alter course—their whole life must be like walking on a sheet of slippery ice. Not only that, but nervous systems are nervous systems. Signals that have to travel a maximum of six feet are going to be faster than ones that have to cover twenty.

I had to make that advantage count. If I could dance fast enough, maybe I could maneuver Svangar into tripping into a building or something, and run before he got loose.

With the reach that axe gave him, there was no way to get around him without coming into range—and I did *not* want to do that. One hit from that thing, and I'd look like a Rorschach test image.

So I ran right at him.

Svangar bellowed a war cry as the axe came down toward me.

I pointed my staff to one side, focused my will, and screamed, *"Forzare!"*

Even magic can't escape a lot of fundamental physics. Project force at something and it pushes back with an equal and opposite reaction. I used a lot of force, slamming against a brick building to my right. The building slammed me back, and the impact sent me flying to one side—and out from under the axe.

The axe cleaved into the asphalt where I'd been a second before. I flew sideways and forward, dropping into a roll as I came down to the ground. The giant roared, his momentum taking him into his own axe. The handle jabbed him in the gut with a whoosh of expelled air that sound like a miniature gale.

I made my feet again and darted up the street a dozen paces, to force the Jotun to face me and turn his back on the escapees.

Svangar wasn't a dummy, though. He knew he was slower.

So he twisted his blazing axe, melted a bunch of the street's asphalt into a blob of burning tar that could have filled a small hot tub, and flung it at me even before he'd begun to turn.

I dodged that one easily enough—but Svangar had never intended to turn me into a living, screaming tar baby. As the Jotun turned, he simply seized a disabled car in one hand and flung it at me sidearm at the speed of a major-league fastball.

I brought my shield up in time, angling it to my left as I darted right. The car hit the shield, which flared into nearly coherent green-gold light. Broken glass and fiberglass and metal flew out from the impact. The smashed car spun wildly away, but even so, Isaac Newton had his two bits. I was knocked to my right, staggered, and had to put a hand on the street to keep from falling.

I recovered my balance, drew my blasting rod from my coat, slammed my will through it, and shouted, *"Fuego!"*

The raw energy of the terrified city supercharged my spell. The beam of molten-gold energy that lashed out from its tip, as bright as any arc welder's fire, forced me to close my eyes and turn away from its intensity in the smoldering ember light of the burning city, and left a blazon of blue-purple light across the insides of my eyelids.

I blinked them open again frantically to find the Jotun eyeing me, with a large section of the mail over his heart glowing deep orange.

"A little flame like that?" rumbled the Jotun. "Against a son of Muspelheim?"

Dammit. Fire was my go-to exactly because it usually did the trick.

The Jotun snorted contemptuously. Then he swung his axe broadside at a building, which put up about as much resistance as dandelions do to machetes, and sent a cloud of broken glass and concrete and steel at me.

I lifted my arm to cover my face and brought up my shield. Broken glass rattled against the spell-armored sleeve of my duster. One piece got by and my ear suddenly went hot and tingly. The rest slammed into my shield and drove me back until I hit the hood of a parked car, taking my legs out from under me and sending me crashing to my back on the sidewalk.

My heart slammed with terror.

This wasn't a fight; it was an earthquake—and I was running around in the middle of it like a damned fool.

Svangar took a couple of huge strides and the axe came down.

I braced the end of my staff against the hollow of my shoulder, the way I would have a rifle, and screamed, *"Forzare!"*

The air was too thick with energy that night. I'd given the

spell a lot more than I meant to. The staff kicked back against me like a mule. I heard my shoulder re-dislocate with an audible tearing sound and a burst of pain-static—but I held on and was flung violently away from the descending axe.

I fetched up against another car, hard enough to drive the wind right out of me.

The Jotun turned his axe sideways like a flyswatter, took a stride toward me, and raised it.

And that was when I saw Bradley vanish into the haze, the last of the company of escapees—but Murphy hadn't gone with them.

She was standing next to her Harley, and the box labeled CAMPING SUPPLIES was wide open.

I watched her draw out a round tube with a couple of grip points and a control pad, painted olive drab. She extended the tube, flipped up some kind of little doohickey on it, lifted it to her freaking shoulder, and settled her fingers lightly on the control pad.

"You fight like a woman, *seidrmadr*," Svangar snarled.

"Hey, *drittsekk*!" Murphy shouted.

Svangar turned his head toward her, his expression furious.

One corner of her mouth crooked up in a smile and her blue eyes were cold. "Me, too."

And she fired the weapon.

I don't know a lot about military hardware. But if you're going to fight a Jotun, it seems to me a bazooka is about the right caliber.

I didn't really see the rocket fly. That's not how those things work. They move at about the speed of a handgun bullet. There was simply an explosion followed almost instantaneously by another explosion in the hollow of Svangar's throat. *CrackBOOM*.

Resisting fire was a nifty trick, but in the end, again, Sir Isaac will always weigh in on matters. Fire is an absolute, a collection point of energy, and it can always get hotter. Eventually, as with any defense, there's a limit to what it can do, a point of catastrophic failure—and Murphy's rocket found that limit.

Ever see a watermelon get smashed with a sledgehammer?

It was sort of like that.

Flesh and blood exploded from the Jotun in a cloud of aerial chum. I could see Svangar's cracked and blackened collarbone and his freaking *spine* through the hole in his neck. The Jotun staggered, his shoulder smashing into a building, raised his axe one last time— and fell as it dropped from his suddenly nerveless fingers.

The giant's body crushed two cars and knocked over a streetlight as it came down. One outflung hand landed not three feet from my toes.

And suddenly the street was silent and very still.

I got up and walked toward her, taking slow steps, wide around the fallen Jotun. It was a little difficult to keep my balance. I might not have been able to feel it, but the pain was taking its physical toll on me. My entire body tingled unpleasantly.

"Fight like a woman, my ass," Murphy muttered darkly, glowering at the dead giant.

She stood there with the rocket launcher on her shoulder and one hand on her hip and grinned at me as I came close.

"Seriously?" I asked. "A bazooka?"

"Had two. That other one was my practice launch," she said.

"You never told me about it."

Her grin widened. "No, you great gawking man-child. You'd have wanted to play with it."

I put a hand over my heart and gave her a wounded look. "Ow."

"Truth hurts, huh?"

"Drittsekk?" I asked her.

"Norwegian for, ah, scumbag," she said. Then she glanced at my expression and said, "I'm a cop, Harry. There's tradition to consider."

Before I could respond, Rudolph's panicky voice screamed, "Both of you, don't move! Don't either of you scumbags move a fucking muscle!"

I blinked and looked to one side. Rudolph had a shiner on his jawline that had already swollen into a proper mouse. He was standing on his feet, wobbling, his face pasty and his eyes wide and confused. His suit was torn and wrinkled and sprinkled with bits of blood from what appeared to be a broken nose. But he was in a Weaver stance, had recovered his gun from where Bradley had lost it, and had the weapon leveled at Murphy.

"Terrorist!" he gabbled. "You're a goddamned terrorist!"

"Rudolph," Murphy said, "you don't know what's going on."

The whites of his eyes got bigger. "You just killed someone with a rocket launcher!"

Murphy eyed the fallen Jotun. "That was the idea, yeah."

"Hey, hey, Rudolph," I said. "Easy. Easy. Look, we can't be here for very long. There's more of the enemy coming. We all need to go."

"Shut up, shut up!" Rudolph screamed, tracking the gun to me. "Shut the fuck up, you lowlife!"

I began to lift a hand, to flick a wave of force at him, to take the gun out of his hand—but I didn't.

I looked at my arm. I told it to rise. It ignored me. I couldn't tell what was going on behind the cloud of static flooding my nervous system. Christ, that was the shoulder I'd dislocated, again. Without being able to sense the pain of the injury, I hadn't noticed.

"Rudolph!" Murphy said, her voice cracking with authority. "We're trying to help you. Jesus, Mary, and Joseph, man, at least take your finger off the trigger."

Rudolph swung the weapon back to Murphy and began to shriek in a high-pitched voice, pushing the gun forward for emphasis, "I don't need you to—"

The gun went off.

The emptied rocket launcher fell to the street with a metallic clatter, splattered with scarlet.

Murphy dropped like a stone.

Chapter

Twenty-two

Rudolph stood there, shocked at the sudden noise. He stared at the gun. Then at Murphy. "What? What?"

"Medic!" I screamed, rushing forward. "Medic! Medic!"

Murphy lay on the street behind her motorcycle. One knee had bent so that she was lying on her lower leg. The emptied rocket launcher was still rocking where it fell.

I knelt over her. Her eyes were open wide as she stared up.

The fire of the Eye flared again, briefly turned the world scarlet.

I didn't care.

I ripped her jacket and shirt open.

The bullet had gone into her neck, a quarter of an inch above her Kevlar vest. It hadn't gone straight through. It had begun tumbling when it hit and had come out under and behind her left ear, leaving a trail of ravaged flesh in its wake. Blood came out as from a fountain.

"Karrin," I said. "Oh God."

I ripped the duster off, tore my shirt in my haste to get it off over my head, wrapped it into a pad, and put pressure on the gaping wound. As long as I didn't try to move it at the shoulder, my injured arm functioned a little. I could use both hands. "Medic!"

There was so much blood. It soaked my shirt through.

I heard footsteps running toward us.

"Karrin, I'm here," I said. "Help is coming. Hang on."

She coughed blood.

"Harry," she said.

Her lips went red with blood when she said my name.

Her voice was ragged.

"I'm here," I said. It was hard to see her. The world had gone blurry. "I'm here."

The blood was making a pool around her golden hair.

The running footsteps came to a sudden stop.

Murphy made a couple of gurgling, choking sounds.

I looked up to see Waldo Butters standing ten feet away, staring at Murphy.

His face said everything.

"No," I said. "No, no, no, Karrin? Come on, Karrin."

She looked up at me for a second, and the corners of her eyes wrinkled as she smiled weakly. Her face had gone grey. Her lips were blue. "Not from you. I like Murph from you."

"Okay," I said. I could barely choke the words. "Murph."

She reached across her chest and weakly touched my hand with hers.

"Harry," she said. "I lov—"

Her eyes were on mine, and I couldn't look away. I felt the soulgaze begin.

And I saw the flame of a candle go out.

Her eyes emptied. Just emptied, like the windows of an

abandoned house. One moment, her body had been gasping for breath, straining, her face full of pain and confusion.

Then . . .

It was just an empty house.

"No," I said. "No, no, no."

I bent over her. Airway, breathing, circulation. I opened
her mouth, tried to make sure it was clear. But it was
pooled with blood.

I couldn't see her then. Was weeping. I bent over her
anyway, breathed into her mouth.

"Harry," Butters said. His voice creaked.

I breathed in five deep breaths, tasted blood. "Keep the
pressure!"

Butters knelt down, his body moving on autopilot, his
face stunned. He put his hands over the pad, and I did
compressions.

On an empty house.

I leaned down to breathe for Murphy again. Then more
compressions.

"Harry," Butters said. "Harry."

Five breaths. Compressions. It was hard work. In a couple of minutes I felt dizzy as hell.

"Harry, you can't," Butters said. "You can't."

"Come on!" I screamed. "Murph, come on!"

I breathed for her again.

I broke her rib on the next compression.

But it didn't matter.

It was nothing but an empty house.

I felt Butters put his hands on my wrists. He drew them

gently away. "Harry," he said, his voice thick. "Harry, even if she'd been on a table when it happened . . ."

I didn't look away from her face. From her eyes.

I'd been too afraid to soulgaze Murph. Everyone who had done that with me had seen something that didn't please them. I'd been afraid to lose her, and I'd never allowed it.

Now it was too late.

The eyes are the windows of the soul.

And Murphy's eyes were just the windows of an empty house.

There was nothing inside to gaze upon.

I put my forehead against hers and wept. Helplessly. I screamed in rage and denial as I did. I knew the sound was ugly, was hardly human.

I felt Butters's hand on my shoulder.

"Harry, we've got to go. We have to."

I shook him off with a violent twist of my shoulders.

She was gone.

Murphy was *gone*.

And the Winter mantle did nothing, did less than nothing, for the pain.

I put my hand on her hair. Her head was still warm. I could still smell her shampoo, beneath all the iron scent of her blood.

I felt myself start to scream again. But I grabbed onto that scream and coldly choked it to death.

I leaned down and kissed her forehead, closing my eyes. Felt the pain rising in me. And I embraced it. Welcomed it. I watched the futures I'd hoped we would have die before my eyes. I let the pain burn away everything non-essential.

When I opened my eyes again and looked up, the world had gone grey scale.

Except for Rudolph.

Rudolph was bathed in light the color of Murphy's blood.

He flinched as my gaze fell on him.

Butters got what was happening. Somewhere in the distance, I heard him say, in a warning tone. "Harry. Harry, what are you doing?"

Rudolph began taking terrified steps back. He pointed the gun at me and I couldn't have cared less. "Wait. Wait. I didn't mean . . ."

I rose.

"Harry, no!" Butters said sharply.

Rudolph turned and ran.

That made things simple.

I took off after my prey.

Chapter

Twenty-three

Hate is comforting.

Hate is pure.

There aren't any questions, any worries about right and wrong, any quibbles about your motivations or goals. There are no doubts.

Hate is serene.

Rudolph ran. I pursued. And when I caught him, I would kill him. Horribly.

Nothing else entered into it.

I'll give the guy this much credit: He could move. He'd always been careful about his looks, and evidently that meant a lot of cardio as well as expensive suits. He ran well.

But he didn't have my focus, my clarity, and he hadn't been running himself half to death every morning for months and months. He was human. He felt pain. It was an enormous disadvantage.

I gained.

He made funny sounds as he ran. Little gasps and

whimpers. He was terrified. He should have been. In a city of monsters, he'd just pissed off one of the worst.

He took a right turn into a little loading area behind a building, tried a door, and found it locked. Obviously. Everyone who wasn't running was forting up. There were more monsters than unlocked doors in Chicago that night. I don't know what he was thinking.

He turned from the door, desperate, lifted his gun, and started shooting at me as fast as he could pull the trigger.

I raised my shield and slowed to a walk. Some of the shots went wide. Some bounced off the shield. None of them threatened me.

"You can't!" Rudolph screamed. He fumbled at his armpit and withdrew another magazine. "You can't!"

Before he could reload, I just walked forward into him, holding up the shield, and smashed him back against the steel door behind him.

Then I set my legs against the ground and started pushing.

Rudolph made a short, high-pitched sound of pain. The shield caught the barrel of his gun and forced it one way, his wrist another. The idiot still had his finger locked on the trigger. I heard the finger break.

"Dresden, no!" Rudolph screamed.

I pushed harder. Fire might have been good, but my damned arm would make it difficult. This felt better. Felt right. I thought about saying something about grinding his bones to make my bread, but I didn't feel like conversation at that moment. Besides. Why waste breath on a corpse?

We were in pandemonium.

No one was going to ask any questions about one more body.

I pushed harder. Rudolph tried to scream again. There wasn't enough room between my shield and the metal door for his lungs to expand all the way, so it came out breathy and weak. His eyes were wide and terrified, I noted, but that was to be expected. He was dying, after all.

The sour scent of urine filled the air.

I took note of it and adjusted my feet slightly so that I could lean in harder.

He went for his phone, of all the stupid things. His goddamned phone. As if anything there would do him any good. As if it would function and let him call for help. As if it would arrive in time to do him any good.

The phone fell from his fingers as he tried to gasp for breath.

I saw it on his face when he realized what was going to happen. When the panic took him, and the tears. When his hope faltered and died.

It made me feel something hot and sweet deep in my guts.

You killed her.

Feel what I feel, you bastard.

My teeth were bared. I felt sick, and hollow, and *strong*. I pushed harder.

I heard a bone break. I didn't care where it might have been. I just liked the sound and wanted to hear more of it.

"*Bozhe moi,*" came a sudden, startled voice from somewhere behind me. "Dresden. What is the meaning of this?"

"Fuck off, Sanya," I snarled. "Won't be a minute."

Rudolph made a gurgling sound.

"Dresden," Sanya said. His deep voice was troubled, which stood to reason. He didn't have much clarity, like I did. "He is no threat to you. Stop this."

"He killed Murphy," I said. My voice sounded calm. "I'm going to balance those scales real quick. Then we'll get to work."

"No," Sanya said. "That is not your place."

I heard the steel in his voice.

I turned my head slowly and looked at him.

The Knight of Hope drew *Esperacchius* from his side. The saber gleamed with a harsh, threatening light in the dimness of the alleyway.

"Let him go," Sanya said. "You are killing a man. If he has done wrong, he will face justice. But not like this."

"Just a second," I said, as if I was putting together a sandwich.

Sanya's expression was strange. I couldn't track what it was. But I knew it wasn't appropriate to the situation. He stalked closer, moving well. Very well. He was a more worthy opponent. "Harry Dresden. I will not ask again."

Something disturbed the purity of my hatred then. I couldn't tell what it was, but it pissed me off.

What had been a profoundly pure experience had been disrupted. This creature, this Rudolph, didn't deserve even the death I was about to give him. He couldn't even die properly, forcing me to work for it. He was beyond contempt.

"Walk away, Sanya," I said shortly. "This is happening."

Sanya wouldn't walk away. That wasn't the Knight's

style. He wasn't going to let me finish my business. I would have to reason with him.

Sanya closed his eyes for a second, as if in pain.

Which, come on. That was just stupid.

I dropped the shield, whipped toward him, and kicked him in the balls.

I was fast and strong. But Sanya had been fighting for his life against various bad guys for a while now and wasn't going to be taken down by a sucker punch. He managed to move his hips at the last second, taking some of the impact out of the kick. So instead of dropping him to the ground, the blow knocked him back and staggered him, but he kept his feet.

I gave Sanya no time to recover. I followed up, inside the reach of *Esperacchius*, getting my left forearm across his right, driving his arm back and up and not letting it come back down. He was big and strong. I was bigger, stronger. I crowded him against a wall, drove my knee up into his belly, once, twice, hard enough to break boards.

Then the Russian's head snapped forward into my face. There was a burst of static pain in the general area of my head, and then I was on my way back across the alley. My shoulders hit the wall, hard. There was a crackling noise, a flash of heat in my shoulder—and then I could move my right arm readily again.

Sanya had driven a fist like a sledgehammer twice into my belly by the time I caught his blow with my right forearm before a third could land. I stomped down as hard as I could on one of his feet, with mixed results—the Russian had worn steel-toed work boots. He staggered a little, then threw a knee at my groin. I blocked it with one thigh, the one I'd hurt earlier, and the world narrowed to a tunnel for a second before I twisted my head to one side, found his ear, and bit down as hard as I could.

Sanya screamed and his weight shifted back.

I used that change of weight, set my legs, and drove him across the alleyway with the full power of my body and the strength of the Winter Knight. He hit the wall with a vicious impact. I felt it drive the air from his lungs, and I let out a shout of triumph as he bounced off, stunned for maybe all of a second.

I hit him, hard, three times in that second, driving my fist into the side of his neck, into the base of his jaw under the ear, and into his temple, wham, wham, wham.

The Sword fell out of his hand.

The Russian toppled. He hit the ground stunned, making gagging sounds.

"Self-righteous loudmouth," I snarled down at him. "This is no concern of yours."

The hate was calling me. I had no time for further distractions, as satisfying as they might have been.

I spat the taste of blood out of my mouth and turned back to Rudolph.

He was on the ground, curled into a ball, gasping with pain, making choking sounds. He'd lost control of his bowels as well, and the stench made me want to tear his arms and legs off, one at a time.

But he wasn't alone.

Waldo Butters had taken a knee beside him.

The little Knight faced me. He stood up, slowly. I could see that he was shaking, trembling in every limb. His face was pale. The white cloak with its red cross was stained with blood and worse, dirty from the chaos it had been through.

But it fit him.

"Harry," he said. "I can't let you."

"You saw what he did," I said. My voice sounded like my throat was full of rubble and broken glass. "What he did to *her*."

"You have lost it, man," Butters said. His voice was pleading. "Harry, I can't let you."

"You'd protect that thing?" I snarled.

"He's *not* the one I'm trying to protect," he snapped back. Something hard came into his eyes, and the trembling vanished. He rose, the broken hilt of *Fidelacchius*, the Sword of Faith, in his hands. "I'm trying to protect my friend."

Again, my clarity was broken. Again, I felt the rage surge through me. I didn't even bother with the words to a spell. Let it burn. I lifted my hand, and with it my rage, drew upon the wild power in the air, and ripped lightning from nowhere and nothing, sending a thunderbolt at Rudolph with an incoherent scream of rage.

Sudden white light flared, blinding. The confines of the alley were filled with voices louder than thunder, an angry chorus singing a warning note. From the broken hilt of the Sword of Faith came a blaze of light that intercepted that thunderbolt and sent it crashing into the wall above and behind Rudolph.

Which was a fine trick. But I knew the Sword's secret. I wouldn't have to incapacitate Butters to get him out of the way.

I strode forward, winding up with my left hand.

"Harry," Butters said, tears in his eyes. "Don't."

I lashed out backhanded, striking at Butters's face.

He held up the very nonphysical Sword in a parry.

. . .

And my world *became* pain.

. . .

There was no warning, no anything. The second my arm touched the plane of the blade of light, everything shifted. The power of the mantle wrapped around me vanished like mist before the morning sun. Every injury, every hurt, every ache and scratch and bruise and strain, all came crashing onto me at once. I staggered, my limbs weak, as if I had suddenly gained several hundred pounds.

I felt Rudolph. Felt his terror. His agony. His confusion. His humiliation. His remorse. His sick self-hatred. I felt them all as if they were my own. I *saw* myself through Rudolph's eyes, huge and vicious and deadly, implacable as an avalanche.

And Murphy.

Oh God. Oh God, Karrin.

My clarity withered before that light, before the star-bright blaze of pain in my left arm. I had to shield my eyes against the light of the Sword with my right hand, though the mere movement caused me pain enough to threaten the contents of my stomach.

The stench of my own charred flesh filled my nose, somehow laced with the scent of sulfur, brimstone. There was a blazon of blackened flesh along my left forearm, starting just above my shield bracelet and running to my elbow, straight as a ruler.

I fell to my knees.

I dropped to my right elbow, cradling the burned flesh against me.

The scream of pure pain that came out of me wasn't loud. It was hardly human.

And in its wake, I broke.

I sobbed.

While Sir Waldo, the Knight of Faith, stood over me with that blazing Sword, between me and Rudolph's curled, helpless form.

"I'm here, Harry," Butters said, his voice thick with tears. "Harry, I'm here."

The light dimmed and went out, and I felt him crouch in front of me, felt his arms go around me. "I'm here, man. I'm here."

Oh, Hell's bells. Oh God.

What had I done?

I had almost . . .

If not for Butters and Sanya . . .

Murph would have been so ashamed. So terrified for me.

Oh God, Murph.

I leaned against him, sobbing, unable to control myself. Though he was only a little guy, he was wiry and tough. He didn't waver. Not even when my whole weight leaned against him.

"He took her," I heard myself say, the words barely understandable. "He took her from me."

Butters's arms tightened on me. "He took her from all of us," he said. "And he'll answer for it before the law, Harry. But it can't happen like this. You can't let it happen like this." He abruptly hauled me upright to face him, and his expression was intent, hard, though tears ran down his cheeks. "We *need* you. You, the good man. I can't let you hurt that man. Too many of us need him. Your daughter needs him."

It was that last phrase that did it. It hit me like a bucket of cold water.

Maggie.

Despite all the pain, despite the tears, my loss, I could see her there, in my mind's eye. I could imagine her, awake in bed at Michael's place, as safe as anywhere in this town, but too wise to believe that everything was all right, holding on to Mouse and waiting in silence to understand events that were well beyond her ability to change.

Oh God. What had I almost done to her?

Everything hurt.

But there was enough left of me to feel shame.

"I'm sorry," I said. "Butters, I'm sorry."

His face twisted with empathy, and his tears fell harder.

"Sanya," I choked.

"Am all right," I heard a groggy voice say from down the alley. "*Bozhe moi*, you fight dirty." I felt a large hand come down on my shoulder. "Like a Russian."

"Sanya's here, too. He'll be okay," Butters said.

I teetered forward abruptly, unable to stay upright.

My friends caught me.

They held me.

"I'm here, Harry," Butters kept saying. "I'm here."

"She's gone," I whispered.

"Yeah," he said. "I know. I'm here."

And for a time, there was nothing else to be done.

I wept.

And the city burned.

Chapter

Twenty-four

Sanya and his people had gotten their act together pretty quick. They'd come in numbers, down three parallel streets, the one we'd been on and the street on either side of it. They'd gone with a simple tactic—advancing in a line and shooting anything that didn't look human with lots and lots of slugs and buckshot.

Those largest Huntsmen were a big job—but many hands make light work. The way Sanya told it, the first one to come roaring out of the haze had been scary—but he and his appointed uniformed officer had managed to stand and shoot, and enough of the volunteers had stood with them to bring it down before it could complete its charge. And after that, after they saw with their own eyes that the enemy could bleed and die, things changed. The volunteers just stalked forward, killing Huntsmen, whose spears, while terrifying and destructive, really weren't up to exchanging fire with pump-action guns while outnumbered five or six to one.

The enemy and creatures of Winter alike gave way before that kind of pressure, much to their mutual dismay.

The humans that those beings would normally consider their prey had opened their eyes and armed themselves and were willing to fight. For now, the volunteers outnumbered the foe, and the Fomor fell back, ceding the area to the Scattergun Brigade.

I don't know how long I was out of the fight. Butters told me later it had been only a few minutes. All I know is that after a time, the physical pain began to recede, and I felt the Winter mantle settle around me again.

Sanya had broken my nose for me, I realized. Not that I hadn't earned considerably worse. Sobbing hysterically with a broken nose isn't real dignified. Or practical, for activities like breathing. It took me half a minute of coughing and spitting to get things cleared up. By the time I had, and had swiped at my eyes with a cleanish portion of my coat's sleeves, the burn of my broken nose and the aches and pains had once more faded beneath the staticky curtain of the Winter mantle.

Except for the burn on my arm.

That one hurt. Period.

I'd dealt with burns before. This one wasn't the worst I'd ever gotten. Even so, it throbbed and pulsed and made me feel a little queasy and shaky.

And it made me feel . . . human.

I'm not saying pain is what defines us as human beings. But it is, in many ways, what unites us. We all recognize other people in pain. Damned near all of us are moved to do something about it when we see it. It's our common enemy, though it isn't, really, an enemy. Pain is, at least when our bodies are working properly, a teacher. A really tough, really strict, and perfectly fair teacher.

I didn't enjoy the steady, throbbing pain coming from the burn the holy Sword had given me.

But I did find it immensely reassuring.

The pain on the inside of me was something else entirely.

Carefully, I put that aside. I didn't try to bury it or freeze it. I just set it in a different room of my mental house and swung the door mostly shut.

Later, there would be time to feel it. All of it.

But I'd lost people before. That's the thing about being an orphan. Grief is a known quantity. Loss is your family. Sure, it was going to hurt. It was going to tear me up. The empty place where she had been would make me its bitch for a while.

But that was for later.

First I was going to finish what we'd set out to do: protect the city.

And I was going to provide Murph with a fitting escort to what came after while I did it.

Butters walked over to me with my staff. He passed it to me.

I nodded at him. I didn't know where Rudolph was, or what Butters and Sanya had done with him. I didn't want to know. Rudolph wasn't my problem. He couldn't be. I had too much responsibility to the city, to my friends—to my family.

I slammed one end of my staff onto the asphalt and shoved myself back to my feet. I think someone was trying to talk to me on the way. I didn't listen. And without a word I walked back to Murph's body.

It really was so tiny.

Now that she was gone, it seemed even smaller.

I picked Murph up. She weighed almost nothing.

I cradled her body against my chest and then walked, briskly, my arm throbbing, through the blocks back to Millennium Park, where Mab still waited behind her cohort of warrior Sidhe—but instead of facing the oncoming threat, her gaze was waiting to find me as I emerged from the haze.

She gave no visible signal, but the unicorn moved, nudging its way through the Sidhe as the Queen of Air and Darkness rode out to face me.

She regarded Murph's pale face, my bloody form, and said only, "You have returned."

"Yes," I said. "She's a Jotunslayer. She deserves to be laid with dignity."

"And so she does," Mab agreed.

She turned and pointed a finger at one of the blocks of waiting Sidhe warriors. Half a dozen of them peeled off from the formation instantly, in unison, and marched over to us.

"See that this warrior is laid in state," she said, and moved her head in a curt gesture toward the Bean. "She has shared our enemies and earned our respect, and so shall it be known amongst my vassals and to the furthest reaches of my kingdom."

The Sidhe saluted, fists to heart, their weird faemetal armor ringing with tones like bells or wind chimes where it was struck. One of them offered up a long, narrow shield, and they took position on either side of it.

She wasn't heavy.

But I couldn't carry her and do what we'd set out to do.

I put her down on the shield, as gently as I could. I composed her as best I could. The grey, somehow shrunken remains weren't Murph. But they deserved more respect, more grace, than I could offer.

I put my hand on her head one more time. Touched her hair one more time.

Then I said, "Okay."

The Sidhe carried Murphy's body. I went with them, enough to make sure they behaved.

They did. Could be it was the bloodied, bruised, angry Winter Knight standing over them that inspired it. Could be that it was real respect. The Winter Court and death are distant relatives. The only times I'd seen Winter volunteer something like humanity was when someone had died.

Maybe it was all they had left.

My left arm throbbed and burned as they laid Murphy down atop a bier made of the cases the weapons had been stored in.

The warrior Sidhe saluted the body. Then they filed out.

It was only then I noticed that they were all female.

I looked at Murphy's body lying on the crates. Except for all the blood, and the grey skin, she might have been asleep.

But she wasn't asleep.

"I gotta go," I said quietly. I wasn't sure whom I was talking to. I suppose her death could have left a shade of some kind, but that wasn't it. It took a little time for a shade to condense. After I had briefly participated in it, the whole afterlife thing had become even more confusing to me, not less. "Ethniu is almost here. Mab's ready to make her play. I have to be there."

One of her curls had fallen over her eye. I moved the curl back. It promptly fell over her eye again.

I smiled, through tears.

Even dead, I couldn't make her do a damned thing.

I leaned down and kissed her forehead.

"I already miss you so much," I said quietly. "Goodbye, Murph."

I rose to leave and almost bumped into Mab, she was standing so close behind me.

I wavered and didn't. One does not bump into the Queen of Air and Darkness. It simply isn't done.

Mab stared silently at the body for a breath, her eyes unreadable. Then she looked searchingly up at me. She was at her human-disguise height, a little less than a foot shorter than me. The starlight in her hair was truly beautiful.

Silently, she reached out and took my left arm. She pushed the sleeve of my duster up, despite my discomfort, and studied the burn for a moment. Then she said, with a slow, quiet, ever so slightly *jealous* tone, "That must hurt."

"It does," I said.

She closed her eyes for a moment and took a breath.

When she opened them, it was all business again. "Can you fight?"

"Watch me."

"I shall," she said. "And you shall see something the world has not seen in many a year."

"What's that?"

"Mab at war," she said simply. She glanced to one side.

"Your little ones have found King Corb. He has come ashore upon the beach east of here and joined Ethniu. It is time." She looked up at me. "When the moment is right, it must be you who calls out her name."

I knew whom she was talking about. There was no need for explanation. "Why me?"

"She will answer you," Mab said. "She has before."

I exhaled. "Oh. Got it."

"Good." Mab touched my burned arm again and then withdrew her hand. "It is possible that I shall fall this night."

"You're immortal," I said.

"Immortal. Not eternal. There is power here of the truly ancient world. It is enough to ensure the deed." She narrowed her eyes. "Should I fall, I have one last command you would be wise to fulfill."

I tilted my head.

"Kill Molly Carpenter," she said calmly. "As quickly as possible."

"Funny," I said.

Mab stared at me.

Of course. She hadn't been joking.

On a normal day, I would have been more upset. Today already hurt so much that I hardly noticed. Mab wanted me to kill someone. She usually did. It was sort of my job description.

I frowned dully at her. "Why?"

"As Winter Lady, she shows promise," Mab said. "But she is not ready to become Mab. The consequences would be . . . unsettling. For both of you. Perhaps for all of Winter."

I tried to think of the kind of situation that would unsettle *Mab*. My mind shied away from it.

"That's not going to be an issue," I said. "Because you aren't going to get killed tonight. When I bury Murph, she's going to be holding the shattered key to that Titanic bitch's cell on Demonreach in her hands."

Mab's face blossomed into a carnivore's sharp grin. "Not the Eye?"

"Fuck the Eye," I said.

She actually lifted her hand to cover her mouth. But I saw her eyes . . . smile. It was damned eerie. "All upon the field tonight want that weapon. Your own White Council included. It is the primary reason they fight."

I blinked.

I looked out at the ruddy haze outside and spat a curse.

Of course. That's why everyone was fighting beside Mab. Not to honor the treaty, at least not for all of them. But to secure a weapon that would give them an enormous advantage over any of the other Accorded nations. One that could be a threat even to immortals like Mab. I could imagine what the Senior Council would be saying about it if I accused them, too. *Too dangerous, could cause havoc, can't let those monsters have it, we'll be able to lock it away and keep it safe, harrumph, harrumph.*

"Should we be victorious, that will be the real fight, you know," Mab said. Her gaze, always penetrating, made me squirm. "Who shall possess the Eye?"

Outside, said Eye filled the night with light and destruction again. I heard the building fall this time, clearly. Hell. It was only a couple of blocks to the north. It might have been the one with Bradley's day care in it.

"I can wreck buildings just fine all by myself," I said,

and tapped the center of my forehead. "And I got three eyes already. What the hell do I want with another big ugly one?"

"What indeed," Mab said, as if I hadn't spoken. She closed her eyes and said, "I confess, it has been long since I have taken the field in earnest, my Knight." She showed me her teeth. "I think this shall be . . . fun."

I blinked. *"Fun?"*

Mab opened her eyes, and they *twinkled*. Just *twinkled*.

And then she turned in a wave of silken hair and starlight and strode out of the Bean and onto the battlefield.

"Hell's bells," I muttered after her.

I didn't hear it, of course. But my mind provided me with a perfect reproduction of Murph's drily amused chuckle.

I turned back to Murph's remains and touched her cheek with the backs of the fingers of my left hand. Then paused.

Her Sig, her favorite handgun, was still riding in its shoulder holster beneath her coat.

Heroes are traditionally buried with their arms.

But this fight was still going.

I took the gun from its holster, very gently. It wasn't a large weapon, but it fit my hand nicely enough as a backup.

"Backup," I said. "You mind if I borrow her for a while?"

Murph couldn't say anything.

But with a whisper, where I'd moved it to get the gun, her coat fell open a little more, showing the spare magazines she had prepared.

"Thanks, Murph," I whispered.

I took the magazines and *Backup*.

And then I stalked out to fight for the city.

Chapter
Twenty-five

I walked out of the Bean and into the soundtrack of a B horror movie: The Fomor forces didn't use drums to send signals in the haze.

They used clicks.

I supposed that made sense. Drums wouldn't sound like much underwater. But two rocks banged together are two rocks banged together. I just hoped that they weren't enough like dolphins to be able to *see* through the haze using the clicks, too. I didn't think so, since dolphins had an absolutely enormous biological investment in their natural sonar, but I'd had unpleasant surprises before.

I strode through the ranks of the Sidhe cohort, and this time there were no games. They made a path for me with crisp precision. But I could sense their eagerness as I passed by. The Winter Court makes very little distinction between sex and violence. Their confrontation with me earlier had been foreplay, but now they were ready for the main event.

Normally, before a big fight, I felt as intensely as they

did, if differently. The adrenaline. The fear. The eagerness to get it over with.

This time I didn't.

It wasn't that I didn't feel anything. I felt plenty. I just couldn't care too much about it, in the face of my loss. That was dangerous, both for me and for the people I was protecting. Battles are not graded on a curve, ever. You survive or you don't. And everyone you'll ever face in a battle to the death is undefeated.

I had to get my head into the game.

I strode across the park to the pavilion, where Sanya and the volunteers waited, and as I went, the scarlet-hazed air filled with eerie clicks that sounded hideously organic. They came echoing through the heavy air, from multiple directions, north and south alike.

The Alphas fell in around me as I came to the volunteers, and Butters appeared from the haze to silently take up a position behind me and to my right, where he could watch my back. Or stab me in it if I went all monstery, I supposed.

Good.

"Harry," Sanya said cheerfully. One of the volunteers, damned if it wasn't Randy, was busy wrapping a bandage around the big Russian's head, to secure the pad over his torn and bloodied ear. "You are just in time, *da*?" He gestured out at the unseen sources of the clicks. "What kind of monster you think we get to kill now?"

"Doesn't matter," I said. "If it bleeds, we can kill it. And they all bleed. Let's go."

"*Da*," Sanya said firmly, and raised his voice as Randy finished with the bandage. "All right, everyone! Offense, time for us to make them sorry! Defense, stay here and kill anything that comes from the north!"

Sanya's chosen officers started calling out to their groups, and they began to spread out in a line, facing east. The officers weren't being subtle about it. They physically shoved people into position. There were a lot of worried faces on that line. I could feel their fear, the kind that makes your limbs feel hollow and your forehead bead in a cold sweat.

But through the banner, I could also feel their determination, and the aggression radiating off that hideous unicorn that was seeping into them. They were terrified and furious and ready to spill blood.

Sanya came up beside me.

"I'm sorry," I said.

Sanya snorted.

"Thanks," I said. I lowered my voice. "They're amateurs. If we run into enough trained professionals, like Listen and his people, they're going to be slaughtered."

Sanya gave me the side-eye. "You think they do not know that?" He clapped a hand to my shoulder. "We all must die, Dresden. There is no shame in dying for something worthwhile."

"I'd rather the Fomor died for something they thought was worthwhile, if it's all the same to you."

"Hah," he said, grinning. "*Da*. That is plan. And it is time."

I held up a hand, sharply. "Wait."

Reports came in from the malks, through my banner. They were once again out ghosting through the haze. I tasted stagnant seawater on my tongue, there was so much of the scent in the air. Malks were not, on the whole, very bright—too much of their brain was devoted to blood-shed. But my scouts' estimates were not optimistic, and in some cases almost fearful.

Grimalkin, I thought. *I need an accurate assessment of enemy position and numbers.*

The Elder malk's reply came buzzing through my head in his creepy, creepy voice. *They are legion. Between five and seven thousand. They march west through the park.*

Holy crap.

There was no way for about eight hundred amateurs with shotguns to fight that and win.

Unless . . .

"Dammit," I said. "They're coming right at us. We have to beat them to Columbus. It's a double-wide separated roadway, and it's at ground level, maybe fifteen feet lower than the park. There's a pedestrian bridge across. The bridge is higher than the park and it will give them a firing position down onto our people, as well as an easy way across Columbus—otherwise, they'll have to climb straight walls under heavy fire."

"Destroy bridge?" Sanya asked.

"And hold the line for as long as we can, do all the damage we can," I said.

Sanya took a deep breath and then looked at the volunteers. *"Da,"* he said quietly. "Then we must move quickly."

"Yeah," I said. Then we jogged out in front of the volunteers, and I called, "Follow me!"

And we took off at a trot across the Great Lawn, our northern flank shielded by the defensive positions at the pavilion, with stealthy little monsters moving in a screen in front of us, serving as my eyes.

What I had not considered was that eight hundred people running together make a thunder of their own. As we ran, I heard the alien clicking sounds stop—and then resurge in a furious, faster tempo.

Hah. They hadn't been expecting something like this. And now that I thought about it, I wouldn't want to run into eight hundred angry people with shotguns on an average Chicago evening, either.

The retaining wall on this side of Columbus came into sight, and I poured it on, aiming for the pedestrian bridge. Sanya started screaming orders to his officers, hard to hear over the sound of that many people moving.

I didn't see the enemy team holding our end of the bridge through the haze until they popped up from under cloaks like ghillie suits and opened fire. Angry wasps hissed through the air and someone hit me in the stomach with a baseball bat and drove the wind out of me.

For a second, I couldn't tell what was happening. Some of my volunteers had raised their weapons and returned fire immediately, but most were confused. I knew the feeling. Getting shot at often confuses the hell out of me, and only training and experience allow you to respond with the kind of instant aggression necessary to counter that kind of surprise attack. I lifted my left arm, and only a lifetime of practice and dedication allowed me to bring up my shield through the pain.

Pain?

I looked down at my belly. There was no blood.

I felt a hit on my shoulder. Another on my cheekbone, even though nothing had touched my shield.

And then I got it.

My people were dying. I could feel it. Feel their pain. Their terror. Their confusion.

The air *seethed* with magical potential.

I drew my blasting rod, gathered my will, dropped the shield, and screamed, *"FUEGO!"*

Because nothing cuts through bullshit like a proper fireball.

The lance of energy that emerged from my blasting rod was an order of magnitude more potent than any I had thrown before, thanks to the cloud of terror over the city. The very air boiled and shrieked in protest, and when the blast hit the ground among the enemy fire team, the thermal bloom that erupted was a sphere of white-hot light. The concussion of that expanding heat slapped me in the chest so hard that it rocked me back a step.

The enemy fire stopped.

All that was left a few seconds later as the fire boiled away was a black circle on the ground maybe thirty feet across, in a mound, where the heat had sucked the very earth up in a low scorched dome, some unrecognizable lumps, and a small mushroom-shaped cloud of sullen red flame that vanished into black smoke.

There was a second of stunned silence, and then one of the volunteers, damned if it wasn't Randy, shouted, "We've got a goddamned wizard! Fuck those guys!"

The rest of the volunteers roared their defiance. I ran forward, and they followed.

While we did, two of my people bled to death from their wounds. They . . . just went out. One moment, I could feel their terror and pain as if it were my own. The next . . . there was only silence.

Eleven hundred and eighty-five.

And I didn't even have time enough to find where they'd fallen and look at them.

The footbridge isn't just a simple, straightforward bridge over an underpass. It's this enormous, gleaming, serpentine thing that winds like a river, made out of concrete and gleaming polished steel. It's solid. Like, really solid. And the only place it could reasonably be taken down was over Columbus itself, where it thinned out to normal bridge proportions.

I drew up to a halt at the mouth of the bridge and turned to Sanya. "Deploy our people in two ranks. One along the side of the bridge and the other along the wall over Columbus."

"And you?"

"Those trees are blocking our line of fire. I gotta take them out, then go out on the bridge to take it down," I said. "Be right back."

"Not alone," Sanya said.

"He isn't," Butters said, firmly.

I eyed the little guy and didn't have time to argue. So instead I grunted, jerked my chin to indicate the direction, and started off.

I couldn't get over how easy it was to use magic in the boiling air. I'd already performed several spells that by all rights should have left me in need of a breather and a meal. Instead, the latent magic in the air made me feel exhilarated, eager to do more. Which isn't different from any other kind of power, I suppose. And it held the same dangers. So I was careful about how much force I used on the trees. Just enough to rip through each trunk and send them crashing down toward the street below.

Once that was done, I raised my shield preemptively and hurried forward, following the curve of the bridge, even as some of the volunteers pounded out onto the bridge to take up firing positions overlooking the underpass.

The enemy clicks became louder and more erratic, and I saw them for the first time as I stepped out onto the bridge.

The Fomor army seemed to be organized in warbands. Each one had maybe three hundred creatures in it, in a distinct group, gathered around a central standard. No two groups looked the same. Some were simply a collection of turtleneck handlers, each holding a pair of large, hairless, vaguely canine animals. Some were packs of shapeless, deformed . . . things, naked, neither human nor animal, their faces and bodies twisted and ugly, the cruelest combinations of expressed genes imaginable. Some were orderly ranks of armored warriors, their arms a little too long for their bodies, their shoulders too wide. Some looked like troops of more modern militaries and were armed with rifles. And at the center of each warband was a knot of Fomor proper, frog-faced jerks in badly clashing clothing, seven feet tall.

There were a couple of thousand of them. And those were only the ones I could *see*. The haze must have been concealing the rest.

When I was spotted, things got a little crazy.

Shots rang out and my shield lit up like a disco ball.

Butters yelped and jumped behind me. I pressed forward. I had to get far enough up the bridge to bring it down.

Someone shrieked something, and one of the groups of those tormented abominations came howling toward me, their locomotion ragged and swift.

Butters peeked out from behind me and said, "Wow, red carats everywhere."

I blinked and poured more energy into the shield. With this much available, it wasn't hard to hold it up. "What? What the hell do vegetables have to do with anything going on right now?"

"It's kind of a Knight thing."

I crouched low and got out of the worst of the fire. The walls on either side of the footbridge were about five feet high, and there was no way for them to get a clear line of sight to us. I felt clever as I hurried forward.

And then I heard several *phoont* sounds.

Grenades began to fall.

Some of them went right on by and over. Trying to land a grenade inside the sheltered area of the footbridge was a damned tricky shot. But the enemy did what the enemy always does, and showed up with more skill than they had any right to possess.

I shoved Butters against one of the walls, pressed my lower back against his chest, and melded the shield's edges against the wall behind us.

Half a dozen grenades went off in the space of maybe fifteen seconds, and the world was just one enormous crunching sound after another.

"Down," I growled as they stopped falling, and I lowered my shield. We dropped to hands and knees, below the level of the bridge's walls, and I started crawling forward faster than I would have believed humanly possible. Butters followed.

Evidently, they figured dozens of grenades had done the job, because we didn't take any more fire—until we rounded a corner and found ourselves face-to-face with fifty turtlenecks in full tactical gear.

"Forzare!" I shouted, and unleashed a broad stroke of pure kinetic force. I hit them harder than I'd meant to. The first three ranks of them went flying back like they'd been on wires, and collided with the men behind them. The impact brought instant massive confusion.

"Butters!" I shouted. "Kill the bridge!"

And I charged, slamming my right hand forward, screaming, *"Forzare!"* with every stride, knocking the turtlenecks around like ninepins.

"Harry!" Butters screamed.

"Kill the bridge, dammit!" I shouted back.

I heard the Sword of Faith come alight in his hands, and a glance over my shoulder showed him hacking through the bridge at his feet as if it had been made of so many soap bubbles.

I spun back to the enemy, brought my shield up—and stood tall.

"You!" I said, relishing the moment. "Shall not! Pass!"

They replied with a hail of automatic weapons fire. The impacts against my shield all but blinded me.

And a freaking Fomor sorcerer popped out from behind a veil that had concealed him from me and lobbed a viscous-looking ball of quasi-liquid at me.

I'd been burned once before, hah hah, by assuming my

shield would be ready to stop whatever came at me. I ducked and skittered forward and to one side, and the blob hit the bridge where I'd been standing.

Whatever that stuff was, the xenomorphs' blood had nothing on it. It started chewing at the concrete and the steel itself, bubbling and hissing as those substances were dissolved, and a hideous stench filled the air.

The Fomor smiled his froggy smile at me and tossed another, to my other side. I dodged again, but I had less space to do it in—I did not want to walk in one of those puddles. Whatever that vitriol was, it would probably devour my feet in seconds.

And then one of the turtlenecks lobbed a grenade high, aiming for it to come down behind my shield.

A flicker of will and a muttered word, and I batted the grenade out of the air and back down among the turtlenecks.

There was a fine amount of screaming and confusion as it went off, and I checked over my shoulder.

Butters had hacked through the bridge, but the thing hadn't fallen yet. He dashed twenty feet back and started chopping again, to drop that entire length out of the bridge.

I held my shield and my ground as the turtlenecks recovered, way too swiftly to be acceptable, and poured it on again. The Fomor sorcerer had vanished. Those creeps didn't like to expose themselves to danger when they could whip their minions forward into it instead.

"Harry!" Butters shouted.

I started backpedaling, my shield bracelet beginning to overheat from use now, dribbling green-gold sparks everywhere.

I made it back to Butters and he slashed down with *Fidelacchius* one final time, before both of us rushed back, around the curve of the bridge, and out of the line of sight of the turtlenecks. There was an enormous groaning sound, then a rumbling crash and a scream of ripping concrete and twisting metal.

And now that we were out of the line of fire, the volunteers on the bridge started hammering away at the turtlenecks. Yeah, those guys were professionals, but they weren't bulletproof. I saw several go down before they started returning fire and . . .

I felt phantom rounds hit my chest, my head.

Eleven hundred and seventy-nine.

I fought not to throw up. There wouldn't have been much to come up anyway.

The clicks rose to a sound like heavy canvas tearing, and the Fomor army came rushing forward in a storm of shrieks, wails, and screams.

With the bridge out, their only option was to cross Columbus on foot—and they went bounding and leaping forward, jumping off the higher ground and down into the underpass without hesitation.

And nothing happened.

"What?" I demanded. "Where is Sanya?"

"Beats me," Butters said, panting. He was covered in concrete dust.

The enemy massed on the far side of Columbus and then rushed forward, toward us. They crossed the first traffic lane without being fired upon. They reached the median of the divided road while more of their numbers piled into the underpass, a wave of flesh and steel and weaponry.

They crossed the median and the first lane of traffic.

And Sanya bellowed, *"NOW!"*

Eight hundred men and women of Chicago popped up from behind the wall overlooking the sunken drive and opened fire with shotguns from a range of as little as thirty feet.

The slaughter was indescribable.

Shotguns are not precision weapons. But at thirty feet, and in the hands of an amateur, they don't have to be. The volunteers' fire swept the enemy's front ranks like a broom, killing and maiming without prejudice or mercy. The sound of it was a roar like I'd never heard before, with too many individual blasts to distinguish any one round going off, a deadly martial thunderstorm.

The volunteers fired until their weapons ran empty, and if they'd killed fewer than a thousand of the enemy, it was only by a couple.

The enemy howled in their dismay and tried to run, but there was nowhere to go. Some tried to run up or down the street, but Sanya had positioned people all along the ground overlooking the sunken road, firing from defilade, and they enfiladed the ever-loving hell out of the Fomor army. Volunteers screamed their fury and defiance at the enemy. The volume of fire was so heavy that it magically turned a couple of stalled cars the enemy tried to take cover behind into Swiss cheese.

Blood ran down the street in small rivers. The air grew thick with the iron stench of it.

The enemy wasn't done. They took up positions of their own, across the sunken road, behind just as much wall as my volunteers had. Then it became a gunfight. At that range, the professional weaponry of the turtlenecks wasn't substantially better than the volunteers' shotguns. Arguably, the shotguns were a better weapon for the shooting-gallery scenario, since they needn't be aimed as carefully or as long. But that only made it something like a fair fight.

Men and women who had followed me died.

I *felt* them dying. There were very few instant deaths. Even the people shot in the head had time to thrash and scream for a handful of seconds before the end. Some of them were so close I could hear them pleading for mercy. But Death plays no favorites and makes no exceptions.

Eleven hundred and fourteen.

"Hell's bells," I muttered, shoving away the phantom sensory input to the best of my ability. I'd lost seventy-three volunteers, while the enemy dead numbered in the hundreds.

We were winning.

Granted, we weren't going to get any more effective surprise attacks. From here on out, we'd have to work for all of them. But we were doing it.

We were holding them off.

Until the Titan appeared.

Ethniu strode out of the haze, nine feet of terrible bronze beauty. She walked forward through the ranks, and while the enemy wilted and died all around her from my volunteers' fire, she herself was unscathed, as if she'd been walking through a gentle rain instead of a storm of slugs and buckshot. She stood observing our positions for a moment or two, utterly ignoring everything the volunteers tried to do to her.

"Jesus," I said, realizing her intent. "Butters, get them off the bridge!"

I took off, screaming for the volunteers to follow me. I ran back until the bridge met the park on our side of Columbus, then hopped up over the sidewall and slid down the shining steel slope on its other side to the ground. Then I ran toward Sanya.

He had seen what was happening, too. He was screaming for a retreat, but over the roar of gunfire no one could hear him.

Then Ethniu turned the Eye upon our side of the street.

The world went red and howling. She simply tracked the Eye up and down the retaining wall, blasting it into a slope of finely ground rubble.

Some of my people saw it coming in time, and ran.

Most didn't.

They died. They died badly, consumed in a fire made from the raw, seething hatred of a Titan. Whatever pain they feared most, they felt as they died. Images of despair and doom flashed in that fire, and so much fear that many of my people went mad in the partial second of suffering they had left before their bodies were broiled and blasted to dust.

And I felt it with them.

Seven hundred and thirty-two.

It hurt so much that I couldn't breathe.

In the space of a long breath, Ethniu had wiped out more than half of the offensive component of my little army.

Winning. What a joke.

Mortals could not stand against *that*.

The Titan lifted her hand, the gesture elegant, and pointed forward with one finger.

And with a roar, the Fomor army surged forward, down into the sunken road. The wall on our side of Columbus had been blasted into a slope, one the enemy would have no trouble climbing en masse. If we stayed, we'd be swallowed up in moments—and the enemy came at us eagerly, scenting victory, literally baying for our blood.

"Retreat!" I screamed. "Retreat!"

Most of the volunteers were way ahead of me.

But many, eighty-seven, in fact, had been injured and could not run.

They went down fighting.

Six hundred and forty-five.

The rest of us ran for our lives.

Chapter
Twenty-six

It isn't a very long run from the bottom of the bridge to the pavilion. It's maybe a couple of hundred yards.

That distance feels a hell of a lot longer when there's an army chasing you. Without the pall of smoke and dust, their shooters would have gunned us down. It was bad enough for a while anyway: The enemy soldiers on the far side of Columbus fired furiously into the haze. They couldn't see us once we were maybe ten feet back from our side of the street, but there wasn't anything to stop the bullets from coming, either. I felt phantom wounds tear into me as more of my people were hurt by pure, merciless statistics.

I threw up my shield as wide as I could and turned to face the enemy while walking backwards. "Get behind me!" I shouted.

Some did, a little knot of defenders gathering around Butters and Sanya. The Alphas came hurtling out of the haze, muzzles bloodied, and also crouched down in the shelter of my shield. Both groups huddled behind me, and I kept my steps slow and steady so that they could match my pace. The volunteers reloaded their weapons in the safety my shield offered.

"How long can you hold it, Harry?" Butters asked.

"Won't have to be long," I shouted back. "They'll stop shooting as soon as—"

The enemy fire abruptly stopped.

"—their vanguard gets to the other side of the street and obstructs their fire," I shouted into sudden quiet. I dropped the shield. "Hell's bells, move!"

We ran. Every single volunteer who had followed my banner was willing, but not all of them were terribly able. The folks who had gathered around Butters and Sanya were almost all older citizens who weren't going to be winning any marathons anytime soon. I'll give them credit, though—they still held their weapons as if they meant business.

"Weapon," I snarled at one of the more weary-looking men, and he passed me his shotgun. "Keep going, head for the pavilion!"

I dropped back to the rear of the group and found Sanya, Butters, and the Alphas already there ahead of me. I passed the shotgun to Butters, who reduced the Sword of Faith to a wooden handle again, stowed it, and checked the firearm with, if not professionalism, at least confidence. Without a word, I traded looks with Sanya, and then the three of us spread out and turned to scuttle along backwards, Sanya and Butters with their weapons raised, me holding up the glowing tip of my blasting rod. The Alphas, meanwhile, darted out to our flanks, their furry forms vanishing swiftly into the haze.

The first shapes to emerge from the haze were those

hairless canine things, of course, running across the ground at a low rush.

"Get some!" I shouted, and raised my blasting rod. *"Fuego!"*

Butters's shotgun bellowed, and Sanya's Kalashnikov hammered away at a metronome's pace. Creatures snarled and screamed and fell. Fire bloomed among them, sending dozens running and screaming with their injuries. Our pursuers, though clearly still desperate to reach us, juked back and forth, both exposing their fellows to the fire and slowing the entire mass of them, until we could see the shapes of those broad-shouldered, long-armed, armored figures approaching behind them.

We had discouraged their advance, but we couldn't stop it. We kept going backwards. And the enemy kept getting closer. I plied my blasting rod without slowing down, hurling one blast of green-gold fire after another, sending some of my foes screaming with dread and pain while others took their place and closed the distance between us.

"That's it!" bellowed Sanya, somewhere just a bit behind me.

"Dresden, down!" I heard Butters yell.

Something got behind my knees and I tumbled onto the grass.

"Fire!" Sanya bellowed.

And a thunderstorm erupted in the air around me.

I lay there gasping for breath and instinctively raised my arms to shield my head. I saw Butters, who had hit me in the knees in a friendly tackle, lying as flat as he could and doing the same. I realized that we had backpedaled all the way to the fortifications the svartalves had prepared.

Maybe a quarter of the defenders left behind at the fortifications had come to our aid. A hurricane of buckshot swept the field. It wreaked havoc among the charging canines and sent them scurrying. One or two of the armored figures dropped, but the others retreated in good order, dragging the wounded with them.

"Cease fire!" Sanya yelled. "Cease fire!"

The fire trailed off as people emptied their guns, mostly, but it ended, and the survivors managed to clamber into the fortifications all the same.

"Contact!" screamed someone from the other side of the fortifications. "Fire!" Shotguns roared. The spears of the Huntsmen shrieked.

"Sanya!" I shouted.

"On it!" the Russian called back. He vaulted past me, into the fortifications, and headed for the north side to take command of the defense there.

"Find a firing position!" I shouted to the rest of the defenders. "Reload!"

Butters and I got up and hurried inside, where probably too many of the defenders were trying to figure out what had happened to the mobile force. They were gathered around Randy, who was on his knees, sobbing. "They're dead. They're all dead!"

"Butters," I said.

"Yeah," Butters said. He went to Randy's side, put an arm around the man, and started speaking quietly.

I looked up to find all the people who had followed me

staring down at me. From their expressions, they didn't want it to be true.

"It's true," I said in a firm, steady voice. "The enemy hit us hard. And they bled to do it. There's a thousand dead bad guys lying on Columbus right now, and the rest of them have to climb over the corpses of their buddies to come forward." I looked up and down at the people watching me. "I've got no claim on you," I said. "If you want to run, I can't stop you. But by now, the enemy is pressing us from three sides. Maybe four. It might still be possible to retreat if you leave here and go straight west. If you want to do that, go for it. But if you borrowed a gun and ammo, leave them here. The people who are going to fight will need them. Because if we don't stop them here, nothing is going to stand between them and the rest of the town."

On the far side of the pavilion, fire rose into a thunder and died away again, to occasional barks of weapons discharge. The enemy's first rush at the fortifications must have failed.

"You came here to fight. So did they. If you've got loved ones somewhere behind us, you've got a reason to stay. If you don't, the weapon that just killed most of the mobile force is going to be used on them. Make up your mind. Now."

There was a long silence while everyone stared at me.

I turned and hunkered down by Randy across from Butters.

"We can't fight that," Randy sobbed. "No one can."

I put my hand on his shoulder.

The skinny man looked up at me through tears. He

wasn't a coward. He just hadn't been ready for what he'd been forced to see.

"No one can fight that," he whispered.

I made a dangerous moment's eye contact and said, hard, "I can." I stood up and offered Randy my hand. "But I can't do it alone. I need your help."

He stared at my hand.

The volunteers stared at us. I could feel the moment hanging in the air, brittle and tense as crystal. They were terrified. The survivors of the earlier action were terrified, and the defenders were terrified.

And all of them were watching Randy for his reaction.

The man closed his eyes for a moment. Then he whispered, "My little girl was born early yesterday. She's still in the hospital. They couldn't move her."

"Well," I said. "That makes it pretty simple. But that's not the same thing as easy, is it."

His jaw clenched.

And when he looked up at me, his eyes were hard and cold. "No. It sure as hell isn't."

The sound of his hand smacking into mine was loud in the hazy quiet.

Butters and I pulled Randy to his feet.

Something like a long exhalation went through the volunteers. They turned back to their positions, watching the ruddy haze for any incoming enemy.

Sir Knight, came Grimalkin's creepy voice. *I report.*

"Officers!" I called. "Get them into firing positions and make sure everyone has enough ammo. If you don't, there're cases of the stuff. Assign a runner to bring more."

Then I turned and walked several paces away, muttering, "Go, Grimalkin. Report."

I am near the enemy, the Elder malk said. *Hear them for yourself.*

And suddenly my senses surged, and I was elsewhere.

". . . a ridiculous mess," hissed King Corb's voice. "You said there were no mortal forces in the field."

A steady baritone answered. "And there weren't. This one came from nowhere."

"Nowhere!" snarled Corb, furious. His voice bubbled like a teapot. "Would you like to see what nowhere truly looks like, slave?"

I looked around me. I was crouched in a hollow space beneath a mound of rubble, my fur compressed on all sides, and the ground was hard and vicious against my paws. The air was full of the scent of blood, human and monstrous alike, and the smell made me flex my claws in and out repeatedly in instinctive reaction.

Ah. I was getting Grimalkin's sensory input, then.

Ethniu spoke, and the Titan's voice was thoughtful, rich, vibrating pleasantly through octaves of sound I could not possibly have heard with human ears. "Corb," she said, "cease your whining. Listen has proven his ability repeatedly."

"Yet he could not see a small army of mortals ready to bleed us dry."

Listen spoke, his voice steady. "It is hardly reasonable to expect millions of people to lie down and die for our convenience. Especially not in a place with so many interests in the supernatural world. We knew they would fight. The battle plan proceeds smoothly enough."

"Smooth!?" Corb spat. "A fifth of my legion fills the gutters with their blood."

"They shouldn't have advanced without hearing from my recon team."

"Your team was dead!" the Fomor king shrieked.

Listen replied without passion or uncertainty. "Which should have been an excellent indicator that it was not safe to attempt the crossing."

The air suddenly crackled with sorcerous power.

"Corb," Ethniu said. "Put your hands down or I will rip them off."

Corb burbled a curse in some language that sounded absolutely disgusting.

"Better," Ethniu said. "Captain Listen?"

"The enemy is in fortified earthworks around the pavilion," Listen said. "And even if we had sufficient squids remaining, we couldn't use them here. The svartalves appear to have prepared the lattices over the pavilion to prevent them."

They had? Hell's bells, I hadn't noticed that, and I'd been standing in the place. Granted, I'd been a little distracted, but how the hell was Listen smart enough to know that?

"Mab appears to have taken position here, in front of the *Cloud Gate*," Listen continued. "She has a single cohort with her."

"Even a battle cohort of the Sidhe is no match for us," Corb said. "Attack."

Ethniu's voice was acidic. "Naturally. Mab will be an easy kill, I am certain. Listen?"

"We have no intelligence of One-Eye taking a position on the battlefield," Listen said calmly. "This is obviously a trap."

Dammit. I mean, he wasn't *wrong*, but . . .

"Of course it's a trap," Ethniu said. "That woman is a spider. The question is why she is allowing us to see it so easily."

"The surprise attack took her off guard," Corb said.

"The bodies of better than five hundred mortal troops we never knew existed would suggest otherwise," Listen noted.

"Those were not soldiers," spat Corb. "That was merely an armed rabble."

"An armed rabble that killed a fifth of your legion?" Ethniu asked. "Perhaps I chose my ally poorly."

Corb made a sputtering sound but didn't speak. Which showed he had at least a few brains.

"The ambush was well set," Listen said. "Partisans always fight that way, strike and flee. It is necessary given their lack of training and discipline."

"We must pin them down," Ethniu said.

"And we have," Listen replied. "They are trapped inside their own defenses. My people and the Huntsmen press them from the north and have circled behind them in the west. They will not have another opportunity to inflict such damage. We only have to hold steady and finish pushing the blade home."

"Your recommendation, Captain?"

"Destroy their fortifications with the Eye," Listen said

promptly. "Assign a cohort to mop them up after. Then turn everything upon Mab."

Ethniu was silent for a time before she said, "Mab is too close. Should I use the Eye upon those fortifications, it will give her a window of opportunity in which to strike."

Ah-*hah*. The superweapon wasn't a wonder weapon. It had some kind of cooldown period. Good to know.

"Bring up the heavy weapons teams and bombard the fortifications," Listen said. "It won't be as decisive, but they're only earthworks."

"Will it be done before the mortals arrive with their mechanical weapons?"

"Difficult to say," Listen said. "You saw who was leading the rabble."

"The Winter Knight," Corb spat.

"He is canny, resourceful, and stubborn," Listen said. "It could be that he wields enough influence over them to keep them in place and fighting for a time, despite the bombardment."

"Stupid Jotnar," Corb muttered. "Dying to mere mortals. Were they here, they could simply stomp the fort flat."

"They died killing the Einherjaren," Listen noted. "Frankly, given what the revenants can do, I regard the trade as one in our favor. And we have a second group of Jotnar in the south. Could they be summoned?"

"Our messengers keep getting swarmed by these thrice-damned Little Folk," Corb spat. "Who knew they were here in such numbers?"

"I did," Listen said in a flat voice. "And my reports

from the various scouting missions mentioned it specifically."

"Mind your tongue, you jumped-up bed boy," the Fomor snarled.

"Enough," Ethniu said in a tone that made me clench up a little. When she spoke again, it was in her usual voice. "Captain Listen, the fortress is yours. Suppress it until such time as Corb and I have destroyed Mab. Once she is no more, I will reduce the fortress."

"We attack!" Corb said, his tone enormously self-satisfied.

"Unwise," Listen said.

"Time flees from us," Ethniu replied. "Risks must be taken. I need someone competent on the fortress."

"What?" Corb said.

"She said she needed someone competent," Listen replied, in a polite, helpful voice.

"Prepare your warbands, King Corb," Ethniu said in a placating tone. "We will destroy Mab together, and your people will have their vengeance upon the Sidhe."

Corb made a sound that would have been more appropriate coming from a teakettle. Then he stalked away, followed by a retinue of Fomor as his personal bodyguards.

"He will kill you in your sleep one night," Ethniu predicted.

"I'll be waiting for him," Listen replied.

"For a mortal, you are uncommonly capable—and insouciant," Ethniu said. "If I did not need you for later, I might kill you myself."

"But you do need me," Listen said calmly. "And you haven't got anyone else as good as me."

"I find it pleasant to have the service of someone who can think," the Titan replied. "Yet you are mortal. One is much like another."

"How many starborn are there wandering about, this close to the endga—" Listen's voice broke off abruptly. "Sergeant, I want a light on that mound of rubble, right now."

The world blurred as Grimalkin moved, and gunfire roared painfully loud and near—

Gunfire crackled out in the haze somewhere, and I staggered and nearly fell as I found myself back in my own body fully once more.

Grimalkin? I thought.

Not now, Knight, came the pained and furious reply.

Muh? I thought, experimentally.

I heard, my Knight, came Mab's voice, throbbing in the vaults of my mind. *It would be ideal were you in position behind Ethniu when the time comes.*

I ground my teeth. *You don't ask for much, do you?*

Whinging does not become the Winter Knight, Mab said.

Listen and his people will wipe my volunteers out if I leave them.

Mab's mental hiss was painful. *They will also die if Ethniu is not defeated, along with your city. There is no time for arguments. Choose.*

Dammit.

Mab's logic was cold and inhuman.

And it wasn't wrong.

"Get me Sanya," I snarled.

The Russian showed up a minute later.

"Professionals are coming," I said. "Bad guys."

Sanya couldn't really blanch very well, but I saw him swallow. *"Bozhe moi."*

"Good news is, they're pretty conventional," I said. "Bad news is that it's Listen running them. He's smart. Smart enough to have been running various operations for the Fomor in Chicago for freaking years, as a front for scouting the place out for tonight."

Sanya lowered his voice. "I cannot hold this place with these people. Not for long."

"Hopefully, you won't have to," I said. "You don't need to fight so much as survive for a little wh—"

My head snapped back as a sledgehammer swung by someone on a speeding train hit me right in the middle of my forehead. I staggered.

One of my volunteers fell from his position. Pretty much all that was left of his head was his mouth and jaw.

"Down!" Sanya screamed. "Heads down!"

Then we heard a number of hollow booms. And, a second later, a chorus of whistling sounds.

"Mortars," Sanya snarled. "Incoming! Everyone down!"

"Butters!" I shouted.

I took off at a sprint and felt Butters on my heels. The little guy could really move. The training he'd been doing with the Carpenters was serving him well tonight.

I whipped up as much of a veil as I could around us as we ran. It wasn't going to keep anyone from seeing that something was moving, but as long as we *kept* moving, it should make it a lot harder to shoot us.

We dashed out of the pavilion as the mortar shells began to fall among the fortifications, and my people began to scream and die behind us.

Chapter

Twenty-seven

The svartalves had built the earthworks around the pavilion proper, the auditorium and concert hall. The Great Lawn had been stripped down to bare earth and Styrofoam packing in the process. Running across the broken earth was easy enough, except for all the bullets, and since the sidewalks around it had been made to be even with the lawn at its usual level, it meant that we had to hop up about three and a half feet onto the sidewalks to get back up to the park's "ground level."

We got lucky with the bullets, or at least we didn't get unlucky. The shimmering field of the veil around us made us look like blurs in the air, maybe a little bit more obvious than a Predator. Between the veil and the pall of smoke and dust, trying to actually aim at any specific point on our bodies was hopeless, and the dimly seen enemy was mainly focused on dropping mortar shells on the earthworks. They couldn't get enough guns pointed at us to simply fill the air with lead, not in the few seconds we were in the open and running, though the weight of enemy fire increased with every step.

I hit the ground with my staff and vaulted up to the ground level of the park, sliding on concrete for a few yards before springing up and continuing. Butters just jumped, hit the edge of the sidewalk at about belt level, and scrambled up with the agility of someone with a higher power-to-mass ratio than his build would suggest.

We sprinted forward, through the trees and onto the concrete in the square around the Bean.

"Friendlies!" I shouted into the haze, as the vague forms of the Winter cohort resolved themselves into the shapes of the ranks of armored Sidhe.

The entire formation snapped into battle posture, shields rising, knees bending, weapons lifted, when we appeared, and it did not relax from it as we approached. I dropped the veil as we did, and slowed my pace to a swift walk as I reached the ranks and plunged through, sword tips just barely moving out of my way.

"Stay close and keep mum," I muttered to Butters over my shoulder. "Especially with Mab. Don't get caught making anything that could sound like a promise. Don't accept anything that could be construed as a gift."

"That include advice?" Butters asked.

I glowered at him. He grinned at me—and then his face suddenly went slack as we emerged from the troops and he faced the Queen of Air and Darkness on her Winter unicorn.

"Well done, my Knight," Mab said to me without preamble. "You wounded them enough to plant the seeds of doubt."

Mortar shells continued to fall on the pavilion. Occasionally, small bits of dirt and debris would plunge down from overhead, pinging off Sidhe armor or clattering against the concrete. My skin felt as if someone had slapped it with a large grid of barbed wire and then dragged it several inches. The earthen fortress was down to six hundred and twenty-two defenders, with more than two hundred of them wounded, and I could feel each and every scratch. I buried the sensation behind a wall of pure mental discipline, hard-earned over my entire lifetime.

But I was feeling grouchy. I assure you.

"Oh good, doubt seeds," I said. "If we water them and wait and eat all our vegetables, maybe they'll grow into doubt saplings."

"Do not be ridiculous," Mab said. Her lips peeled slowly back from her teeth. "They grow into fear."

"Which makes them angry," I said. "Fear always becomes anger."

"Precisely," Mab said. "An angry foe is predictable. Easily manipulated."

"Well, you've manipulated Corb and Ethniu into coming right at you," I said.

A chorus of chirruping clicks erupted from the far side of the park and began to grow steadily louder.

Mab cast a gaze across the field that on most females would have been reserved for their lovers. "Yes. Corb will whip his people into a frenzy. They will charge us, howling for blood, blind to anything but our deaths."

I eyed her and said, "Oh. Good."

Mab glanced at me and said, "Do not be afraid of Corb, my Knight. He and his were destined to be sacrificed from the moment Ethniu conceived of this plan."

"I know the Sidhe are dangerous," I said. "But there's not enough of them. Not for what is coming at us."

The clicking grew louder.

The Queen of Air and Darkness cast back her head, her eyes going wild, her smile widening to inhuman proportions. "The numbers stand at one Mab to none. That advantage shall be sufficient."

Suddenly I was aware of the creatures of Winter beneath my command, racing to join us. The temperature around us abruptly plummeted. White winter frost began to crackle across the face of the Bean, and Mab shuddered and arched her back, her eyes closing, as the breath of Winter itself gathered around us. White mist began to thicken the grey haze of the city. The air suddenly became close, intimate, as the cloud of cold vapor enveloped the cohort.

The faemetal weapons of the Sidhe began to creak and moan as deathly frost formed upon them

And I realized that I could suddenly see no farther than maybe fifteen feet, tops.

"We won't be able to see them coming," I said in a low voice.

"Irrelevant," Mab replied.

In the shadows of the Bean behind us gathered the malks and Black Dogs, the rake and the ogre, the gnomes and double dozens of the viciously mischievous Little Folk of Winter.

Before us, the Sidhe abruptly began to chant and sing, gesturing with their hands as they did. Flickers of light glittered over the cohort in a dome. Shapes and sigils, runes and formulae, crackled briefly in the air, as two hundred sorcerers gathered their power from the hyperenergetic air.

What the hell? I held up my staff, opening the channels to the energy storage structures inside, and drew that energy down into it. The task normally took an hour of intense concentration and exhausting effort, when I had to provide the energy for the staff myself. With the air gone mad with power, the staff charged in seconds, which should not have been possible, not without the excess energy overflowing into waste heat and burning the thing to a crisp.

Instead, it simply let out a low hum, the runes carved into glowing green-gold, and the faint, excellent scent of scorched wood edged the night.

Mab surveyed her troops, evidently waiting as the various shields and wards and charms and abjurations were assembled from mystic energy. She glanced aside and said, "This is the new Knight of the Sword?"

"Sir Waldo," I said, lifting a hand to Butters down at belt level, in warning. "He's been my ally many times."

"All grown up," Mab noted, in the voice of someone looking at a cow and seeing only steaks. "Welcome, Sir Knight."

Waldo cleared his throat, bowed slightly at the waist, and said, "My pleasure, ma'am."

"Your new Sword," she said, "has shed its mortal limits. Now it harms only the wicked."

My arm throbbed.

The clicking grew steadily louder.

The weapons of the Sidhe groaned with cold and bloodlust.

"The Sword defends the defenseless, ma'am," Butters said. "As it always has."

The chanting of the Sidhe rose to a swift, fevered climax. Flickering sparks began to dance over their weapons and armor, dazzling as a pool of paparazzi's cameras, in every hue imaginable and some that I couldn't remember ever seeing before. It was the opposite of a veil—an enchantment that forced you to notice it, an irritating distraction that simply would not cease being a nuisance.

Mab lifted her head in time with the fevered chanting of the Sidhe and let out a scream that somehow blended perfectly with the song.

The sound of that scream pulsed through me like the most powerful music I'd ever experienced, like the hardest rush of adrenaline I'd ever felt.

I couldn't help it. I drew in a breath and answered the scream with one of my own. As did the Sidhe. Even Butters lifted his voice in a furious shriek.

And then, without conscious command, we were moving, the Sidhe cohort darting forward with unnatural fury and grace. That power that carried them forward wrapped around me, drawing my feet with more surety and dexterity and power than I could have managed alone, and Butters kept pace despite his diminutive stature.

We moved forward together, as lightly as any troupe of dancers, and as we did the formation changed as smoothly as if choreographed. Mab, upon her dark steed, surged forward, through the ranks of armored Sidhe, until she was at the head of the formation, with *me* behind her and to her left, Butters opposite me, and the Sidhe and creatures of Winter dropping into an arrow-shaped formation behind us. Mab's hand fell to her saddle and drew forth a long, jagged blade of what looked like ancient glacier-blue ice. She raised the sword as icy vapor billowed around us, the whole cloud flashing and flickering with faelight like a thunderstorm.

Like I said. When Mab decides it's time to do business, she doesn't just sit around waiting for things to happen.

And that's how maybe two hundred and fifty fae charged five *thousand* Fomor at the Battle of the Bean.

We moved together, all but blinded by mist and vapor, following Mab's will, and suddenly the enemy was there in front of us, hundreds of twisted abominations armed with clubs and rocks and claws and teeth.

Mab howled as the dark unicorn lowered his head and plunged straight down the enemy's throats.

Mab struck left and right with her sword, flickering cuts as swift and light as the beating of a hummingbird's wing. She struck at arms, shoulders, faces, leaving nothing but little incisions the depth of a fingernail's width in soft spaces of flesh—but covering a space as big as my spread hand around the wound with vicious, bitterly cold Winter frost.

There was barely any time to notice anything but the flying limbs, weapons, and furious faces of the Fomor abominations. Where Mab rode on her unicorn, a nexus of terror followed. Those abominations closest to her recoiled and were struck with bitter wounds, even as they blocked their allies from getting close enough to strike Mab. This left her riding forward into a vacuum of space that could never quite close around her—and which left those of us running in her wake an opening to exploit.

Butters and I plunged into that limited space of confusion around Mab. Butters brought *Fidelacchius* to life and began striking, sending the Fomor's hideous troops reeling in reaction. On my side of things, I began laying about me with my staff, each blow dispensing a thunderclap of kinetic energy and sending my target flying a good ten feet in the direction of the blow. I simply left the energy channels in the tool open, drawing in from the power-laden air on a continuous basis as I hammered wider the opening Mab had created.

Behind me came the Sidhe, their weapons shrieking and wailing as the cold, cold faemetal sank into flesh and tasted hot blood, and vapor boiled away from the wounds the supernatural weapons inflicted, their bloodied lengths bubbling as new-drawn blood hissed into plumes of vapor. The light of the Sidhe's armor and weapons and eyes was terrible in the vision of the Fomor's slave-soldiers, and the abominations howled and tried to shield their eyes from the painful hues.

We plunged entirely through the enemy's front line in seconds, taking them completely off guard in the thickened haze—and I almost didn't see what had *really* just happened.

Behind me, I could see one of the abominations, reeling back from the surprise attack from Mab's flying wedge, clutch at a long, shallow, frost-covered wound in its arm, probably Mab's work, and suddenly begin to scream.

The creature clutched at its wounded arm, holding it straight up, rigid, as if it had been holding a mannequin's arm.

I saw the skin along the edges of the wound writhe and suddenly turn black.

And that black began to spread.

The abomination screamed in piteous terror for several seconds, as the black color from the edges of its frostbitten wound raced throughout its body—bringing a terrible stillness in its wake. By the time the black had wrapped around the abomination's torso, the screaming had stopped.

It died screaming.

And a second later, all that was left was an agonized-looking statue of dark stone.

I heard more, even more painful screams behind us, and realized that the weapons of the Sidhe had apparently carried the same curse. We had cut a swath through the enemy, and those we had wounded had . . . simply turned to dark, rough, sandy-textured stone.

And it had, as a consequence, split the group of abominations into two much smaller groups of abominations, separated by a wall of statues.

Without hesitation, Mab wheeled on the nearest group, screamed again, and led the charge through it, her scream carrying me, Butters, and the Sidhe warriors forward, through another round of desperate nightmare time. And once that group had been split, whatever will drove them could no longer keep them on the field. The abominations began to flee, screaming, vanishing into the Winter mist around us.

The Sidhe cut them down without mercy. Lethal blows were kinder: They left nothing but a dead horror upon the ground. Mere wounds began to blacken and petrify, carrying those struck to an agonizing final ending.

Die swiftly or die slowly. That was all the compassion Winter was willing to show.

Mab whirled on her steed the moment the enemy broke, and lifted a hand. As she did, a cold wind descended upon Chicago from the north, the scent of it dry and sharp like at the beginning of proper autumn. It howled across the park, and the billowing vapors of mist and frost fled before it, sweeping the field clean of dust and smoke and mist, leaving the park suddenly clearly visible.

And I saw what Mab had *really* been up to.

As I watched, about fifty yards away, Mab led a cohort of Sidhe into a formation of octokongs, their weird arquebus weapons bellowing to little effect. A dozen yards beyond that, Mab led a cohort of Sidhe into a formation of dog-beasts and their handlers. Beyond them, maybe four or five more Mabs were hammering their way through several formations of those heavily armored ape-things.

And behind us, more Mabs were doing the same thing. The enemy screamed and fought. From one side of the battlefield, sorcery suddenly struck, with a round like a thunderbolt and a spreading cloud of bilious green smoke that . . . just dissolved a pair of hapless octokongs that got in the way.

Glamour.

All the other Mabs, all the other cohorts of Sidhe, all the casualties inflicted upon the enemy by them—they were illusion. Figments of Mab's imagination, given life by all the energy in the air.

I stared in awe. Producing an illusion is, honestly, a task that might be slightly more difficult, magically speaking, than actually creating the illusory effect for real. Every detail, every wrinkle in fabric, every stray hair, every blade of grass that bent beneath an illusory boot, every footfall, every exhalation, every faint scent—they all had to be held and wielded by the conscious thoughts of the source of the illusion.

Imagine one person running two thousand puppets at once.

Mab was doing that in the *back* of her mind, while hacking at the enemy with her frozen sword. She took stock of the battle and lowered her hand, and mist and haze once again fell like a curtain as the cold wind ceased.

Outnumbered dozens to one, Mab had pitted the sheer power of her mind against a supernatural legion—and she was winning.

As long as the enemy couldn't find and target Mab herself among all the duplicates, we weren't fighting an army: We were holding a narrow pass where only a single unit of the foe could see us in the haze and engage us at the same time. Chaos and confusion and terror filled the minds of her enemies, and from them she built a fortress where their numbers counted for nothing.

If left unchecked, Mab and her killers could destroy the entire enemy legion, one unit at a time.

She let out another cry and the Winter unicorn leapt lightly into the haze, the rest of us following her like a comet's tail. She hit a second group of abominations, and if they hadn't been monsters, there to kill us, I would have felt sorry for the things. We dispatched that band, and then a third before the enemy gathered enough wits about them to respond.

A bolt of purple lightning came down out of the haze like the hammer of God and struck Mab squarely.

There was a flare of light so intense that I staggered and

fell, dropping to a knee and barely staggering up again before the Sidhe warriors behind me trampled me to death. There's a reason *he fell* became synonymous for *he died*. Losing your feet on a battlefield is an all-but-certain death sentence.

Blinking my eyes against the dazzling leftover image of the lightning bolt, I saw Mab's slender body arch into a bow, curling around the spot where the lightning had struck her, her long, thin-fingered hands clenched around a ball of white-hot light, the edges of her nails blackening and smoking with the heat. Then, with a banshee wail of pure, terrifying scorn, she straightened again and sent the bolt of lightning raging ahead of the unicorn, plowing an even wider and more fearfully murderous path through the enemy ranks, blasting a burial deep furrow in the earth as she went.

Hell's bells.

I gave myself a stern reminder not to piss her off.

We plunged out of the wreckage of the third unit of abominations, and Mab, her face splattered with deep purple-maroon blood, let out a scornful snarl. "Corb should have shown his hand by now, the coward."

"Fine by me," I panted. There is no more difficult cardio than fighting, let me tell you. "The longer he lets us fight small groups one at a time, the happier I am."

"That part of the dance is done," Mab said, her eyes searching the haze. "These piteous lifespawn are helpless to us. But his other troops carry the Bane."

The Bane, by which she meant iron. For reasons no one I know of has ever figured out, the Fae—and the Sidhe in particular—were vulnerable to the touch of iron and many of its alloys. It burned and sickened them, simultaneously acting as a branding iron and radioactive uranium. I knew the faemetal armor they wore would offer them some protection from the wounds—but the mere presence of too much of the stuff in their proximity would grind away at their endurance and mental cohesion. The Sidhe might be able to fight it for a while—but long-term, it was a losing proposition.

Don't get too worked up about the phrase *cold iron*. Sometimes people insist that it means cold-forged iron. It doesn't. The phrase is poetic metaphor, not instructions for building a chemical model. Sufficient iron content is what does the trick.

If I was fighting the Sidhe, I'd want dump trucks of the stuff. And also the dump trucks. Plus any machines and tools that had been used to load said trucks. Hardly a shock, then, that Corb had so equipped his troops.

Mab had just wheeled in preparation to charge again when there was a deep, ugly note in the air, almost below the range of my hearing, the kind of sound that you hear during disaster movies that have a lot of buildings collapsing, and maybe during earthquakes.

At the same time, my wizard's senses were assaulted by a serious, heavy-duty pulse of earth magic.

There wasn't even time to shout a warning. I called upon the Winter mantle for strength and speed and dove at Mab. The unicorn whirled to try to keep her away from me at the last second but wasn't quite quick enough, and its movement was impeded by several abomination statues.

I was airborne when I saw the attack coming—jagged

spears of metal, made from what looked like rebar scavenged from the wreckage of demolished buildings.

There wasn't one spear.

There weren't a dozen.

There were *hundreds*.

If the Winter unicorn had not reared to protect Mab, I figure I'd have died right there. Instead, the creature's body intercepted maybe a dozen of the spears. I had leapt so that my back and the spell-armored duster that covered it would be between the spears and the Winter Queen.

I hit Mab and carried her off the back of the doomed unicorn.

Two spears hit me. One of them in the small of my back, and one of them directly in the center of my right butt cheek. The damned things were heavy enough to carry considerable force, and while my duster stopped their jagged ends from spearing right through me, it couldn't do nearly as much for the pain of the impact, and half of my body vanished beneath a cloud of tactile white noise as the Winter mantle masked the pain.

I came down on top of Mab and sudden, hot, scarlet blood sprayed against me.

I lifted myself off her rag-doll-limp body, even as I felt another powerful wave of earth magic building.

The Queen of Air and Darkness stared up at me with wide, glassy, grass green eyes.

Three feet of bloodied cold iron stood clear from the center of her torn, spraying throat.

"Butters!" I screamed.

I grabbed Mab by the nearest handle, her hair, and dragged her into the shelter offered by the body of the screaming unicorn thrashing weakly on the ground, just as another tsunami of metal spears flew our way.

I fell over her as much as I could and heard the spears thwacking into the unicorn, which ceased its thrashing and screaming, and into the earth all around us.

The haze was suddenly burned away in a circle around us as the Sword of Faith sprang to life, its fire singing in angry angelic chords. Butters advanced, whirling the Sword rondello style, slashing spears out of the air with shrieks of protesting metal.

He reached my side, threw himself down behind the dead unicorn, and took one look at Mab.

"Jesus," he blurted. "Again?"

"Shut up and get it out of her neck," I said.

"Harry, there's no point."

Mab's green eyes tracked to Butters and narrowed.

"She's immortal, dummy," I snapped. "Get the rebar out of her and she'll be fine."

A dank, fetid wind that smelled of swamps and decomposition began to blow from the east. The haze around us began to clear.

"Dammit," I snarled. "Don't get cute with it. Just rip it out of her neck."

"I could use a little help here."

I checked behind us. I was staring at a bamboo forest of cold steel, rebar standing sharply up from the ground. Twenty or thirty of the Sidhe had been killed outright. The rest were nowhere to be seen. I couldn't even feel the Winter forces under my command through the banner. The forest of steel had cut me off from them.

More whistles and explosions came from the fortress.

We were taking heavy casualties, and I *could* feel the mortals who had followed me. We were down to five hundred and eleven men and women, all of them terrified, their heads down, praying for survival.

And I could see long, lanky shapes approaching through the haze, flickering bubbles of sorcery glowing around them.

A dozen Fomor sorcerers were walking straight toward us.

"I've got to talk to some people about some things," I said. "You're on your own, man. Hurry."

Chapter
Twenty-eight

Magical duels are about two things: anticipation and imagination. When you're up against someone who literally wields the leftover power of Creation itself, they can bring forth damned near anything they can imagine with which to attack you. If you haven't considered their attack and imagined a way to counter it, you lose. It's that simple.

Fully a quarter of my training with my safely dead mentor, Justin DuMorne, had been in magical duels. The man had been grooming me to be his attack dog, and he played hardball. When it came to trading magical punches, I knew what I was doing. Anyone on the level of the Senior Council could probably hand me my ass, but they'd know they'd been in a fight, even so.

One-on-one, I was a beast.

Twelve-on-one, *nobody* is a beast.

I checked on Butters. He had extended the blade of *Fidelacchius* again, this time only a few inches, and was lifting Mab by her head. The head of the length of rebar had been shaped into a hooked point, like a harpoon, only duller. Had he tried to pull it out, he would have had to rip most of Mab's neck open along with it, and I can't imagine that would have been good for her combat effectiveness, immortal or not. Instead, he sliced it away as easily as a seamstress snips a thread, before beginning to lower Mab's head again.

I let myself look concerned, drew in a breath and my power, and waited.

The Fomor Sorcerers' Club chose to attack me when I looked distracted. I mean, who wouldn't, but especially these jerks.

Predictable.

They lobbed those bilious green spheres of acid at me.

I spun toward them, my hand lifted, fingers spread, and pulled out an old one. I sent forth my power in the same moment that I drew on the silent gale of magic in the air, shouting, *"Ventas servitas!"*

On an ordinary night, the gale that my spell conjured would have been able to toss furniture around a room.

Tonight, I could have tossed furniture *trucks.*

The gale caught the spheres in midair, hurtling them back toward their origins on a nearly flat trajectory. The FSC was pretty good. Of the dozen orbs, eleven of their creators were quick enough to unravel the spell that held the acid in its sphere, which the furious gale promptly atomized and dispersed over an area too large to remain dangerous.

That twelfth, guy, though. Maybe he was somebody's nephew, because he didn't figure out that his own spell was coming back at him until it broke on his chin.

As endings went that night, his didn't make the top ten. But on any other night, I'd have been impressed at the results. The acid was considerably more destructive to flesh than it had been to steel and concrete. It even turned his square yellow teeth into slurry.

I dropped the wind spell, struck a cheesy karate pose, and said, "Waaaaaah!" in the style of Bruce Lee. "Which one of you has brought me my nunchucks?"

My humor is wasted, *wasted* upon most of the super-natural community. I mean, my God. They really need to get out into the world more. For instance, the FSC hesitated and glanced at one another, as if to ask if anyone had understood me. Or, hell, maybe they were so ignorant of the mighty Bruce Lee that they didn't even get that it was a joke and were looking for some kind of traitor among themselves.

In that time, I glanced back at Butters, who was tugging on the other end of the rebar now and seemed to be having little luck. Mab's flesh had engulfed the rebar tightly enough to form a vacuum seal, and Butters was having a hell of a time getting it out.

"Boot to the head!" I shouted at Butters.

He blinked, and said, "Nah, nah?"

"Augh, you nerd!"

The FSC had decided to stop worrying about whatever I'd had to say, meanwhile. They turned their focus on me again, and I felt them gathering power to strike—and they wouldn't go with the same attack a second time.

I shook out my shield bracelet, sending power coursing into it, building up layers of magical defenses in a half-dome shape in front of me. My shield bracelet went scorching hot almost instantly: Even if I'd had the additional magical fuel from all the power in the air, the tool wasn't designed to handle all the extra juice—but it was my only chance of surviving a strike from all of them.

"Boot to the head!" I shouted again.

"Nah, nah?" Butters sang back tentatively.

"No, dammit!" I screamed. "Boot! Head!" I lifted a foot and waved it.

Butters's eyes widened in sudden comprehension. And then went a bit wider in pure intimidation.

The FSC struck at me with black lightning in staggered bursts. The bolts rained in like a thunderstorm, irregular and savage, spaced maybe half a second apart. I stumbled, fell to a knee, and poured everything I could into the shield, and for a few seconds the world was blinding, deafening fury.

When it passed, my shield bracelet was actually glowing red-hot at the edges, and I could smell my own scorched hair and flesh, even if I didn't feel much of it. (I still felt the burn Butters had given me, though. That one wasn't stopping.) Except for a half circle in front of me, the concrete was scared black for ten feet in every direction—the burn's end was precisely described by the glowing edge of my shield. There was no sound, no sound at all, other than this ringing sensation in my skull.

I looked drunkenly back at Butters.

The little guy stood, put his boot on Mab's forehead, grabbed the rebar with both hands, and strained to tear it out of her neck.

Mab's thin body arched in silent agony.

The rebar began to slide, slowly at first, as Butters

threw his whole weight into it, and then suddenly tore free. Butters went sprawling to one side.

Mab's lips moved, and her voice sounded clearly inside my head, even though I couldn't hear anything else. "Finally."

She rose, just levitated the hell up, stiff as a board, like in the old vampire movies, her hair and battle mail covered in blood, and as she did, she lifted her left hand—and suddenly squeezed it into a fist.

The surge of magic that came out of her was so dense, so intense, that it sent several pieces of stray Styrofoam fill nearby spiraling into the air on what looked like a helical sine wave around her. I looked back at the FSC. The Fomor sorcerer on the left end of the line . . . just sort of . . .

Did you ever squeeze a handful of red Play-Doh?

It was like that.

The Fomor sorcerer hovered suspended, maybe a foot above the sudden large splatter of blood on the ground.

Mab turned her head to the next sorcerer in the row and flicked her wrist.

The remains of the first Fomor went flying at the next sorcerer in the line at maybe five hundred meters per second. The impact was . . . really, really messy. And confusing.

Mab turned to the next Fomor sorcerer, her eyes cold.

The FSC turned out to be smart enough to know when they were outclassed. And they *were* outclassed. Mab's magic had crushed their defenses like empty beer cans. They turned to run, vanishing behind veils as they went.

Mab watched them flee. Then she turned, still cold, and stalked over to Butters.

The little guy popped up to his feet and gave me a beseeching look.

"It would appear that we are in your debt, Sir Doctor Butters," Mab said. Her voice came to me dimly now. It was ragged and rough, though it grew smoother by the word. The wound on her neck was already nothing more than an angry scar, lightening even as I observed it. The tread of Butters's boot stood out in blood on her forehead. "Should we both survive the battle, in need you may call our name. We will answer."

Her hands flashed out and seized Butters's white cloak.

The Knight stiffened. Judging by his hair, he was about two breaths away from panic.

Mab calmly lifted the cloak to the hem and tore off two large squares.

Butters looked at me with wide eyes. I made a "go easy" gesture toward him with one hand and with the other put my forefinger over my lips.

The little guy swallowed and nodded.

Hey, Butters has got way more guts than sense. But he wasn't crazy. Mab offering you a favor was an even scarier concept than Mab herself was, generally.

"Do you find it acceptable repayment?" Mab asked.

Butters gave her a jerky nod, without speaking.

"Excellent. Done." Mab turned to the fallen Winter unicorn and, using the fabric torn from Butters's cloak like potholders, began drawing rebar spears from the creature's broken body. There was nothing tentative about her motions: They were workmanlike, and she removed the impaling steel with superhuman ease. To my shock, the creature started thrashing and screaming again after a few of the lengths of steel came out, and upon the last one being removed, it heaved its way to its feet, shaking its head and trumpeting in outrage.

So the scary horse was immortal, too. Check.

Mab vaulted to the unicorn's back with about as much effort as I used to fall into bed, and said, " 'Ware," before snapping her fingers.

All her blood that had been scattered around, and the unicorn's, too, abruptly went up into heat and light like flash paper. It left my face and part of my neck seared as if by a sunburn. Butters very briefly managed a Human Torch impersonation and whirled on Mab in shock, the skin of his forehead and cheeks and hands as red as if he'd had them soaking in hot water. "What? Why?"

"I warned you," Mab said calmly.

"She can't leave her blood lying around," I said. "Corb and his people use magic. If they get their hands on it, it'd be bad."

Butters frowned. He knew a lot more about how magic worked than most people. He was something of a neophyte at sorcery himself, and could manage a few fundamentals, and I could see him running through the possibilities of someone getting a magical handle on Mab through her blood. "Even her?"

"It is foolish for most to attempt to chain a tigress," Mab said. Her wide eyes swiveled to me. "Yet chains can be forged—and tigresses can be caged."

"Kind of a solid rule, man," I said. "Doesn't matter how big something is. If it bleeds, you can bind it."

Butters surreptitiously examined his own hands, presumably for any leaking cuts.

Mab showed her teeth and said, "Indeed."

The chittering clicks in the haze ahead of us rose to a crescendo and then suddenly stopped.

So did the fire falling on the fortifications.

The night air changed.

It stilled.

Everything went completely silent and heavy. Sounds suddenly became immediate, close things, like on a winter night in falling snow.

The unicorn threw its head back and shook its mane. Mab laid a hand upon the creature's neck and shivered, leaning forward, her eyes brighter than stars.

"Ahhhhh," she said in a slow, sensual exhalation, barely more than a whisper. "Now we come to it."

I swallowed and kept my voice low. "She's here?"

Mab narrowed her eyes, as if peering through the haze. "The Titan and her"—she glanced aside at me—"frog prince."

"How tough is Corb?" I asked.

"I have heard it said that it is not his destiny to perish before the deepest ocean meets the sun."

"Fuck destiny," I said. "Maybe I'll free will his ass. How tough?"

Mab's teeth showed. "He is your better in power, your better in experience, and your better in treachery."

"But I bet he doesn't have as many friends as me," I said.

I held out my fist without looking.

Butters rapped his knuckles against mine without looking, either.

"Mortal wizards," Mab sighed. "Forever meddling in things you do not comprehend."

I dredged up a quote from someone I rarely agreed with about anything. "What's the point of free will, if not to spit in the eye of destiny?"

"How to phrase this so you will understand," Mab said calmly, facing the night. "Ah. Destiny is a . . . stone-cold bitch."

Which, given the source, was really saying something.

"There are always consequences, wizard," Mab continued. "Always a price to pay, to create a new branching of the universe, to bend the course of the great river."

The haze of dust and smoke before us suddenly glared scarlet.

And then, like a curtain, it parted. Just unreeled away from the entirety of Millennium Park, leaving the air clear and clean, so that we could see plainly what was going on.

"Oh," Butters breathed. "Oh crap."

I swallowed and didn't say anything.

I could see the fortifications clearly. One of the walls had slumped inward rather badly, so that I could see the actual amphitheater stage. I carefully allowed input from the banner, and it made my entire body ache with empathy at the sheer number of wounds my people had sustained. Only three hundred and ninety-eight of the volunteers were still alive. Of eleven hundred and eighty-seven, barely a third remained. Most of them were wounded. All of them were terrified.

Behind us, the forest of rebar was still blocking our

retreat in a half circle maybe forty yards across. Beyond that seemed to be nothing more than an empty park. The Sidhe cohort had deserted the field, and I could sense the Winter creatures through the banner, staying out of sight, wary of showing themselves in the now-cleared air.

There were some wounded in sight, of both sides, struggling weakly on the field where they'd fallen.

But for all practical purposes, the only ones still standing were me, Butters, and Mab on her nightmare unicorn.

Four of us.

And across the field from us stood the enemy.

Even counting the casualties Mab and her cohort had inflicted, we were outnumbered maybe twelve hundred to one, and that was if you included the unicorn. And even as I watched, the enemy cheated *again*. Veils shimmered out of existence, revealing more warbands gathered around their banners, mostly of those heavily armored ape-looking things. We'd thought the enemy had come with about seven thousand bad guys. It looked like they'd managed to conceal another three or four thousand of their hardened troops from us.

I didn't know the specific numbers in the moment. That came later. I just knew that they'd added a couple of hundred yards' worth of ugly to the block of bad guys facing us.

"Wow," Butters said quietly. His voice was flattened, numbed. "Sure are a lot of them."

"It only looks like that because they're all in the same place, standing close together," I said.

Butters eyed me. "Yeah. That's probably it."

All that fighting hadn't been enough.

It hadn't been anything like enough.

In the center of the enemy line stood the Titan.

Even across a battlefield, Ethniu's sheer presence drew the eye with a terrible fascination. The ruddy light from the haze that yet surrounded everything that wasn't the park gleamed from her armored flesh. She had shed everything that was not made of Titanic bronze, and her form was perfection of beauty, but for the smoldering glare of the Eye. Her presence was a kind of weight on my mind, a gravity that strained space around it and could not be ignored. Somehow, even from a hundred yards away, I could see the loveliness of her features clearly, too magnetic to ignore. She was a creature of sorrow turned to such rage that her beauty had become a knife that stabbed at the eyes of any who looked upon it.

To look upon her was to look upon an older, more savage universe, a place where Titans strode the formless night and crushed mortal insects beneath their feet—to see a place so brutal and terrifying that even in our legends, humanity had chosen not to remember.

Her hatred seethed through the smoldering glare of the Eye, in the light of fires of destruction she had brought to my city, a power far older and deeper and more deadly than I had yet known. Beside that power, the massed ranks of the Fomor around her seemed as frail and as transient as fleeting shadows.

I tore my eyes away.

Butters was staring at Ethniu, too. He gripped the empty hilt of *Fidelacchius* in both hands, white-knuckled.

I nudged him and he jerked his chin toward me, his face pale.

"Army doesn't seem nearly so scary now, does it?" I said.

He stared at me for a second. Then his lips lifted in an awful, sick-looking smile, and he exhaled several unsteady breaths that were laughter's closest double in that moment. "Heh. Heh, heh, heh. Heh-heh."

Moving at exactly the same time, Ethniu and Mab stepped forward.

"Stay behind me," Mab murmured as the unicorn's deadly presence brushed between Butters and me and took position between us and Ethniu. "Be ready."

I knew precisely how scary Mab was.

I gotta say, it felt pretty awesome to watch that creepy unicorn plant its feet as if it intended to hold its ground before an onrushing train, bracing between that threat and us. Mab lifted her chin, faced Ethniu, and raised her slim pale hand.

Her voice snapped out over the ground, sharp and threatening, like sudden crackling sounds from the face of a glacier. "Hold, crone. You will come no farther."

Ethniu faced that statement in silence and stillness for a moment.

Then she simply smiled and strode a step closer.

The two monsters faced each other for an endless beat, before Ethniu's voice throbbed through the air, vibrating painfully through my bones, making my teeth buzz unpleasantly.

"You began a mewling mortal," Ethniu replied. Her

voice was as loud inside my head as outside, infused with sheer undeniable power. When that voice spoke, reality itself would bow to suit it. "You will end the same way. Powerful as you are, you come of a younger world. A weaker world."

"A world that left you behind," Mab said, mockery ringing in defiance of the power before her.

Ethniu took a further step forward, the Eye glaring brighter, now cowling her head in scarlet light. "Treacherous little witch. The one who would not bow to my father. You *will* bow to me or face the Eye."

Mab pulled a play from my book.

She threw back her head and laughed.

It was a silvery sound, one that somehow shattered the stillness and closeness of the night. Scorn rang in that laughter, and genuine amusement—the cold, alien amusement of a spider. The laughter made the Fomor troops suddenly clutch at their heads. Their lines wavered as the heavily armored troops dropped their weapons and tried to wrap their long arms around their helmeted skulls.

"You do not know me very well," Mab said, that ear-shredding laughter still lurking in her voice, "do you?"

Ethniu rolled another threatening pace forward. "Your pathetic alliance has abandoned you or waits for death. Your bodyguard is reduced to a pair of beasts. And the mortals will arrive only in time to mourn their dead."

Butters gasped at the force in that voice and staggered a step to one side. Blood had begun to trickle from one of his nostrils. I grabbed his shoulder and pulled him a little more into the shelter of Mab and the unicorn's shadow.

"Harry," he whispered raggedly. "What the hell are we doing standing here? We should not *be* here."

I felt exactly the same way. These were powers older than the modern world of Chicago, beings that had seen years pass beyond the imagining of mere mortals, borne witness to events of myth and legend with their own eyes. To them, this night had simply been a skirmish, not a major metropolitan-scale apocalypse. Tens of thousands of people had died already this evening. Hundreds of thousands more might follow.

And my *daughter* was somewhere behind me.

The fear and rage I'd been keeping safely bottled all evening, all centered around that one little figure, probably sleeping in the safe room at Michael's house, flickered with the most infinitesimal of sparks. That spark found ample fuel and began to burn like a tiny star inside me.

Maggie.

This bitch was *not* going to hurt my little girl.

And with that flicker of knowledge, the kindling of will inside me, the knife at my hip throbbed with a slow, steady, quiet pulse.

It had a heartbeat.

"Steady," I growled. "We're right where we're supposed to be."

Ethniu began striding forward, her giant form taking steps that would have made mine look like a toddler's. "Yield!" she bellowed, and the force of it sent the skirt of Mab's battle-mail dress flying backwards along with the unicorn's unreasonably silken mane and tail, and Mab's bloody starlit hair. "Bow!"

The force of will that condensed on Mab in that word was so dense that I thought it was going to break something. Like maybe the universe. It was a sphere of pure psychic pressure so intense that I knew that if it had been directed at me, it would have compressed my mind into something too dense and inert to function, like a tiny diamond formed from crushed coal.

I'm what you might call oppositionally defiant to authoritarian figures. Someone who doesn't always do as he's told. Maybe even a little bit of a troublemaker.

That will would have crushed mine, flat.

Period.

It wasn't a question of weakness or strength. This was simply power orders of magnitude beyond my ability to contest. The force of that will wasn't even directed at me, and it was everything I could do not to fall to my knees and beg for forgiveness in the face of that terrible rage.

Butters had an excellently ordered mind, but he hadn't had the training I had in mental defenses. He let out a sob of utter despair and would have fallen if I hadn't had his shoulder. I dropped to a knee with him, steadying him as he swayed, his entire body trembling violently.

Except for one hand. It stayed steady on the Sword.

I do not know what power she had won, what knowledge she had gained, what experience she had suffered, or what sacrifices she had made that enabled Mab to defy the absolute force of the Titan's will.

But though her shoulders bowed as if under enormous weight, though the Winter unicorn staggered beneath her, Mab was Mab. She steadied the beast, and her expression locked into a cold, steady mask. She drew in a breath, barely visible as a blur in the air compressed by the Titan's will, and said, simply, "No."

The word rang out in pure silvery truth, her breath condensed into a Wintry plume.

Ethniu's will recoiled, shattering like a sphere of immaterial glass.

The Titan roared her fury.

And with a shriek of power meant to unmake the world, Ethniu turned the Eye upon Mab.

Chapter

Twenty-nine

I felt it in my guts and in my soul when the Eye struck Mab.

She sat ramrod straight on the dark unicorn. Even as Ethniu screamed, Mab lifted her left hand, slim and pale, fingers spread evenly in a defensive gesture. Frost gathered upon her, upon the flanks of the unicorn, crusted the ground all around her, even as the horrible power of the Eye washed over Mab.

The sound alone, as those two sources of power met, was enough to drive a strong mind mad. I couldn't have told you what it sounded like, specifically. It was too huge a noise for that. I can tell you that I started screaming out in pure reflexive protest against that sound, and that my voice was lost in the din. The Winter unicorn reared, trumpeting its defiance, and the dark saber spiraling from its forehead almost seemed to drink in a portion of that fury, while Mab flawlessly adjusted her balance upon its back. The concrete beneath her buckled and shattered into sand. Fire and lightning and wind whirled in a cyclone centered upon her. Bits of her hair, blown wildly by the wind, blackened and disintegrated. The fine mail covering her body was riven by the flood of energy, turning from bright mail to the dark of verdigris, and then tearing as individual rings changed from metal to some kind of blackened residue, leaving smudges of soot over pale skin.

Butters and I were like two men before a flood taking desperate shelter behind a stone.

On pure instinct, I had gathered my shield around us in a half dome that enveloped us entirely. The energy wasn't even being directed at me—I was just trying to stop some of the random splatter that got past Mab and came in our direction.

Again, I was operating out of my weight class. The mere backwash from the Eye was almost more than I could handle. My shield bracelet heated again, and I knew I was going to have a fresh band of burn scars to go along with the old burns on the hand itself. The effort I put forward to protect us would have killed me on another night. Tonight, the power in the air made it simple, and a dozen layers of my best shielding took the brunt of the wild expenditure of energy without faltering.

I could *feel* the power of the Eye as it touched my shield, feel the pure, raw, undiluted *hate* that drove whoever wielded it. This hate wasn't any mere mortal emotion. This was hate of the original vintage, hate as old as the universe itself, hate as hard and sharp and cold as steel, hate as hot as the fires of Hell, hate so vital, so vicious, so vitriolic, that it surpassed the understanding of my merely mortal mind.

Ethniu hated me. Me, personally, though she did not know me. The Titan hated me, hated me on a level I could not begin to understand. That I walked the earth and drew breath was enough to earn her everlasting fury.

But that was just a shadow of what she felt toward *Mab*.

That was *personal*.

Mab, slender and beautiful and deadly on her black unicorn, defying the power of the Eye as it blasted away bits of her hair, as it rent and rendered her armor. Her will manifested around her as cold, pure light, a sphere of diamond radiance that dispersed the most vicious efforts of the Eye, sent power spilling out from her and around her, like a fast-flowing river crashing into an obdurate stone. In that withering light and fury, she was a being of distilled intellect and will, pure determination and cold defiance. In that fury, she was a shadow, an outline, dark and terrible and undeniable, standing against the tide unmoving.

In that moment, I saw with my own eyes why she was called the Queen of Air and Darkness.

And, somehow, she did it. She stopped the Eye. She stood before that undeniable power and was not moved.

The red glare of the Eye faded.

For a long moment, Mab was still, her body clad only in remnants of her mail, in blackened residue and scarlet streaks and burns, her left hand raised and extended in defiance. Smoke rose from her.

Then she fell, suddenly boneless, from the unicorn's back, collapsing to the ground as if too weak to remain upright.

Ethniu stared forward for a moment before lifting her face to the sky and crying out in vicious, spiteful triumph. She raised her hands and threw them forward, and like puppets directed by her will, the entire Fomor legion groaned and began to pace forward in stomping unison, gathering momentum like a single massive beast.

The silence gave way before the sound of boots tromping upon the ground. Like a tide, the Fomor advanced across the field, eerie signal clicks coming before them like rain before a truly terrible storm. They crossed the open field and there was nothing further to stop them.

And, I realized, nothing to shelter them.

They had marched into the open field.

And in the vaults of my mind, Mab's voice rang out in sudden exultation. *NOW, LADY MOLLY.*

From the north, a fresh, chill zephyr swirled down through the city and into the park. Somewhere along the shoreline of Lake Michigan, a gull cried out in sudden excitement.

And music began to play.

At first it was just a few electric guitar notes, almost at random, bouncing among the buildings and echoing over the haze-covered city. Then I recognized the song.

The opening notes of the Guns N' Roses hit "Welcome to the Jungle" began to echo from the buildings behind us, Slash's guitar sending those tones bouncing around the concrete and towers, somehow resonating with the steel and stone of the streets and buildings of the city. Chicago herself became the speaker, music ringing off every surface, setting the ground to quivering in resonance.

Chicago. The place that invented the phrase "concrete jungle."

Molly had chosen just the right song.

The enemy hesitated, eyes shifting left and right, scanning above and below. Fear hit their ranks like a slow, powerful wave, causing steps to falter, formations to stretch and warp.

And then the primal opening vocals and the lead guitar line came in.

And Winter came with them.

Mab's cohort of personal guardsmen came flying out of the night, as nimble and graceful as if they'd been on wires, and they landed around us, congealed into a formation, and locked shields.

The northern sky split with a sudden rush of wind that carried the dry, frozen clarity of the arctic, and with it came a rush of . . . not snowflakes, so much as frozen chips of arctic clouds, hurled forward in a blinding wave. I had to lift a hand to shield my face and eyes, and when I lowered my arm, figures in armor of blue and green and deep purple hues had appeared in ranks on the street, on low rooftops, crouching on the frozen corpses of automobiles. Each succeeding gust of wind seemed to blow more of them into reality. First by the dozen. Then by the score. Then by the hundred.

I turned and saw the Winter Lady step from a particularly dense swirling cloud of frost crystals at street level, at the head of her army. Her long white hair streamed before her like a banner, hiding her face above her smiling lips, and she was clad in sparkles, a few patches of frost, and little else. The serpent tattoo that wove from one of her ankles to her wrist writhed and swirled *inside* her skin, slithering wildly in animated excitement. In one pale hand she bore a slender white sword. A squad of freaking trolls, each one a twelve-foot-tall, leathery, warty monstrosity with more muscle than the NFL, emerged from the suddenly swirling ice with her. Each of them held a sword as long as I was tall, which they lifted with dull-minded eagerness as they stepped out of the sleet and took position around the Winter Lady.

Power surrounded her, violent and lightning quick to my wizard's senses, the power to turn heads and bend minds. To look upon her was to want, desperately, to throw yourself upon her sword, if that was what would please her, and the Winter mantle in me thrummed in pure primal resonance to her presence. The pure emotional *need* to either kill or die for that presence washed over me in a flood.

The Winter Lady let her head fall back and let out a banshee shriek that could have been heard from one end of Chicago to the other.

It was answered from thousands of throats, a great, baying chorus of screams.

Ah. So that's what had been keeping Molly so busy lately.

She'd been building an army.

She lifted the pale white sword, and thousands of gleaming weapons rose in response. Then she dropped the sword, and the army of Winter went abruptly silent and rushed forward across the sleet-riddled ground.

Ethniu took this in without expression for several seconds and then whirled toward Mab, striding forward, as if intent upon finishing her—only to draw up short as Mab was surrounded by her bodyguard again, and as Grimalkin and the contingent of local Winter Fae appeared with them and fell in around Mab, adding their mass to the group protecting the Winter Queen.

Mab was not strong enough to do much more than lift her own head, as the Sidhe warriors surrounding her picked her up and drew her back into the solidity of the formation.

But she did that much and gave Ethniu a smirk of pure defiance.

The Titan screamed, and the Eye flared brighter for a second—before dying down again almost instantly.

Apparently, using the Eye before it was ready was inadvisable. Ethniu's scream of rage turned into a shriek of pain, and she clamped both hands over the Eye and staggered.

Meanwhile, behind Ethniu, I finally spotted Corb, in the center of the Fomor legion and at the rear. He was shrieking orders, and the clicking along the enemy lines became frantic as they attempted to wheel their force to face the army of the Winter Lady.

But Mab wasn't going to stop there.

ONE-EYE! called Mab's psychic voice.

And the sky began to growl.

Lightning crashed down to the earth in a sudden curtain of spears of light, setting half a dozen of the trees in the park aflame, and then leapt *back up* into the sky, burning the air clean and clear as it went. There it formed a blazing cloud of electricity that suddenly flattened into a line that split open in a ragged tear as, maybe four thousand feet up, the sky burst open and a rider emerged, mounted upon an eight-legged steed. The rider surged out of the hole in the sky.

And the Wild Hunt followed him.

Horns blew, wildly, a sound of haunting beauty and

pure terror, as from the rip in the sky came scores of dark mounts and dark hounds, running as if on solid ground and ridden by the darkest talents of Winter—and they all followed the leader of the Hunt, an eight-legged horse half again as big as any of the others, and ridden by a dark, terrifying shadow bearing a bolt of living lightning in one mailed fist.

Beside the great rider, the Erlking himself lifted his horn to his lips and blew, and on that wailing note, in time with the percussion of Guns N' Roses, the Wild Hunt dove down toward the earthbound forces of the Fomor, and terror went before them.

The enemy's voices lifted in wails of dismay, and one of the cohorts of octokongs simply started scattering, turning upon their Fomor masters when they tried to restore order. And it got worse for the Fomor: The whole army had been in the midst of attempting to adjust to the presence of the Winter Lady's cohorts, and they looked waddling and clumsy compared to the Winter cohorts, like . . .

Like seals or sea turtles caught on land.

In a flash of insight, I realized that Corb's forces were used to operating and practicing underwater. Down there, stumbling into a comrade in arms during maneuvers was no big deal because it wouldn't make anyone fall down, or trip up the following troops. Down there, there was about triple the physical space to operate within, and an extra dimension of possible movement to boot.

Dry land was a less forgiving place for imprecision. And they hadn't been able to practice on land—not while maintaining their centuries-long seclusion underwater. As a result, the Fomor army couldn't react or maneuver anywhere near as quickly as they should have been able to. They were too used to the sea.

If we'd fought them down there, I expect we wouldn't have had a chance.

But we weren't down there.

This was a realm of Air and Darkness.

The Wild Hunt swept down upon the most vulnerable and exposed troops in the enemy line—the poor saps on the very outside of the wheel—and it was like watching automated machinery in a meat-packing plant. Down swept the Wild Hunt in a great vertical wheel led by that monstrous eight-legged steed. There was a huge humming tone, like the buzz in the air around active Tesla coils, but bigger and more eerie, and a *continuous* lightning bolt as wide as a lane of traffic lashed out from the right hand of the shadowy leader of the Wild Hunt as he soared along the enemy line, wreaking carnage and chaos among them.

While the rest of the Hunt did not wield weapons so spectacular, their swords and spears, gripped by hands with centuries of experience, were plied to deadly effect. At the speed of their dive, the lightest brush from the edge of a blade carried terrible, focused power. Heads and limbs flew. Blood sprayed.

My Knight, came Mab's psychic voice. *We have perhaps sixty seconds before the Eye is once again loosed upon us. You must call her by then.*

"There's an army between me and there," I protested. "Literally, an army."

Gee, thanks, Sir Obvious, came the Winter Lady's merry, excited, somehow panting psychic voice. I caught a glimpse of Molly across the battlefield, watched a heavy axe shatter upon the frost glittering upon her skin even as she flicked her white sword left and right with almost delicate motions, the lightest touch of the blade engulfing each of her foes in the obdurate ice of Winter's heart. The smile on her face made her look wild and terrible and delighted, as the mountainous group of trolls behind her shattered each frozen foe to ice cubes with vast sweeps of their crude weapons.

There was an enormous exhalation, and the Winter unicorn suddenly stood in front of me, stamping its spiked hooves impatiently.

Mab took the psychic phone back, her thoughts mildly reproachful. *Have I ever asked you to accomplish an easy task, my Knight? Tonight seems an unlikely place to begin.*

Well. She had me there.

Butters, evidently, was not privy to Mab's conversation with me. He was staring at the unicorn. "Uh. Harry?"

"Dammit," I muttered.

I swallowed and took a deep breath. Then I seized the unicorn by the mane, hoped to God it didn't notice how much my hands were shaking, and leapt onto its back. I turned back to Butters and offered him my hand. "No time. Trust me."

"Ah hell," Butters said in a note of open complaint. But he'd already put his hand in mine before he began speaking, and I hauled him up onto the unicorn's back with me.

If our weight was any burden to the unicorn, it wasn't obvious from the way the creature moved. I could feel the thing quivering in its desire to spill blood. No sooner had Butters swung up behind me and gotten settled than the beast took off. If I hadn't ridden a supernaturally powerful equine earlier that year, both of us would have fallen off on our asses—and even so, Butters had to cling to me hard to keep from taking a tumble. The unicorn forged through the little sea of blue- and purple-armored allies who glided from its path, and then we were on open ground and racing toward the enemy.

I've ridden horses more than most, and I feel qualified to say that riding a unicorn in battle is an experience I was unlikely to forget.

In the first place, there wasn't really a sense of up-and-down to the way the creature ran. In that sense, it felt more like riding a motorcycle, though I had more experience with horses. The only times I'd been on a motorcycle had been with . . .

Murph.

The pain hit my heart.

Power flooded into me, more than I'd ever felt, all of it in the space of a couple of seconds. My heart rate skyrocketed, my hair stood on end, and my body temperature had begun to climb. My brain took note of those things while my heart kept aching and more and more power rushed in.

Magic and emotion are intertwined so strongly that it can be hard to tell where one begins and the other ends. Emotion makes the most immediate and ready fuel for magical power, though it can have some odd effects on what you're trying to do. Fuel a love spell with rage and you're likely to get some odd side effects, for example.

But for causing pain, there wasn't better fuel than pain itself. So, though it hurt, viciously, I fought to take hold of that power and started shaping it with my thoughts as the unicorn rushed forward. But I'd never had that much energy rush into me that quickly before.

Hell's bells, what had just happened to me?

Flickers of green-gold light began to gather along the unicorn's central horn, and I suddenly understood.

I had various tools, like my staff, created to help me gather, focus, and direct power.

As did Mab.

It was everything I could do just to hold on, and the unicorn had more acceleration than a Maserati. We started closing the distance to the enemy with alarming rapidity.

I shoved my staff at Butters and shouted, "Hold this!"

He fumbled and managed to take it, and I leaned forward and laid my right palm on the unicorn's neck.

The creature's horn flared with pure power, became incandescent with gold-green light, and I *felt* the humming channels of power rushing through the body of the immortal creature, just like when I sent energy into my staff— only that was like comparing a drinking fountain to a firefighting company's equipment. I might have been holding more energy than I ever had before, but this creature had been designed to focus and enhance *Mab's* power. I couldn't have overloaded it if I'd tried.

So when we were about fifty yards from the enemy, I sent that stored energy through my right hand into the Winter unicorn, focused my will and intent, modified the shape of the spell on the fly, and howled, *"Forzare!"*

By the time I'd done that, we were upon them.

A wave of pure kinetic energy, amplified by the unicorn's horn, rushed out ahead of us like a fast-moving river and broke upon the enemy in a tsunami. Bodies flew from our path as if swatted away by God's heaviest driver. I don't mean they flew back, either. I threw them *up*, like thirty feet *up*, and before they could come down again we'd sprinted underneath them, so that the unicorn's hooves were constantly coming down on open ground. From a distance, it must have looked like some enormous gardener had taken a hurricane-force leaf blower to the enemy.

"Holy moly!" shouted Butters.

The unicorn let out a bellowing sound that would have been more appropriate to maybe a bear or a tiger or a low-flying Concorde, and for several seconds the world became a confusing blur of bodies twirling into the air, screams, and flying thunderbolts of excess energy bleeding into the night.

The unicorn blew past the enemy lines and into the clear on the other side—and we started taking gunfire almost instantly. The unicorn didn't slow down but started running serpentine, snaking left and right with what felt like enough g-force to give me whiplash. Targets moving like that are difficult to hit even in a practice scenario, much less in adrenaline-charged real life, but I was so busy holding on for my life that I couldn't possibly have brought a counterattack to bear. I couldn't even see *where* the fire was coming from.

I looked over my shoulder and caught a frenzied glimpse of King Corb bearing a staff of what looked like coral, pointing a finger at the ground ahead of us and shrieking.

And I realized that the problem with having all that

power to work with was that the enemy got to work with it, too.

The ground ahead of us suddenly darkened. The unicorn tried to twist and evade it, but Corb had timed it perfectly and the creature was moving too fast.

I poured my will into my beleaguered shield bracelet, bringing it up in a tight sphere around Butters and me.

The unicorn hit the patch of darkened earth and plunged into it as if it were liquid. Salty brine had mixed with the earth, rendering it into the next best thing to quicksand, arresting the unicorn's momentum abruptly, and Butters and I flew over its head, hit the ground on the other side, and started rolling.

We were heading straight for Columbus, bouncing like a cannonball. If we hit that concrete wall along the upper level of the park, we'd be splattered against the inside of my own shield, so I started layering its interior with kinetic force and letting the outer layers be ripped off by our impacts with the ground, slowing us and shedding our energy in the form of heat. We left a trail of bouncing ball prints in scorched earth and concrete, and by the time we hit the wall, we'd shed enough momentum that it didn't feel much worse than a moderate traffic collision—which is to say it was loud and terrifying and painful, but we survived.

It left me and Butters lying on a sidewalk against a concrete wall, alone at the rear of the enemy lines.

And it also left us staring at Listen and a platoon of his turtlenecks, not fifty feet away, operating several infantry mortars and holding enough guns to invade Texas.

Listen and I moved at the same time.

His gun snapped up.

I thrust out my hand at the earth and snarled, *"Forzare!"*

My intention had been to use the spell to bulldoze a berm of earth into place between us. But I still wasn't used to this turbocharged magic thing.

Oops.

The energy I'd sent out formed a berm all right—and then it kept on pushing and building it, like a rogue wave on Hawaii's North Shore. Maybe eighteen or twenty tons of earth hit Listen and his people and swamped them.

And at the same time, someone punched me in the belly on my left side, right under the floating ribs, and drove the breath out of me. The whole left side of my abdomen suddenly felt wet.

Harry! screamed Molly's psychic voice, full of alarm.

I *felt* the gaze of the Titan as her head swiveled toward me like a machine-gun turret, and her features, her presence, became suffused with pure rage.

I managed not to foul my underwear and fought to draw a breath as Ethniu kicked a panicked octokong out of her way and began striding toward me.

"Oh boy," Butters breathed. He crouched over me and ripped my shirt open. His eyes widened as he stared down at me; then he shot a glance over his shoulder at the Titan, who was rapidly drawing nearer.

Butters drew my hands to the spot where I'd been punched and pressed them down. "Hold them here, Harry. Keep up the pressure. I'll be right back."

And then the little guy stood up, his limbs shaking, his face ashen, and put himself between me and a goddamned Titan.

I felt my teeth stretch into a wolf's smile. Hell. If Butters could do that, I could do my part. It was hard. But I drew in enough breath and focused my will, infusing my voice with Power.

"Titania," I wheezed. "I summon thee."

Maybe half a dozen of the armored foot soldiers around Ethniu, confused and looking for direction, sensed her intent and went flying forward like hounds on a trail.

I labored for another breath, and to hold my hands where Butters had put them.

Butters lifted *Fidelacchius* and brought the blade to life in a buzz of angelic choral fury.

"Titania!" I rasped, louder. The Name echoed weirdly, or it seemed that way to me. *"I summon thee!"*

The first of the heavily armored ape-armed troopers reached Butters.

And the little guy went full Jedi on his ass.

Fidelacchius sliced the trooper's weapon in half and took part of the arm with it. A second swing split the trooper's heavy shield in half with the rest of him, and the pieces fell in separate directions. The other five hesitated— and Butters went up the middle like a human Cuisinart, striking down three more in less time than it would have taken to call his name.

Ethniu strode closer, shouting something in a tongue I did not understand, seized the corpse of one of my volunteers from the earlier engagement by the calf, and flung it overhand at Butters and his remaining opponents, smashing all three of them out of her way.

But the little guy had bought me time enough.

I drew in my third wheezing breath as the fire of the Eye began to kindle, poured my will into my voice, and screamed, *"TITANIA! I SUMMON THEE!"*

Chapter

Thirty

Titania doesn't like me on the best of days.

It's hard to blame her; I killed her child.

So when I completed the summoning, without anything like any kind of control over the being I was calling in, I wasn't really expecting roses and chocolate.

Neither was I expecting to get struck by a bolt of lightning.

But here we are.

There was an enormous sound, a flash of light, a shock against my body like a spray of frozen fire. And the next thing I knew, I was lying flat on my back, wheezing, with chunks of concrete and other debris pattering down around me. I tried to get up and I think my legs and shoulders twitched. But other than that, nothing much happened.

I lived static interference for a while, waiting for my brain to start tracking again. The next thing I knew, Butters was helping me sit up and saying something like, ". . . lucky that the bullet didn't puncture the abdominal wall. The lightning actually cauterized it, or you'd still be bleeding."

"Tough love," I gasped. I got a look at my bare chest. I had a lot of blood and what looked like a horrible burn along the entire horizontal length of flesh beneath my ribs on the left side, shaped vaguely like the spreading branches of a tree, or maybe wave patterns in sand. At least that would be kind of a cool scar. Everything I could feel was encased in fuzzy white static, and I was grateful for the insulation the Winter mantle was giving me against the pain.

I couldn't feel it, but I knew my body was taking a terrible beating. While I could keep driving it forward, this kind of thing was taking a toll. I still had limits, even if it didn't feel like I did. If I didn't respect that, I could tough-guy myself right into a grave.

I lay there quietly for a moment, staring up at the sky. It was like being in the eye of a hurricane. Everywhere around us was smoke and dust, lit only by smoldering fires. But from where I now lay, it was like looking up from the bottom of a well, a long column of clear air that stretched up into the night sky, where clouds were boiling into existence out of nowhere, while thunder rumbled with low menace.

When the Queens of Summer and Winter took to the same field, there were always storms.

And then my awareness rushed back together again and I got my head back into the game, looking wildly around to determine what had happened.

Battle was raging in the park. The incoming charge of the Winter Lady and her troops had hit the wobbly lines of the Fomor like a wrecking ball, centered around a point of silver-white light and hulking trolls. I could hear the haunting shrieks of the Winter Lady, and the answering screams of her troops, as their offensive punched deep into the enemy formation and devolved into the pure chaos of frantic hand-to-hand combat.

Except that Molly's troops were *cheating*: They'd brought pistols and submachine guns and plied them to devastating effect along with swords and axes. Though the enemy still outnumbered them, the Winter Lady's charge had been potentially deadly, threatening to cleave the enemy lines entirely.

King Corb and his retinue of sorcerers and their bodyguards charged frantically toward that threat, to pit their sorcerous might against the Winter Lady—and to entrap her charge in their own superior numbers if she could be stopped from breaking through their lines.

The great wheeling death machine that was the Wild Hunt rolled over the Fomor legion with frantic abandon the whole while, too frenzied in its lust for blood to care which particular targets it struck, terrifying in the absolute random fatality of its selections.

And standing ten feet off, facing away from me, the Queen of Summer, Titania, faced Ethniu, eye to eye, standing as tall as the Titan. The Summer Queen wore leather armor, all in flickering shades of green, like sunlight passing through fluttering leaves on a warm spring day. Her silver-white hair was braided with ivy and flowers. She carried no weapons, and she stood alone—but the legion of the Fomor, it seemed, could hardly bring themselves to so much as look at her, much less approach.

Titania's voice rang into the night like a silver bell. "Clever of you, Ethniu, to attack my sister at midsummer, when she is at her weakest." A growl of thunder added punctuation to the end of her sentence. "But it was shortsighted to assume she would stand alone."

There was a thrumming in the air, a quivering sensation of nauseated terror that went through me like a bullet, and suddenly the silver-grey eight-legged steed whom the legends named Sleipnir thundered out of the night sky, its hooves digging up mounds of earth to arrest its momentum. The great horse reared, kicking the scorched air with all four forehooves, and the terrible shadow upon its back lifted a hand that suddenly clasped a bolt of lightning.

When the Erlking landed, he did so in total silence, despite the heavy faemetal plate he wore over his usual hunting leathers. He landed in a crouch, flanking the Titan opposite the terrible rider, and drew his antler-handled hunting sword as he faced Ethniu.

I wanted nothing at all to do with this fight, and I started trying to worm out of the immediate blast radius without being noticed.

"I give you this single opportunity," Titania continued. "Withdraw from the mortal world. Return to your sanctuary. It will end here."

"As if you could offer or deny me anything I chose to take," Ethniu snarled. "Petty little demigod."

And with that she unleashed the power of the Eye.

Titania was waiting for it.

The torrent of destructive fire struck out at Titania— but rather than trying to oppose or endure it, she did the opposite. She spread her arms wide, rolled at her hips and lower back in a peculiarly dancelike motion, and rather than striking her, the torrent of energy bent and twisted, sending all that heat and hate spiraling up into the night sky.

Up into the sky that had, only a moment before, been full of freezing air and sleet, courtesy of the Winter Lady.

To call what happened next "rain" is something of an understatement.

Great, grinding thunder raised its voice in a throaty roar, and the air turned to falling water.

Water and magic are awfully finicky around each other. Enough running water tends to disperse and ground out magical energy, so much so that entities whose existence most depended on magic dared not cross even a running stream.

Titania didn't so much summon a thunderstorm as she created an improvised waterfall.

Down smashed the rain so thickly that I had to cover my mouth with a hand in order to be able to breathe.

And I felt the shift in power happening.

The terror of the city and its hovering magical potential in the air began to melt away like a sandcastle before the tide. The water sluiced down over the city, washing the air clean once more. Magic began to bleed out of the air and sink back into the earth, drawn along by the heavy rain.

It couldn't come down that hard for very long. It was maybe thirty seconds. Definitely no more than sixty. And then the rain abruptly stopped, as if a switch had been thrown, and only a few light, sporadic raindrops continued to fall. The city went from a roar to almost complete silence. The quivering reservoir of concentrated dread, ready to be collected and used, had withered and melted away.

And with its energy supply abruptly missing, the sullen fire of the Eye guttered and nearly went out.

Ethniu let out a short, sharp exhalation and lifted her left hand to the Eye.

Titania lowered her face, gleaming from the flood, and focused bright green feline eyes upon the Titan, her expression as set and immovable as the earth.

Sleipnir screamed and reared again, the great beast straining against the reins, eager to fight, while the blue-white fire of the living lightning in the hand of its great rider cast flickering nightmare shadows upon the ground all around them.

The Erlking gave her a wolfish smile.

And then the immortals went to war.

It happened fast. Everything was a blur of motion and energy. Sounds tumbled one upon another so rapidly that it was impossible to pick out or identify any given portion of it. Lights flashed so brightly that I had to cry out against the intensity.

None of them bothered with physical weapons. They all threw Power at one another. They all had been using it for century upon century. They were all better than me, with minds capable of shaping and forming multiple workings of Power simultaneously. I couldn't have *tracked* that duel, not even if I'd been at one hundred percent and had signed guarantees of safety. Participating in it? Laughable.

There was so much power there that my Sight started picking up images, like a light so bright that it hurt even through closed eyelids. Each of the combatants blurred, as if multiple layers of the same image had suddenly started performing multiple separate actions. I was struck by the sudden overwhelming perception that I was looking at potential realities, possible realities, all overlapping while immortal minds fought to see into the future and adjusted and counteradjusted their actions based upon what they could perceive there. So not only were they all doing multiple things at once; they were all *thinking* through *every* available possibility. That was like . . . simultaneously playing an entirely mental game of 3-D chess while juggling a running chain saw, a lit torch, and a bowling ball, all while balancing on a slack rope.

And then they took all that vision and Power and potential and condensed it into a single instant. When they cut loose, the immortals fought one another all at once: They brought the totality of their being to the table, expending their energy all in the smallest area and time frame possible, concentrating their enormous Power with inhuman precision.

So there was light that tore at my eyes and sound that clawed at my ears, a nauseating ripple in the air caused by so much energy being unleashed in so small an area, and a clap of thunder.

And then there was a smoldering crater in the ground where the four of them had been standing faced off against one another.

Where the Erlking had been there was only a burned shape. Half of it was a skeleton, charred black. The other half looked like a lot of melted metal and cooked meat.

Sleipnir lay on his side, stunned, several yards away. Beside him lay his rider, his dark cloak and hood smoldering.

And Ethniu stood in the center of the smoking crater, her feet planted wide and confident, holding a limp, apparently unconscious Titania by the throat, the Summer Queen's feet dangling six inches off the ground. Ethniu's Titanic bronze skin-slash-armor had been scorched but not dented. She was breathing hard and looked unsteady, her eyes wide.

"Pathetic," Ethniu purred to Titania. "I don't need the Eye of Balor to deal with a goblin with delusions of grandeur, a starved, emaciated old god, and a little girl playing at being a queen."

And with a casual motion, she slammed the Summer Queen's head into the earth at her feet, leaving the rest of her limp body awkwardly sticking out.

I stared. Just stared.

One-Eye wasn't moving.

The Erlking's skeleton had begun twitching. Nerve fibers and ligaments were beginning to regrow on the blackened bones. It was like watching stop-motion capture of creeping ivy. But it would take him hours to recover.

Titania was down.

Titania.

Even Mab had been TKO'd.

Ethniu looked around at the three fallen opponents and let out a little-girl giggle, a sound that was frightening in how hysterical it sounded.

And her balance wobbled.

Not a lot. But she wavered.

She showed weakness.

The Winter mantle in me suddenly focused on the Titan and licked its chops.

The fight had cost her something. Though she might be powerful and well equipped and tough as hell, the Titan still had limits. And if she had limits, then she could be pushed beyond them.

She could be beaten.

It could be done.

Ethniu hadn't even glanced at me. She paced over toward One-Eye's fallen form, making a softly reproving clicking noise with her mouth. "I warned you, fool. Look at what the mortals have made of you. We needed their terror. Never their love." She shook her head and leaned down, reaching out.

One-Eye gripped an ash-hafted spear in his right hand. Flickers of blue-white electricity played over its head.

"You are barely sustained by the faith of children," Ethniu murmured. "While I am made stronger every time they cry out in fear in their sleep. Every time they feel a moment of dread after they turn out the light. We were never meant to be their protectors. We were meant to be what lurks in the dark." She lifted the spear and studied it with narrowed eyes for a moment. "The mortals have become arrogant, in their well-lit world. Proud. Boastful. It is time to remind them of their insignificance."

She lifted the spear into the air, narrowed her eyes, and

suddenly it became a blazing thunderbolt in her hands, ready to be hurled at any who might dare oppose her.

So, naturally, of course, she turned to me. Lightning crackled overhead, seemingly eager to get started. Armies fought in the background, and the riders of the Wild Hunt screamed and blew horns, dark and horrible shadows against the lightning flickering between clouds overhead.

And Murph was gone.

It looked and sounded and felt like the end of the world.

"Starting," the Titan said, her beautiful face framed in brilliant blue-white glare and heavy shadow, "with you, little wizard. Empty night, but your breed is annoying enough to be worth killing."

I'd just been proximate to a divine beatdown and smiting.

I'd just been struck by *lightning*.

My snark projectors were out of alignment. But that was no reason not to try.

Heck, every insult was essentially a different way of saying the exact same thing.

"Yeah?" I wheezed. "Well. You suck."

Ethniu stared at me for a few seconds.

Then she tilted her head back and laughed. It was . . .

Giddy. Pure. It came right up out of her belly in a kind of brittle-sounding joy.

It didn't sound right. At all.

"What's so funny?" I asked.

"Oh," Ethniu sighed. "Me." She shook her head. "Hav-

ing a conversation with a talking cockroach. I suppose con-
gratulations are in order, insect. I've actually noticed that
I'm killing you. I'll even enjoy it a little."

And she stepped forward and lifted the bolt of living
lightning over her head.

Chapter
Thirty-one

My body was still shorted out enough that I couldn't move much. And I'd seen the kind of power that spear put out. Without the supercharged atmosphere, I couldn't put up a defense sufficient to the task of defeating it. Maybe if I'd been able to keep her talking for a minute, I could have recovered enough to at least attempt to run away.

But I could see it in her face and in every line of her bronzed form: She wasn't going to be swayed or denied or distracted. She'd had her own brief moment of weakness after battling several immortals, and now she was back on task—a task she'd been planning for thousands of years.

There wasn't much I could do.

That was when it was too much. Everything. The injuries. Not so much the physical ones. I had seen too much for one night.

Lost too much.

That was when I broke.

When you're in that kind of condition, your brain does weird things. I didn't feel scared or angry or upset anymore. I felt like a bystander, a member of the audience. Once you realize your ticket has been punched, you see things differently. I could see everything that was happening around us. It didn't really involve me any longer.

The Winter Lady's charge had been met by a wall of sorcery from Corb and his inner circle, and they'd stopped her and her trolls' charge, ba-dump-bump, cold. Molly's army's furious strike had stalled short of cutting the Fomor's legion in twain, simply lacking the mass it needed to finish the deadly stroke. Even as I watched, I saw Winter troops being pushed back, cut down. One of the trolls fell, its head a smoking ruin, as King Corb lowered his staff and howled triumph. A bolt of green lightning shattered upon the Winter Lady's flank. I saw it scorch flesh to bone, saw her ribs burned black, saw her stagger a step and then turn like Juggernaut, relentless and unstoppable, and keep fighting as another troll fell, nearly crushing her.

Winter's momentum had stalled in the sultry summer night. And the Fomor legion, terrified and furious, smelled blood and began smashing their way into the forces of Winter, killing with wild abandon.

The last defenders of Chicago were falling.

And from the south, where our allies had been holding the enemy, came the long, low blare of a Jotun's horn, sounding the attack.

I couldn't see, through the armies and the park and the smoke, what was happening to the south. But the Jotun horn sounded again, nearer.

Our allies there had fallen. The second arm of the enemy force was sweeping toward us.

And when it arrived, they would crush whatever resistance was left.

My city was falling.

There wasn't anything I could do. I couldn't even lift a hand to make a dramatic gesture, and I only would have needed to move one finger.

The world was just too heavy.

The Titan stared at me, triumph in her gaze, the spear she'd taken from One-Eye's fallen form lifted.

I'd been through a lot in my time. But I knew an ending when I saw it.

The Titan had won. The old world, the old darkness, had come back at last. Chicago would be laid to waste and ruin.

And I would die with it.

I met Ethniu's gaze, and in that moment I knew that I probably wasn't even going to be aware of it when I died: There was no chance at all that I could soulgaze that being and keep my mind intact. I would die mad.

Only it didn't happen.

And I saw a truth even more hideous.

It didn't take a wizard to see the Titan's soul. It was already all around us. The sheer desire for ruin and destruction that filled her soul and had allowed her to master the Eye had been made manifest in the world. This was the world that Ethniu longed for. The terror, the death, the blood, the destruction, the senseless chaos— this was who and what she was. This madness was the fire that had fueled the Titans, that had made their destruction a necessity in the first place.

Blood was their art. Screams were their music. Horror was their faith.

Mortals could not stand before this.

I watched my death coming for me and wept in sheer despair.

I knew that it wasn't just the actual pain. I knew it was also the dark will of the enemy, now unopposed by Mab's battered will, and that that awful psychic pressure was running rampant with my emotions. I knew it was a lie.

But it was becoming the truth, right in front of my eyes.

And . . .

And then . . .

And then Waldo Butters stepped up.

The little guy appeared from behind me and put himself directly between the Titan and me.

He wasn't an impressive figure under the best of circumstances. Standing in front of the towering Ethniu, he looked even less impressive. Even if they'd both been humans and the same height, she'd have had more muscle. Combined with everything else about her, her aura, her power, her grace, her armor, her height, her beauty, the war and ruin and mad-lit, dying city behind her . . . Butters didn't even look like a human being. He looked more like a badly animated marionette standing *next* to a human being.

He looked small.

Dirty.

Tired.

Bruised.

Frightened.

The little guy glanced back at me, his face sick and pale. Then he turned to face the Titan.

And he squared his shoulders.

And he raised the Sword, a sudden white, pure light in that place, an unseen choir providing hushed music around it.

In that light, Ethniu's armor looked . . . sharper somehow, harder, more uncomfortable, more inhibitive to her movements. Her beauty seemed flawed, harsh, as if it had been a trick of the light, and in her living eye I could see nothing but a desperate, empty hunger, a void within her soul that could never be filled.

Before that light, even the ancient terror of the Titan hesitated.

"Begone, Titan," Butters said. His voice was quiet, mellow, resonant. It wasn't a human voice at all. Though the volume never lifted, it could be heard over the battle, over the thunder, over the crackle and roar of fires. "These souls are not for you. Begone to the depths of your hatred and rage. There is no world for you here any longer."

Ethniu's face became a thundercloud, her lips twisting into a snarl of pure hate. "Do you *dare* give me orders, you lapdog, you traitor, you coward."

"Ethniu," murmured that voice, and the depth of compassion in it was like a deep, quiet sea. "I only offer vision, that you may avoid suffering."

"You're no more powerful than your instrument now." Ethniu spat toward Butters, and the spittle actually began eating a hole in the ground, it was so virulent. "You chose the side of the insects. Be crushed with them."

She straightened, whirled the spear as if it had been a reed, and smashed at Butters with a bolt of lightning that sounded like some enormous, angrily buzzing waterfall.

Butters screamed, in his dirty, tired, terrified, normal human voice, barely audible.

He lifted the Sword, and again I understood, on an instinctual level, that the blade of the Sword of Faith, though made of immaterial light, was for this purpose far *more* solid, more unbreakable, more *real* than it had ever been when made of steel. Had the Sword been lifted in this purpose before, mere molecular structure would have been shattered by the forces brought to bear upon it—but now, unpolluted by the material world, the true power of the blade could be brought to bear, and in that bar of silver white light was a galaxy of subtle color, of immovable power, of something so pure and steady and fixed that the universe itself had been built upon its foundation, and in the background my addled brain could hear the faint echoes of a Voice saying, *Let there be light.*

The mortal man holding *that* blade met the Titan's fury.

And he would *not* be moved.

Like a rock in the sea he stood, as a tide of power crashed against him. The light could have struck anyone too near it blind through its sheer intensity. The heat ripped and tore the earth around him, rendering the ground down to bare earth in a furious flood of energetic violence. For the space of seven slow heartbeats, Butters stood before that tide, gripping the Sword, and the light and fury and shadow and flying debris formed a shape in the air behind him, of a tall, indistinct form that folded graceful wings around him like an eagle protecting her young from the rain.

Then, like even the most terrible, hungry tide, that power passed.

And an utter silence fell.

Untouched in the center of a circle of destruction stood the Knight of Faith, shining in the white light of *Fidelacchius*, and that fire had done nothing but leave him untarnished and clean, dirt and grime and impurity burned away while he was left untouched, his white cloak stirred by the heat rising from the ground around him, his dark eyes glittering with determination behind his goofy sports goggles.

Ethniu only stared.

"You know what?" Butters said, and in the center of what looked like the end of the world, his merely human voice sounded, not epic, not mighty, not bold—not even scared or angry. He merely sounded . . . normal. Human.

And if there was anything in the universe more defiant of the world the Titan was creating than that, I couldn't have imagined what it might be.

Butters nodded thoughtfully and said, "I believe you aren't as tough as you think you are."

Ethniu's lips peeled back in a contemptuous smile. "Behold your champions, the young gods, the forces of your world, lying helpless upon the ground, mortal."

Butters looked around and nodded. And then he said, "You know who's come out ahead of every one of these guys at one time or another?" he said, and jerked his chin over his shoulder toward me. "Harry Dresden. You haven't killed him yet." Butters lifted the Sword again and his voice hardened. "And as long as I'm standing here, you aren't going to."

The Titan's eyes narrowed in sheer hatred. "Little. Man. Do you think you can stop me alone?"

"It's not about me," Butters said. "And I'm not alone."

"Look around you, fool."

I heard the smile come into his voice, though it grew no less hard. "I. Am not. Alone."

I shed a tear for Butters and his courage.

But the Titan was right.

The horn of the Jotnar, of doom, sounded again, nearby. It was the sound of my city's death.

I saw a massive silhouette appear in the haze bordering the south side of the park.

Ethniu glanced that way, then turned back to us, contempt scorching the edges of her smile.

But the fool, the Knight of Faith, held his ground.

And it turned out that I was wrong, and the fool was right.

Sometimes that's all faith is.

Sometimes that's enough.

The enormous form in the haze dwindled with the rapidity of a backlit shadow, and suddenly River Shoulders staggered out of the pall of destruction into the clear air of the park. His old tuxedo had been torn away completely. One of his shoulders hung as if dislocated, and his fur was singed and matted the grey of falling ash, darkened in places with blood. But he'd apparently found his spectacles, and one of their lenses was sharply cracked.

And over his good shoulder, he lugged the horn of a Jotun.

The Sasquatch's gaze swept around the park and his expression lit with an abrupt fierceness. The enormous muscles of his arm bulged and strained and hauled the horn into position, and he blew three long, wailing blasts from the instrument that shook the air with the clarity of their tone and sent fresh cracks spreading through the bone of the horn.

And in response, there was a throaty roar from beyond the wall of vision-obscuring haze, and golden white light suddenly burned the pall away.

From the south rose a light like the first of morning, as if a star had fallen to street level. There was a flutter of silver motion, and then standing atop an abandoned refrigerated truck was the breath of dawn in the shape of something like a horse. Rivers of light poured from it like water in the shape of its mane and tail, and the sword of light atop its head shone like visible music. Astride his back was Sarissa, the Summer Lady, clad in falling swaths of curling silver hair and random flower petals. She held a staff of living wood covered in freshly bloomed flowers— and tipped with a copper spearhead stained with blood.

Seated behind her was an armored figure bearing a flaming sword. Fix, the Summer Knight, my opposite number. As the Summer unicorn stirred and reared, fore-hooves flashing color, he lifted the sword in defiance.

At the same time, the Summer Lady threw back her head and let out a scream that was a single vibrating note, and a column of glorious golden light suddenly burned a hole in the haze and the cloud cover, turning the few remaining raindrops to spectrum-shattered mist and steam.

From the desperate clash of battle came an answering

shriek—and a column of cold, defiant blue light rose into the night, centered on the darting, tireless form of the Winter Lady.

Movement stirred around the truck at ground level.

And the Baron of Chicago led the way.

Marcone strode into the light and clarity provided by the Summer Lady and came forward as though he meant to walk through a steel wall. He had shed his suit jacket in exchange for a pair of freaking pirate bandoliers hung with, I kid you not, what looked like seventeen or eighteen flintlock weapons—and he was carrying one in either hand.

To his right was Hendricks, dressed in a mix of tactical gear and what looked like samurai armor, carrying one of those automatic shotguns in one hand and a broadsword in the other. To his left, Gard strode along in silver armor that gleamed even when there wasn't any light shining on it, over a mail coat that flowed like silk rather than steel. She carried her battle-axe in her hands, its blade shining with the power of glowing runes, so bright they left after-images blurred into my vision. The two champions followed Marcone.

And I could feel, from there, the banner of his will streaming behind him.

Following in his wake came hundreds of Einherjaren, including that poor bastard on guard duty whom Lara had taken out, looking furious and still a little blurry with apparent drink. With them came Marcone's troubleshooters, cold professionals whose job it was to find trouble—and shoot it. Behind *them* came the svartalves, or what I presumed were the svartalves—a block of troops that were kitted out for war in some kind of armor that had a veil built into every suit, so that the figures were mostly just blurs in the air about the right height to be a svartalf.

With them marched LaChaise and his ghouls, giggling like drunks, all of them gathered like an honor guard around an open space in which whirled a number of heavy objects, as if they had been moons captured in the gravity field of some small, incredibly dense planetoid—and at the center of that deadly spinning atomic model of whirling junk marched a slim figure that I presumed to be the Archive.

They came into the open and Marcone broke into a slow jog, and, following his banner, those coming behind him fell into step in unison. More figures came. And more. And more.

Spreading out to the right of Marcone's group came the White Council of Wizardry. My grandfather, the Blackstaff, led the way, the left side of his body shrouded in a deathly shadow that made me feel cold to look upon. On his right marched my friend Ramirez, grim and battered as hell, but keeping the pace, his silver Warden's blade in hand. Cristos kept on his left, and the earth quivered around him as if some kind of heavy machinery was running wherever he walked. And overhead, I heard an eagle's cry, and the sky rumbled with thunder in response. Listens-to-Wind was still in. Behind them marched a column of Wardens, grim men and women in grey cloaks, bearing staves and silver swords in their hands.

On Marcone's other flank was a crew of ghostly white figures, covered in cloaks and shrouds of some kind of filmy white cloth and moving with inhuman grace. I felt the Winter mantle tug toward those figures in a movement of pure hunger, now that Lara and her people had also come to the fray.

And behind them came people. Just people. Hundreds of them, armed with shotguns of the exact same make as the ones that had been stored in the Bean, hundreds of them following the banner of the Baron of Chicago's will, frightened and *furious* and coming to destroy those who had brought death to their homes, who had challenged their territory, their very right to *be*.

I stared.

Hell's bells.

Marcone had rallied whatever troops he had left after the fight with the Jotnar. He had gathered his people together and then had to have circled down to help the southern defenses at the svartalf embassy. He must have gathered up a following much like I had—and he'd been able to arm them, and brought them sweeping unexpectedly to the aid of the southern defense.

Who had then been free to come help us in turn.

And now the enclosing arms of that force were about to spill directly onto the Fomor's legion as they blindly encircled the Winter Lady, hungry to destroy her.

Marcone, at the front of his own army, supported by some of the most powerful beings it had been my pleasure or misfortune to encounter, lifted one of those damned old guns, aimed it at Ethniu, and pulled the trigger.

And he got lucky. There was a sudden *buzz-thump*, and the Titan twitched as sparks flew from her armor.

The Baron of Chicago dropped the gun, drew another, and lifted his chin in sheer defiance.

And the Titan's face twisted in utter fury.

"What?" she spat, so furious that spittle flew from her lips and spilled between her teeth, burning the ground where it fell. She twisted in place, feet scraping the earth like a furious child's, only more apocalyptic, and Butters flinched in physical pain at the sheer rage and hatred in the Titan's voice. "These mortal *beasts*. These *worms*. I will grind that man's teeth to *dust* beneath my *heel*."

It was seeing that helpless fury that had taken her, that frustration and rage that did it, I think. I'd felt that way before. And I could handle it way better than she could. I had seen the Titan's weakness: She had the vices of her virtues.

In a way, it wasn't her fault. Ethniu was an elemental being, a primal force of the universe. Such beings had been meant to shape worlds from raw matter, not to cope with their wills being frustrated. Her own personal power meant that she could demand and get her way in nearly every circumstance.

But when she found a circumstance that wasn't like the others, she was confounded. She had been able to make things happen her way for so long, she was not used to coping with opposition, had grown rigid in her habit of victory. She never needed the reflexes to deal with an agile opponent, with adversity, with unpredictability. She re-acted to them the way a child would, confronting such obstacles for the very first time.

She spent precious seconds throwing a tantrum.

And hope rekindled and flickered to life.

Just this little light inside. That made everything matter again.

That reminded me that I had a job to do.

"Heh," I cackled. "Heh. Heh, heh, heh, hehehehehe-heh." My voice came out creaky and cracking, but genuinely amused. "You noob."

Ethniu glared at me, and my heart skipped a little beat. Because fear was a thing again, too. Fear that I might still lose this fight.

Because I knew that I could still win.

Marcone's shot had evidently been the signal to charge. The Baron of Chicago and his forces broke into a run, their voices rising in fury as they came, the earth trembling, white-shrouded vampires leaping as if on wires through the tide of light and resolution flooding from the Summer Lady's beacon, the unseen battle of minds and wills being waged every bit as viciously as the physical conflict unfolding before me.

If the newly arrived allied force hit the Fomor legions before order had been brought upon them, Marcone's charge would shatter them.

"Don't let her get to the Fomor!" I shouted.

Ethniu swept the spear at the earth between her and Butters, and another bolt of lightning howled from it—not at Butters, but at the ground itself, rending the earth between us and sending a truckload of torn ground flying at Butters and me. I covered my head with my arms and felt glad I was wearing the spellbound coat. It meant I had just collected a new round of bruises instead of broken bones. By the time I lowered my arms, Ethniu was on the last few degrees of arc on a fifty-yard leap that had carried her to the rear of the Fomor army, where she slammed the haft of her stolen spear into the ground and instantly arrested the attention of the surrounding Fomor troops. Her will flared out to enfold all of those around her, and they turned at once in lockstep, hundreds of the heavily armored warriors of the Fomor turning to face the Baron's charge.

The return to myself had meant the return of input from my own banner. I had one hundred and eighty-seven people still in the fight, most of them wounded.

And, from the battered ruin of the earthworks around the auditorium, there was a sudden flood of light, as *Esperacchius* appeared on the walls, along with a sudden ragged roar of defiance, and I realized with a start that when I had swamped Listen and his troops, I had also taken the pressure off the fortress.

I shoved myself to my feet, found my staff, and shouted, "Butters!"

"Here," came his voice, panting and pained but game.

The white-shrouded forms bounded through the air in graceful arcs and suddenly blurred in all directions as the Baron's army closed with the enemy, a dizzying display as the two masses crushed together.

"Come on!" I shouted.

"Where?"

I pointed at the clashing armies.

"What!?"

"Marcone gave us a shot," I said. "But if she kills him, his banner falls, and the people behind him will scatter. Then it's an army of them against a few of us. Then we all die." I gripped his shoulder and felt myself giving him the crazy grin, the one I know I get sometimes.

And with my other hand, I grabbed the handle of the knife.

It was time.

The heartbeat of the city, panicked and furious, flooded through me.

Butters's eyes got a little whiter.

I pointed at the army and said, "Cut me a way through there."

Butters looked at me. Then at the armies clashing. Then at me again.

"Yeah," he said. "Why not?"

We didn't charge into the fray so much as aggressively shamble.

But into the fray we went.

Chapter
Thirty-two

What came next was . . .

Look. I've been in a few fights. I even did my bit in a war.

None of it was like this.

What I remember most was how unsteady the ground was. The earth had been torn to dirt by the forces brought to bear upon it, and then doused in rain so dense it needed a new word to describe it. Then thousands of beings started fighting to the death on top of it.

The ground was a mixture of terrain so slippery you couldn't get your foot planted, terrain so boggy you couldn't tear your foot back out of it again, blood, and the fallen bodies of the wounded, the dying, and the dead, mixed liberally together.

The hell of it was, the most solid place to put your feet was on the fallen.

It would have been a hell of a workout, moving across that field, even if no one had been trying to kill us. But there was a war on—and outside of a few tightly gathered knots of troops around Marcone, Ethniu, Corb, and

Molly, there was no order to be had at all. No real lines to speak of, no uniforms—just pure pandemonium.

Fifty yards away, I heard River Shoulders roaring in fury, a sound that stunned and weakened friend and foe alike around him—but since he was concentrating only upon tearing the Fomor literally limb from limb, it worked out pretty well for his friends. Parts were flying into the air where the Sasquatch rampaged, and his presence on the field sent the enemy fleeing in terror, or at least in search of easier foes.

From the remains of the fortress, Sanya lifted his Sword and led my people forward into the fight. Even though they were battered and bleeding, the Knight had recognized that the matter would be settled in the next few moments, and the light of *Esperacchius* led a wedge of my people directly toward Ethniu, a rare knot of coordination in the melee, a fragile arrow aimed at the enemy's heart.

Then we were in the thick of it, and all I could see were struggling, mud-covered bodies. Frequently, it was impossible to tell friend from foe.

For everyone but Waldo Butters.

I don't know how, but the little guy went through that fight, the chaos and horror and filth—and none of it so much as *touched* him. When his feet hit the cloggy parts of the ground, he was so little that he had no trouble getting out again. On the slippery bits, his feet and balance shifted, legs taking the motion as naturally as a pro skateboarder out goofing around, and I recognized someone operating on something like angelic *intellectus* when I saw it, though I doubted Butters was even aware that he was doing it.

The Knight of Faith had decided where he needed to go. Mere physics would not be enough to gainsay him.

A unit of heavily armored Fomor troopers got in his way, six or eight of the enemy who had grouped together and were pounding the stuffing out of a small group of slim, armored fae brought to the fight by the Winter Lady—or at least, I was pretty sure that's what was happening. The mud of the fight coated everyone. In the stark light and the sheer chaos, it was all but impossible to tell a friendly face from a hostile one until the subject in question was so close that there was only time to strike, block, or attempt to flee.

Butters hit the entire group like a tornado—absolute, deadly, and bizarrely selective. The angelic chorus around *Fidelacchius* rose to an exultant crescendo as the weapon whirled and struck down everyone who got in our path— absolutely everyone.

When the Sword of Faith struck the soldiers of the Fomor, the slaves of the Titan's will, it did so with gruesome, precisely egalitarian effect, cleaving armor and weapon and flesh with equal precision and disdain. And when it struck the defenders of the city, that same weapon swept away grime from eyes, cleared muck from ears, and burned away some of the environment hampering our allies, leaving the ground steadier under their feet.

Butters, flowing with the grace of absolute concentration, struck what I presumed to be a friendly with the Sword, shattering the bent and stricken helmet clear off the head of what turned out to be a rather unremarkable-looking young woman with medium brown skin and the arched cheekbones and angular eyes of a native of the far northwest of North America, her face twisted with utter terror—and I saw it when the Sword passed, and its light burned that fear out of her. She blinked twice, as if waking up from a nap that had been plagued with a bad dream, set her jaw, and rose with her weapon in her hand.

"Sir Knight," she bade me, by way of greeting, gave me a short nod, and rose to drive her sword into the throat of an enemy soldier that lay on the ground, clutching at the place where its arm had been.

I had to turn to keep pace with Butters, or he'd have left me clambering through the muck after him. But I looked behind us and saw the wake we were leaving—not only of felled enemies, but of allies, seared free of the dark pressure of Ethniu's will, their courage renewed.

Behind us, Sanya and his people angled into that opening that Butters's passing had left, filling it with sudden friendly forces—and others struggling in the havoc around us saw that opening and rallied toward it, toward the two Knights, as their allies called encouragement and flung themselves upon an increasingly uncertain foe. Sanya managed to meet up with Butters with a cheerful *whoop* of greeting, and then the big man covered Butters's six, simply following the smaller Knight, blade whirling, and fending off attacks that came at his flanks and rear.

In that moment, I *knew* what Michael had meant when he said that the most powerful part of the Sword of Faith had nothing to do with the word *sword*. Or even with the artifacts the two men held in their hands. Neither of the Swords could have done anything without the minds and hearts and hands of the men bearing them. And now Butters was, himself, the edge of a blade that was carving its way into the enemy, filling the empty space left behind with members of the alliance, surging with renewed energy, with the big black Russian behind him, laughing in a steady roar of amused defiance.

There was no way I could have taken myself through that mess without making it a hell of a lot messier. Butters made it look easy.

On that field, in that chaos, not even the mud stuck to him. Where the light of the Swords went, everyone knew who was who—there was no confusion to be had. Only choices. And everywhere the Knights went, the enemy fell, and our allies roared back into the fight.

Having those two going before me was not like having two allies. In that terrible, desperate place, it was like having hope and faith *themselves* standing beside you, and *that* power was deeper and ultimately more meaningful than any enchantment or mystic weapon around.

Long story short—the Swords cut a hole through the chaos, leaving bad news for the enemy everywhere they walked. Granted, a lot of the beings fighting on our side weren't exactly angels. But whatever their reasons, that night they stood in defense of life, and evidently, that was good enough for the Power behind the Swords.

The physical trauma the Knights actually inflicted on the bodies of the foe was insignificant compared to the wreckage they made of enemy morale. For every Fomor trooper that went down before them, fifty more saw their companions falling beneath blades of terrifying light, saw the enemy surging to the fight with rising ferocity. Worse, beneath the light of the Swords, the dread will of the Titan held diminished sway—and without that psychic pressure to oppose them, the troops that the Winter Lady brought to the fight came at the enemy with pure, intelligent aggression.

And somewhere along the way I realized that the Winter troops Molly had brought to the battle were kids. They were a batch of goddamned kids, even younger than the Wardens. Kids fighting like stunt doubles in martial arts movies.

There had been rumors on the Paranet that the faeries had begun stealing children again.

Maybe they had. God, given what was in front of my eyes, I wasn't even sure it was a bad thing.

The Winter Lady shrieked over the battle again, her voice pure, contemptuous fury, as one of her dwindling bodyguard of trolls smashed its way through the blocks of ice left in her wake. Another wave of enemy magic crashed upon the battlefield around her, and if she walked through it mainly untouched, the trolls around her screamed their pain and rage as fresh waves of enemy troops, driven by terror of Corb and his coterie, flung themselves at the Winter Lady.

My heart went into my throat as I saw a sword strike her and wedge itself into the flesh of her naked shoulder as if she had been a block of ice. Molly contemptuously touched the hand holding the weapon with her blade and snapped a kick up into the ice, shattering the frozen hand. She knocked the sword casually out of her flesh. Then she leaned down and almost sensually ran the edge of her icy blade beneath the edge of the enemy's helmet. The blade opened the trooper's throat in a wash of blood that burst into steam as it touched Molly's pale, cold flesh, and she bubbled into chill, hungry laughter as it did.

God.

I'd heard that laugh coming from other lips.

Yeah.

No wonder she hadn't gone home to visit the family for Sunday dinner.

In any other circumstance I could have imagined, I would have gone charging full steam toward Molly to assist and protect her. But the Winter Lady didn't need my help.

She was the anvil.

As long as she and her little legion held together, the enemy was trapped, forced to try to finish them off. As long as the Winter Lady stood, if the Fomor fled, the Winter Fae would be among them, cutting them down without mercy. While Molly stood, the Fomor legion would be exposed, disorganized, vulnerable to the very attack that was happening now. Professional militaries were professional because of their ability to operate in unison more effectively than militaries with less training—like armed civilian defenders, for example. Chaos and disorganization among the enemy strongly favored our team.

Charging off to Molly's rescue would defeat the entire point of what she was doing.

She had chosen to be the anvil. It was up to the rest of us to be the hammer.

So when Butters started turning to go toward her, I shouted, "No!" and pointed over his shoulder, with my staff, at Ethniu and her embattled cohesive knot of Fomor troops.

And I left my former apprentice to fight for her life against the King of the Fomor, his elite bodyguard of sorcerers, and overwhelming numerical odds, in the hope that I could help bring down a Titan before the Fomor did the same to Molly.

Butters fought through another forty yards. I know that doesn't sound like much. You had to be there. The mud and water on the ground made every step a slightly different trap. The lighting was worse than a dance floor's, alternating patches of mud and shadow and brilliant white light from the whirling Swords. And fighting is the most difficult cardio there is. Ten yards on that field would have been a stiff workout.

He did forty without slowing down. And there was nothing at all that was little about the Knight of Faith that night.

The shotguns of my volunteers, coming along in our wake, were being plied more sparingly now. Ammunition was low, but we'd lost so many people that finding more on their remains wasn't out of the question the people who were still alive were largely ones who had been to places like this before, or been taught by those who had When they shot, they did it smoothly and in cold blood. And they shot once and moved on. Watching them wasn't like watching an action movie. It was like watching a well-coordinated work crew all moving to the same song. Steady, rhythmic work, as they advanced under cover of their companions, fired two or three rounds on any available targets, then covered the advance of the companion rank coming behind them, reloading.

The hard part, during that advance, was not pitching in. The air wasn't supercharging my use of magic any longer, and that meant I couldn't be epic for very long before collapsing. If I'd tried another leaf-blower spell, it would have dropped me unconscious in the time it took us to move forward. It was simply too high an energy requirement now. I had the magic that was available to me and nothing more—and I had to save every punch I had for Ethniu.

And that meant that people died whom I maybe could have saved.

It wasn't like I did nothing. My staff was still charged up, as if I'd loaded it up nice and heavy, and I knocked some bad guys around who would have wounded or killed my people. But I missed some. I don't know. Maybe I could have done more. Or done it smarter somehow. But if you weren't there, you can't know how desperate it was. How everyone was terrified. What it does to you to see the power of darkness, of real, genuine terror, on gruesome display. Hell, even when it's on your side, it ain't pretty. Witnessing wrath and death being visited upon another being, no matter how righteously, is no easy thing.

The Knights of the Sword, some of the Sidhe we'd relieved, and my volunteers cut me a path through an army.

We got there first, but farthest out.

Ethniu had positioned herself atop a mound of corpses. And incipient corpses. There were plenty to go around, and they'd piled them into a hill maybe ten feet high. It meant that she could see the battlefield all around her, ply the blasts of her stolen spear with deadly effect. When the Eye had drawn in enough energy once more, she would have her choice of targets.

But it also meant that she could be seen.

She had arrayed her troops on the mound of corpses

around her in thick ranks. These were the heavy guys, strong and spooky-quick in their thick armor, with their too-thick torsos and overlong arms. I only got to see one face, behind the helmets, and that was of a hairy, rough-looking humanoid. It was hard to see much. He'd been hit with a heavy club or hammer, hard enough to shatter his helmet, and there was only so much left of the face. Neanderthal? Hell, how long *had* the Fomor been enslaving humans?

They faced us now in solid, disciplined ranks, and Butters slowed. Even he didn't think he was going to just waltz through that.

On the far side of Ethniu's defensive position, Marcone's forces broke through the chaos.

First through was the Archive. She looked like a girl, not terribly remarkable in any way, in her early teens, wearing a formal school uniform. The objects whirling in a lethally swift orbiting cloud around her started with broken fire hydrants and got bigger and heavier from there, up to and including a big police motorcycle. They were moving so fast that it was hard to *see* what the object was, until it hit something. Then there was a gruesome spray and it slowed down enough for you to see a hundred-and-twenty-pound dumbbell tearing an octokong in half, or a bundle of rusty barbed wire the size of an Earthball smash its way through entire troops of Huntsmen at once. None of them got it in the face, either—when they saw the gruesome machine that was the Archive coming, they tried to flee. The ground and the chaos of the battlefield didn't always allow it.

When it didn't, the results looked like some kind of

accident involving pressurized tanks of various colors of paint.

The Archive hadn't come here to fight.

She was just mowing the lawn.

A few yards down the line from her, a block of enemy troops fifty yards deep and thirty yards across abruptly contorted—and then they just *died*, falling like broken puppets. One moment, chaos raged. The next, there was a sudden block of absolute stillness and silence.

The Blackstaff strode into the vacuum, Ebenezar McCoy in the fullness of his power, the left side of his body buried in a shadow so deep that it had to be taken on faith that he still had that half of his body at all.

Beside him strode Ramirez and Cristos. Cristos was doing something to the ground that solidified it into hard clay about a foot in front of Ebenezar's toes, and the old man strode forward with dust coating him and a bleeding wound on the side of his mostly bald pate, his jaw set at a pugnacious angle.

A Fomor officer, probably one of their lesser nobles, had been pressured toward the old man by the inexorable power of the Archive and had the choice of the lawn mower or the tiger. He chose tiger, howled, and flung himself and his personal retinue at Ebenezar.

I had never seen Ramirez cut loose before.

Maybe a dozen froggy Fomor warriors came at them. He gathered his good hand in across his body, like a farmer drawing seed from a seed bag, and unleashed it with a ringing word and a flash of dark, dangerous eyes. A wave of translucent pale blue energy washed across them and . . .

And they just fell to wet, mushy dust. To their component molecules, maybe, as if the bonds of energy that had
held them together had somehow been broken. Taken
apart. Disintegrated. I noted, somewhere in the academic
vaults of my head, that magic like that was like unbaking
a damned cake back into its original components. Where
would you even start?

Even more impressive, from an academic standpoint,
was that breaking the energy of those bonds must have
provided most of the fuel for the spell, because Ramirez
never so much as broke limping stride. He could pull that
one over and over again.

Ramirez was good. Better than me, on a technical level,
by a considerable margin.

He blew them into water and dust. It wasn't even fair.

In a war, nobody plays fair. That's what war is.

A group of panicked, fleeing octokongs went by as Lara
and her people came bounding out of the chaos, their
flowing, shroudlike white robes stained in various shades
of blood. None of them looked hurt, and I saw one take a
panicked blow from an octokong's emptied arquebus. The
shroud material *twitched* and *moved*, gathering thickly beneath where the blow began to land, and the body beneath seemed to briefly lose mobility and stiffen as the
arquebus struck—and rebounded, the shroud actively
pushing the weapon away, as the White Court vampire
wearing it dealt a pair of lethal blows and breezed on by in
a little twirling dance step. When Lara's people landed in
the open, they did it together, coordinated, somewhere
between Hong Kong cinema and *Charlie's Angels*.

Ethniu raised the spear and it transformed again into

lightning in her hand. She swept a baleful gaze around the battlefield, choosing which target was the most dangerous.

She focused on me for a second. Then, longer, on the Archive. But then her eyes settled on my grandfather. On the Blackstaff in his left hand. Something about it seemed to stoke the furnace of her rage.

"Little boys should not play with adult tools," the Titan snarled.

The old man's answer was to raise the Blackstaff, shadow engulfing his head and shoulders, and to make a sweeping, beckoning gesture.

The front rank of the line of Fomor troopers died in their tracks, clattering to the ground.

Ethniu howled and unleashed the lightning against my grandfather.

The stocky old man vanished farther into shadow, raising the Blackstaff, the weapon's darkness devouring the lightning, drinking and drinking endlessly—until I could see actinic fire gathering in the cracks of the old man's skin. It did weird things to the shadow he cast, twisting and distorting it until it looked like a hideously twisted old woman, complete with the classic witch nose and chin, looking somehow darkly amused.

The instant Ethniu brought her fire down upon the old man, the Archive tilted her head slightly and lifted a single finger. In that instant, the whirling screen of big heavy things went flying toward the Titan in rapid succession like stones loosed from a giant's sling. They hammered Ethniu, striking clouds of sparks from the Titanic bronze armor over her skin, battering her back off the top of her mound of bodies, and sending the bolt of energy trailing up into the sky.

My grandfather staggered and fell to a knee, silver light seething from beneath his skin, showing the dark shadows of liver spots, the lines of the bones in his right hand. Then he lifted that hand, holding what looked like a blazing gemstone the size of a softball, and with a word and a gesture sent damned near every erg of energy he'd just received sailing back at the Titan's position, wreaking havoc among her troops.

Just as Baron Marcone and his people hammered their way through the confused Fomor and into Ethniu's makeshift redoubt.

The troubleshooters on either side of Marcone led the way, rifles at their shoulders, advancing with a weird, slow little shuffle that left their shoulders steady and even, even in the sketchy terrain. They fired into the mass of troops. The Fomor's armor wasn't up to stopping heavy fire from military-grade arms at close range. Their shields were made out of something heavier, though, and they wound up dropping into a version of the old Roman tortoise formation, shields lifted and interlocked to form a wall against them.

Ethniu bounded back into position atop the mound and lifted the spear again.

The old man shouted and hammered her with a flying wedge of raw kinetic force that struck her like the blade of a guillotine, sending a shower of fire up from the surface of her bronzed flesh and leaving a glowing, smoking line across her upper torso—but it didn't break the armor. She ignored the blow from the deadliest wizard of the

White Council as if it had been delivered with a pillow, not the foundational forces of the universe, and focused her rage on the defiant Baron of Chicago.

Ethniu screamed her primal fury toward the man, and in response the formation of troops began a groaning chant, moving forward toward us behind the cover of their shields. Marcone's troubleshooters lit the tall, unbowed form of Ethniu up, but they'd brought guns to an epic mythology fight. They inflicted some losses on the troops, but to the Titan they were so many annoying mosquitoes doing nothing but proving how necessary it was to crush them.

"Harry!" Butters called, his voice twisted with rapid breathing and rising distress. "What's the plan here, man?"

"Uh, uh," I said.

I'd never been in an epic mythology fight quite this epic before.

The Archive gestured, the ground shook, and a sudden fissure opened in the earth, swallowing enemy troops and the bodies of our fallen allies alike, and nearly took Ethniu with them. The Titan staggered, and I could see the slight tug of exhaustion in her response, the signs of slowness that showed how much energy she had been expending.

The biggest guns around weren't putting her in the ground.

But they were weakening her. Slowing her.

This was our chance.

"Get her!" I screamed.

On the other side of the field, Marcone shouted something to his people that probably sounded cooler than me and meant "Get her." They came forward aggressively, and Marcone led the way, drawing pistols and firing them one at a time, in alternating hands—and where they struck, they smashed through shields and armor and flesh alike.

Butters and Sanya rushed forward on either side of me. Sanya was bellowing laughter like a madman. Butters shrieked the battle cry of maybe something like a leatherback turtle—but there was a long swath of ground he had taken from the enemy in his wake. Behind them, our volunteers shouted exhausted, terrified cries and came forward.

I used to wonder how people could run forward into things like that. I think it's about the environment. There's just too much confusion, too much fear, too much pain, to think rationally. It's not a rational place. When death is all around, forward can get to looking like a pretty good way out. And humans can only bear tension, fear, and worry for so long. We aren't built to sit quietly under such burdens. We're built to go out and deal with whatever is causing them.

We aren't built to sit and take it. We were made to take action.

Eventually, too much pressure will bring a willing fight out of anybody. Even in a nightmare hellscape. Or especially in a nightmare hellscape. Eventually, it's better to go forward into it and have things settled than to huddle in terror for one second longer.

I think we'd all had as much as we could take.

It was time to settle it. One way or another.

So I charged in and felt others following me, the light

of the Swords casting an implacable, inexorable glare ahead of us.

I had a couple of seconds to see everything, absolutely everything about the charge. Time slowed, as it does sometimes in such circumstances. I could see the interplay of the plates of armor worn by the enemy, the skill with which they had been made. I could see individual droplets of mud flying, almost floating, through the air. I could smell mud and blood and viscera as clearly and vividly as a fresh, steaming pizza put on your table. I could see dead eyes and broken bodies, shifting as they were walked upon, giving the illusion of animation.

And then we crashed into the foe, and everything was flying weapons and screams and balance and trying to get enough air into my lungs. There was no music now—few clicks, few calls. Just panting breaths and grunts and cries of pain. Weapons hitting one another. Curses. Bodies slipping, falling into the mud, visibility of no more than a few feet.

Absolute chaos.

But we had the Knights of the Sword and the enemy didn't.

The light of the Swords blinded the enemy to everything else. If there were missiles flung, it was at the Knights. A froggy minor sorcerer tried his hand at them, to no success, his magic blocked by the light of the Sword of Faith. The Swords filled our foes with fear—as long as the Knights were coming at them, they had little thought for the most intelligent response and reacted to their fear instead.

We cut our way toward the weakened Titan, step by step.

I saw things. Ebenezar set a squad of octokongs on fire with an absent word and a flick of one hand. Cristos began making fists and just yanking the enemy down into the earth, right down past the tops of their heads, killing and burying them all at once, very efficient. Ramirez hustled over to the Archive, melting bad guys along the way, and covered Ivy while she kept ripping at the earth beneath the Titan's feet in an effort to keep her stumbling and off-balance.

And Marcone walked straight into the melee, firing flintlocks and dropping them as if he had an unlimited supply. Gard and Hendricks fought on either side of him, and his people covered his rear as they all pushed forward together, closing to a range too short for even pistols to be practical. A lot of people were down in the mud, fighting and biting and gouging. Bad idea, to wrestle Neanderthals. We didn't get the best of those fights, and once they realized it, the enemy threw themselves forward with berserk abandon, and if you didn't have a friend to shoot the berserk trooper off you, you got slammed against the ground until you died.

The champions got to the Titan at about the same time.

Gard went in first.

The Valkyrie spun full circle with her axe to build momentum, called something in a voice almost like a note of music, and the head of the axe blazed with runic power. She struck Ethniu in the ankle. In the back of the ankle.

In her Achilles tendon.

And for the first time in millennia, mortals heard a Titan scream in pain.

It was like a psychic bomb went off. A wave of agony hit my nervous system with the clarity and intensity of dental pain, pure and unfiltered. The world staggered to one side. I'd have fallen if Sanya hadn't caught my arm.

Ethniu lurched, her foot not bleeding, but brutally broken and no longer supporting her weight—and Hendricks hit her at the hips like the linebacker he'd once been. Titan and professional bruiser went down together—and without an instant's hesitation, Marcone drew his last and largest pistol, shoved the barrel into the Titan's natural eye, and pulled the trigger.

There was a howl of sound, a flash of purple light that seared my retinas, and Ethniu's head jerked back and to one side.

Again, without hesitation, Marcone dropped the pistol, drew a knife, and knelt to drive it into the same eye.

Ethniu kicked. There was the sound of multiple wet sticks snapping. Hendricks gasped. Gard raised her axe again, but the Titan simply seized her leg around the knee and twisted. Bones and ligaments snapped. Gard went down screaming.

Hands shot to Marcone, supernaturally swift, but the Baron of Chicago hadn't waited around to see them coming and was already in a roll over one shoulder and away before she could seize him.

The Titan sat up. There was a ring of powder burn around her natural eye, a little redness, and otherwise not a mark on her. She kicked Marcone's legs out from under him as he began to rise, sending him sprawling to one side.

Ethniu lifted the spear.

"No!" I shouted. I triggered the last couple of blasts of kinetic force from my staff, emptying it, but the press was too close, and armored troopers soaked up the blasts before they could get to Ethniu.

The spear came down.

Hendricks took it.

The big man, the gangster's long-term bodyguard, threw himself in the way of the spear.

It struck home, hard and clean. It transfixed Hendricks diagonally, going in above his collarbone, coming out around his kidneys. The resistance of his body guided the head of the spear off course. It struck into the earth beside Marcone's head.

Hendricks glowered up at the Titan. And spat.

And died.

Eyes still open and on his foe.

Gard screamed in simple, ancient, human anguish.

And Marcone slid around his dead friend's back, seized the automatic shotgun from its harness on Hendricks's chest, swung the barrel up into the Titan's face, and emptied the magazine.

Ethniu reeled back, shielding her face with her arms and screaming in fury. She was showing more weakness—she had ignored fire that had come at her earlier, but Marcone's rounds had caused her pain. She swung the spear to one side and back, slamming Marcone with Hendricks's limp body with a hideous finality of impact. Then she whipped the spear free, sending a column of lightning tearing into the Archive's position. Ramirez grabbed the girl and yanked her out of the way, but Ethniu had regained her footing.

A needle of fire so bright that it hurt my eyes lashed into Ethniu's body at the waist, where she had to twist and bend, and where the armor just couldn't have been as thick. It drew a hiss of discomfort and annoyance from her, and she whirled the spear and smashed back at my grandfather with more lightning. The old man got a shield up in time, but Cristos had been a half heartbeat slow. He was flung to one side, burning, body going limp and rag doll in the violence of the explosion.

Then, as my grandfather recovered, Ethniu bounded forward, superhumanly agile even mostly on one leg, and struck him with the butt end of the spear.

My grandfather was a quarterstaff fighter with lifetimes of experience. And he was in damned fine condition for a man who had seen birthdays in four different centuries. But he was about five six and mortal. She was a nine-foot protogoddess. He pulled two deflection parries he should never have survived, much less made cleanly, and then she kicked him with her wounded leg.

She didn't break his ribs. Her virtually invincible shin hit him with a low roundhouse in the hips, the side of the pelvis.

It was like a kid snapping a stick.

My grandfather went down hard. Unmoving.

The Titan's lips twisted in disgust. She bent down, tore a head from a corpse with about as much trouble as me plucking a grape, and flung it at the Archive. Her aim was perfect. The girl was just struggling up out of the mud when the flying head hit her at the top of her sternum and hammered her back down.

Hell's bells.

There was a bounding sound in the darkness, and River

Shoulders flew through the air at Ethniu. She slammed at him with a bolt of lightning, but the bespectacled Sasquatch had evidently watched some home improvement videos or something. He was still airborne as the lightning hit, and he had timed it perfectly. There was nowhere for the current to latch on and ground out, and he passed through the bolt of lightning with little more consequence than some of his hair being set on fire.

The flaming Sasquatch hit Ethniu like a runaway truck—hitting a runaway truck barrier.

The Titan simply dug a heel into the ground and accepted River Shoulders' charge. She arrested it completely. Then she got ahold of his good arm and dislocated it with a twist.

River Shoulders screamed.

Lightning struck, a hawk cried in fury, and then a god-damned grizzly bear *fell out of the night sky* and onto Ethniu's head.

Don't care how Titanic you are. No one expects an orbital-drop grizzly.

The bear's fangs and claws raked at the Titan, leaving smoldering, glowing marks on her armor, but she simply hammered the thing with the butt of her spear until it dropped away, stunned. She swung the spear like a club, screaming in mindless rage, and broke the bear's back like it was made of balsa wood.

The bear screamed in pain and fear—and suddenly Listens-to-Wind lay where the bear had been, prostrate and racked with obvious agony.

In seconds, she had killed or crippled virtually every other major hitter on the field.

Hell's *bells*.

Divine combat. Heavy-duty magical combat. Physical combat.

We were playing rock, paper, scissors with the Titan, and each of us could only do one. She could always pull scissors to our paper, paper to our rock, rock to our scissors. And if she got bored, she could always pull out Even Better Scissors, Rock, or Paper. God, from what I'd seen and heard about her, she wasn't even an experienced warrior. She was a noob. She was simply a power an order of magnitude beyond anything facing her. And she was beating us.

But she was breathing hard now. She was paying a price for her victory.

How do you eat a Titan?

One bite at a time.

Sanya and Butters didn't speak to each other. Simultaneously, they simply flew forward at the Titan as we finally broke through the troops and had a shot at her. Butters went right. Sanya went left. The light of the Swords could have illuminated a stadium.

But here's the thing about the Swords. The thing no one had told me, that I'd had to learn through years of observation.

The Swords could work miracles when it came to facing off against the forces of darkness. But it wasn't their job to decide the fight. The Swords, and the Knights, weren't given power to crush their enemies wholesale. They existed to level the field—to create a choice where one wouldn't have otherwise been possible. The Swords gave the Knights an absolute power to contest the will of darkness.

But the Swords could not give them victory.

Swords don't do that. Swords have never done that.

Victory comes from the mind, the heart, and the will. From people.

What is the sword compared to the hand that wields it?

All around us, the battle hung in the balance, poised. It could have gone one way or the other, and a feather's touch could have made the difference in which way it fell.

I lifted a hand. I had retooled the top of my staff weeks before. It had been fit very closely, so close that you couldn't see the seam when it was closed. The svartalves had used lasers when I commissioned it. I unscrewed a four-inch section from the top of the staff, where a simple bolt and socket had been set.

Then I drew the dagger from my belt.

My heartbeat thundered in my ears.

The handle of the dagger had been set with the same size socket as the cap of the staff. I set it on the end and spun it, and the well-oiled bolt whirled into place and locked with a simple hinged hook over one side of the dagger's hilt, to keep it from unscrewing.

Then I gathered power. The runes of the weapon's haft flared into green-gold light that pulsed in intensity along with the thunder of my heart.

The knife at the head didn't burst into flame or anything. It just became . . . colder. The edges harder, sharper, more real—so real that anything that you looked at in the background beyond the spear seemed . . . blurry. Symbolic. Transitory.

That weapon carried reality woven into it, dark and hard and unalterable. I felt my will and the weapon's head vibrating in harmony, along with my heartbeat.

I slammed the butt end of the Spear of Destiny on the ground, and green and gold fire leapt up in a ring around me.

The impact vibrated against my hand and I felt it go out into the ground through the soles of my sneakers. I could sense the substance of the Spear stirring, forming, almost awakening. It drew some of its energy from me. My heart rate started to climb.

"Hey! Regina George!" I called, and my voice echoed over the field as if on loudspeakers.

Thrum-thrum, went the power of the Spear. *Thrum-thrum. Thrum-thrum.*

Ethniu's head whipped toward me, her eye focused on the Spear, wide and alarmed—while Butters and Sanya rushed to flank her.

"Yeah," I said, and started wearily forward. "Enough foreplay. Time for the main event."

Chapter

Thirty-three

Sanya and Waldo and I rushed the Last Titan, and Chicago hung in the balance.

Around us, armies clashed drunkenly. Marcone's amateurs fought like hell beside mine. They didn't fight well, but they fought hard—and when they went down, they did not go alone. Etri's people were simply terrifying—blurs that moved across the battle, striking from almost complete invisibility, and could sink into the earth and emerge from it anywhere they wanted, at will.

If we'd had a legion of svartalves, we wouldn't have *needed* anyone else. But they weren't a numerous people—and they were directing their efforts to spearheading the attack of the relief force, to join up with the Winter Lady's cohorts.

Lara's people fought beside them.

Watching the two groups work together was like some kind of bizarre outtake from the Cirque du Soleil. Lara's fighters sailed through the air with the greatest of ease, taking thirty-foot strides in great, leaping bounds, moving almost weightlessly, their shroud-armor fluttering and snapping. As I watched, the wavery figure of a svartalf emerged from the earth and dragged a minor Fomor's ankles into the ground. Even as it did, a white figure flashed by, spinning a blade on the end of a pole in a smooth arc, and killed the enemy sorcerer as easily as a beast at slaughter, and I saw the unmistakable silvery eyes of Lara Raith as she went by. She snapped the weapon up in a salute to the svartalf warrior as she passed, then engaged a band of war-beasts and their handlers, only to have half a dozen more wavery figures emerge from the ground behind her foes as they surrounded her, a counter-ambush that annihilated the bunch.

Lara's eyes and mine met for a dangerous second—and she immediately shifted her direction, bounding across the savage battlefield like a fluttering pale spirit, toward Ethniu's back.

Sanya, as tough as Butters and more athletic, got to Ethniu first.

The Titan lashed out with the spear's head, sending it whipping through an arc that would have severed Sanya's neck if he hadn't dropped into a slide. He came through with the old cavalry saber held in both hands and struck at the Titan's other foot.

Ethniu knew the power of the Swords at this point, and she dodged out of the way—forcing her weight onto her wounded leg and sending her down to a knee.

Butters, going by the other side, whipped *Fidelacchius* through a circle—and Ethniu struck him right on the chin with the butt end of her stolen spear with a simple lightning-fast jab while he did it.

Which is why you shouldn't learn fighting moves from the movies.

Butters went flying back into the mud and didn't move.

Half the light on the field went out.

Sanya regained his feet, behind the Titan, and charged as she began to rise, the head of the spear orienting on the unmoving form of the Knight of Faith. Before she could finish him, Sanya slammed into her back and smashed her down into the mud.

Ethniu twisted on the way down and hammered an awkward blow at Sanya with one arm. The Knight of Hope caught the blow on the blade of *Esperacchius*.

And again, a Titan screamed.

Maybe two thousand individuals from both armies simply collapsed to the ground, howling in agony as a wave of psychic pain washed out of the Titan. It felt like my arm had been set on fire.

But it sure as hell wasn't the first time.

This time, I'd been ready, bracing myself against the Titan's suffering, and surged through it like a swimmer breaking through the first wave at the beach. I closed the last few yards, slammed my feet down hard to brace them, and thrust the Spear at the Titan's face.

Ethniu swept her stolen spear from left to right like a windshield wiper, and she was *fast*, way faster than she'd looked when I hadn't been within stab range. I tried to slip the parry but was just too slow, and she batted the Spear aside, seized Sanya by a handful of his mail shirt, and threw him at me with about as much energy as a runaway golf cart.

We both went down in a heap, hard enough to take breath and cause stars and comets to whirl in front of us.

Esperacchius spun out of Sanya's hands.

There was *blood* on it.

The Titan's *blood*.

Ethniu glanced at a smoldering pile of what was mostly corpses, their body fat blazing in flames where one of the bolts of lightning or flying shards of Power had struck incidental targets. With the head of the spear, she flicked the Sword of Hope, smeared with blood too red to be real, into the fire.

And then she thrust her wounded arm into it, her expression twisting with pain as the fire scorched and boiled the wound.

The light of the Sword died.

Hundreds screamed with the Titan's pain.

And the world suddenly got a whole hell of a lot darker.

"Trinkets of the Redeemer," she snarled, her voice absolutely bubbling with hatred. She rose, whipping her burned arm out of the fire. The wound hadn't been a very big one, even struck with *Esperacchius*, and she had cauterized it closed, apparently. Though the surface of her bronze skin was untouched, the flesh inside the wound had been charred like meat on a grill. "Maggots crawling on our beautiful world. Infesting it. *Humans*."

Hate seethed through her, vibrated off her like heat from a fire. The Titan twisted her face in a rictus of concentration.

And the Eye kindled to scarlet life and began to brighten.

"Damn," Sanya muttered, as the Titan turned toward us. The scarlet warlight of the Eye let me at least see Sanya.

The big man was lying on his back. Something in the area of his collarbone was . . . just wrong, under the skin. It wasn't shaped like humans were supposed to be shaped. His voice was thready, and he panted as though each inhalation was of pure fire. "Was pretty sure that would work."

"Get her," I said. "Not much of a plan."

"No. For next time, need better plan."

I blinked and looked at the Russian as the red glare brightened.

"Next time?"

He grinned at me, though he couldn't move, in sheer mad defiance.

Supercool magical pokey stick or not, I didn't have what it took to stand up to power on the order of magnitude of the Eye of Balor. My heaviest magical punch was nowhere close to what my grandfather could throw, and that hadn't gotten through her armor, either. Even if I was a lot better, even if I threw it out as a death curse, the best spell I had wouldn't surpass what the old man could do.

And I still hadn't gotten to her blood.

If I was going to bind the Titan, I needed that. And I needed her closer to the water.

The Spear quivered with power, and I could feel the sheer metaphysical *mass* of the thing, its utter reality. It was, in many ways, just a spear. But it was a spear to *everything*. If I could stick it in the Titan, she would bleed.

But she was twenty rough feet away. And I'd have to get close enough to even have a shot at hitting her. And she'd have to be so slow that merely human reflexes could manage the task.

None of which was going to happen before she unleashed the Eye.

But I shoved myself to my feet, Spear in hand, brought forth my shield, and stepped forward, in front of the fallen Knight of Hope. No particular reason to do it. Not a lot of hope to be had.

The enemy had come at us, out of nowhere, far stronger than we had expected, and we'd done everything we could.

It hadn't been enough.

I faced the Titan's hate and fury and acknowledged that I couldn't beat it. But I figured I could die as well as Hendricks had—on my feet, face to the foe, between her and my friend.

And, twenty yards away, the swirl of battle stirred, and I saw One-Eye's shadowy form on the ground where he'd fallen.

He lifted his head.

He opened his eye.

It gleamed like a smoldering coal in the shadow.

And Odin, Father of the Aesir, spoke, his voice a deep resonance that shook the air with gentle power. *"Gungnir."*

I knew the translation of the weapon's name, a bit of useless trivia that had stuck in my head.

Swayer.

A rune burst into scarlet light upon the Spear's blade.

And, like a snake, the weapon of the gods the Titan had stolen turned in her hand, whipping about with lightning speed. As it did, runes burst into light all along the length of the blade and haft alike, suddenly blazing with energy.

And the weapon plunged with vicious, absolute precision into the Eye of Balor.

A wall of light hit me. I don't mean it was bright. I mean I got hit with a physical force the likes of which I had seldom experienced. If I hadn't had the shield up and ready, it would have obliterated me.

Shield or not, I was flung to the ground, and I fought to keep myself between the torrent and the fallen Knights. The world was white. Sound was just a high-pitched, endless tone. Reality was pain.

When the world came back again, Ethniu was on one knee. Her right hand rested on the ground. Half of her skull was burned to the bone. Black. The Eye glowered within its socket, flames and semisolid plasma gathered around it. The arm that had been holding Gungnir was gone. Just gone, right around the elbow, the flesh burned to a withered stump. Blinding light seethed from what looked like cracks on the Eye's surface.

And.

Stars and stones.

The damned creature lifted her maimed head. Half of her face was untouched. And she focused her gaze, equal parts mind-numbing beauty and screaming horror, and brought the Eye to bear on me.

Lara rose from behind that hideous head, leaping from a good fifty feet off. She sailed through the air with a grace that was more like that of an insect than a bird, spun as she came, and delivered a kick that could have inspired poetry to the back of the Titan's skull. She put everything into it as she came, the full power of a White Court vampire unleashing her stored strength all at once. Lara could have driven that kick through a battleship's hull.

She hit the Titan in the base of the skull.

The kick couldn't hurt Ethniu.

But the Eye, the *Eye* flew out of its socket and landed on the muddy ground, a little bigger than a softball, glowing with sullen rising fire.

A fire that had the potential to consume anything that was.

Including Ethniu.

The Titan clutched at her maimed face and her expression suddenly became subsumed with terror.

She lurched for the Eye.

So did I.

So did Lara.

We hit in a tangled confusion of bodies. The Eye skittered away.

It bounced and rolled and came to a stop against the boots of Hendricks's corpse.

And John Marcone popped out of the shadows near Hendricks's body, seized it, gave me a ferocious glare, and sprinted toward Lake Michigan.

Ethniu thrust her good hand at me, but Lara was quick. She kicked at the Titan's arm, deflecting some of the power of the blow, and it only sent me rolling across the muddy ground.

"Go!" Lara screamed, her eyes as bright as mirrors. She whipped her weapon—I think the Japanese called it a *naginata*—at the Titan, to no more effect than leaving sullen red lines of heat upon the Titanic bronze coating Ethniu's form.

Ethniu batted Lara aside like a rag doll and rose—only to stumble, as Lara's shroud-armor writhed off the vampire like a living thing, like some kind of bizarre invertebrate from the deep sea, and wrapped around the Titan's knees, binding them together. Ethniu fell back down again and was forced to briefly struggle against the living cloth.

Lara, naked as a jaybird, her pale skin gleaming, almost glowing, scrambled to one side and thrust her weapon at the Titan's fingers, trying to keep them from getting hold of the binding armor.

"She wants the Eye!" Lara screamed. "Go, Harry!"

The Spear felt heavy in my hands. It still had the power to hurt the Titan. But even with the backup of the Winter mantle, I was too battered and slow to get through to her.

And I needed to get her to the water anyway.

Marcone knew the plan. And he'd been thinking about it harder than me.

So I flung myself after him, plunging out of the clear air around the battlefield and into the choking, smoky haze over the city.

It was getting hard to tell where the park had been. The ground had been torn apart by the forces unleashed there. We got to where the footbridge had stood and found that Ethniu had used the Eye to facilitate the crossing of the avenue below for her army. She had blown the bridge and the retaining walls into slopes of rubble. And the area beyond was even worse. Streets, buildings, trees, light poles, everything that had not been able to flee had suffered destruction as if she had risen from the lake and pounded everything in her line of sight to rubble with the power of the Eye. The retaining wall beside the water was . . . just kind of a really, really rocky beach now.

I caught up to Marcone as he scrambled across the rough ground, running wherever possible. When I finally drew up beside him, he increased his pace, and I was hard-pressed to stay with him. Granted, he didn't look like he'd been through as much physical discomfort as I had that night, but even so he moved damned well, and like he'd been to places like this before.

"Can we use the weapon?" he asked in a terse tone as we ran.

Behind us, Ethniu let out a scream of rage, and there was a sound like metal cables tearing.

Then she screamed again. And it was closer.

"Maybe I could," I panted. "If I had a lifetime to study it. But probably not. Something like that isn't meant for mortals."

"Then we have no other option," Marcone said. "What do you need for the binding?"

"Her blood," I said.

And I started tearing at the bag I'd carried tied shut on my belt for most of the night.

Ethniu screamed again, closer. She wasn't moving much faster than we were. She'd had one hell of a night, too. Hell's bells, for all I knew she was using echolocation. She had every other damned advantage.

"I take it your weapon can accomplish that?" he asked.

"I don't know," I said honestly. We'd reached the beach by then, and clambered down the slope of broken rock to the edge of the water. "But it was good enough for the Son of God. I figure it's in the right league."

Marcone's eyes widened. One of his hands twitched. "And the adults let *you* have it?"

There was a clatter of rock on rock behind us.

"There's not much justice in the world," I said. "This thing might work. It might not. Takes some pretty serious power to hurt her. Like, angel-level power."

"The Swords," he said.

"Butters is new," I said. "He did something without thinking. This is what we've got."

In the haze, in which visibility had dropped to maybe thirty feet, I heard something breathing, the bubble of a slight snarl on every exhale.

Marcone crouched, tense.

"Do you at least have a gun?" I asked. "Maybe you can distract her."

"I have a knife," Marcone said.

"Jusht like a gangshter," I said. "Bringsh a knife to an apocalypshe fight."

Marcone gave me a level look and then said, in a much more conversational tone, "Honestly, Dresden. If you used your mind half as much as your mouth, you'd be running the place by now." He held up the Eye and spoke patiently. "I have what she *wants*. I will distract her." He clambered over several yards away from me and fell silent, watching the murky shadows.

I wanted to say something back, about how he was a running mouth, but instead I fell silent, gathered up some of my power, and shaped it into the mildest, softest veil I

could around me. Too much power in it, and Ethniu
might become aware of the energies in motion.

She was wounded now. Hunting. Hurting. Furious.
Frightened.

Like one of us.

She'd be focused on retrieving the Eye, focused on securing its power, on wiping away her enemies, who were
everyone, forever.

I wouldn't matter unless I got between her and the Eye.

So I stood still and silent and let the haze of the battle
and the more subtle effort of my will gather around me.
And waited.

It wasn't long.

Ethniu came down the slope on all fours, crawling with
perfect grace and mangled limbs, like a wounded spider,
holding herself up on the stump of her arm as easily as if
she'd been born that way. Her burned face was . . . sort of
seething, with some kind of thick mist or steam, as her
body fought the injuries Odin had inflicted.

Her eye locked on Marcone and she let out a low, cackling exhalation.

"The mortal who thinks himself a lord," the Titan
purred.

"Fool," Marcone replied by way of greeting, his tone
polite and pitched to carry loudly.

"What?" Ethniu demanded.

"If you had a mind," Marcone said, "you would have
used restraint. You would have arisen from the water with
no warning to anyone. You would have unleashed a wave
of expendable troops on the city, blown down a building
or two, and returned to the sea to watch the havoc un-

fold." He shook his head. "I will simply never understand the need some people seem to feel to be proven correct in front of their enemies. It's quite childish."

I blinked.

Was Marcone . . . talking smack?

"Give me what is mine, mortal," Ethniu snarled. "And I will kill you swiftly."

"Your negotiating skills would seem to need work as well," Marcone added.

Behind us, there was a series of roaring detonations, from back by the park. Sorcery, maybe.

I was an idiot. An exhausted, terrified idiot. Marcone didn't do anything just to be doing it.

He was providing cover for me.

So I started moving whenever they spoke, as soft and quiet as I knew how. It wasn't as quiet as usual. I'd just been too battered. Even now, I didn't feel pain, exactly. Mostly my body just seemed very confused about what the hell was going on. One moment it would be too hot, the next freezing, and nothing felt like it was moving quite right, so my balance kept wobbling. The Winter mantle had been stretched to its limits. Or rather, it had stretched me to mine.

It felt like I was getting closer to Game Over than I had before.

"You aren't anyone," the Titan said. "You're nothing. Just an animal. An animal near the top of its class on one little world."

"And yet, I walk where I will," Marcone said. "I sleep where and when I please. I eat when I hunger. I choose what to make of my life. I am free."

I crept closer.

"Who are you?" Marcone asked back, his voice ringing defiance. "A daughter unloved by her monstrous father? Sold and traded like a horse? Hiding in a dark cave with her useless hangers-on for millennia? And now lashing out with her daddy's gun." He shook his head and bounced the Eye in his hand. "It appears that it is better to be a mortal than a Titan, these days."

She crept closer, vibrating with tension. "Give me," she seethed, "the Eye."

Marcone stared at the Titan and appeared to choose his words the way a surgeon would his implements. "Be a good girl," he said. "And go get it."

With an expression of absolute nonchalant contempt, he tossed the smoldering Eye over his shoulder and into the waters of Lake Michigan.

Which instantly began to boil.

I was close.

The Titan bared her teeth in a hideous grimace, enraged beyond making a sound, beyond even attempting communication, and came at him.

A rock rolled beneath my ankle.

Without an instant's hesitation, Ethniu spun and flung a rock at me with her good hand.

I saw it coming and felt like a moron. Ethniu had had no reason to have a conversation with Marcone. She'd known I was there all along, but she hadn't known exactly where. So she'd been using the slight sound of my own movements to get a fix on my location. The rock was enough to give me away.

But Marcone had struck her where it hurt—in the feelings. What he'd said had been defiant enough, disrespect-ful enough, to send her into a rage. She could have flicked that stone at me carefully, like a dart thrower, beaned me in the head, and that would have been that. But she didn't. She threw it hard, sidearm, like a major-league pitcher, her rage giving the motion away so that I had an instant to counter her.

I turned my shoulder into the stone and it hit me like a sledgehammer.

My coat stopped the worst of it, which meant that all I got was a broken arm. Left one, middle of my forearm. The rock shattered against me, and if the coat kept me alive, it still felt like I'd been kicked by a particularly pow-erful and hostile horse.

I went down with a cry.

My body felt like a car that didn't want to start, and my limbs filled with a bone-crushing weariness. The toll the night had put on me was becoming physically unsupport-able. I slammed a hand to the ground to push myself up, or tried to. The actual movements my body performed seemed a lot feebler than I had intended. But I got back up, just as the Titan slithered across the rocks to Marcone.

Steel gleamed in the Baron's hand. Maybe a four-inch blade, black composite handle, modern diver's knife, very plain. Very much not epic or apocalyptic.

Marcone stabbed at her. A child would have done bet-ter against a professional wrestler.

Ethniu's good arm blurred. She seized him by the throat, lifted him with no noticeable effort, gave her arm a little bob, a little twist, and broke his neck.

I watched Marcone jerk and go limp.

She rose to a knee, her good leg planted in the boiling water, and threw the corpse away like an empty beer can.

The Baron of Chicago landed on the rocks, boneless and broken.

A roar went up from the battlefield behind us.

The blue beam of light rising into the night like a vague, glowing moonbeam, above the embattled forces of the Winter Lady, flickered and dimmed.

Ethniu let out a bubbling, almost disbelieving laugh. Then she prowled like a beast down into the roiling water and slipped beneath it. I could see her reaching out a hand toward the light of the Eye.

I staggered over to Marcone's body. Broken neck didn't kill you right away.

Nobody ought to die alone.

And when I got there, he sat up.

I fell back with a manly high-pitched scream.

Marcone's head was twisted way too far around to one side. He rolled his neck as if stretching out. There was series of hideous little pops in his neck and then he shook his head back and forth as if easing a cramp, and his neck just . . . unbroke.

Marcone gave me a bland look and held up his knife.

Its blade was covered in blood, too bright red to be real.

I blinked and stared at the knife. Then up at him.

"What the actual fuck?" I asked.

I felt my eyes widen.

Celestial power, they had said, to get through the Titanic bronze.

Or *infernal*.

Marcone's eyes wrinkled at the corners in genuine amusement. "Honestly, Dresden. Did you think I'd stop with the title?"

And in the center of his forehead, his skin flushed and stirred and then began to glow in a lambent purple light in the shape of an angelic rune.

A pair of glowing violet eyes etched in light opened on his forehead, just above his own eyebrows.

And with a little ripple, black thorns that would have been at home on particularly wild roses began to emerge from his skin, in a pattern on his face and stirring beneath his shirt.

"I believe you needed this," he said, offering me the handle of the knife. "And I believe time is short."

I took the knife, staring.

Sir Gentleman Johnnie Marcone, Baron of Chicago, Knight of the Blackened Denarius, the bearer of the Master of Sorcery, Thorned Namshiel, calmly rose and divested himself of the pirate bandoliers. He reached up to undo his tie and tossed it to one side. Then he loosened his collar so that the thorns in his skin weren't pressing on it, and unbuttoned the shirt, evidently to make himself more comfortable there, too.

The coin of Thorned Namshiel, one of a set of thirty, rested on an almost unbearably fine silver chain against Marcone's chest.

"I believe Namshiel and I can play for a draw against her," he said. "But not for long. You must complete the binding as quickly as you can."

"I," I said. "Buh."

Marcone turned and slapped me.

"Hell's bells," I spat.

"Focus," he snarled. "I know it hurts. I know what you've lost. I know you're tired. But you and I are all that stands between that creature and this city."

I clenched my jaw.

"If we fail now," he continued, "everyone who has been lost has been lost for *nothing*. Your people. And mine."

The water of Lake Michigan flared with red light.

Gulp. Ethniu had reclaimed the Eye.

"Dresden," Marcone hissed, giving my chest a little push. "Are you going to sit there while that happens?"

I thought of Murphy's body, silent, small, back in the Bean.

I thought of my little Maggie, in her pajamas, small and vulnerable.

I snarled at my sluggish brain, forced the gears to start grinding again. Then I met the eyes of tiger-souled John Marcone and said, *"No."*

He bared his teeth. And the weird purple eyes . . . smiled.

Marcone rose, turned to face the water, and started spinning off defensive spells. Different ones. From each hand. Simultaneously. Evidently, a few years in private tuition with an angelic master of magic as a teacher really got some results.

Maybe if there was a later, I needed to get back to school myself. The very thought was exhausting.

Christ, it had really been a very long day.

A Titan was about to send the world into a new Dark Age while Knights of Winter and Hell tried to get in her way. Several Queens of Faerie had been beaten bloody, half a pantheon of supernatural terrors had smashed one another to pieces in Millennium Park, and they'd knocked buildings down like Legos while they did it.

Double Dragon boss fight beside Hell Knight Marcone now?

Yeah.

Sure.

Why not?

Chapter

Thirty-four

Ethniu didn't arise from the waters of Lake Michigan so much as explode from them, her raw power and agility belying her mangled limbs. Stars and stones, she was functionally halfway to being a quadriplegic— biplegic, I guess—and she still moved like a damned gymnast.

Marcone began muttering in a language I didn't recognize and pointed a finger at the ground twenty yards away and to his left. He indicated another position to his right with his other hand, at a point equidistant from the first, said something, and there was a crackling sound in the air, like . . . broken wind chimes, maybe.

Ethniu came out of the water with the Eye already bursting forth in a tidal roar of red energy, lashing out unstoppably at Marcone.

Marcone simply stepped to his left and vanished into a chorus of broken wind chimes—reappearing at the point he'd pointed to with his left hand, clear of the beam.

Ethniu shrieked in rage, slewing the gaze of the Eye around wantonly, though the motion was slower than it should have been and seemed to take physical effort from her straining neck muscles as she swept her gaze around, searching for Marcone. She spotted him with another scream, but he simply took a second step, vanishing from the first point of the triangle he'd indicated, and appeared in the second in another shower of clinking-crystal sounds.

Holy crap. Direct point-to-point translocation was something that the White Council kept in a section called "Highly Theoretical and Dangerous Magic" in the wizard's library at the complex in Edinburgh. I knew, because years ago when I'd asked about it, I'd been put on the no-access list for the entire section.

Which . . . well, to be fair, probably wasn't entirely unwise.

Ethniu spent the energy of the Eye's blast while Marcone played freaking peekaboo with her, using magic I wouldn't care to touch until I'd had another forty or fifty years to practice, at least.

And while Marcone kept her busy, I got to work.

I grounded the Spear next to me. Working with one hand was a pain, but my left hand wasn't cooperating very well and couldn't do much more than wave vaguely and grasp Marcone's bloodied knife. I opened the bag I'd had tied closed, rested my palm on the skull inside for a second, and said, "Bob!"

The eyes of the skull kindled to light, even as I held him up so that he could see what was happening. "Did Radio Mab go off the air? Is it over? Are we . . . Oh my freaking God!"

Beyond us, Ethniu seized a boulder the size of a basketball and smashed at Marcone with it. The gangster stood there calmly while the rock shattered on a dim violet aura around him, the pieces flinging themselves violently back into Ethniu's face.

"Oh *hell* no!" Bob declared.

I had to reach across to fumble in my opposite pocket with my good hand and withdraw the crystal I'd brought from Demonreach for the purpose. It flickered, deep down, with the faint green light of the crystals in the catacombs under the island.

"Bob," I said. "We're going to bind a Titan."

"Fuck *that*!" the skull sputtered. "I'm going to Utah! Stuff like this *never* happens in Utah!"

"Buddy," I said, turning the skull to look at me. "I need you."

Bob the Skull's eyelights dwindled down to little points and he said, in a tiny voice, "Dammit." He shuddered in my hand and then the lights brightened again. "Think of all the girls we'll get when we lock her up!"

Such a long night.

"That's the spirit," I sighed.

"Oh! I see what you did there."

"Dammit, Bob, focus!" I snapped grumpily. "You're the circle. And if we survive this, you get a twenty-four-hour pass. Shore leave."

"Whoop!" Bob whooped, and campfire sparks soared out of the skull's eye sockets and into a swiftly moving cloud in the hellish air.

Ethniu recoiled from the rebounding stone, snarling in frustration, and started clubbing Marcone with one arm, the motion primal, brutal. His shields were comprehensive, if not really first-class in strength—but he just kept spinning *new* ones off his fingers, defenses akimbo. Ethniu's furious blows would shatter the shield they struck, but by then Marcone would have spun up another one.

She switched tactics, kicking a cloud of stones at him with her broken foot—which already looked steadier than it had been. Marcone had to drop a new shield low to intercept the stones, which scattered off in random directions as the spell fractured, breaking the rhythm. He had to dive to one side before Ethniu compressed his spine into his tailbone, and she surged after him, snarling.

I took the bloodied knife and swept it over the smoldering light of the crystal, and it flared to life as the blood of the Titan touched it. It might have been really bright. I could barely tell. The world was turning into weird shadows and odd streaks of color. My good hand was shaking hard.

I drove the crystal down into some rubble so that it stood up from the ground. Then I smeared more of the Titan's blood onto the tip of the Spear.

My heart suddenly skittered along even faster. *Thrumthrumthrumthrumthrum.*

Marcone did something that made greasy black smoke condense into a thick, choking cloud and sent it zipping toward the Titan's face, where it clung in a wobbly bubble of impenetrable fog. The Titan swiped at it uselessly.

"Namshiel," she snarled. "You greasy little snake!"

Marcone spoke in a different voice even as he ducked behind a chunk of fallen concrete the size of a tractor trailer. It sounded like him, mostly, only with a very formal British accent. "You haven't changed much, either, darling."

In answer, Ethniu screamed and surged directly forward and *through* the concrete and the rebar inside it alike. It exploded and came sloughing over Marcone in an avalanche. Marcone played a desperate move and threw a telekinetic strike at his own feet. Magic is awesome, but physics are still physics. Throw a bunch of force at the ground, and the ground throws just as much force back at you.

Marcone exploded out from under the avalanche of shattering concrete, flew up at maybe a twenty-degree angle, and landed a good fifty feet out into Lake Michigan.

And the Titan's furious gaze immediately whipped toward me.

"Filthy little *thief* of Power," Ethniu snarled. Spittle and foam were falling from the skullified side of her face, along with a steady patter of some kind of yellowish slime as she came skittering toward me over the stones. "I will feed you to the Eye."

"Bob!" I screamed, and seized the Spear, holding its point up above me.

The cloud of campfire sparks swirled in a helix up around the Spear, touched the blood at the tip like a hound picking up a scent. I whirled the Spear in a circle, gathering up the substance of the spirit around it along with my will, and murmured, *"Ventris cyclis!"*

Wind and spirit flew toward the Titan, too swiftly to be seen as more than a single blur of light that whipped thrice counterclockwise about the Titan and then settled into place, a whirling cyclone of motes of light, a solid bar of my will that encircled her.

Thrumthrumthrumthrumthrumthrum.

I sent my will into the Spear, my own power flooding out along with Bob, infusing his essence, just as my will could have infused a circle of chalk or silver.

Ethniu staggered as the lights surrounded her, shielding her eyes—and then she let out a choking sound and screamed in denial as the circle closed around her.

Wizards are the gatekeepers, the defenders of this world. Or at least we are when we're at our best. And if some immortal thing rolls in here from Somewhere Else, we can say something about it. We can pit our will against them. We might not win, but with a proper channel and a circle of power, we can make them stop to fight us.

The circle closed on Ethniu, and suddenly I found myself pitted against the mutilated will of a Titan.

There was a horrible pressure, a whole-body crushing agony, as if I had suddenly blinked to the floor of the sea. And that was what it was like, with the force of that mind pressing against mine—like trying to hold off the weight of the tide.

But the sea had tried to wash my mind away before now, and I knew the secret of facing the will of supernatural beings. I might be nothing but a grain of sand on the shore of that ocean—but pound as it might, the ocean couldn't destroy that grain of sand. Not if it was stubborn enough to hold together. Though the ocean might wash the sand here and there, might batter and rage at it, when the ocean's rage is gone, and the waters once more serene, the sand will remain.

So I took the pressure. Though my head felt like someone was trying to squeeze my brains out through my nose, I kept my will on the Spear, on the circle.

The snarling rage of the furious, terrified Titan filled my head. Literally. Her voice was echoing off the surface of my skull, deafening and inescapable and really, really uncomfortable.

"Mortal," she snarled. "Do you think you can pit your will against mine?"

"Obviously," I muttered. "That's why you're in a circle, genius." I took a slow breath and in that deep, echoing voice called, "Ethniu, daughter of Balor! I bind thee!"

The Titan wailed and shook her head violently, spittle and slime and worse spraying everywhere. She thrashed and suddenly there was a hideous power raking at the circle.

Bob screamed in agony. The sparks began to fly apart.

"No!" I said, and sent my will rushing into the Spear, out along the stream of sparks still connected to it like some kind of bizarre whirling lasso. I fed power and will to the familiar spirit, fighting the pressure from the Titan, binding together his immaterial substance and preventing her from tearing it apart.

"Insect!" Ethniu hissed, flinging herself from the edge of the circle and pacing back and forth in it like a frantic big cat. "The advantage of immortality is that one can take the time to be thorough. Do you think we did not plan for this?"

"Yeah, kinda," I said, "or you wouldn't be stuck in my circle. Ethniu, daughter of Balor, I bind thee!"

Ethniu didn't scream this time.

She smiled.

And then she . . . *thought* at me.

The lake and everything else went away.

And I found myself standing on a quiet lawn in a darkened neighborhood I knew well.

I was in Michael Carpenter's front yard.

The lights were out. And the sky was beginning to fill with dust and smoke and the red glare of the Eye. But I could still see the moon a little. This was earlier in the evening.

She was showing me a memory.

And I watched, as Listen and maybe thirty or forty of his turtlenecks advanced into the yard in full tactical gear. They came in, in multiple stacks, heading for Michael's front door, the kitchen door, the garage, and the door to the backyard.

I watched as, in a handful of seconds, the men set breaching charges on the door, blew it, and went in.

Michael Carpenter, stolid in his blue plaid work shirt, was waiting for them, shotgun in hand.

He wasn't really a gunfighter. He was retired now.

It was over quickly.

They left his body in the entry hall and walked over it. Enemies, mortal enemies, twisted people but still people, flooded into his house to the chattering thumps of suppressed weapons. I knew there were angels on guard at Michael's house. I knew they would have burned any supernatural attacker with the fires that ravaged Sodom and Gomorrah.

But these were mortals. People.

Angels weren't allowed to gainsay people.

Listen and his team were thorough. They must have

found the safe room, because charges went off again. Then some screams.

Some very high-pitched screams.

And gunfire.

And then the Fomor squads filed out with the same silence with which they'd filed in.

Listen stopped on the front lawn, next to where I stood in the vision, lifted a radio to his mouth, and said, "Tell her the target has been cleared and confirmed. We're moving back to the shore to meet the rest of the company."

I pushed forward, toward the house, toward the front door, and could see blood running from the second floor, from where the safe room was, and I ran up the stairs to the hidden entrance and found it twisted and torn with the violence of the breaching charges, and behind the door . . .

I saw them.

Saw *her*.

Charity and the Carpenter kids all lay between Maggie and the door. Even little Harry, who was almost as young as Maggie, had stood in her defense.

It had been efficient.

And suddenly I was standing on the shore of Lake Michigan again, cold and more brutally weary than I'd ever been, struggling against Ethniu's will.

You see, mortal? the Titan's voice said in my head. *Listen and his people scouted this target thoroughly. They planned countermeasures for all of your kind here. And they planned something in particular for you and the Winter Lady. All those targets in one place just made it too tempting.* Ethniu paused, and her mental voice became poison-ously sweet. *Your child is dead. Your ally and his family are dead. They were destroyed hours ago.*

My stomach dropped out.

This is the world I bring to you, mortal.

And then she thought at me again. She showed me the world she desired. A world of blasted cities, of smoke, of tears, of screams. Blood ran in the gutters rather than water. And columns of greasy black smoke rose from altars, from temples, from shrines decorated with skulls and crusted with the blood of sacrifices.

This is what is coming. And there is nothing you can do to stop it. Just as well that your daughter will not see it, I think. Just as well that you won't, either.

And I felt her will gathering again, preparing to shatter mine.

Everything felt spinny. Empty.

Bob let out a wordless wail. I could feel my hold on the circle weakening. I could feel the Titan beginning to burst free of the binding.

Maggie, I thought. *I'm so sorry. I should have done more. I should have been there.*

"Dresden!" Marcone screamed from the water. "We'll never get another chance at this!"

Ethniu's will began to rip mine apart. Slowly. Almost sensually. I could feel her pressing against my mind. Pressing inside. She found my pain and my horror and she slithered inside while I gritted my teeth and held on to the Spear for simple support to keep from falling.

. . . thrumthrumthrumthrumthrumthrumthrum . . .

I couldn't get the image of my daughter's little shattered body out of my head.

Ethniu's savaged face twisted into a hideous smile.

I should have done more, taken more measures to protect you than just leave you with Mou . . .

My head snapped back up.

I stared at her for a second.

And then I clenched my teeth in a sudden wolfish smile.

"Hey, Bubbles," I said. "You forgot the dog."

Ethniu's smile vanished. "What?"

"The dog," I said. "The dog was with them. Maybe your guys could take him out, maybe not. But it wouldn't be fast. And they'd only get to my daughter over his dead body. But he's not there. Question, where is he? Answer, with my daughter. That's the only place it's possible for him to be. Ergo, she wasn't there. She was never there. In fact, none of them were, because the dog's absence was a message, to me, from the person responsible. This girl I know had places to be this evening. Man, she really has been busy."

Ethniu looked baffled.

I took a deep breath and said, "Honey, you're fighting faeries. It was staged for your benefit. Wouldn't be shocked if we went back there and found a bunch of bundles of wood where those bodies were."

The Titan's living eye widened.

"Listen *betrayed* me," Ethniu hissed, spitting in her fury.

I stared at her for a second. For a second, I almost felt sorry for her.

Then I sighed.

"Sure, that's the takeaway here," I said. "Nice knowing

you." I set my jaw, kept my will on her, and cried, in a voice that echoed from the vaults of the apocalypse sky, *"ETHNIU, DAUGHTER OF BALOR, I BIND THEE!"*

A storm hit my mind. Even after Ethniu had expended such energies, after she had fought so many foes, after she had laid low a high school gymnasium full of supernatural heavyweights, the raw strength of the Titan's remaining will was overwhelming. It tore at my perceptions, flooding them with random images and smells and sensations. It was like standing in a sandstorm, only instead of inflicting pain, every random grain forced you through an experience, a memory, so disjointed and intense and rapid that there was nothing to focus on, to hold on to. A flash sensation of summer-warmed grass between my toes. Plunging into a pool of chilled water in the hour before dawn. An image of watching warmly over a field worked by people with bronze tools. Another of strangling someone to death with my bare hands. And the images doubled, redoubled, multiplied into thousands of separate impressions all coming at me at once.

Memories. These were the substance of Ethniu, the pieces of *her* that railed against my will. She was going to hammer them into my mind as I tried to complete the binding, sandblast my psyche to pieces with an overwhelming flood of impressions.

I had to get to an image, a moment, that was mine. Me. That was strong enough to hold all the rest together.

I found one image.

Maggie, holding on to me with all four limbs, her little heart beating against my chest, while Mouse leaned against me, a solid presence of utter faithfulness and love.

And that was enough.

If the Titan shredded away everything else I had, this would be enough to build on. Friends. Family. Love. I focused on that memory, of my girl holding on to me with desperate strength, my fuzzy friend beside us, while her father's arms held her safe.

The storm of the Titan's will raged. But I found myself standing in the eye of the hurricane with the most quiet, defiant smile that had ever landed on my face.

The world came back to me. I could feel the Spear in my hands again, the broken rock and concrete beneath my feet.

Ethniu writhed and twisted in the center of the circle of campfire light, coming up off the ground as if gravity had suddenly stopped functioning.

"Bound, bound, bound!" I called. "Thrice said and done! Begone!"

The Titan shrieked in outrage.

My left eardrum exploded. Or maybe imploded. Whatever, it wasn't there anymore. The world turned into one of those barrel rides where they spin so fast you stick to the wall. Only I didn't have a wall to lean on.

I had the Spear of fucking Destiny.

THRUM THRUM THRUM THRUM THRUM THRUM THRUM

It was as if I had started some vast and momentous engine.

"Alfred!" I screamed, and kicked the crystal out into the water of the lake.

The moment the bloodied crystal hit the water, there was a sound. A deep, deep sound, like a rumbling in earth miles below us. The surface of Lake Michigan went suddenly still—and then began to jump and vibrate like the indicator bars of God's biggest stereo.

A light appeared in the water. I don't mean like a spotlight or a glowing aura. This thing was huge. Hundreds of yards across. And it came through the water at a speed so great that it couldn't readily be estimated.

But it pushed a bow wave ahead of it. A huge one.

"Oh crap," I muttered.

In the water, Marcone snapped his head toward the wave, then calmly murmured something. He abruptly zipped through the water as though being pulled by a friendly dolphin and attained the shore.

"Dresden!"

"Go!" I said. "I've got to hold her here!"

Marcone gave me a look and said, "Of course you do." He eyed the incoming wave, gold and green and across the entire horizon. Then he muttered something in a language I didn't know, answered himself in the same language and a different voice, and then said, in English, "No, I don't have any gopher wood. No one has any gopher wood. I'm not even sure it exists anymore." Then he shook his head, looked at the ground, and started muttering and drawing in power.

The wave loomed larger. Ethniu screamed again, but I put my shoulder up against my right ear, so that was fine.

There was a hideous smell in the air. I looked around and saw broken concrete beginning to melt into slurry while Marcone chanted in some harsh-sounding language.

The wave loomed up, millions of tons of water, coming at us fast.

And then the breadth of the wave condensed. Intensified. It built higher and higher in the last hundred yards to shore, focused, piling into a curl a city block wide and towering like a skyscraper.

For a second, the gold-green tower was poised at apogee, graceful, beautiful.

And then eyes opened at the top of the wave. Green, furious, hostile, and implacable eyes.

The wave came down.

And Demonreach came down with it, great stony hands the size of pickup trucks outstretched.

That vast wall of glowing green water crashed down over the Titan, who screamed once more.

And then that huge form, a magical servant of my will, surged through the binding of my will held around the Titan and enfolded her in its vast, implacable form. The Titan fought, but her strength was spent. It was like watching a seal get pulled down by something big and dark and unseen—a desperate struggle with a foregone conclusion. Not because the Titan was strong enough to fight something like Alfred—but because this was what Alfred did. This was the purpose of its creation. Ant lions aren't all that much bigger or stronger than ants.

But ant lions kill ants. It is what they do.

This was what Alfred *did*.

I saw Demonreach drag the Titan, screaming and thrashing, into the pitiless waters of Lake Michigan. I felt it when my will prevailed.

THRUM. THRUM. THRUM. THRUM.

The Spear quivered in time with my heartbeat. Steady and rumbling, the tactile equivalent of a big rig's engine.

The rest of the wave that had hammered the Titan back into the water hit us, icy cold despite the glowing light that infused it. Stinking greyness rose around us, and I was thrown into something hard, the sky and the city whirling overhead, and then there was darkness and cold water all around.

I started trying to find my way out. I was underwater. There were cold, hard walls. And a ceiling. I was in an enclosed space. I was exhausted. My battered body was so bruised and numb, I could barely tell when I actually touched something. I tried to summon up some of my will, at least enough to bring some light into my staff or amulet, and . . . just couldn't. There was just nothing there. My tank was on absolute E.

I tried to find a way out, by feel, in the dark, with the water making me colder and slower, with my lungs slowly beginning to burn.

Then there were three points of violet light that resolved into the eyes and the rune of Thorned Namshiel.

I felt Marcone thump my shoulder. Then he fumbled at my hand. I took it, and the Baron of Chicago led me through the darkness, to an opening in the solid barrier surrounding us. I lost some skin but I scraped through, kicked weakly at the water, and eventually got my head above it again.

Marcone broke the surface at the same time. He started dragging me toward the shore.

I peered at what looked like an enormous concrete . . . teacup, I supposed, since it was about the same shape, up-ended, maybe twelve feet across.

"What?" I asked.

The waters were rough, waves surging back and forth—but the beach, such as it was, was empty, except for us.

And a massive form of green-gold light was vanishing, slow and steady, back into the depths of Lake Michigan.

Marcone slogged onto the shore and made sure I was able to get out of the water.

"What?" I asked, panting, "The hell. Is that thing?"

Marcone plopped down on a rock and said, "There's no reason a concrete vessel couldn't have handled that wave, structurally speaking. I must have made it too top-heavy, and it rolled on us."

"Yeah, well," I panted, gasping sweet, sweet air. "That's because you suck. And you're an amateur. Who sucks."

"I didn't see you doing anything about it."

"Yeah, because I was holding the freaking Titan!" I shot back. "I was doing the grown-up stuff."

"You just almost killed us both as an *unintended side effect* of that binding," Marcone snapped. "And you call me an amateur."

"I saved your life from a Titan," I panted, exhausted. And I think I had picked up a couple of cracked ribs, despite the last-second shield of concrete that had risen to stop most of the force of the wave. "You almost drowned us. Fake wizard."

"I just broke down the molecular structure of concrete and then chemically re-formed it inside a mold of pure will, saving both of our lives from that wave in the process."

"Fake," I said. "Sad."

Marcone let out a low, weary chuckle.

My stomach twitched a lot while breaths went in and out of my exhausted body.

We did *not* laugh together.

And he was no less an asshole.

But we won.

Chapter

Thirty-five

We should move," Marcone said eventually. "Without Ethniu's will to counter those of the Ladies, Corb's forces will break. They'll run for the water, and we are in their path."

He was right, but there was no sense letting him feel that way. And I was too tired to move. "How about you fight them all with your new buddy? Look real good in front of everyone."

"You first."

I started to say something childish, but there was a particularly loud ripple of water from the shoreline, and both of us came up ready to fight. Some of us more drunkenly than others.

An ivory sphere a little bigger than a softball, glowing with sullen fire, tumbled out of the waves and onto the beach.

The Eye.

Pulsing with power.

Throbbing with it, really.

Power that could lay gods and monsters low.

I glanced aside.

Marcone was staring at the Eye.

It lay approximately equidistant between us, down at the waterline.

It might have been six inches nearer to me.

He turned and looked at me thoughtfully.

He looked at the Spear.

He didn't move or reach for weapons. No demented angelic eyes appeared on his forehead. He just looked at me.

I returned the look. I knew what Marcone was. I'd taken his measure, and he hadn't changed. He was, above all things, a dangerous predator. It was simply his nature. And you don't let predators know when you're scared.

Because I was.

Marcone the gangster had been bad enough. Marcone the supernatural power broker had been nerve-racking. Marcone the Knight of the Blackened Denarius was a nightmare I had barely considered.

But it didn't matter what else you added to it. He was Marcone. And one of these days, he and I would settle things between us.

Maybe today. Right here. It would be a good time for him. I was exhausted after that binding, and he had to know it. If he acted, he could eliminate me and gain the Spear of Destiny and the Eye of Balor, all in an evening. In all this confusion, who was to say what had really happened?

The victor. That's who.

Marcone hadn't survived as long as he had without being able to read faces. And from the look on his, he'd figured out what had been going on in my head. I'd seen his small sharklike smile before. But it was more frightening now.

Because I wasn't standing outside an aquarium. I was in the bloody, desperate water with him. And he was more than large enough to rip me to pieces.

He smiled and stared at me without blinking while those cold pale green eyes did the math.

Evidently, the numbers didn't turn out far enough in his favor to suit him.

His smile for a second turned almost human, and he said, "Not today."

Water lapped on the shore. Shouts and cries and desperate clicks drifted down to us, seemingly from another world.

"Why?" I asked.

For a second, a look of contempt touched his face—but then he became pensive. His fingers came to rest lightly against his chest, and then he regarded me more seriously. "Because I am beginning to learn what it means to think in the long term," he replied, his voice serious. "And time favors me. You and I will face one another eventually. But for now, I think it best you take the Eye for safekeeping, wizard."

I scowled. "You're just yielding the Eye to the White Council?"

"Do I look like a moron? Certainly not," Marcone said. "To the Wizard of Chicago. This was, after all, your kill. By the terms of the Accords, you deserve first claim."

"We did it together," I objected warily.

Marcone's smile sharpened.

"Prove it," he purred, "hero."

He twitched two fingers and vanished behind a veil.

And I sat there in the cold and the damp, exhausted, momentarily safe, and certain in the sinking sensation that the future I was facing had suddenly become about a thousand times more complicated.

Footsteps began to sound in the haze nearby, along with desperate clicking noises.

I grabbed up the Eye and dumped it in my duster's pocket. Then I reached up and unlatched and unscrewed the dagger from the end of my staff, sticking it back in its sheath at my hip. There was a sense of frustration from the weapon, as I undid it, but the throbbing power behind the blade eased and quieted.

Then I slopped up a veil that would do and shambled back up the rock-and-gravel beach to the street level of the city. I staggered to one side and sat down on a bench and watched as the coalition led by Baron Marcone and the Winter Lady drove the Fomor legions from the field—first in a trickle, and then in a wave.

I was too exhausted to do anything but sit there as the enemy was driven away—and the rest of my team wasn't much better off than I was. Once the defenders had driven the foe to the waterfront, they staggered to an exhausted stop themselves, casting weary cheers and jeers after the fleeing foe, and swiping with exhausted, half-hearted energy at the enemies who were still fleeing past them.

It was odd seeing citizens of Chicago, armed with baseball bats and shotguns and whatever else had been at hand, standing shoulder to shoulder with armored warriors of Winter, even the high-and-mighty Sidhe, shouting defiance and scorn in unison at the fleeing foe.

And then we all heard it together.

Whupwhupwhupwhupwhupwhupwhupwhup.

We'd all heard choppers coming before. But not like this. This was magnified tenfold over anything I'd heard from the machines. This sounded more like *weather.*

Our side immediately began withdrawing from the shoreline, and the enemy broke into a desperate sprint for the water. I saw King Corb and his retinue leading the way, mainly because they blasted to death any of their own people too slow to clear their path and leapt over their bodies. They hit the water maybe ten seconds before the cavalry came.

It was just poetry that the broken overcast had begun to lighten out over the lake, and that the first rays of dawn turned the eastern horizon to a band of gold.

The enemy did their best to get away—but the very destruction they'd leveled in order to come ashore laid them bare to the guns of the Apache attack ships that came overhead. Those big cannons under their chins started going *chunk-chunk-chunk-chunk-chunk*, like a thundercloud playing steel percussion. Explosions started ripping through the Fomor as they tried to flee.

What came next was every bit as hideous and savage and thorough as anything that had happened that evening.

But it was a lot more impersonal.

That cavalry unit swept the "beach" clean. Which was an odd turn of phrase to use, given what a mess they made of it. By the time they were done, everyone there looked like they had gone through a food processor.

I bore witness, too tired to care about the odd clatter of shrapnel that came near. Then I turned my back on it and started slogging my way back toward the Bean.

There would be a lot of people in uniforms asking questions soon. I wanted to get Murph clear of them.

As I walked, a gentle, steady rain began. At first, it almost seemed black—even with what had already fallen, there was so much particulate matter in the air that the rain literally came down muddy. But after a few moments, that lessened, and then the water began to fall clean over the war-torn city.

I stopped for a moment and let it fall over me, too, with my eyes closed.

When I opened them, a pair of large wolves sat on the street in front of me, and I realized they'd been standing guard. The bulkier of the two looked at me with obvious relief. The taller and leaner came and leaned against my side a little.

Will and Georgia had come through okay.

We all walked together toward the Bean.

There were knots of order, here and there, of the city beginning to lurch into motion again as the light began to gather. A group of EMTs and medics had arrived and established a triage station for the injured. They were working frantically to save the wounded defenders of the city. I saw Lamar crouching down beside a dazed-looking Ramirez, pressing a bottle of water into the Warden's hands as medics bundled Ebenezar onto a stretcher. I saw my grandfather wave a vague, irritated hand at a medic trying to press an oxygen mask over his mouth, and part of me sagged in relief that my friend and the crusty old bastard had survived.

There were plenty of wounded to work with. They were piling them up around the base of the Bean.

"Harry!" boomed Sanya as I approached. He waved an arm from where he'd been stretched out on the concrete with what was obviously a pair of broken legs to go with his other injuries. "There, you see? Next time, we know better! Make better plan!"

I slogged over to him with my furry escort. Butters was lying next to Sanya, carefully flat on his back, his arms folded in a funeral pose. There were two more wolves lying on either side of him, and both looked as though they'd tear to pieces anything that tried to harm him.

"Sir Butters," I said gravely.

"Nngh," Butters said. "My jaw. My back."

"Is fine," Sanya boomed cheerfully. "If it was really bad, you feel nothing at all. Is good, all this pain!"

Butters squinted at me without moving his head and spoke without taking his teeth apart. "So you got her?"

"It's done," I said.

"Sweet," Butters said, and closed his eyes. "I'm going to sleep for a week."

"Good, good, you rest until we can find some food," Sanya told him. "I am *starving*."

"Cheerful for a man in your condition," I noted, peering at him.

"We are too alive to not be cheerful, eh, wizard?" He

reached up and clapped my forearm. The burned one. Cheerfully.

I winced. And laughed a little.

Lara's people were doing a lot of the work, I realized. The members of the House itself were gathered together over to one side, a good fifty yards from anyone, and the pale glitter of hungry vampire eyes told me why. But her hired help, led by Riley, was assisting with the wounded, sharing out water and sorting those in need of immediate care from those who could wait by the Archive—who sported what looked like a broken nose and radiated a sense of . . . not command, but the tangible, absolute authority wielded by those with sure and certain knowledge in an emergency.

Well. The living repository of the accumulated knowledge of mankind probably had a real good idea of the most appropriate measures to take in any given emergency. If she told me what to do in this situation, I'd probably listen and pitch in as well.

I lost track for a bit after that, and found myself seated in the shadow of the Bean, a cup of water in my hands, my staff at my side, the Eye heavy in my pocket. Molly, now wearing what looked like a fireman's coat, put her fingers under my hands and lifted, nudging the water toward my lips. I drank.

I looked up at her, coughed out some smoke, and then croaked, "Where'd you hide them? Our family?"

She glanced at me and then smiled faintly. "Right across the street. Where they could watch the whole thing. Like in *Fellowship*."

"Clever girl," I said.

She showed me a vulpine smile.

"They're calling you the Eye-Killer," she said. "Rumors are spreading about how you defeated a Titan."

"She had gone through a few sparring partners before she got to me," I said. "I was just batting cleanup." I looked around us and said, "Look what we've brought upon them, Molls."

She looked. There were a lot of hurt people. Most of them bore their pain quietly. A few couldn't. And a lot of them would never make another sound, except during decomposition.

"We have to answer for this," I said quietly. "We have to help. The wounded." I didn't look back at the dark opening in the base of the Bean. "The dead. We owe them. You know I'm right."

"That could be a tough sell," she said in quiet answer.

"I'm not asking," I said. "My fealty is a two-way street. I have gone above and beyond my duty to Winter, right in front of God and everybody, by doing what no one else could. Now Winter will respond in kind, by helping as no one else can. You will help them. Every one of them. Do it in secret, no connections. We've interfered in their lives enough. This will happen."

The Winter Lady gave me a very long, very intent stare.

And then she shivered and bowed her head.

"Already you have bound a Titan. And now a Queen. Sometimes," Molly whispered, "I'm very proud to be your friend, Harry. And sometimes you frighten me."

Sometimes *I* frightened *the Winter Lady*.

I shook my head. Molly was soon called away to her

royal matters. She had plenty of wounded of her own who needed tending to.

I looked over at a slight rise in the ground where Mab and Titania stood, their respective unicorns standing nearby. The Winter unicorn was mostly coated in thick mud. The rain was washing it slowly clean. The two Queens simply faced each other, silent.

I propped my chin in my hand and watched, fascinated.

"The rain was a kind touch," Mab said finally. "There were a number of fires it checked."

"You understand what has happened," Titania replied quietly. "What it means."

"I expect you to do your duty," Mab said.

Titania's expression flickered in pain. "When have I not?"

Mab nodded. Titania matched the gesture. Then a warm southern wind blew a curtain of gentle rain around her and the Summer unicorn, and when it faded they were gone.

Mab walked over to me, moving as if her bones were made of fragile porcelain. She stood staring down at me for a moment.

"And so. The man who has bound a Titan. What will you do with her, I wonder."

I squinted up at Mab. Then snorted. "Leave her buried. Bury her deeper if I can."

Mab stared at me. "The creature is bound to you, Warden. Your will can compel her now. The power of a Titan, at your beck and call."

Which was true enough, in its way. Ethniu was my prisoner. I could . . . extract service from her. It would be tricky and treacherous as hell, but wizards had done it before, with beings of tremendous supernatural power. It was possible.

Just . . . massively, massively unwise.

"My will causes enough trouble," I said wearily. "Until I get the sense to use it wisely, why don't we just let sleeping gods lie."

I shoved myself to my feet as sturdily as I could.

"Easy, my Knight," Mab said quietly, glancing around. "You show weakness."

"National Guard is going to be here soon," I said. "I don't want to leave Murphy here for them."

Mab lifted a hand and physically stopped me from taking a step. "The honored dead will be cared for," she said. "You have my word on that."

Which settled that. When Mab gives her word, it is good. Period.

"And there is another matter which must be settled ere we are through," she said.

I glanced back and saw Lara Raith coming toward me.

Behind her, in a circle of empty space maybe ten feet across, were Justine and Goodman Grey. The man looked like thirty miles of bad road. His clothes were in rags, and he was covered with bruises that had gone to school and graduated as contusions. One of his eyes was completely shot with red, his nose was broken, and when he snarled at someone who stepped a little too close, he was missing some teeth.

But no one was getting within an arm's length of Justine, either.

"Dresden," Goodman Grey demanded. "Deed done. Contract over. Here. Delivered, one female, cute, no damage."

He gave Justine what could have been a rough push but wasn't, and she crossed the space to stand beside me, her expression dismayed. "Harry, my God, what have they done to you?"

"Explain this, Dresden," Lara Raith snapped. "This lunatic put half a dozen of the security team I had watching her in the hospital."

"What?" I said to Grey. "I didn't hire you for that."

"You hired me to make sure she was all right," Grey spat. "And when the lights went out a bunch of goons went rushing at her apartment."

"To get her to safety," Lara insisted.

"I didn't know that!" Grey protested. "Just be glad you've still got them. I didn't have to settle for broken bones, you know."

"This creature is your hireling?" Lara demanded of me.

I fumbled in my pocket and found the envelope with the crumpled, baked dollar. I passed it over to Grey. "I mean. Barely."

He snatched the envelope, muttering darkly. ". . . running all over the damned city, fighting every damned thing that popped up, all for a pretty face . . ." He gave me a dark glower, then one for Lara, turned with a limp, nodded politely to Justine, and stalked lopsidedly away.

Lara was giving me a furious look. "How dare you interfere with the protection of one of my own."

"Yeah, well, Thomas wanted me to," I said. "And she's one of mine, too. What was I supposed to do?"

Lara threw her hands in the air and said, as if the word held terrible significance, *"Communicate?"*

I spun my finger around at the general everything. "Been a little busy, right?"

"Oh," Lara said, glaring at Mab.

"I did warn you," Mab said. "He is independently minded. Did he repay you as I ordered?"

"I mean, barely," Lara said, imitating my voice but making it sound a lot dumber.

"Time flies from us," Mab said. Her gaze shifted to the south. "Mortal armsmen approach."

Lara nodded and squared off in front of me, glaring. "I have a request."

"Seriously?" I demanded.

Lara's eyes hardened. "What you did tonight, Dresden. What you took from me on the island. That should be balanced."

My insides went queasy and I lurched a foot to one side. "Yeah," I said. "It should."

Lara looked blank for a second, and I think I had said something that actually surprised her. Some of the coldness went out of her eyes as she pointed at Justine. "She wants to see him. You should be the one to take her."

I turned to look at Justine. The young woman was wearing pajamas that had been through the hellish cityscape and holding her arms tightly across her chest. She looked exhausted and terrified. She'd been crying at some point recently. "Harry," she said. "I'm scared. No one will talk about him. Is he . . ."

"No," I said. "No. But . . . it's complicated." I thought of explaining his condition to her and quailed, but that was just too bad. She deserved to know. I also thought about all the svartalves in their invisible armor and glanced around warily. "And we shouldn't talk about it in the open."

Lara eyed me. And I saw the tension and the damage

wrought by the evening's terror in her face. "Justine has given much to my House," Lara said. "And I take care of my people. Show her. Now. She's been kept in the dark long enough. That's what I ask of you."

Again, that vicious pull on the inside. God, I was tired. I wanted to fall over somewhere and cry for a while. Or drink for a while. Or both.

I wanted to make sure Maggie was all right with my own eyes, my own hands.

I lifted my lip in a snarl at Lara.

But then I looked down at Justine, at her weeping eyes.

I'd done enough harm for one evening.

Maybe I could help someone a little. Start paying off that karma.

And suddenly it was too crowded here. There was just too much. The silence of the island sounded wonderful by comparison. And I think I knew where I'd left at least half a bottle of whiskey, back in the cabin. I could put the Eye in safe storage with the other artifacts I'd acquired. And it was probably a good idea to check on Alfred and the state of the island's defenses, after the spirit had exerted itself in such an epic fashion. "Fine," I said. I glanced at Mab. "But I'm not walking to the boat."

"It is a unicorn," Mab said, "not a . . . ride-sharing service."

I sat down and glowered.

"Well. That was terrifying," Justine said a while later. "It wasn't like being on a horse at all, really. More like . . . riding a living train. That might eat you."

We were on the *Water Beetle*. The Winter unicorn had

dropped us off, seething in fury and apparent hunger, and I had gotten the boat going, even as the first hint of dawn began to touch the sky. As the light rose, I saw several other vessels out on the lake. Apparently, fleeing the little-A apocalypse on one had been a valid idea, and there were enough engines sufficiently old and well maintained to have escaped being disabled by the Eye. So that was good. I'd have hated to be the only thing moving and to attract the attention of more helicopters.

I got the *Beetle* settled on course and locked her steering there. The gentle rain had continued, washing terror and leftover black magic out of the air. The coming day was going to be a hot one, but with the rain the current temperature was just about perfect. So I shrugged out of my coat and just turned my face up to the sky for a while.

When I looked down again, Justine was looking up at me from the deck with the first-aid kit. "Harry," she said, "come into the cabin. We should cover those burns up, at least, so they don't get infected."

She was right. I was just about too tired to understand English, but she sounded pretty right. So I stumped down to the cabin. She took some time to clean and cover the burns on my left forearm. I'd lost my shield bracelet along the way somewhere. Dammit. I'd have to make another. A real one this time.

I'd need a lab.

I answered questions mechanically as she worked on me.

"So he's alive. He's safe," she said.

"For now," I said. "He's in cold storage until we can figure out a way to help him."

"But . . . I can speak to him?"

I shook my head. "In theory. But he's been through a lot. He might be recovering for a while."

"But . . . I can be near him? See him?"

No reason she couldn't see the crystal Alfred had put Thomas in if she was willing to walk the stairs. "Yes."

Justine put her arms around my neck and gave me a gentle hug. It was a mark of how weary I was that the Winter mantle sent no surge of desire through me. Justine's hugs are pretty distracting.

"Thank you, Harry. For saving him. For taking him there. It was a terrible risk. Lara might have killed you. The svartalves would be very angry at you if they knew"

"He's family," I muttered wearily.

"Do . . ." She took a deep breath. "Do you know why? Why he tried to kill Etri?"

I shook my head.

"Was it me?" she asked, her voice sick. "Did someone use me against him?" Her hand went to her belly. "Use *us* against him?"

"He wasn't in any shape to explain," I said. "Maybe he'll be able to share something with us when we get there."

Justine bit her lip and bowed her head.

I patted her shoulder clumsily. "Look. I'm gonna close my eyes for a couple. Don't let me sleep more than twenty minutes. Okay?"

"Of course," Justine said. "Of course. Rest."

She said something else, but I had already closed my eyes. I didn't even bother to lie down first. I was sitting on a bench seat, one that would fold out into a bunk, but it seemed like too much work to do it. So I just let my head fall back against the wall, which on a boat is a bulkhead, and closed my eyes.

You don't exactly sleep, in situations like that. You close your eyes and stop moving, and then a lot of complicated things happen in your brain.

Mine started replaying the tapes of the evening. Not in order. Not even a highlights reel. Just . . . random images of the past couple of days.

Murphy, gasping. Not in a bad way.

Murphy, at peace. In the worst way.

Maggie, her eyes worried.

I thought of Butters, tense and in pain—and victorious.

I thought of Chandler, just vanishing. Of Yoshimo and Wild Bill, maybe worse than dead.

I thought of the faintly surprised look on the dead face of glamour-Michael.

And my brother.

Thomas, telling me about his child.

Thomas, beaten so badly.

Thomas, struggling to speak.

I thought of my brother's face, crushed and swollen out of shape.

Junghg. S'Jnngh.

He hadn't been able to say "Justine."

Or maybe he hadn't been trying to say it.

I thought of the island, disturbed at the great powers expended that night.

The last thing I needed was something slipping out of the prison during all the hubbub.

S'Jnngh, he'd told me.

Why *had* my brother gone after Etri?

S'Justine, he'd told me.

It's Justine.

Hell's bells.

It was Justine.

He'd told me.

My eyes opened suddenly, and too wide.

The cabin was empty.

I got up, slowly and carefully. And I walked very slowly and quietly out onto the deck of the *Beetle*. I wasn't sure how much time had gone by. My eyes felt like there were a couple of ounces of sand rubbing around under each lid.

Justine was standing at the front of the ship, looking out into the darkness ahead of us. Toward the island.

She looked over her shoulder at me in the predawn darkness. She was just an outline.

"You're sure the baby will be all right?" she asked me. "I've heard things about that place."

"If you just dropped in, it would be kind of rough on you," I said. "But you're with me. Come in as an invited guest, you'll be perfectly safe. And that's what you are. I'm bringing you there myself."

She gave me a smile that was both worried and relieved, and looked back out at the water.

For a second, I thought about picking up something I might whap her unconscious with, and then discarded the idea. After the night I'd had, I was too exhausted to make such a thing practical. And no matter what you saw in the movies, hitting people in the head was dangerous. I could kill Justine. So instead, I gathered the shreds of what was left of my will and prepared to use them.

"But that was the plan the whole time," I told her. "Right?"

The figure at the front of the boat went completely still.

"See, there were just too many threads being pulled," I said. "The attack on the Outer Gates especially. And the Titan herself . . . God, what a blunt instrument. What a big, loud distraction. So that you could get inside."

Justine's head turned to face me. The lightening sky was behind her. There was nothing to be seen of her expression but blackness.

I limped forward a couple of paces. Nothing specific was any worse than it had been an hour ago, but even the immunity of the Winter mantle had its limits. My joints felt like they'd been dipped in plaster and were slowly drying stiff.

"And every single living family member of mine, personally, was placed in danger. All of them. To make sure I had the maximum amount of personal worry to distract me."

Justine has incredible cheekbones. They shifted, slightly altering her shadowy profile as she smiled.

"Something about Justine wasn't . . . quite right, earlier, in the apartment," I said. And I let my voice harden. "How long ago did you possess the girl?"

Justine was silent for a moment. Then she shook her head and said, "I think the problem is, you just don't *sound* all that bright, wizard. Perhaps it's skewing my expectations."

She turned toward me, slim and graceful, steady on the deck.

I faced her and tried not to pitch over the rail as the *Water Beetle* bumped along the waves. It had been a long night. And I didn't have much left, physically or otherwise.

"Tell me your name," I said, and slid some of my will into my voice.

"You know who I am," Justine purred in answer.

Then she reached out with one hand and ripped a four-foot section of the ship's steel handrail off its metal struts.

I blinked wearily and fancied I could hear grains of sand pattering to the deck from my eyes. Now I knew what Ethniu had felt like at the end. "Humor me," I said, with more of my will. "Tell me your name."

Justine, or whatever being was driving Justine's body around, turned toward me and began slow, stalking paces forward. It made some abortive, choking noises in its throat, and then said, the words drawn from it reluctantly, "It will do you no good once I've caved in your skull, Nemesis am I called."

There. Bingo.

For years, shadowy forces had been driving events in Chicago and in the wider world. For years, I'd been picking up threads and finding them connected to others. For years, I'd been flailing around trying to get an idea of the forces that had been arrayed against me.

And tonight, one of the players was in the open.

Right there. Behind Justine's eyes.

And I was going to get answers.

I didn't have much left in me but pure, stiff-necked, muleheaded contrariness.

But even after the night I'd had, I still had plenty of it.

"I don't care what they call you," I spat. The effort of maintaining my will made it impossible to move my feet as the slender girl stalked forward with her steel bar. "Thrice I say and done. Tell me your name."

The slender figure froze in front of me, shuddering.

Then she exhaled in a slow, utterly sensual voice, "I am the doubt that wards away sleep. I am the flaw that corrupts, the infected wound, the false fork in the trail. I am the gnawer, the worm in the book, the maggot that burrows in the mind's eye."

She shuddered in bizarre ecstasy and panted, in a frantic whisper, "I am He Who Walks Beside."

Hell's bells.

A Walker.

And if I hadn't twigged to its presence, I would have set it loose on Demonreach—*the* prison for the great nightmares of the world. Ethniu wasn't the biggest thing in it—not by a long shot. And an Outsider with the power of a Walker, turned loose inside the island's defenses, might well be able to destroy them and set loose every horror inside.

Hell. There'd have been an Ethniu for every city, if the place got emptied out.

The weight of my will, once finished forcing the information from the possessing being, flooded out of me and left me barely able to stand. I staggered back, away from the slender figure in front of me.

Justine, calmly, pursued.

"I hope it felt good to scratch that itch," she purred. "This is the end of your story, starborn."

"How long?" I asked. "How long have you been in Justine?"

Justine waved the steel bar in a vague gesture. "Mortal time is such a limited concept. A few years. Ever since she became close to Lara."

I glowered at her. "You conceived my brother's child intentionally."

"Obviously," Justine purred. "That ridiculous instinct, honestly. It is your kind's greatest weakness. Once he understood that his mate and his offspring would die if he did not follow my instructions, well . . ." She shrugged.

"So you sent him at Etri. At the svartalves, someone almost everyone respects. Why? To shatter the Accords?"

"Apocalypse isn't an event," Nemesis murmured. "It is a frame of mind."

I probably would have staggered anyway, but the phrase hit hard.

"This was less a plan than . . . an act of faith, I suppose you would say," the Outsider continued through Justine's lips.

"Faith?" I asked.

"In what is coming," the Walker said. "The unraveling of all things into darkness and silence."

"Empty Night," I breathed.

"Empty Night," the creature echoed, in the hushed tone of a holy phrase. "So we pressed the attacks at the Outer Gates. While I sowed havoc within the walls of reality. We loosed some of the primal forces of your own precious Creation against you. Undermined Mab, her people, the Accords, the delusion of order you force upon the universe with your useless presence." She smiled, dropping lower, the motion feline, sensual, hypnotic. "You may have survived the day. But the deed is done. We are the tide. Infinite. Unrelenting. And one day, starborn, make no mistake, we will wipe away all that you know. All we need is a single opening."

"Must suck," I panted, "to get whipped by some stupid punk from Chicago. 'Cause it looks to me like I beat you."

Something ugly went through her voice. "There was never a victory for you to gain," Nemesis hissed. "The mortals have been given terror they have not known in centuries. There is nothing more that need be done. They are your death stroke. Now I need only wait."

I finally reached the back of the boat and said, "Funny you should mention waiting."

Justine tilted her head, too far, silent.

"You know how you don't want to arrive on Demonreach, Walker?" The rear railing hit the backs of my thighs. "You don't want to show up all on your lonesome. Alfred hates that. That would be like sprinting into a meat grinder."

The gathering light showed me Justine's face as her eyes widened and she whipped her head over her shoulder.

The black mass of Demonreach, backlit by the golden sky, loomed directly ahead of us, swiftly larger, as the boat chugged toward its shores.

Justine whirled back and lunged toward me. "No!"

I smirked at her, spread my arms, and fell over the back of the boat, into the freezing waters of Lake Michigan.

With the last shreds of my will, I called to Demonreach.

And the last thing I felt before things went black was green-gold light, and a huge stony hand clamping down on my shoulder, tearing me away from the Outsider's desperate grasp.

Chapter

Thirty-six

Those next few days remain a montage in my head.

I woke up bumping along the surface of Lake Michigan in a rubber boat being run by Lara's people. I vaguely remembered reaching shore and having Alfred store the Eye safely away. Demonreach had allowed Riley and two of his men to approach and pick me up off the shoreline, after throwing poor Freydis two hundred yards out into the lake. They'd found me unconscious with my legs still in the freezing water and were treating the Winter Knight for hypothermia. Which is a bit like fitting a polar bear for a fur coat—it doesn't help the bear and it makes him sort of grumpy.

But they got me back to shore.

I remember insisting where Riley was to take me when we got there.

To her.

To her body, I mean.

Everything was chaos in Chicago, but it was the kind of chaos that people were more used to. There were soldiers and police everywhere. Emergency vehicles of all kinds were everywhere. The air was constantly full of the chop of helicopter blades.

If you knew what to look for, you could see signs of the presence of the Little Folk. They were everywhere in the wreckage, at the will of the Winter Lady, leaving enough signs and clues to lead rescuers to the wounded among the rubble—as they would later ensure the recovery of the dead. They wouldn't find absolutely everyone, but you'd hear newscasters remarking on the unusual dedication and success of the search-and-rescue teams in Chicago for years after.

In the area around the Bean, the cops were see-through, to me anyway, members of Mab's personal retinue underneath glamours that were more emotional than physical. When a Sidhe pretending to be a police officer spoke to you, you *felt* the authority more than you thought about it or saw it. In the chaotic aftermath of the battle, that was worth more than validated ID codes.

There, where Mab's people had control, they had brought in as many EMTs as they could scrape together for the wounded, both of my volunteers and of Marcone's.

For the first time in hours, thinking of my volunteers triggered no instant awareness of them. I poked around in my head with my wizard's senses, a sensation sort of like trying to count your teeth with your tongue. I found nothing. The banner was gone.

I walked silently through the wounded. Those who had been dying mostly had.

I walked up to the Bean.

I stopped at the door and took a breath.

The fight was over. There was nothing left to distract me from this. And it was going to hurt.

I bent over and climbed into the structure and turned to face the improvised bier.

It was empty.

She was gone.

Where she had lain, there was a symbol scorched into the crates as if by a white-hot stylus. Three triangles, interlocking. The valknut. The knot of the fallen warriors. Symbol of Odin.

I stared at the empty crates. Her blood was still on them, drying black.

Something dark began to stir, down deep. Something angry.

"Nothing has changed," said a soft, slightly slurred voice behind me. "She's gone. She isn't coming back."

I turned and found Miss Gard sitting on a pile of crates. There was a bottle of whiskey in her hand. There were four empties at her feet. She looked like she'd been through almost as much as I had.

I closed my eyes for a second. I was bone tired. I felt the rage down there.

But this wasn't the time.

Let the deep things stay deep.

"Hey, Siggy," I said in a gentle voice.

"It's the same," Gard slurred. "Where Nathan died." Her red eyes welled. "The damned knot. It's part of our inventory system. A check mark. One Einherjar, picked up and in transit."

"Nathan . . ." I said. Then it clicked. "Hendricks. Huh. He never looked like a Nathan."

I slumped down onto the crate next to her.

She passed me the bottle. I probably should have been drinking water. It's a far more adult drink than whiskey. But I took a solid pull and let it burn down.

"He hated that name," she said. "His mother . . ." She shook her head. "Well. That doesn't mean anything anymore."

"Einherjar," I said. "Murph didn't 'die well.'"

Gard's eyes flashed. "She died slaying a Jotun," she said roughly. "She did it to protect you. And she got results. She died a warrior's death. One without personal glory. The one that happened because she was doing what was necessary."

I tilted my head at her.

She waved a hand vaguely at her temple. "It's a limited *intellectus*, of the honored dead, of their deeds. I know who she was now, Dresden. Don't you dare cheapen her death by suggesting it was less than the culmination of a life of habitual valor."

Well.

There wasn't much I could say to that.

I leaned my head back against the crate behind me and began to weep steady tears that somehow didn't affect my breathing at all. "Dying sucks more than not dying. She should have stayed put."

"You'd be dead now if she had," the Valkyrie said. "So would I. So would a lot of people. And the world would be in chaos."

"Wait for it," I said darkly. I drank some more and passed the bottle back. And I added, "I want you to tell him something for me."

Gard looked at me, suddenly wary. "Before you speak, know this: The being you have dealt with is . . . only a facet of the being whose symbol that is. His guises are created to diminish him into something a mortal mind can readily accept. But though he may not have the strength he once did, that being is yet an elemental one. He does not accept insults or threats lightly."

"Good. Because I'm not delivering them lightly," I said, a low thunder growling its way into my quiet words. "You tell *Odin* that *Harry Blackstone Copperfield Dresden* says, upon his Name, that if he doesn't treat Murph better than I would myself, I'm going to kick down his door, pluck his fucking ravens, knock him down, kick his guts out, drag him to the island, and lock him up in a cell with Ethniu."

Gard blinked at me.

"I beat a divine being once," I said. "If I have to build a nation to get it done, I'll do it again. You tell him exactly what I said."

Gard stared at me for a moment. Then a slow, if sad, smile touched her face. "I'll tell him," she said. Then she added, gently, "It will please him, I think. If not the twins. Have no fear for your shieldmaiden. In our halls, warriors who died for family, for duty, for love, are given the respect such a death deserves. She will want for nothing."

I nodded. Then after a while, I said, "If she's an Einherjar now . . ."

Gard shook her head. "Not until the memory of her has faded from the minds of those who knew her. That is the limit not even the Allfather may cross."

"She, uh," I said. I blinked several times. "She wasn't real forgettable."

"She was not," agreed the Valkyrie. "And she has earned her rest."

"She earned better than a bullet in the neck," I spat.

"All warriors die, Dresden," Gard replied. "And if they die in the course of being true to their duty and honor, most would count that a fitting end to a worthy life. She did."

I nodded.

"Fuck worthy," I said quietly, miserably. "I miss her."

Silent seconds went by while I went briefly blind.

"I'm sorry," I said. "For . . . Nathan He was a loyal friend to the end."

"Oh, man up, Dresden," Gard said. "You're still here."

But she nodded as she said it. And she cried, too.

We had a funeral followed by a wake at Mac's a few days later, the Paranet crew and me.

Everyone was dazed, struggling to adjust to the reality that had confronted them.

Tens of thousands had perished. The final count of fallen humanity that night would have overflowed Soldier Field—which was being used for refugees, of which there were more than a hundred thousand.

Ethniu had been even harder on Chicago real estate values than me. Wakka wakka.

The Huntsmen, in particular, had ravaged every neighborhood they went through, killing about ninety-five percent of the occupants—until they got to the South Side.

Then it was like the robbery of the First National Bank of Northfield, Minnesota. Too many people were willing to fight—and they were armed. Sure, there were a lot of bad guys—but there were a lot more citizens, a higher-than-average percentage of them had guns, and once they understood what was happening, they turned the streets into shooting galleries. That was when things had started to turn on that flank of the battle, providing an opening for Marcone.

Apparently, even the legions of epic mythology had better plan for trouble on some of the toughest streets in the world.

The power was out and stayed that way for a while. There was just too much to replace. That made clean water hard to move around. More people got sick and died, and things could have gotten really bad if we'd had a harsher summer. But the weather stayed unseasonably mild and cool, with frequent rains. Maybe a Queen of Faerie ensured that. Or maybe the universe figured the city had earned a break.

Either way, it was raining when we gathered at my grave in Graceland.

We filled a coffin with pictures. I used one of me and Murph arguing that some joker in CPD had taken when both of us had cartoonish expressions on our faces. It felt truer to what we'd had, somehow.

It hadn't had a lot of chance to grow.

Other pictures went in. No frames. There wouldn't have been room. If they'd given their life for the city, their picture went in. We used copies of the drivers' licenses of the volunteers, when we couldn't find anything else about them. Hendricks's picture went in. So did Yoshimo's and Wild Bill's and Chandler's. Everyone in the Paranet community, hell, almost everyone in the *city* had lost someone they knew or were related to.

When people you know die, that gets attention. That was the beginning of the change in Chicago, where the supernatural had just become a threat that was too great to be denied or overlooked.

Butters, moving comically in his neck brace and backboard, stood with me throughout the memorial service. Of the survivors, fifty or so of my volunteers had been willing to attend. In a ceremony that was half comedic and half gut-wrenching, I pronounced them Knights of the Bean and Defenders of Chicago. And then I pinned a dried lima bean glued to a steel backing to their chests, and I made each of them a promise:

"If you or anyone you love is ever in danger, come and find me. If it isn't you, tell them to show me this. I will help. No questions asked."

Promises are a magic of their own, with a little will behind them. And when I made each one, I felt it leave a signature on the pin. I'd know it if someone tried to pass a fake one on me.

After that, I tried to give a speech about Murph.

"Karrin Murph—" I said.

And nothing else would come out.

Butters took over, speaking a little stiffly due to his jaw, and said some things to the gathering, which they took very well. People had seen Butters in action, and word had spread. They looked at him like he was a big damned hero.

Which he was—but he didn't see it that way, because of course he wouldn't. .

They didn't look at me like I was a big damned hero, though.

In fact . . . mostly, people weren't looking at me at all.

I guess people had seen glimpses of me in that fight, too. Plus I'd just incinerated a bunch of guys, in front of God and everybody. And word had gotten around.

Ever see a video clip of a shark swimming through a school of baitfish? Where the fish all make sure to stay well out of his path?

I was the shark now.

Except for a few friends, no one came within arm's reach of me.

And . . . that suited me, somehow. I felt raw, as if my skin had been peeled off and the world was made of salt and lemon juice. Maybe a little distance was a good thing, for a while.

After Butters finished, old Father Forthill came out and spoke a gentle prayer for the dead. Then we closed up the casket and filled my open grave. I had my tombstone removed and replaced with one that simply read, THEY DEFENDED CHICAGO, and the month and year.

I was the last one at the grave.

Except for Michael. My friend wore a waterproof overcoat and fedora. I'd shown up in shirtsleeves. I hadn't even brought an umbrella. Back before the Winter mantle, I'd have been shivering. Now the rain felt nice on my bruises.

Michael stood with me in comfortable silence, waiting.

"Marcone was right," I said quietly.

Michael frowned. He said nothing.

"Marcone built a base of power," I said. "He prepared for this. If he hadn't, the city would have fallen. Period. I would never have succeeded without him."

"What are you saying, Harry?" Michael asked gently.

"I can do more," I said quietly. "I need to do more."

"Like Marcone has?" Michael asked.

"Somehow," I said quietly. "I don't think I could do it his way. Too many suits."

"Corporate thug doesn't really fit you," Michael agreed. "What did you have in mind?"

"Wizard of Chicago?" I suggested.

"Good to stick with what you know," Michael said. "But you're talking about more, aren't you?"

I was quiet for a moment, looking down at the rain splashing on the casket.

"Do you know why I wanted Murph to stay out of the fight?" I asked.

"Because you'd given up on her," Michael said.

"No, it was because I'd given up on . . . Oh, yes." I cleared my throat. "On some level, I had written her off. I knew I was going to be out there without her watching my back."

Die alone, whispered a voice in my memory.

"She didn't agree with your assessment," Michael noted.

"No," I said quietly. "She had, you know. Hope. Faith. That what she was doing was right and necessary and worth it." I squinted at him. "Death isn't when your body stops working. It's when there's no more future. When you can't see past right now, because you stopped believing in tomorrow." I shrugged. "There should be a place where people can borrow a little hope and faith when they're running low."

My friend's eyes wrinkled at the corners. "Oh, I'd say there's one or two."

"Well. You folks talk to a lot of people. But not everyone speaks in the same language. Maybe there're folks who just wouldn't understand what you've got to say. Maybe they need to hear it from someone like me."

Michael smiled and said, "The Almighty gave each of us our own utterly unique voice. Surely there's a lesson to be learned there."

"Will you help me?" I asked.

"Always," he said.

"Good," I said. "I think I'm going to need a carpenter."

His face slowly brightened over the course of a moment, a deep, intense satisfaction radiating from him. It was like watching the sun rise on his soul. "I love to give that kind of help. And my rates are very reasonable . . ."

There were footsteps in the wet grass behind us.

We turned to find Carlos Ramirez facing us from beneath a grey umbrella. He wore his Warden's cloak. His expression was fatigued and grim. He looked like he hadn't slept in days.

"Carlos," I said quietly. "Good to see you."

He nodded, once. When he spoke, his voice was ragged, as if he'd been shouting a lot. "Harry Dresden," he said in a formal tone and cadence. "Greetings from the White Council."

Not *Warden Dresden*, I noted. Not even *Wizard Dresden*.

So.

Michael glanced between us and said, "I'll excuse myself, gentlemen."

"Thank you, Sir Michael," Ramirez said quietly.

Michael turned and limped back toward the cars.

"The vote," I said. "Forgot all about it. Guess it didn't go my way."

Ramirez shook his head.

"You're out," he said. "You are no longer to associate yourself with the White Council or harass its members. You will refrain from the public practice of magic to standards of discretion determined by the Council or face the consequences. Wardens will periodically inspect you and your residence for residual black magic. You know the drill." He shook his head and reached into his coat. "There are some documents. They list all the terms."

"Terms," I said. "Pretty bold for the Council to boot me out, then dictate terms to me."

Ramirez stared at me for a second. Then he said, his voice low, "You had to know this was coming. It's been coming for a long time. We've given you chance after chance, and you keep—" He broke off and looked away. "You never should have gotten mixed up with Mab, Harry. That changed everything."

"Carlos," I began.

"You sold out to the monsters, Dresden," Ramirez spat, his voice harsh. "Don't you see that? Can't you see it even now? As beaten as you are, you shouldn't even be able to stand up. Sixty degrees, windy, and raining and you're standing there soaking wet and enjoying it."

"What did you say?" I asked, low and hard.

"You heard me," he said. He wasn't budging, either. "I don't know, Dresden, if what happened here could have been avoided. But I know you were mixed up in it in ways you aren't saying." He stared at me beseechingly, shaking his head. "You should have *trusted* me, man. And you pull that stupid hex on me instead?" Something in his face broke. "Chandler's *gone*. Bill and Yukie are *gone*. And maybe if you'd been willing to talk, that wouldn't have happened. Maybe it would have made things different."

"I had to," I said. "I didn't have a choice."

"Yeah," he said, his voice weary. "I know you think that. And that's the problem." He took his hand out of his coat and tossed a thick legal envelope at me. I caught it. "Read that. Believe it. Because as far as the White Council is concerned, you're one of the monsters now, Dresden. Push us and we'll push back. Hard."

"Who's going to do the pushing, 'Los?" I asked. "You?"

"No," he said quietly. "McCoy." He cleared his throat. "We were friends once, Dresden. So I'll tell you this last bit of gossip. The Senior Council voted in emergency session, while Listens-to-Wind and McCoy were in surgery. They found witnesses who saw you directly murder human servants of the Fomor by means of pyromancy."

Which was true. "You've seen what those guys have done," I told him. "Would you call them human, strictly speaking?"

"Doesn't matter what I think," Ramirez said. "You

know how broadly they interpret the First Law. And why it has to be that way. By unanimous vote, they have already given the Blackstaff the order to execute your death warrant, and suspended it. If you cross the line, they'll send him. And if he won't do it, he'll be charged with treason. So for your sake—and his—don't make us take action."

"You son of a bitch," I said quietly.

"We don't fight monsters fair," he said. "I learned that from you."

We stood there quietly for a moment.

"It doesn't have to be like this," I said.

"It *does*," Ramirez replied. "You made that call when you didn't talk to me. And *sixty thousand people died*."

I let out a frustrated breath.

"One of these days," I said, "you're going to look back at today and feel really stupid."

"Is that a threat?" he asked.

"No, you knob." I sighed wearily. "Just a fact."

"The Council has spoken," he said, just as tiredly, and turned to go.

"No," I said.

He paused. "What?"

"No," I said again, a little firmer. "The White Council has gotten to bully wizards for a long time, and they think they have the right. I say they don't."

Ramirez tilted his head. "Don't talk yourself into something I can't ignore, Dresden."

I grimaced. "Carlos. I mean to live my life. You've cast me out, and you think that means I'm vulnerable. Maybe you ought to rethink that."

"Meaning what?"

"Why don't you ask Ethniu how vulnerable I am?" I said quietly. "We can. If you'd like."

I let that one hang there while he stared at me.

"To say nothing about how Mab would react to the death of the Winter Knight," I continued. "The Winter Lady might not take it kindly, either, and you saw what she's capable of doing."

Carlos's cheek twitched. "Yes. I did."

I paused and said, "*That* was a threat, Carlos. I'm going to live here and do what I've always done. I want you to leave me in peace. And I'll do the same in return. The way things are in the world, I don't think the Council can afford to push things that far. Not for little old me."

Ramirez exhaled. "You're taking one hell of a risk, Harry."

"I don't like being told what to do," I said. "I let you push me around, who the hell am I?"

"Yeah," Ramirez said. "Who the hell *are* you?"

It was quiet.

"Goodbye," he said quietly.

And then he left.

Back at the car, Michael said, "That looked grim. What happened?"

"Rest of the White Council was pretty nervous about the guy who soloed a Titan, I guess," I said. "They voted. I'm an outlaw. Like the old days."

Michael considered that for a moment. Then he said, quietly and firmly, "Those *fuckers*."

I stumbled on the slippery grass in the rain and fell on my ass.

And it didn't stop there. Michael swore. My friend

cursed a blue streak like a dozen sailors picking a dozen fights. He swore profanities that would have made a fallen angel blush. He swore in three different languages that I recognized, and in a dozen I didn't. He swore like a man with a forty-year pent-up hurricane of ranting profanity in his chest that had been looking for a way to come out.

When he was finished he looked up at the rain and said, "I'll be happy to do penance, Lord. But some things need to be said." Then he turned to me, extended his hand, and said, firmly, "You are always welcome in *my* house, Harry Dresden. In fact, Charity told me to invite you and Maggie over for Christmas Eve and morning with us. It's hard for us to think of Christmas without her. And you're still coming for Sunday dinner, aren't you? The place is still pretty cut up from where those lunatics came in the house, but I think a couple of weeks of work should set it right. . . ."

I took my friend's hand.

There was rain in my eyes.

It took only days for rumors to spread that there were beings in town sniffing around for my trail, bad guys I'd crossed or annoyed at some point in the past. I didn't have the imprimatur of the White Council anymore. And while Mab would speak very loudly if anyone moved against the Winter *Court*, if her Winter Knight got himself killed because of his own stupid choices, she wouldn't lose much sleep, apart from the stress of finding a replacement.

That, combined with my injuries, kept me indoors for

a few days. I got my arm set and put in a cast. I was pretty sure my joints had voided their warranties at the very least, but those first few days were full of desperation where medical care was involved, and every church and hospital overflowed with the wounded. It took the broken bone and the fact that I knew Lamar to even rate acknowledgment in triage, in the battle's immediate aftermath.

Fortunately, I had access to Charity Carpenter, who had been patching up her husband and his idiot friends for years. So, in addition to my cast, I got stitches in several places, a painful shoulder relocation I didn't know I needed, a bunch of bandages, a shoulder wrap, elbow wraps, wrist wraps, knee wraps, ankle wraps, a couple of two-gallon bags of ice for my knees, and Tiger Balm.

(Which not even the Winter Knight can ignore when it gets in a cut, it turns out, and which is one ingredient and a little will away from being an excellent ointment against fae glamour, if you can keep your eyes open. Seriously, that stuff is borderline magical off the shelf.)

By the time the needs of my body had been seen to as best as possible, I looked and felt like a mummy, wrapped and way too herbal scented, dried out and too stiff to move when I finally crashed into the bed in the Carpenters' (original) guest room. They had some extras now. I think I slept for about a day. I remember eating ravenously a couple of times. And then I just lay there with my eyes closed for a long time, weeping silently. And I woke up holding a sleeping Maggie, with Mouse curled into his tiniest ball on the bottom two-thirds of the bed, on what

I think was the second morning, and felt battered and exhausted and mostly human.

I made my daughter breakfast. And I did a lot of thinking.

Those first few days, when I moved around Chicago at all, I was careful. Real careful. Like, having four full-grown werewolves with me or nearby at all times careful. I got out, got my bearings, and started moving.

Will and the Alphas came with me to the session of the first-ever Unseelie Accords Executive Ministry meeting. War with the Fomor had been declared by unanimous consent within the Accorded nations, and the Ministry was supposed to determine what to do about it, starting with dealing with the aftermath of the Battle of the Bean.

No one invited me to the Ministry meeting, in a private club in one of the gorgeous old stone buildings in Oldtown, so I did it myself. The place was hidden behind a web of veils and glamours so thick and intricate that it made me a little dizzy just sensing it. If I hadn't known exactly where I was going and exactly what I was looking for, I'd have wandered right past the place.

When I came in, there was a waiting room where several people came to their feet—a Sidhe warrior from either Court, Miss Gard, a svartalf I didn't recognize, and Freydis, who was covered with bumps and bruises and still-healing cuts and looked relaxed for the first time since I'd seen her.

"Easy, people," I said. "I came to talk."

They all eyed me warily, which was to say down the

barrels of their guns. Except for Freydis, who kept reading her magazine and just looked amused.

Well. Granted I looked like ten miles of bad road in my battle-stained black leather duster. And my eyes were watery from the damned hurry-up Tiger Balm antiglamour ointment I'd whipped up to help find the place. And also I had four battle-hardened werewolves with me.

I guess I can see it.

I got out a cloth and wiped the ointment off my cheekbones, blinking more tears out of my eyes, while making uncomfortable noises. It's difficult to be intimidating when you look ridiculous. By the time I was done and could see properly again, most of the guns were half-lowered.

"Gard," I said. Whenever you're facing a bunch of people, do whatever you can to face one person. It takes some of the psychological advantage of numbers away. "You know me. I need to speak to them."

Gard lowered her weapon entirely, without holstering it. "The Ministry is meeting in closed session."

I faced her and said, quietly and firmly, "I have earned the right to speak. By deed. Or none of us would be here."

Gard stared at me for a long moment.

And the corner of her mouth twitched.

The Ministry had met in a ballroom big enough for a basketball game, its curtains drawn against any view from outside. The interior of the place had been filled with light so brilliant and omnipresent that shadows had nowhere to fall. There was no furniture in the place—just light and open flooring, and a circle of beings facing one another.

I closed the door behind me and limped forward into the light, squinting as my pupils got more of a workout than they'd had in a while. I suppose sunglasses would have defeated the point.

There were things out there that lived, and listened, in shadows.

I walked forward into shocked silence.

Marcone stood there, in his suit, looking unstained by recent events. Vadderung looked like an older, leaner version of approximately the same creature, a wolfhound standing beside a mastiff. Mab had adopted her corporate appearance for the meeting, apparently keeping in theme with the pair of them, and Etri's sister, Evanna, had kept up the motif. Beside her, Lara Raith was as stunning in a white suit as she was in nothing at all, while Sarissa, the Summer Lady, had gone office casual in laconic defiance of the trend.

And the Archive stood there, slightly to one side, not quite part of the circle. She'd collected a number of cuts from flying bits of debris, probably, and her nose had been broken rather badly. Black rings had spread around the base of her eyes.

I walked around the circle to Mab's right hand.

The Queen of Air and Darkness gave me a peeved look.

I stared back at her, willing her to get it.

And so help me, she just looked at me and *did*. Her expression became very serious, and she nodded firmly, once, twitching one finger and somehow conveying that I was to wait.

"Please pardon the disruption. Mistress Archive, continue the report."

The Archive nodded once and flicked a hand at the air. There was a shimmer, and a television screen appeared there, a news report that I suppose had been inevitable, even if the ongoing loss of power meant that we hadn't had the chance to see it yet.

It was helicopter footage, along Chicago's waterfront. It showed the destruction in graphic detail. Basically the Bean reflected the lakeshore now, a wide swath of pulverized bits of former city. I could imagine the magazine covers. Or the thumbnail images. Whatever.

The chyron running at the bottom of the screen read: AFTERMATH OF MAJOR TERRORIST ATTACK IN CHICAGO. WIDESPREAD CHEMICAL WEAPONS AND POSSIBLE WEAPONS OF MASS DESTRUCTION USED. AS MANY AS 20,000 DEAD. PRESIDENT DECLARES STATE OF NATIONAL EMERGENCY.

Hell's bells.

"In aggregate," the Archive said, speaking with a little more Stallone than one would have expected out of a teenage girl, "the coverage of the event would strongly indicate that the mortal powers that be have decided to obfuscate."

"Optimistic," Vadderung murmured.

"Gaslighting eight million people?" Lara asked. "They've done that by breakfast each morning." She glanced over at me and gave me a faintly quizzical look and a dip of her chin. "The military is controlling traffic in and out of the city. Power, communications, and humanitarian aid are funneled in through them. The official version of events will have a very large lead and a much louder voice than any truth tellers who may come along, and the disruptive effects of the Eye make it unlikely that any photographic or video evidence was obtained. Add in a fictional toxin which caused hallucinations, possibly long-term and recurring, in those exposed to it and they'll be able to muddle things thoroughly."

"Not within the city," Marcone said. "They're building a psychological wall around the place. That will unify those held prisoner by it in a way that would not otherwise be possible."

"Meaning what, precisely?" Mab asked.

"Meaning that the human factor will be . . . greatly intensified, within the city," Marcone said. "Uncertainty and insecurity will cause people to gravitate toward the security offered by group identity and support. People are, frankly, terrified. That's going to cause them to cling to the veneer of normality. By day." He shook his head. "By night, expect them to acquire arms. Expect them to become wiser and more dangerous. Expect some of them to make bargains with the powers they've been exposed to. And expect others to hunt anything they perceive as supernatural through the streets in packs. And that's a best-case scenario."

My stomach twisted.

I mean, he was right. Everything he was saying was exactly accurate.

And yet . . . also wrong.

Yeah, darkness could make things really, really bad. Frightened people in large groups rarely acted wisely.

But sometimes that foolishness came out as kindness and compassion, when there was every reason to look out only for yourself. Sometimes it came out as irrational courage in the face of overwhelming terror. Sometimes our madness leads us to choices that make us better and nobler and kinder than we were before.

People like Marcone made me think that everything is falling apart.

But people like Michael, like Murphy, like the brave men and women who had fought and died in defiance of what must have seemed like the world's ending, make me think that maybe we're falling *forward*. Like a child learning to walk. Sometimes we lurch and stumble. Sometimes we fall. And each time we learn. But each time we have to make up our minds to get up again, to take the next step.

So that one day we can walk with our heads held high.

The fight for Chicago had gotten started when Ethniu attacked. But it was far from over.

"Baron?" Mab asked. "Can you maintain a functioning society within the city?"

"No one could," Marcone replied. "However, I judge that, for now, the city will have a strong self-interest in maintaining its current power structure. That gives me what I believe is the most practical available leverage of the direction of events within it."

"Do you have control or not?" Mab asked.

"Does a man in a canoe have control over the rapids?" Marcone replied.

"But you believe they can be navigated?" Mab clarified.

"To the limit of my foresight, yes. That makes no allowance for federal interests, however. My reach there is more limited."

Mab contemplated the reply and then nodded. She considered Lara. "Can you nullify their involvement?"

Lara thought for a moment before answering. "On the political level, there's more profit to be gained from engagement than nullification. On the practical level, however . . . there's no way to keep the Librarians out entirely now."

"A complication," Vadderung said, in the wry tone of a man engaging in understatement.

Lara grimaced.

"Who are these Librarians?" Evanna asked.

"The Library of Congress, Special Collections Division," Lara provided. "Also known as the Librum Bellum. Men in Black."

"Government agents," Evanna noted. "What danger do they pose?"

"They're the eyes and ears," Lara said. "They're smart, skilled, dedicated, professional, they've got several centuries of collective knowledge through the Masons, and they will absolutely be coming to *learn* whatever they can They are *extremely* dangerous."

"Assuming they haven't been here in the city all along," Vadderung pointed out mildly. "Perhaps they've already identified each of us."

Lara winced. "Optimist."

Vadderung's mouth twitched at a corner.

The Summer Lady cleared her throat and glanced at Mab, who nodded. Sarissa turned her gaze along the circle as she said, "Make whatever preparations you wish. But the truth is out. And spreading. All of these stratagems, from the mortal authorities or from us, can only delay that."

"Sweet Summer child," Lara murmured wryly.

Mab held up a slender hand as if to forestall bickering. "We must prepare for as many futures as possible, not merely the ones we prefer. If we can slow the mortals' collective hand from striking until we have dealt with the Fomor, then it is worthwhile to attempt. If nothing else, it lets us focus upon a single foe at a time."

I felt myself freeze for a moment at that.

Humanity.

A foe.

I glanced around. Yeah. No wonder there wasn't a representative from the White Council here. Like it or not, they were pretty much the spokespeople for humanity at large, within the Accorded nations. A lot of wizards had family in the mortal world, close ties to it. Martha Liberty was still close with members of an extended clan of whom she was the founding matriarch, down in New Orleans, for example.

And . . . well, even *I* had Maggie. Friends. It mattered to me. The environment those people existed in, their society, it mattered to me.

Sarissa looked a little disturbed. But other than that, I realized that there was no one else in this room for whom that was true.

Stars and stones.

Ramirez hadn't been wrong.

I was working with monsters.

But I wasn't them.

I leaned forward slightly, as if preparing to take a step,

and Mab said, "Ladies and gentlemen, my Knight requests audience. In light of his recent service to the Accorded nations, I believe it right and proper to grant it. Will anyone here gainsay me?"

Marcone suddenly looked more alert.

I gave him a little smile. I didn't quite blow him a kiss. But I let him know it was coming.

"This should be interesting," Vadderung murmured.

Mab turned to me and nodded, tilting her head in toward the center of the circle.

I shambled forward into it and felt the gazes of very dangerous people upon me.

And for the first time, I didn't have any of the weight of the White Council backing me up.

It was just me. That was intimidating.

But it also meant that I had me on my side. And I liked the way that felt.

Don't fight all of them, Harry, I thought. *Fight one of them.*

And I turned to Marcone.

"The Summer and Winter Courts care about balance," I said. "And what the Accorded nations have done to Chicago has created a terrible imbalance. More than just the political and military consequences of our conflicts, we have violated the spirit of laws so old that they have never been written down. We were guests in Chicago. And we brought our troubles to their home."

An uneasy ripple went through some of those in the circle: Vadderung, Mab, Evanna, and Sarissa all stirred uneasily.

Lara and Marcone took careful note of that.

"Choices have consequences that ripple out in all directions," I said quietly. "And our choices have hurt the people of this city. We can't possibly scramble to minimize the consequences to our lives without acknowledging the debt we have incurred by inflicting our conflict upon them."

I met Marcone's eyes. "Our world isn't supposed to cross with theirs, for the most part. And in return, they mostly ignore us. Now you say that the mortals are going to be sending eyes and ears in. Well, maybe it'd be smart for them to see some things."

"What do you suggest?" Marcone asked.

"The Accorded nations provide humanitarian aid and assistance," I said.

That got a reaction from everyone, from Vadderung's eyebrow lift to Evanna's incredulous sputter.

"I'm not saying make open diplomatic contact," I said. "I'm saying we act. We help. Indirectly, in secret. If they're looking, they'll see what you're doing. Let them see us do what we can to balance the scales. Ethniu's attack changed everything. It was too big, too loud. They've seen us. And we'd better show them from the get-go that we aren't trying to murder them all. Because we made a bad first impression. And because it's smart. And because it's right." I met Marcone's eyes. "I called, and men and women of this city answered. They followed me. They fought. And I felt them die."

Something flickered in Marcone's face.

His chin moved in the faintest vertical tilt of acknowledgment.

I dropped my voice to something that was just between

me and Marcone. "We owe them more than just washing our hands of the mess. And you're going to make a fortune rebuilding things anyway."

Marcone's eyes flickered with amusement, acknowledging the truth of my point.

"The Accords," he said, carefully, "are not a charitable organization."

"Nor are we beggars, unable to pay our debts," Mab answered. "My Knight makes a fine point: Our fight did them harm. They had to choose to shed their blood in defense. Innocents were slain. Value lost. Specifics can be argued, but the direction of the debt is clear." Her head swiveled to me. "What recompense do you recommend?"

"The money stuff, they've got insurance and things for. There are economic safety nets everywhere. It's the people we need to take care of. Anyone injured in the attack, we pay for it. Whatever they need, healing of the body or mind. We pay to bury the dead. And we pay a weregild to the survivors of anyone slain. I don't care if they find buried gold or get a mysterious winning lottery ticket or what, but we owe them a debt for something priceless. And we owe them the gesture of helping to make their future more secure after what we took from them. And there's a man in this room who can get down everyone's freaking chimneys every year if he has to, so don't tell me that there isn't power to make it happen."

"These numbers are very large," Mab noted.

"Our debt," I said, "is larger. Ask any child of the men and women who died."

Mab looked faintly troubled at the thought.

"The Accords," she said, "provide for reparations to damaged parties. This business of guest-right disturbs me greatly and demands care and respect. Making right the damages wrought upon the mortals seems meet to me—with the understanding that we will apply the resources expended for such repayment to the debt of those ultimately responsible, namely, the Fomor, once our conflict with them has been resolved."

And it turned out that by unanimous vote, everyone in the Accords agreed on that, because everyone in politics enjoys giving other people's money to good causes.

Whatever. I got people some help, did a little good.

But I wasn't finished.

"There is also the matter," I said, to Mab, "of personal debt. Ethniu was my kill, before all the Accorded nations, in defense of the demesne of Baron John Marcone of Chicago." I turned to face him. "Acknowledgment of that act is due."

Eyes turned toward Marcone.

"The Eye seems ample reward for such a deed," Marcone noted.

"To some," Sarissa said, her voice very dry.

"Do you have it?" I asked Marcone innocently.

He stood there, suddenly very wary.

"I mean, I'm not sure where it is," I said, which was technically true—Alfred had it stashed somewhere and I'd told him not to tell me where, specifically for this conversation. Technical truth was, at the moment, the best kind of truth. "But if you want to hand it to me . . ."

"I assumed you claimed it from Ethniu," Marcone said.

"I don't know what to tell you," I said.

"Are we to believe that you just left a weapon like the Eye lying upon the ground?" Marcone asked.

"Dude, there was an apocalypse on," I said, in a very reasonable tone. "The earth shaking. Giant waves. I almost drowned, you know, in this giant stupid concrete teacup some fool made. It's all kind of blurry."

Marcone narrowed his eyes.

"The point is, my people fought and died for your land," I said, my voice suddenly harder. "I fought and bled for your land. And if I hadn't, you wouldn't have a territory to defend. I defended your home. And I lost my own home doing it."

I pointed at Evanna.

Everyone looked at her.

"There was . . . damage to that apartment during the attack," she politely lied. "No replacement apartment is available at this time. As such, he may no longer be our guest."

"See?" I said. "A debt is owed. And we take our debts pretty serious in Winter."

I felt Mab's gaze over my shoulder, like a cold draft in the room.

Only it was focused on Marcone.

Marcone eyed me and then Mab, and then Lara. "Surely you don't believe him."

A little smile played on the corners of Lara's mouth. "The last I saw," she said, "*you* were the one running off with the Eye, Baron."

"Queen Mab," Marcone said in protest.

"He has given me no reason to disbelieve him, Baron," Mab said. She knew all about technically true things, too.

Marcone turned to me with his eyes narrowed. He regarded me and said, "I know you have it."

Marcone had put me on a pedestal by telling people I'd taken out Ethniu. That act alone had probably scared enough members of the White Council to get me voted out. But if he was going to put me up there, he shouldn't be too terribly surprised if I kicked him in the face.

I took a breath, enjoying the moment.

"Prove it," I said. "*Sir* Baron."

Marcone eyed me. Then glanced past me to the Queen of Air and Darkness.

Mab's eyebrow went up so far that it threatened the line of her skull. Then she said, as if to Marcone, "Much is explained."

Marcone's gaze slid around the faces of the Ministry, weighing what he saw there. He yielded with reluctant grace. "Very well, Sir Dresden." Marcone sighed. "What is it you wish of me?"

I leaned down to look him in the face.

"I want my *lab* back," I said. "Move your stuff."

I'll give this to Marcone: When he gives his word, he's good for it.

He emptied out the little castle built on the site of my old boardinghouse within twenty-four hours. Soldiers, personnel, furniture, lights—by the time we arrived the next day, all of it was gone. The castle was empty of Marcone's presence, right down to the stones.

"What do you think?" I asked. I turned on a heel, regarding the main hall. There was still a big hole in the roof where Ethniu and the Eye had provided incentive to install a skylight. I pointed at it. "Maybe get one like Doctor Strange's window, right?"

Molly looked around the place speculatively. "It looks . . . cold and slightly damp and gloomy. Like one big basement."

"Glorious," I said. "Your dad is coming over later to help me figure out how to make it a little more human-friendly. I mean, you could fit a basketball court in here. And I don't need a throne room."

"And you do need a basketball court?"

"It's an idea—that's all I'm saying."

She shook her head. "Have you noticed all the enchantments on the place?" Molly asked skeptically. "There is some really old stuff here that is still working."

In point of fact, I had Bob going over the entire thing now for an in-depth assessment. The defensive systems built into the castle had been laid up by a wizard with a particularly thorough breed of the crazies. My first read was that Marcone's use of them had only touched the surface of their potential—maybe Thorned Namshiel hadn't yet had time to teach him to make full use of them. Hell, the only reason I felt like I knew what I was talking about was that the enchantments hardwired into the stones of the castle bore a startling structural resemblance to those that had been used to create Demonreach. It was entirely possible that the castle's magical defenses had been the work of the original Merlin or one of his inheritors.

It would take time to be sure, but if I was right, by the

time I was done with the place, I'd have a redoubt damned near as hard to crack as the island, and a heck of a lot more convenient to live in.

"Yeah. Kind of like having a smart house, I guess," I said. "There're all sorts of features I'm going to have to work through and figure out."

Molly gave me a rather wan smile. "Sounds fun."

"Maybe a little," I said. "Gotta make sure Marcone didn't leave me any magical surprises behind."

"Do you think he would?"

"Not really," I said. "But home's a real good thing to be thorough about." I looked around. "He was supposed to be bringing the keys by. He's late." I caught a look on Molly's face and scowled. "Wait. Did you come down here with me to distract me?"

"Not distract, precisely," Molly hedged. "But . . . perhaps it's better if you don't butt heads with Marcone just now, Harry."

"Indeed," came Mab's cool, calm voice.

The Queen of Air and Darkness entered the great hall through the same doors Ethniu had ducked beneath a few days before and surveyed the bare, clean walls through the shafts of sunlight falling through the hole in the roof. She wore the same business wear she had in the Ministry meeting. "Something of a fixer-upper, isn't it, my Knight?"

I scowled at her. "Did you collect the keys from Marcone on my behalf?"

"No," Mab said.

"Because you thought I'd pick a fight with him?"

"Of course not," Mab said.

"You don't trust me," I said.

Mab gave me a bland look. "Do not be ridiculous. I trust you as much as anyone." She glanced over her shoulder to a second figure entering the shadowed hall.

"Lara," I said calmly.

The power behind the throne of the White Court entered the room with a faintly cautious air, examining the bare walls curiously. One, two, three dangerous women here with me, and a definite sense of conspiracy-for-my-own-good in the air. It was appropriate to start feeling a little wary, I thought.

"At Mab's suggestion, I took it upon myself to run the keys down to you," Lara said. "I pointed out to the good Baron how it made everything happen in front of witnesses, very official and aboveboard, and avoided any possible moments of . . . negative emotional interaction between the two of you."

I grunted and said, "Between the two of us, eh?"

"Oh, Marcone is furious with you, in his own way," Lara said. "I'd say you won the round."

Which did not make me feel a little surge of petty satisfaction. At all. Ahem.

"But you've got the keys?" I asked her.

She held them up. She was wearing white gloves to go with the business suit.

"And you guys arranged everything so us boys don't get all emotional and start punching each other to impress the girls," I said.

"Or start making out with each other," Lara volleyed back. "The two of you were looking very warrior-bro chummy, I thought."

"Ew," I said, and held out my hands. "How do I know you didn't make a copy of them for yourself?"

"Mab was with me," Lara said. She crossed the room to drop the keys in my hand without touching me. "And as if you weren't going to change all the locks first thing, anyway."

I bounced the keys, two copies of a single master key, in my hand, then slipped them into my pocket. "I wouldn't have punched him in the nose. I would have been nice. As long as he was."

"Of course," Lara said, nodding firmly. "You're both very mature."

I sniffed haughtily.

Both of us were kidding around, rather than moving right into what was coming next. Neither one of us liked thinking about the fact that not only had we lost Thomas; we'd failed him, too.

"Did your people find anything else?" I asked.

Lara's expression sobered. "The ship was found sunk in two feet of water off a beach in Indiana. Recovery operations underway."

I exhaled and nodded my thanks to her. "So, Justine made it to shore."

Lara nodded. "But where she went after that, we don't know. My people are looking, but it's a very large world."

"Finding people is what I do," I said. "If you hold down your end, I'll start from mine. Between us, we'll catch her."

"If we do," Lara said, "do you really think you can cast out . . ." Her voice lowered. She never said the word *Nemesis*.

"I don't know," I said. "But we owe it to Thomas to try to save her. And the child."

Lara's eyes became grim, and she gave me a small, firm nod and offered me her hand. "Shake on it, wizard?"

I nodded and traded grips with her. "Agreed."

And a flickering something went between us. It wasn't White Court mojo, I didn't think. Just . . . a shivering note of energy. A harmony.

It was a promise both of us had put a measure of will behind. It was a promise both of us meant to keep.

We both had the same feelings about family.

"Excellent," said Mab from behind us. "Lady Lara, upon due consideration, your third favor is granted. You have my permission to court my Knight. The wedding will commence at sundown."

"Uh," I said, "what?"

Lara arched an eyebrow. "What?"

"WHAT!!??" sputtered Molly.

I blinked at her. Then at Mab. Then at Lara. And then Lara and I both more or less simultaneously jerked our hands out of the grip they'd been in.

"The third favor requested of Winter," Mab clarified. "Lady Lara desired a binding alliance with Winter. This seems wise to us. It will be done."

"Not that part," I stammered. "The part with a wedding."

"The fusion of bloodlines is how these things are generally arranged," Mab said in a deadly reasonable tone. "And you passed responsibility for such decisions to me when you swore your oaths, my Knight."

"Hey, didn't nobody say anything about *weddings*," I protested.

Mab stared at me for half of a frozen second before saying, "You knew."

Yeah, well. There wasn't any weaseling out of that one. When Mab had staked her claim, she had done so in . . . an unmistakably intimate and thorough fashion. Mab had laid claim to my *life*. And I'd agreed to it. Also unmistakably.

I looked away from Mab, because she was probably in the right. I'd made a deal and sworn my oaths. Mab, as my liege, had not only the right, but the *obligation* to marry me off if it meant a more stable and secure Winter.

But that didn't matter.

Because I'd had a long damned week.

And Murph was *gone*.

And the Winter mantle didn't do a thing for that kind of pain.

"You know what you can do with your wedding?" I asked Mab pleasantly, and even though I knew I was about to offer her open defiance in front of witnesses, and that there was only one way she could react to such a thing, I felt the words coming up.

Mab's gaze turned icy and settled on me.

And some part of me said, *What the hell?* and started looking for the most childishly insulting thing I could possibly say to her.

But before I could come up with something really good, open my mouth, and doom myself, Molly and Lara had both come between us.

"This is inappropriate to force upon him at this time,"

Molly said in a cool, rational tone to Mab, as she put a hand on my shoulder. Her fingers closed in an icy vise, hard enough to make my arm go numb. It wasn't quite as effective as slamming a gag over my mouth would have been, but it was close. "In the immediate wake of the battle and his personal losses," Molly argued, "there is nothing to be gained by putting further strain upon him."

"Your terms are acceptable," Lara said immediately upon Molly's heels. "But the customs of both my people and his own call for a more graceful and appropriate period of time before a formal union is commenced—as well as for a mourning period after the passing of one of the honored dead. To ignore either of these requirements would be for you and me to openly disrespect each other. It would send mixed messages to our vassals upon the very foundation of our alliance."

Mab looked coldly furious, but her gaze flickered aside to Molly and to Lara for maybe a tenth of a second. She stared at me and then arched an eyebrow, daring me to defy her. "Do you concur with this assessment, my Knight?"

The part of me that missed Murphy and was sick of hurting wanted to scream, *Go pound sand, you frigid witch. I am not your Ken doll.*

Molly's hand clenched me hard enough to make things in my shoulder crackle.

Maybe she and Lara hadn't shown up only in an effort to keep me from losing it on Marcone. Maybe they'd come in an effort to protect me from something a lot more dangerous.

I couldn't stop from glaring defiance at Queen Mab.

But the part of me that wanted to survive rasped, "Yeah. What they said."

Mab stared daggers at me for a solid thirty seconds of frozen silence. Then she said, "In the interests of building a solid foundation, Lady Lara, and in making best use of our Knight, Lady Molly, I will grant him the period of a year of mourning," she said.

"Do you know what you can do with your year of mourn—" I began to say.

"Agreed," Molly said hurriedly over me, and gave me a look that said, *Dammit, Harry.*

Mab gave Molly a narrow-eyed glance. Then she lifted a finger and added, "With the proviso that they make regular public appearances together. War does not wait for the mending of broken hearts. We must project the image of improved solidarity at once."

Mab looked from Molly to Lara and back.

Molly looked like she was biting back a whole lot of what she had to say. But she inclined her head slightly and nodded.

Lara grimaced. She gave Molly a look that contained something like an apology. But she nodded as well.

"Excellent," Mab said, her tone frozen. "See to the details, Lady Molly. Yourself."

Lara winced.

Molly looked as if Mab had just punched her in the belly.

But she nodded.

Mab shook her head and said, "The world we have been building is at risk. Now is not the time for defiance. From any of you. Do not make me regret my investments."

Something very like fear touched Lara's face for a moment. She didn't look up to challenging Mab. I knew how she felt.

"I would speak privately with my Knight," Mab continued. "Lady Molly. Lady Lara. Thank you for your time."

Mab didn't exactly dismiss them, not directly. But her tone made it perfectly clear that they had been dismissed, nonetheless.

Lara turned to go. Molly hesitated for a second, her expression uncomfortable.

The way I understood it, Molly didn't exactly have an option when Mab gave her a direct order. Power always comes at a price.

"It's okay," I told her. "I'll be out in a minute."

My ex-apprentice gave me a faint smile. Then she traded a guarded look with Mab, inclined her head to the Queen of Winter, and walked with Lara out of my secondhand castle. There was some definite coolness between Lara and Molly: Actual frost formed on the floor at the Winter Lady's feet.

And that left me alone with Mab.

Mab raised a hand as I began to speak and said, her voice tired and uninflected, "Yes. You defy me. Obviously. You always do. In the interests of efficiency, let us assume you have uttered some mystifying reference to mortal popular nonsense, I have glared at you and reminded you of the power I hold over you, you have confirmed that you continue to understand the circumstances that require me to tolerate your insouciance, and we have both agreed to continue this ridiculous dance in the future, presumably for the remainder of time."

Which made me blink.

Mab didn't usually get into meta-discussions about the nature of our relationship.

She took a step past me and looked around the bare walls of the great hall. "The Baron has garnered the lion's share of respect among his elders by surviving a storm this violent at all, much less proving to have prepared for it, seizing the initiative, and fighting for his territory successfully. Yet you have claimed a choice prize of him, and he has had the grace to yield it to you. And there are many who suspect you have claimed the Eye by right of victory as well—a circumstance far more favorable to you than if they actually knew whether you had it or not." She pursed her lips. "You begin to understand how to armor yourself with your enemies' doubts. Your reputation grows more formidable."

"Formidable enough the White Council doesn't want anything to do with me," I said.

She waved a hand, her voice utterly confident. "Sheep fear wolves, my Knight. And it is appropriate that they do so."

"The big bad momma of wicked faeries just looked at me about a work problem and said, 'Whatchagonnado?'" I sighed. "Maybe that's a bad sign."

Mab stopped under the hole in the roof and stared up at it, her face pale and perfect in the wan shaft of daylight, filtered through thick, sleepy rain clouds. The raindrops that made it through bounced off her and landed on the floor with sharp clicks, as tiny chips of ice. "You begin to see the shape of my problems, my Knight." She glanced at me. "You are a wolf. A predator. One they need."

"I'm the hero Chicago deserves," I said in my best overblown Batman voice. "But not the one it swiped on Tinder."

Mab glanced at me wearily. "You know what it is," she said, "to sell pieces of your soul so that someone who will never know your name will have another chance at life."

I didn't have a response for that.

Silence fell.

I walked over beside Mab and looked up out of the castle at the soft daylight and the falling rain.

When droplets hit me, I just got wet.

"I always figured," I said, "that when you sold your soul, it went all at once."

She smiled faintly. *Click, click, click.*

"You didn't even understand who would be receiving it," she said. "Honestly, why you children keep making such bargains with old serpents like me, I shall never understand."

I frowned up at the light.

"When big, bad, hungry evil showed up at the door," I said, "I wanted the people of Chicago kept safe. So I fought it. With everything I had."

"Yes," Mab said.

"So did Marcone," I said. "End of the day, when push came to shove, he gave people who were in trouble shelter behind his walls. And he fought to defend the city."

"He did," Mab said.

"I won't forget it."

I eyed her.

"So did you," I said.

She stared up at the light, ignoring me. *Click, click, click*.

"Thank you," I said. "You fought for my city. My people. Thank you."

She looked at me in sudden confusion.

"Thank you," I said, for the third time.

Three repetitions separate the random from the intentional. Repeat something three times, and you make it more real.

Mab shivered at my gratitude.

She closed her eyes.

And for a second, raindrops fell through the hole in the roof.

Then they went *click, click, click* again. And Mab opened her eyes. "Child," she said. "You are welcome."

"I have a question," I said.

"Ask."

"The Eye," I said. "It was made of pure hate. I felt that."

"Yes."

"It destroyed everything it touched," I said. "Except you. Even Titania didn't touch it when she faced it. But you could. Why?"

Mab's mouth turned up into a faint smile.

"Everyone," she said, "thinks that hate and love are somehow opposite forces. They are not. They are the same force, facing opposite directions." She glanced aside at me. "Love is a fire, my Knight. Love turned the wrong way has killed as many as hate. *Reason*, young wizard, is the opposite of hate, not love. Ethniu could not destroy me with a single blast of the Eye. I was quite certain of it. I ran the numbers."

I stared at her for a moment. Then I nodded.

"You need to run a few more," I said. "Because you're asking too much of me. It's more than I can give you."

"Why?" she asked. "Because your lover fell in battle?"

I gave her a furious look.

She took it without noticing, and I was too tired to keep it up. "You will heal. I have buried a cohort of lovers over the years, Dresden," she said, without malice. "We won this battle. Enjoy the victory. But the war goes on— and it must yet be fought."

It wasn't like I saw Murph's shade standing there. That would have been too much. But I could imagine what it would look like, standing there, staring at me impatiently while Mab said things that would become no less true just because I didn't like them.

"You're asking too much," I said.

"You find the pairing undesirable?"

"I find it suicidal, and it wouldn't matter who she was," I said. "You're forcing me into something that shouldn't be forced."

Her voice turned colder and harder than any stone in Antarctica. "Yes. I am." She glanced at me. "Because I judge it necessary. Our world has just become infinitely more uncertain and dangerous. We must become stronger and more stable to face it, securing both the appearance and fact of a secure alliance with a competent partner. That is more important than any given person or their petty desires. Including yours."

"Makes sense," I said. "And it doesn't matter. You should do it."

"Do what?"

"Get married. Lara wouldn't mind."

"Not possible," Mab said. "If it was work I could do myself, I would."

Which . . . I believed, actually. "Why not?"

"Certain aspects of my power have to do with choices I made when I was mortal," she said. "There would be . . . compatibility issues. This is part of the task the Knight was designed for."

"Designed for? I'm not . . . That isn't how it works. It's not a choice I'm making. That's just how it is."

Click, click, click.

"There is," Mab said, a very soft, very gentle tone of warning in her voice, "one year, for it to be different."

"That isn't how it works," I said. "People aren't machine parts. You can't just plug them in wherever. They aren't game pieces. You can't just pick them up and move them around the board, wherever you want them to go."

"Yet the machine still must function. The game must be played," she said, her voice implacable, stating facts, not angry. "Do not test me. There is no margin here for you to dance within. Bend, wizard. Or I will break you."

I drew in a breath and let it out again.

"I guess we'll see," I said.

Her eyes glinted. But she looked like someone who had heard what she expected to hear. She inclined her head to me in an opponent's acknowledgment. "We will see."

Molly's car was being driven by one of the Sidhe who I couldn't quite tell was male or female, and who could presumably kill me a dozen times while I tried to figure it out.

"You hear nothing," Molly told the Sidhe, and the being shuddered a little and nodded.

"Literally," Molly said. "That's my Winter Law voice. The driver is effectively deaf until I say otherwise."

And then she rolled up the privacy curtain between the front and the back.

"Your driver reads lips?" I guessed.

"I find it best to assume," she said. "The Winter Court is just that kind of place." She folded her arms and crossed her knees, which looked very nice in the sharp, rather conservative dress suit she wore. "I can't believe she's just selling you off like a horse to Lara."

"Thanks?" I said.

She waved a hand in a vaguely apologetic gesture. "You know what I mean. It's unconscionable."

"For most of humanity's history," I said, "it was standard practice. Marriage of a couple, symbolizing the actions of a state, bound together in an act of ritual high magic. And it was practiced so long because it worked."

Molly eyed me. "Who exactly do you think you're teaching, here, Socrates?"

I lifted a hand in acknowledgment. "I'm . . . tired, Molly. Sorry."

She grimaced and looked out the window. "No. I shouldn't have pushed." She shook her head. "I can't believe Mab is doing this to you *now*. The dirt's barely settled on Murphy's grave."

No.

It hadn't.

I stared out the window for a while, just sort of letting the world happen to me. Molly spoke, I think.

"You haven't heard a word I said, have you?" she asked me, a while later.

I blinked and tried to recall, but I hadn't really been tracking too well. "Sorry," I said. "I mean, I'm not sorry. I'm hurt, and I deserve consideration for it. But I'm sorry that's a pain for you right now."

Molly gave me a faint, grim smile and shook her head. "No. I get it. Losing someone you feel that way about. Having them taken away. It changes you for a while."

I looked at her and winced.

I started to apologize.

She saw it coming, and smiled and shook her head firmly, even while tears formed in her eyes. "We've dealt with that already. That was pain and it happened and it was real and necessary, and now it's in the past."

I cupped her cheek with my hand. She closed her eyes and leaned against my palm.

"Harry," she said. "She was a good person. I'm sorry."

I nodded several times and couldn't say anything. Or see anything.

"But listen. I don't expect you to be fine. I expect you to maybe behave like an ass for a while, because you're hurting. And while we would all be grateful if you didn't, if you do sometimes, you've . . . earned it. There are people around you who understand what it's cost you to do the things you've done. And if you're grouchy while you heal from the wounds you've taken, it's unpleasant and understandable." She looked up at me. "So, yeah. It's okay if you're a mess for a while. That's how you heal from stuff like this. And when everything shakes out, I'll still be your friend."

"Oh, thank God," I said, and even if I laughed, I mostly meant it. "This Lara thing Mab's throwing at me. I can't deal with it."

"I don't think Lara was thinking things would happen at that pace, either," Molly said, her tone dry. "The year was for herself as much as for you."

"Whatever," I said. "It's a year. I don't have to figure everything out right now, today." I settled back in my seat and swept a hand at my eyes. "Good thing. I'm not really up for it at the moment."

"And I'm still pushing," said Molly, her tone even more wry. She took my hand between hers and held it firmly. "You're my Knight as well, Harry. And I owe you a great deal. I am on your side. When you're ready to act, I'll be there. And until then, I'll be here."

"Thanks, Molls," I said.

She smiled at me fleetingly. Then she bit her lip and said, "How do I look?"

Her hair was styled back into the natural golden brown color she'd been born with, and fell in a long, natural cut. She wore minimal makeup and muted lipstick. She looked like she'd gained weight and . . . were those the beginnings of crow's-feet at the corners of her eyes?

"This is approximately what I'd look like, if I wasn't . . ." she said. Then she flailed her hands and said, "How in the hell do you go to your parents and say, 'Hi, Mom, Dad, I'm a faerie princess. The evil sexy kind'?" She looked up at me, and her eyes were a bit desperate. "Harry, this was a bad idea. You can make excuses for me, right? We're really Catholic. We can be polite around problems right in the middle of the room for generations if we need to."

"No, you can't," I said, gently, and squeezed her hands back. "That's not worthy of any of you."

"They're not going to understand," she said.

"Especially if you never talk to them about it," I said.

"It's the look," she said. "The look my father is going to give me. The disappointed look." She shook her head. "Fighting Corb and his buddies didn't scare me. But that does."

"If you love them," I said, "you kinda have to build that on something real. That means telling them the truth. It's not a very good way to build real love and trust. It's just the only way."

She released me and waved both hands as though plagued by a swarm of insects. "Yes. I know, I know, I know." She sniffed and started blinking her eyes clear. "I just wanted a moment to imagine myself panicking and running away. It seemed so restful."

The car slid to a stop outside the Carpenters' home.

"Moment's over," I said gently. "You ready?"

I offered her my hand.

She took it and gave me a faintly puzzled smile. "You never push me about things like this, Harry. But you haven't relented. Why not?"

"Because I'm in your corner, kiddo," I said. "Including backing you on this whole Winter Lady gig. But it occurs to me that what has made you a successful Winter Lady hasn't got anything to do with what Mab gave you." I nodded toward the house. "It's mostly about what you learned from them. I know you're all about the job right now. But keep yourself, Molly. It's easy to lose perspective if you don't have somewhere solid you can plant your feet from time to time."

"You think that place is here?" she asked.

I opened the car door and got out, drawing her with me. She murmured something to the driver and then followed me into the early Sunday afternoon sunshine, behind clouds that promised more rain before too much longer.

We walked up to the porch and I knocked on the door.

Somewhere in the house, Mouse let out a single basso woof, and then heavy paw steps sounded on the stairs.

"I don't know of many more solid places," I said.

The door opened, and Michael smiled out at us. His smile became radiant when he saw Molly. "Oh, oh my goodness, you look so . . ." He huffed out a quick breath of laughter and nodded. "Perfect."

"Dad," Molly stammered. She glanced up at me for a second and then plowed doggedly ahead. "There's something I have to tell you."

"Molly," Michael said.

"Dad, this is important," she said. "I haven't been saying much about my new job, because I knew you wouldn't like what you heard."

"Molly, we know that—"

"No, wait," she said. "Because I have to make sure that we are absolutely clear."

"That you're the Winter Lady now," Michael said. "Yes, obviously. You think your mother and I are blind as well as old?" He kissed her hair, turned to me, and said, "Hello, Harry."

Molly blinked.

"Now, we've checked all the glassware and we've gotten out your grandmother's silverware," Michael said. "I had no idea how much the tradition of silverware for guests is bound up with the idea of being able to prepare a proper dinner for the Fair Folk, should they come to visit, and I suppose this is technically the same thing. The silver shouldn't be a problem for you, should it?"

Molly blinked several more times, then smiled slowly and carefully at her father and said, "That will be fine, Dad."

"Good, because your mother says you're not getting out of helping in the kitchen just because you're a faerie princess now. She got you those long kitchen gloves so that you can still wash dishes."

Molly blinked several more times.

I just sort of drank it in.

Michael saw the expression on his daughter's face. He put his hand on her shoulder. Then he enfolded her in a slow, gentle hug.

"Don't think that you're getting out of a talking-to, either, young lady," he said, his big voice gentle and deep. "Your mother and I have concerns, and we're going to address them with you because we love you and we know what happened to the last young woman with your job. But that's for later. For now, I'm just glad that you're home to see us. And you still eat meat, don't you? Your mother found this fancy flavored salt for the roast and it really is quite good."

"Oh, very meat-friendly, is Winter," Molly stammered. She looked at Michael, her expression faintly baffled and very much full of affection, and said, "I love you, Dad."

Michael smiled and kissed her hair again.

Then there was a high-pitched shriek and Maggie came

flying over the doorway and into my arms. I caught her without too much trouble. She was such a little thing.

She hugged me with improbable strength. I think she cheated, by using her legs as much as her arms. I hugged her back, as gently as I knew how. She always laid her head against my arm and closed her eyes for a moment when she greeted me like that.

I would close my eyes with her when she did.

Because that was my solid place.

I'd taken a horrible loss.

But I'd lost before, and survived it.

And it wasn't just me, now.

I felt a gentle bump and looked down to see Mouse leaning sleepily against my leg, his great tail wagging gently. My little family.

Michael and Molly went into the house arm in arm. From within, Charity and Sanya exclaimed their enthusiastic greetings.

I held on to Maggie for a moment more.

Michael stuck his head back out, saw me, smiled, and went inside.

Michael knows about taking a moment.

Life in the supernatural world was about to get a lot more complicated, for everyone. Every bad guy I'd ever angered out there was going to reevaluate whether or not they could take me down, now that I was out of the White Council. Mab planned to marry me off to the nice vampire queen next door. And I had a whole castle to furnish on a limited budget.

Because we were going to need the castle. There was more than one kind of threat to Chicago, and I was going to be ready for the next one.

Thunder rumbled on the horizon.

"More rain coming," Maggie said.

"When it gets here, we'll run out and dance in it," I said.

"Why?" Maggie asked.

"If we don't, life has just as much rain," I said, "but way less dancing."

"You're silly, Dad."

"I'm *hungry*," I complained.

"I stole us both rolls!" Maggie said. "If we hurry, they're still warm!"

"Stole?"

"Well," she hedged. "I sort of helped make them. They're kind of like commission."

"Hmm. I can work with that. Let's ask for some jelly for them."

"Okay."

At that moment, Marcone was probably plotting his next cache of emergency weapons. My enemies within the White Council were probably getting their next scheme together. Nemesis was still out there, running around with my brother's girlfriend and their baby, trying to literally end the world. Mab and Lara had schemes in motion. And a planet of consequence was about to fall on all of us, no matter how the exposure of the danger of the supernatural world got spun to the mortals.

Trouble was coming.

Murphy was gone.

And I had a hole in my chest that was going to take time to heal.

But after a lot of time, and hurt, it would heal.

And right now, I was about to have a nice meal with people who cared about me, and about one another.

There are a lot of ways to get ready for trouble.

You get ready to fight. That's one of them.

But it's even more important that you build something worth fighting for.

CHRISTMAS EVE

A DRESDEN FILES SHORT STORY

For my readers who, for whatever reason, aren't sleeping tonight. Merry Christmas, you magnificent weirdos.

'Twas the night before Christmas, and all through the house, not a creature was stirring except me and Mouse.

I sat in the middle of a lopsided circle of parts that spread out before me in a one-hundred-and eighty-degree arc, glowering at an instruction manual. "Why do they bother putting the assembly instructions in twenty different languages," I all but screamed, "and then just have a drawing with numbers and letters and arrows!?"

"Woof," Mouse said, commiserating. He was more than two hundred pounds of patient grey floof and was better with people than I was.

I went back to trying to assemble the stupid bicycle. Maggie needed to learn to ride a bike. A lot of little girls would have wanted the pink-and-purple bike. But Maggie's favorite color was red. She insisted that the red ones go faster.

"You need a degree and a NASCAR pit crew to do this!" I muttered darkly.

Mouse sighed. Then he nudged my hand with his nose

until I dropped the part I was trying to assemble. Then he picked up a different part in his huge, patient jaws and handed it to me.

"What am I supposed to do with this?" I demanded. "Other than wipe your drool off, you moose."

Mouse chuffed and nudged my other hand with his nose.

"I know you want to help," I said. "But these two parts don't—"

The parts clicked together and locked, easily.

Mouse's tail went *thump, thump* against the floor.

"Nobody likes a wiseass," I said darkly.

Mouse's tail went *thumpthumpthumpthump* and he grinned a doggy grin at me.

"Are you laughing at me?" I demanded.

Mouse sneezed.

I sighed and ruffled his ears. "Fine. If you can't beat them, join them." I held up the paper so Mouse could peer at it. "Which one is next?"

Mouse selected the next part, and I started bumbling around with it until I got it right. Then we did the next one. The fire in the fireplace crackled and popped. It was the only light.

There were quiet footsteps and then Michael Carpenter appeared, a large man in his fifties with a thick, powerful build. He wore a comfortable robe belted over his pajamas, and carried a coffee mug in his hand. He paused in the doorway to his own living room and regarded me struggling, smiling quietly.

"Maggie and Hank crashed about an hour ago," he said. "So you have the rest of the night to get it done."

"Just say it," I muttered.

"I wouldn't dream," he replied. He took a sip of egg-nog from his mug. His wife, Charity, made wicked-potent nog. "It just wouldn't be fair."

"You must have done a million of these things," I said.

"Or two," he said, nodding.

I spread my hands over the parts in exasperation. "Well?"

"Oh," he said, his voice serious—but his eyes were twinkling. "Harry, I wouldn't dream of taking this joy away from you. This is what being a father is all about."

"Staying up all night cutting myself while I try to fig-ure out this stupid thing?" I demanded.

"Don't forget being woken at the crack of dawn by ex-cited children," he said.

I groaned.

Michael smiled faintly. "Don't moan about it, Harry. I got pretty used to my Molly showing up at my bedside at five a.m. with a cup of burnt coffee she made herself." Something sad and tired touched the wrinkles at the cor-ners of his eyes. "It's the most annoying thing you'll ever miss once it's gone."

I sighed.

I looked up at him.

"Most of my memories of my dad are of Christmas mornings," I said. I swallowed and looked down at the potential bike. So much thought had to go into preparing it. Getting it ready for the world. "I just don't want to screw it up."

Sympathetic pain flickered on his face. "Harry," he said, "what do you remember most?"

"Coffee," I said instantly. "My dad would let me drink coffee on Christmas morning." I smiled, remembering. "I mean, it was more like a cup of milk and sugar with a little coffee thrown into it, but I thought I was pretty big stuff. We'd make breakfast together and then he'd sit with me and open my presents and we'd spend the day playing with them."

Michael took a sip of nog and nodded thoughtfully. Then he smiled at me and said, "I think you'll do just fine." He cocked his head slightly, as if listening to a comment coming from an earbug. He let out a little snort and shook his head.

"What?" I asked him warily. I looked around the room at any potential unseen angelic presences and demanded, "What?"

"Spoilers," the ex-Knight murmured. "Merry Christmas, Harry." And he limped silently from the room.

I squinted at him, feeling very much as if I had somehow been bamboozled. Then I muttered something dark about the duplicity of paladins, retired or not, and went back to trying to figure out the bike. I got into it, focusing with as much intensity as I would spend on any spell. This was a mere child's bicycle. It was no match for the intellect of the Wizard of Chicago.

Plus I had Mouse to help.

I'd been going along for a goodly while when there was a sudden gust of wind outside so cold that it came flooding down the chimney, so intense that it made the flames flicker and gutter before they sprang up again. I looked up sharply, as my wizard's senses told me that power was in motion. The flames in the fireplace guttered again, leaving the room in almost absolute blackness. When they sprang back up, the flames were green and blue and purple, dancing merrily.

And the Queen of Air and Darkness stood above me.

Queen Mab was as tall as me tonight—it changed, based upon her mood and her intentions. Her skin was white as frost, her lips as dark as frozen mulberries, and her hair had been made from the first snowflakes to fall through the virgin air. She was stunningly beautiful, immortal, had the power of a demigoddess, was the unquestioned queen of the wicked Fae—and she was my boss.

"My Knight," she murmured, inclining her head.

I wasn't sure what protocol dictated for this particular circumstance, so I bowed my head slightly and said, "Good evening."

"Guardian," Mab said. She bowed her head rather more deeply to Mouse.

I get no respect, no respect at all.

Mouse regarded Mab solemnly. His tail had stopped wagging. But he thumped a paw twice on the floor in response.

Mab regarded the circle of parts around me, her head tilted. "A conjuring?"

"Yeah. Kind of," I said, scratching at my hair. "You aren't here to call me in to work, I hope."

"Do not be ridiculous," she said. "It is Christmas."

I lifted my eyebrows. "Christmas spirit? You?"

She lifted her chin slightly. "Christmas falls within the realm of Winter, does it not?"

I huffed out a little laugh. "Yeah. I guess it does. But I thought you had people for that."

"I do," Mab said. "Yet . . ." She frowned, as if concentrating to make sure she repeated the phrase correctly. "It does not do for the boss to spend too much time in the office." She paused for a breath and then said, "I have brought your gift."

I think my jaw bounced off my knee before it landed in the pile of parts. "What?"

"You are participating in the holiday this year," Mab said. "I have an obligation to my vassals."

"What?" I repeated.

She took one hand out from behind her back and presented me with a small gift bag of wintry blue, covered with cheerful silver snowflakes.

I eyed the bag. "Is it going to explode? Or try to eat me?"

"Do not be tiresome," Mab sighed.

"Faeries don't give gifts," I said. "What kind of trick is this?"

"The kind that isn't," she replied. "I am not giving you a gift. I am fulfilling to you an obligation."

I felt a smile touch the corner of my mouth. "Obligation, eh? Suppose I don't accept?"

A pained expression touched her eyes for about a tenth of a second. "That would be your choice. As would be the consequences."

"Well. That's the first time I've ever been threatened into accepting a Christmas present," I said.

I took the bag. Inside was a jewelry box. Inside the jewelry box was a plain band that probably wouldn't have fit on my pinky. It was made from some kind of silvery, opalescent metal. I brushed a fingertip over it. It hummed with stored energy.

"Potent," I said. "What does it do?"

"It is meant for your daughter," Mab said. "And it will give her powers."

I snapped the box shut and eyed Mab. "Excuse me?"

She made an impatient sound. "Not like that, wizard," she said. "If you give her the ring, she will . . . have a certain amount of influence, until next stroke of noon, over the forces of Winter." She sighed. "And it will play music."

I narrowed my eyes. "What music?"

Mab leaned over, opened the box, and obligingly touched the ring. It immediately buzzed and the room filled with a swirl of music, as a woman's voice sang, "The snow glows white on the mountain tonight . . ."

I shut the box on the sound and eyed her. It was just possible that I'd already heard that song enough to make my teeth itch.

"Now I understand," I said drily.

"You are welcome," she replied.

"Just out of curiosity," I said, "is it going to be possible for her to freeze someone's heart and turn them into an ice statue?"

Mab looked baffled. "Those are the powers in the motion picture. Should I have cheated her?"

I rubbed at the spot between my eyes. "Got it. We'll go someplace nice and quiet to play with this gift."

"Make sure she knows who gave it to her," Mab said.

Then the fire guttered again. When it returned to life, it was golden and merry, the way fire is supposed to be—and Mab was gone.

"Leave me!" I called quietly to the empty air where she'd been. "Take me back! Haunt me no longer!"

Mouse's jaws dropped open in a grin.

"Seriously?" I said. "You've read *A Christmas Carol*?" *Thumpthumpthumpthump.*

"Yeah, well," I said. "Let's get back to work."

And we did. We'd been going for a while when sleet suddenly rattled against the windows outside, the silent snow turning into a quiet chorus of clicks and pops. Wind gusted again—and there was the sudden sound of a key in a locked door.

The front door of the Carpenter house opened slowly and quietly, and a tall young woman with white-blond hair and ruddy pink cheeks, wrapped in a long and stylish winter coat, came in out of the cold.

"Molly," I said, smiling.

My former apprentice, now technically also my boss, beamed at me, crossed the floor, and promptly gave me an enormous hug, which I returned.

"Merry Christmas, Harry," she said.

"Merry Christmas, Molls," I said. "Tell me it wasn't you who talked to Mab about Maggie's present."

"That was Sarissa," Molly said. "She showed Mab the movie."

I tried to imagine Mab watching a Disney movie. She did not like Disney—not the company, and not the man. Disney had, in Mab's opinion, done too much damage to the old faerie tales by sanding off all the unpleasant bits. According to Mab, it had weakened humanity in the face of supernatural forces, when they found out that the actual wicked Fae were nothing like Disney promised.

Trying to imagine her watching musical numbers made my brain hurt.

I tilted my head and said, "You're here to bring me a gift?"

"Part and parcel of the whole Winter Lady gig," she said, smiling. She rummaged in her coat and came out with a silver envelope decorated with white snowflakes. She presented it with a flourish and a little bow. "It's a little symbolic, but I think you'll like it."

I opened the envelope. It had one piece of paper in it. On it was written a very large number.

"What is this?" I asked.

"The total of everyone's medical bills from last summer," she said, her voice quieter, soberer. "Everyone who got hurt. It's all paid for."

I didn't want to think about the peace talks.

Pain. So much pain.

"What about the funerals?" I asked. My voice was bitter.

Molly was quiet for a long moment before she said, gently, "Those, too."

I bowed my head.

I counted my breaths.

"I'm sorry," I said. "You're trying to be kind and I'm just . . ."

"Don't," she said. "It's supposed to hurt, Harry. I'm glad you hurt. It means you're still you."

I looked in the direction of the den, where Maggie and the youngest Carpenter children had fallen asleep watching movies.

"Sometimes," I said, "I can't believe how arrogant I am. If it wasn't for the kid . . ."

Molly leaned down and rapped me sharply on the

crown of the head with one knuckle. I eyed her and scowled. "Hey."

"Stop it," she said. "You didn't choose for things to fall out the way they did. You did everything in your power to stop anyone from being harmed. And you risked an awful lot getting in everyone's face after the battle. It helped a whole lot of people."

"People who might not have gotten hurt in the first place if—"

Molly rapped me on the head again and said, "You're like a broken guilt record." She sighed. "Can I give you a piece of advice, Harry?"

I squinted at her. "What?"

"When I was a kid, my mom spent a whole lot of time telling me how I should behave."

"And that worked out," I said.

She smiled, a flash of warmth that vanished into a little sadness. "Looking back, mostly what I did was whatever my dad did." She put a hand on my shoulder, leaned over, and pressed a cool, sisterly kiss against my cheek. "Maybe you should think about what you want to teach Maggie."

I scowled and looked down.

"You can forgive yourself, Harry," she said gently. "The world won't end. And it would be good for your daughter."

"Cheap shot," I said.

She nodded. "But no less true."

I looked down at the half-assembled bike. "That . . . is something I never learned to do," I said.

"Then I guess you've got some work ahead of you."

Dammit.

I hate it when the grasshopper has me dead to rights.

"I'll try," I said.

"Good enough for me," said the Winter Lady. She laid her cold hand against my cheek for a moment and then rose.

"You're not staying?" I asked.

Molly shook her head. "Still trying to get my cohorts back to full strength. I've got pickups in Japan, Norway, and Siberia tonight. I'll be back in time for morning presents."

"Good," I said. I wanted to see her face when she saw the 110th-gear Princess Leia action figure I'd gotten for her. "You made some enemies last summer. Watch your back, Molls."

Molly gave me a brilliant smile that was just a little too toothy to be warm. "I don't watch my back, Harry," she said. "I make other people watch theirs."

"All the same."

She rolled her eyes. "I'll be careful."

"You'll be dead!" we both shouted together, and grinned like fools.

We traded another quick hug, and Molly left.

As soon as she was gone, I let the smile drop. Mouse made a soft, pained sound and leaned against me.

Six months was not a long time in which to say so many goodbyes.

My dog leaned against me and I stared at the fire and wept for a time. But I was tired of tears. I was so damned tired of them.

I picked up the piece of paper. If you left off the decimal points, it was a prime number. It represented the costs of medical care for tens of thousands, and funerals for thousands more. On a rational level, I knew Molly was right. It could have been worse. Much worse.

But in my heart, all I could see was blood on asphalt, and all I could feel were empty places inside me where people should have been.

I got up and walked quietly to the den, where my daughter, Maggie, was asleep with the other kids, her cheeks pink. She was a tiny girl, the lowest percentile for height and weight in her class, and she'd come back from her first semester of school with a GPA higher than 4.0. All I had was a GED. I didn't even know how to calculate GPA. But I think I had a good idea of what the letters stood for.

I watched her chest rise and fall for a little while, and the pain receded. I took a deep breath.

I've fallen apart before. I've let the madness have me.

But I was a father now.

I no longer had that luxury. Thank God.

Nothing you ever do can change the past. Can't live your life looking backwards or you'll spend it walking in circles.

That little girl was the future.

I nodded. And then I went back to the bicycle.

Mouse was fluffy and faithful, but he was also pretty much just a kid himself. He helped out valiantly for another half hour or so and then just sort of fell over sideways and started snoring. I smiled at him. He'd done enough. I could muddle through the rest on my own.

I cleared my mind of everything except solving the problem in front of me and anticipating Maggie's happiness. The fire crackled. I added more wood. A deep and peaceful warmth settled somewhere between my chest and my stomach.

And then I understood why Michael hadn't helped.

I was just putting the extra bullet-hole stickers I'd picked up onto the bike when the fire crackled and popped and flared up.

"Merciful Heaven, what is this?" I mused aloud.

There was a sound that can only be described as a *foomph*, and a sudden flood of soot from the fireplace and then . . .

Well. Then.

He had a round face. And a little round belly. That shook when he laughed. Underneath all the chain mail.

Kringle was a tall, burly man with long silvery white hair and a magnificent snowy beard. He wore hunting leathers under a mail shirt, and over that was a heavy, magnificent crimson hooded robe trimmed in white fur. He carried an enormous sack over one shoulder—and there was no sword at his hip.

He looked at me and let out a low, rumbling laugh.

"Hey," I said quietly.

Kringle looked down at the bike I'd put together. He knelt by it, examining it closely.

"This was done properly," he said, a calm note of approval in his voice.

"Thanks," I said. "I'm not your vassal. We've worked together on some things, but I'm not even your friend. So if you're here to give me a gift, I'm not sure why."

"Because tonight," Kringle said, "that is what I do." His blue eyes crinkled at the corners as he smiled. "And because you're on my list, lad."

I snorted. "Please."

Kringle eyed me for a moment. Then he winked and said, "Call Kris Kringle a liar on Christmas Eve one more time."

"L—" I began.

But something made me think better of it. I went back to putting stickers on the bike instead.

"Good," Kringle said. "And, yes. I've brought you a gift."

"Tell me it's not a pony for Maggie," I said. "I'll be housebreaking it for years."

Kringle tilted his head back and chortled again. It was impossible not to smile when he did. But I could cover it up with a scowl as soon as he stopped, so I did.

"No. It's not for Maggie." And he put down his sack and started rummaging inside, muttering cheerfully to himself.

In a twinkling, he'd come up with a small cubic package wrapped in green-and-red patterned paper that—I'll be damned—had an image of Mouse's grinning face as part of the pattern. There was a tag on it. TO: HARRY. FROM: SANTA CLAUS.

And the package was warm.

I eyed it and then looked up at Kringle.

"Well, lad," Kringle said, chortling again, and gestured at the package.

I opened it.

Inside was . . .

Was . . .

A plain white coffee mug. The kind you buy at a craft store.

Painted on it in a kindergartner's attempt at writing, the scarlet letters drawn like pictograms by someone too little to understand them, were the words: NUMB3R ON3 DAD.

The handwriting was mine.

The cup was full of a light brown liquid.

Something happened to my eyes and I couldn't see the cup anymore. Just a blur of firelight. But I picked it up and sipped milk and sugar with a little splash of coffee in it.

For just a second, I smelled my dad's old aftershave. For just a second, I heard him laughing, laughing so hard that tears had to have been rolling from his eyes. For just a second, I felt a hand, his hand, on my shoulder.

I drank from the cup I'd given my father on our last Christmas together, and the entire time I did, the memories of those Christmas mornings, of the laughter and hugs and the play, ran through my mind in IMAX, so vivid that I felt myself losing my breath at the memories of chasing my father around the yard with my new plastic lightsaber.

I left the last sip in the bottom of the cup, kept my eyes closed, and said, "I love you, Dad."

When I looked up at him, Kringle was smiling down at me. He winked. Then he picked up his sack, slung it over his shoulder, and turned to the fireplace.

"Oh," he murmured, laughter in the back of his throat. "One more thing."

I heard a *thump* behind me.

I turned.

My daughter, Maggie, stood in the doorway from the den. She'd dropped a pillow that she'd evidently been carrying. She was staring, slack-jawed, at Kringle.

"Ho, ho, ho," he chortled quietly. He nodded politely

toward Maggie, laid a finger aside his nose, and . . . just vanished up the chimney.

"Oh wow," Maggie breathed. She met my gaze and her eyes were wide. "Oh wow!"

As if the sound of her voice had been a starting pistol, Mouse bounced to his feet, suddenly awake and looking around excitedly.

"What are you waiting for?" I demanded of my daughter. I rose and rushed toward the front door. "Come on!"

Her little face with her big dark eyes went incandescent with joy and she sprinted after me, Mouse hard on her heels.

We all ran to the front door and I flung it open to the night air.

We saw the snow cascade off the roof. We saw the sleigh leap into the air, reindeer and all.

"Oh wow!" Maggie exclaimed. "Santa's real! And he left me a bike!"

I looked down at her, and then back up at the departing sleigh, smiling hard enough to break my face.

"Yep," I said. "He sure did."

And we heard him exclaim as he drove out of sight:

"Merry Christmas to all, and to all a good night!"

Acknowledgments

This one is for the inmates of the Beta Readers' Asylum, who had to go round and round with this one. Thank you for all your help and insight, guys.